All Things Await

Seth Clabough

WITHDRAWN

Savant Books and Publications
Honolulu, HI, USA
2016

Published in the USA by Savant Books and Publications
2630 Kapiolani Blvd #1601
Honolulu, HI 96826
http://www.savantbooksandpublications.com

Printed in the USA

Edited by Suzanne Langford
Cover Image Rory MacLeod|357.365: Starry Day (modified)
License: https://creativecommons.org/license/by/2.0
Cover Design by Jessica Orfe

13 digit ISBN: 9780991562275

Dedication

To my children,
Whitaker, Avie, Elsa, and Oliver
for leading me from these daydreams
and
my wife, Erin,
who helped me
dream them.

Acknowledgements

I would like to thank Aberystwyth University, Sweet Briar College, FAU in Erlangen and Longwood University for their support and contributions at different stages during this project.

I'm indebted to Ralph Doudera for the gift of free writing space in Santa Teresa; Jem Poster for his steady and invaluable guidance; my editor, Suzanne Langford, and my publisher, Daniel Janik, for their insights, patience, and support; and my agent, David Forrer, for his steadfast dedication to the project and me—thank you.

I'm strangely grateful to the cafés where I wrote ATA in Costa Rica including Zwart Art Café, Burger Rancho, and The Bakery—thanks for the extra biscuits and for not kicking me out. I owe an especially huge debt to all the welcoming guides and friends in CR who, knowingly or not, helped the project along: Demian Geneau, Billy and Yada, Aldo, Massimo Varelli, Martjin Glorieux, and the awesome Margriet Zwart.

My biggest thanks to my brother, Casey, for being brilliant and supportive; my parents, Howard and Jeanne, for their unconditional love and continual assistance; my dear children for putting everything in perspective; and my wife, Erin, for her sharp mind, warm love, and restless wanderlust.

All Things Await

Author's Note

Synesthesia: a condition in which the normally separate senses are not separate but cross-wired. Specific digits and letters (whether spoken or heard) often have colors associated with them and words may have *a touch* sensation. Other cross-wirings can present themselves from time to time.

Multiverse/Parallel Universes: a narrative informed by and engaged with quantum physics. Lightly's vision involves aspects of multiple/parallel universes that quantum theory predicts. A scholarly article on the application of quantum theory to *All Things Await* appears in the Taylor & Francis Group's peer reviewed journal *New Writing: the International Journal for the Practice and Theory of Creative Writing*.

We are haunted by the awareness that infinitely many slightly variant copies of ourselves are living out their parallel lives and that every moment more duplicates spring into existence and take up our many alternative futures.
--Frank Wilczek, Nobel Laureate in Physics

All we know is that there are dead feelings, dead ideas and cold beliefs, and there are hot and alive ones; and when one grows hot and alive within us, everything has to re-crystallize about it. And our explanations then get so vague and general that one realizes all the more the intense individuality of the whole phenomenon.
--William James, *The Varieties of Religious Experience*

I think you still have a little lightning in you.
--Wes Anderson, *Moonrise Kingdom*

1

When I told Emerald over dinner at Estes Dining Hall my plan for the summer, she thought I meant I was going to some resort and so she asked to go with me.

"I'm sorry, Emmy," I told her. "I really am, but you can't come on this one. I've got to take my jars down there and fill them up with experiences and fill them up with life and truth and all that junk, and I need to do it alone."

"Alone?" she repeated. Emerald was a tall girl, leggy, with well-groomed hair the color of peach fuzz and nails done twice a month by other people. Against the dark red bricks of the cafeteria wall she pulsated with a yellow glow. Her eyes were green, and she gave me that beautiful pout that sliced me up.

"But you said you were coming to Jennifer's lake house," she complained. "My whole sorority is coming. Even John Allen is coming for Penelope. I'll be the only girl without a guy." There was a little catch in her breath and she put those green eyes in me. "Are you *even* going to come back and play quarterback?" she asked.

"Quarterback? Jeez, Emmy, darling, I'm talking about something bigger than lake houses and quarterbacking and, besides, at least I told you. I'm not even calling my mom and dad."

"I thought you said your dad was dead."

"Well, he is, Emmy. He is and he isn't. It's the cat in the box paradox."

We were sitting at one of those long, rectangular cafeteria tables with the bench attached to it, adjacent to the perfumed radiance of Emerald's sorority sisters. Across the dining hall, Biggs and Thomas Hicks Rambo were crammed in with the other offensive linemen around a tiny blue table, and I could tell by their glowering that they were freaking pissed that I'd left them sitting with Santana Montana Ordóñez again. It was true that they were my athletic family. I knew it was true that even the closest families had disagreements now again, but it was also true that deep down in my heart of hearts I didn't care at all. I felt differently about poor, squat, bespectacled Santana Montana Ordóñez—the "Mexican fairy" they called him. He sat

3

among those giants holding a can of grape Shasta in his lap, staring at his plate as if practicing the art of motionlessness. When I'd brought him over to the table I'd told them that his father was an avid San Francisco 49ers fan and had given his son *Montana* as a middle name out of respect to the great quarterback Joe Montana, but that wasn't flying with the meatheads. God, did I love the strange perfection of that awkward kid in his frumpy sweaters and freshly ironed khakis. Since taking him under my wing, I'd bent my will on getting the o-line to love him, too. Or, at least, to understand his unique perfection, which I felt might redeem them from their awful prejudices.

Emerald picked up her tray, stood up, and put her free hand on her slender hip. I watched her, feeling a little guilty that I'd nearly forgotten she was there at all, yet truly in awe of her hip and the way her long fingers splayed across it.

"I don't know what's happened to you," she said, "but you're not the same guy I started dating. It's like you're a different person. I don't know what you're going through, and I want to be supportive, but you shouldn't assume I'll wait all summer for you."

"I know, Emmy," I said after a moment, for I knew there was nothing for her to wait for anyway.

On the table was the shoebox I'd been carrying with me everywhere of late and inside it was a cocoon spun to a twig from the tulip poplar found alongside the railroad tracks. I didn't know what would come out of it, but I was hell bent on finding out. Emerald lingered above me, the hardness draining from her lovely face. She leaned over, reached around as she so often did in those dreamy hours in bed, a bed which was itself a world entire, to touch the M-shaped scar on the back of my head.

"You're not going to do anything stupid again are you?" she asked. Good Lord, but I was going to miss those mornings lingering in bed—the fresh scent of bleach lifting from her pillows and the gentle friction of starched sheets against my skin. But more than that I would miss the gorgeous lie of order the clean precision of items in her room told: little framed pictures on the wall neatly arranged to form larger groups of perfect squares, the careful arrangement of stuffed animals, books stacked large to small, the constancy of fresh flowers in vases, the order of work supplies on her desk, and so on.

"No, Emmy," I said. "I've got two empty jars, and I'll fill them up with sand and ocean and bring them back for you if I can slip them through customs."

4

"Are you breaking up with me?" she asked quietly. I could tell by the movement of delicate muscles around her mouth that I was hurting her and I sure as hell hated that even though I knew there was no better way.

"I don't know," I said. "Maybe. I'm saying I have to go."

"But a year and half together, Lightly. The things we've done and talked about. You can just turn your back like that on the memories we share?"

"Emmy, darling," I said. "You're the best thing in the world, but never forget that memory is just a corpse we all drag around."

"Is it that you don't think I'm smart?" she demanded. "Well, I've got news for you, Lightly. No one understands anyone when they start talking like you do with your facts about space and particles!"

"Jesus, Emmy," I said. "I'm failing math and physics and have a C average in my own damn major. Meanwhile, you're as sharp as they come and when you're angry, a gorgeous rose blush suffuses the yellow glow of your face."

"No one says *suffuses*," she said. She straightened, no longer vulnerable, but resolute. "You're very weird, Lightly," she said. "But I will miss you."

"I guess that you will, Emmy darling," I said. "And I will miss the daffodil yellow of your voice, and how your name smells like cotton candy and tangerines."

When I get to where I'm going, I will send Emerald a postcard. It will begin, *You've been a garden hose in summer grass.* It will end, *I will miss talking to you on the Pineapple House couch while it is snowing outside.*

2

What was prompting this big adventure I was about to undertake, I didn't exactly know.

Maybe it was the school and maybe it wasn't. Thomas Jefferson College was expensive and small—thirty grand a year in tuition and only an elite two thousand enrolled. Last year we'd been listed in a national survey's top ten in three different private college categories: Most Prestigious, Strongest Academics, and Most Racist.

But wasn't "Tommy Jeffs" a good college with wild nights, soft lips, grabbable hips, and fine binges? Hell, yes. But the nights had the feel of a Carnival cruise ship lurching away on a vast dark sea, and there was something profane about our excesses and effulgence. I guess it was the *privilegedness* of it, but that's not exactly right. Maybe the *exclusionariness* of it. I guess there isn't a word for it and that was the problem.

What the hell could I complain about though? Wasn't I captain of the good old goddamn football team? Wasn't my girl the hottest ticket in a little town of first rate shows? Hell, yes. But it was all coming down. With a week left in the term, the big willow oaks in the quad were heavy with new foliage. Irresolute breezes kept lifting the limbs here and there so that they were restless like nervous arms.

And I wasn't sleeping.

I'd lie in bed channeling strangers. They'd whisper to me through my mouth. Or I'd stand in my room in the dark trying to feel where I was and when I was and what all the *wasing* meant, but I felt nothing. Sometimes a sliver here and there would pass by me like gravity escaping one universe and entering another. It was momentary. Every time I thought I had it, it was gone. There was no one alive who knew what *it* was. There was no one alive who knew what I meant, but still I hoped. Was I crazy? No. Everyone was crazy, but I knew there had to be more: little pockets of people gathering in midnight alleys, faces glimpsed in the red glow of cigarettes and then darkening again, how huddled strangers spoke in secret tongues the secret language of the secret griefs of wild, unknown men. Old Scotty Fitzgerald knew what I meant, but he was too damn weak.

And strange things were happening to me. I started remembering people I'd never met, awakening to messages floating out of the dorm window, or I'd enter someone's room and suddenly everything in it—photos, trophies, books, empty cans, the wrappers of fast food burgers—would seem nothing more than fragments washed up there and the vast improbability of everything around us at any given moment would settle upon me as an unliftable weight.

The biggie was seeing myself—I shit you not—stay behind in the weight room after I'd left. I know how it sounds, but I'd left the *International Journal of Theoretical Physics* propped on the damn screen of a stationary bike and went back for it. When I opened the weight room door, there I was lying on the bench doing a single arm dumbbell press. Hell, I jumped right back into the hall, shook my head, and sung a few lines of "My Country, Tis of Thee" in Latin—"*portus et exulum, et tumulus senum*" and so on—just to, you know, make sure I was real and all, and when I peered back in, I was no longer there. Well, that must have been the last straw, because the very next morning as I walked to breakfast the answer arrived, pulling along its boxcars of truth.

What happened was this: For no discernible reason, I noticed as I walked something different in the world around me. There was, for example, an amber glow from each bush and tree, from each individual brick in the Moreland and Mary Branch dorms. And it wasn't the sunlight making everything glow; each thing seemed to possess some mystical radiance of its own that, though I was certain it had always been there, I'd never noticed before. Like many of those who share my neurological quirk, I was used to the tints and distance of letters, numbers—even words—but this was something more. A chorus of birdcalls issued forth from the hollies, oaks, and poplars. Through the treetops in the quad I sensed an image approaching, a secret of the world about to be revealed. And that feeling rose in me, a feeling that the pieces were all there in the language of everything: the various shades of green in each leaf and blade of grass, the rising of bricks upon themselves, the angle of the boughs from the boles, the geometry of birds fluttering from nest to earth. Suddenly I knew beyond any doubt that these were individual characters in a complex message explaining everything.

Anyway, it was then that my big adventure began to take on solid shape and specific meaning. What I realized sitting there was that I wasn't being driven out any more than something was drawing me out. Some magnetic force was dragging me forward. For no reason I could identify clearly, I felt sure that there was a specific geographical location where all might be revealed and made whole and that I could zero in. In my gut was a corresponding pulsating swell, a charged particle of sorts, promising that all would be laid bare before me, that the unity of all things only necessitated the right eyes in the right place at the right time, that the electric center within me had shifted, and all things were in a frenzy to recrystallize around my new one.

Anyway, after sort of breaking things off with Emmy I cruised on out of Estes without so much as a backward glance at Emmy, Santana Montana Ordóñez, or my glowering o-line. Late evening was coming on steady and expectant like something tame. I shuffled onward toward Greenwood Library for in me was a compulsion to research distant places and locate that one place where the vision I sought would appear. All I knew was that it was somewhere on a tropical coast. Some might say I thought that because my mother had dragged us to so many exotic coasts or that I just wanted it to be some sunny, gorgeous place. But when you know a thing, you just know it— people with weather-induced arthritis would know what I mean.

Maybe it was the way I'd secured the Nike shoebox under my arm like a football as I passed the fountain in the tree-lined courtyard that caused me to think of Coach Sanford. Even though conditioning didn't start until the end of summer, Coach had already started on me. He'd get all worked up about how we had a good shot at the conference title next year. We were only Division III, so it wasn't like a big deal or anything, but to hear Coach talk about it you'd think football was the only thing worth doing.

Each time he'd seen me since our season had ended, he'd shake that prickly crew cut and say, "We've got a lot to build on, Lightly." He'd put his hairy, muscle-bound arm around me in that awkward, fatherly way coaches do and say, "A young man with a mind like yours has to keep himself occupied, focused on healthy things. We can't afford to lose you for part of the season again."

Mom used to say that, too—about focusing, I mean. My fourth grade teacher, Ms. Whitehead, called up my mother one day and told her I'd been staring out the window an awful lot and whispering things to myself. Mom sat me down and we had ourselves a talk. I didn't tell her about reading the messages inscribed in branch and cloud. Hell, I was only ten and could not have said it with any clarity. Instead, I told her I wasn't distracted but intensely focused on the entire scene outside. The Redskins had a bye that week so

Dad was home. He sat on the new leather couch with his biceps still bulging from his just completed workout and a massive bag of ice rising from each knee like glaciers. The sun had come around and the afternoon light caught the lip of the bay window in the living room so that the freshly polished floorboards beneath the raised couch gleamed with unbelievable brightness beneath him. He said Mom would make me a sissy, but Mom didn't want me getting off the task at hand, which was studying hard and getting into a good school. She didn't want me staring out of too many windows. After that she put me on some medication to help me focus and concentrate and not have so many different interests all the time.

Thinking on Coach as I had been, I wasn't entirely surprised to see the old school aggressiveness of his crew cut bobbing toward me when I was half way to Greenwood Library. He strode forward shaking his head *no* as coaches often do, but he was grinning just the same. He turned alongside and got that heavy arm around me.

"Twelve, what have you done to the o-line to make them mad?" he asked. He called all of us by our jersey number.

Coach Sanford's coloring was that of dull urine, and even in the cool evening air he stank of sweat residue and the nylon and plastic of sports equipment. Naturally, he reminded me of my father.

"I'm setting out on a big adventure, Coach," I said. "And god do I love my o-line, but they are racist and homophobic, and I'm trying to help break them of it like one would train a puppy to dump on newspaper."

He stopped smiling, likely because he didn't understand what I meant, and tightened his grip around me in a friendly but serious way.

"I'm worried you're not trying to get our team perfect on the field, Twelve," he said. Each word from his mouth was gravel and just as dusty and gray. "Being voted captain comes with responsibilities."

"Coach," I said, "I want you to know that I left a version of me in the weight room to lift dumbbells up and down repeatedly and whatnot—god, is it boring, but that's the level of a version of me's commitment to our team and yada yada. Coach? Coach, what's wrong? Your face has gone kinda wonky all of a sudden." Coach didn't say a thing and instead stood there like some sketchy, slight-of-hand brain doctor had just yanked his noodle through his nostril and slid a baboon's brain up in his pumpkin head lickety-split and with no one the wiser, which, in truth, neither of us were.

I stared at his mouth as it opened and shut dumbly, feeling sorry and fond of him all at once.

"Did it hurt when the doctor did that?"

"What?"

Boy did I love Coach Sanford for the ridiculous fact of his existence, for the unimaginable narrowness of his vision, which was in its own way a type of achievement. So I put my arm around him, too, and told him how football could become perfect if all the rules and reads bent to your will, when the entire game unfurled and spread itself luxuriously before your mind's eye like it did in the sky for the young genius bastard in that book by Joyce.

That did not put him at ease, though, as he had very little interest in Joyce. His big mitt moved like sandpaper up the back of my neck, and he shook me gently and said my brain was simmering again. When he said my brain was too big for my britches it was hard not to laugh at the clumsy image he'd trotted out into the air between us. I was genuinely touched by the sincere way he was saying that focusing on football would help cool me down.

"You're getting too distracted by things," he said. "It gets you off the task at hand, son, which is football."

I took a step away and smiled at him warmly.

"My tasks include football, Coach," I said by way of farewell, "but are not limited to it. I'm on a quest which is driven by a longing of great intensity, you see, and I cannot afford to tarry."

When I get to where I'm going I'll send Coach Sanford a postcard. It will begin, *You are a compendious piece of music whose lyrics consist solely of the repetition of one word: football.* It will end, *You'll do fine without me next season—just remember there are depths to you which you should truly never attempt to know.*

3

Around midnight, I made the walk back from the library, which was open late on account of exams. It was a warm May night, and the way little breezes kept touching the leaves here and there gently like a doting mother made me think of Margaret, who was long gone from this world.

One of those breezes swooped down from the treetops to play through my hair. The breeze moved on in little swirls and eddies. I turned to watch it go because as far back as I can remember I've been able to see the driftwood-colored wind moving between the things it stirs.

For no reason at all, I thought of Margie—the sadness in her pretty eyes. The color of them was all around me. Something stirred deep and I had to hold my breath, pinch my nose, and shut my eyes to get the feeling to subside. After a moment, the color vanished with a whoosh and noises tumbled to the forefront: the keening of leaves above, distant traffic on I-95, the faint trickle of a clear little creek in the distant foothills of memory and so on.

I spun and dashed into the brightly lit hall of the Moreland Dormitory, leaving the night to attend to the mystery of it all.

Biggs was sleeping in bed with the light out and the tv on when I entered our room. I yanked the tv plug out of the wall and watched to see if he would stir. He'd been sulking since the end of the season and mad as hell with me about Santana Montana Ordóñez. The past few weeks he'd all but given up talking to me and was also, I suspected, beginning to avoid me when possible. I forgave him, of course. Who could hold petty grudges, I reasoned, when the mystery of man's innate longing was about to be solved?

I crawled into bed and watched Biggs' massive form snore open-mouthed in the dimness. He always slept naked, and god did I hate him for it.

Outside, I could feel the trees taking in the darkness leaf by leaf. I lay there for half the night listening to the whistles blow every hour as the trains rolled through Ashland. Biggs' snores were swells rolling out over an utterly brown sea while the train whistles were a shadowy pit and conjured up the total absence of color. The whistle was the lonesomest thing I'd ever heard. They blew with such regularity you could set your watch by them, and they made me somehow nostalgic for places I'd never been.

It was depressing, but my hours of researching tropical beaches at Greenwood had narrowed my search. The images of Central America's shabby-chic coast had called to me from the screen, and so I drank in the longing and the emptiness which was itself a type of presence because I knew soon enough I'd never feel those things again and perhaps they'd be missed. I would have left right then, if I'd known the location. It had to be the right place and I knew I was closing in. When I got there—if I got there—it would be like having trillions of eyes seeing trillions of lives but all set in one head, if that makes sense.

I wrapped the silence between the whistles around me like a blanket and wondered about all the things happening right then in different countries all over the world while Biggs snored his fat-headed life away. I became anxious about the unique experiences I was missing out on. I became aware of how quickly time was passing, of the unwinding clock in my heart, the hurtling of my flickering consciousness—at nearly forty-five hundred heartbeats per hour—toward the abyss.

I couldn't sleep a wink.

Toward morning, but before first light, Biggs woke up and found my wide eyes locked on him from across the room.

"Oh my god, Lightly," he said, shaking his head in disgust as he flipped around under the sheets. "You're so freaking weird."

"I know, Biggs old buddy," I said. "But you will snore half of your life away, and we only have a finite amount of life in us, you know? Even you must have looked up on a clear night and wondered at the man-destroying beauty of the obliterating stars—as that hawk-loving poet wrote it."

He sighed heavily, so I called him a handsome and powerfully built turd of a young man and told him about all the things people were doing in other countries right at that moment, even detailing a group of disenfranchised youths wearing track suits, smoking spliffs in Brussels' Grand Square, trading their pick-pocketing techniques and small-scale dreams with one another like baseball cards.

I stopped when I could hear him snoring.

4

I awoke mid morning to find Biggs already gone. I was feeling increasingly annoyed by his childish behavior and disappointed in him, what with being his captain and all. But he was a simple creature, I reminded myself, and it was dangerous to try to fix simple creatures in complex ways. Anyway, I assured myself, it was all in his best interest.

I had plans to study with Santana Montana Ordóñez at Greenwood, so I struggled to sit on the edge of the bed and knocked over a wall of unopened care packages. There were two stacks of them in the room—one on my side and the other on Biggs' side—all from my dear mother.

Initially, whenever I'd stack one up unopened, Biggs would shake his square head at me and say, "You should treat your poor mother better. I wish mine would send packages like yours."

"Biggs," I told him sadly, "do you think it's because your head is square that you don't know what you're talking about?"

For a while, I'd take them to the campus post office and mail them to random people in rural North Dakotan towns. This was taking something awful and making something fun out of it. It got old though and around the time I gave that up, Mother started sending the packages to my roommate. This was when she realized—probably after being contacted by thoughtful folks in North Dakota—that I was forwarding them to strangers.

Biggs was thrilled. The first one he opened had sticky notes on each item and a twelve page, handwritten letter updating him on the minutia of my mother's day, asking him questions about his life, advising him on how best to deal with me in a multitude of unlikely hypothetical situations (a peanut allergy attack in a Charleston, South Carolina seafood restaurant, a broken kneecap on a snowy mesa in New Mexico—you get the idea).

Biggs, god bless the witless wonder, wrote her back. He placed his big ass in front of our desktop and used his fat pointer fingers to punch up a response to all the questions. It took him two hours.

"That's how you treat a mother," he said indignantly after he'd mailed it off, but a few days later, when another package arrived for him with a note twice as long asking him twice as many questions, offering advice on twice as many unlikely hypothetical situations, and explaining in great detail how to dress for the upcoming week—the look in his bewildered eye sent me into fits of hysterical laughter.

"What's wrong with you?" I asked, stretching out on the bed and propping my chin on my palms. "Write her back, you ungrateful bastard!"

I watched him pull the items out of the care package: a tube of Dr. Ken's All Natural Toothpaste, a pack of Eden Organic Pistachios, a colorless book published in 1972 entitled *Improving the Study Habits of Young Men*. Each item had a sticky note with tiny writing on both sides exhaustively explaining how to best make use of the item. He read a few of them, then gave up, claiming he had a headache. Soon after that he started stacking the boxes unopened, too.

5

After my shower, I made my way across campus toward the Greenwood Library feeling refreshed and taking deep liberating breaths of the late morning air. There was a bounce in my step, and I clutched the Nike shoebox to me with extra tenderness. I couldn't see the mystical glow of things, but I knew it was there waiting.

When I'd told Santana Montana Ordóñez to meet me at the library, I'd been sure to tell him we would not be studying together as it were, because I didn't have much interest in studying to be honest. I had two exams remaining—Dr. Watson's English exam and Dr. Kwell's Introduction to Physics—and I knew I'd feel less bad about not studying notes or course content if I was in the library reading on similar topics of interest such as high energy works of literature and quantum physics. Also, I just loved the place.

I couldn't tell you a damn thing about the Greenwood Library's architecture, being exceedingly ignorant in that area of knowledge, other than it was a long two-story brick and concrete building. It did have a row of columns out front, but the columns were rising, square slabs lacking ornamentation. And yet, except for the orderly perfection of the football field on game days with the uniformly cut grass and the precision of its painted white lines, Greenwood was, in my opinion, the most beautiful place on campus and the place where I felt most comfortable.

Maybe it was the inside of the library, where the bright rooms with high ceilings were "splashed with light," as they say, and the walls were "painted in varying shades of amber" that gave the place its beauty. Or maybe how the airy, book-lined rooms had clusters of high stalked flowers—magenta, rose-dawn, eggshell white—stabbing higher than castle turrets from golden vases everywhere. More likely though it was the books themselves, the feeling of ideas vibrating from the shelves and the air thick with words longing to be read that made me love the place.

I passed between the columns humming a little tune and went up the stairs to the second floor where a row of two dozen chair-lined wooden tables ran the length of the library. And who do you suppose I saw at those tables? Of course, that amazing outcast Santana Montana Ordóñez. He sat alone at the farthest table toward the front of the library. All the way down at the opposite end of the library was a table crowded by six of my offensive linemen and Thelonious Monk, my fullback, nicknamed Rampage on account of his exploits on the field. *Good Lord,* I thought, *this is an illustration of the problem in some way.*

I decided to check in on my teammates first, in part because it was a surprise to see them together in the library—in any such place of learning really. The way a hush fell over them when they saw me approaching made me curious and suspicious all at once. There was something ridiculous about them sitting there in their workout gear, and about the optical illusion their massiveness created by making the large library table and generous Windsor chairs seem like they were built to the scale of preschoolers.

"It's the Tommy Jeffs brain trust," I said when I stood before them. I put the shoebox on the table and asked, "What the hell gives?"

Naturally, Thomas Hicks Rambo spoke up first. He was my center, sort of the brain of the o-line and a fellow captain. He had to call out the blocking scheme at the line for every play based on the defensive alignment and he was sure the hell good at it.

"Nothing, Lightly," he said, rearing back and causing the chair to creak in agony. "Just running a little exam game plan for the fellas here. As co-captain, you know how we can't afford another batch of academic casualties like we had this year. We could have won the division with what we lost instead of coming in second." The patient tone of his voice was a dull, bland blue, the same color I perceived on the rare occasions when I heard politicians speak. I looked around at their wide faces, but they weren't looking at me.

"Wait," I said. "You all look too uncomfortable for that to be the truth. Rampage?" I asked, focusing on my beloved short, thickset fullback and calling his name in a loving, slightly mocking way. "Rampage?" I repeated. Thomas Hicks Rambo glanced at Rampage and then back at me. "My beautiful friend, Rampage, here," I said gesturing toward him, "won't even look me in the eye, Hicksie. That tells me more than I need to know. Do you think I'm an idiot?"

"No," said Thomas Hicks Rambo evenly.

"You think I can't see the lines of what you're doing?"

"No," he repeated.

"Because I see a cherub that sees them," I said. "And those lines make a picture that is ridiculously clear to me."

"I'm not sure I know what you mean," he said.

"I'm not sure that you don't," I said. The four other linemen, being under-classmen and in the presence of their star quarterback, just looked on uncertainly and slightly baffled, while my roommate, Biggs, shook his head. Biggs looked deeply annoyed.

"Go ahead," I said pointing toward the speck at the head of the library that was Santana Montana Ordóñez. "Go ahead and let what you feel about that kid down there outweigh our friendship. I swear to god I love you giant bastards, but your ignorance astounds me. Look around at all these books, the complexity and brilliance of the ideas that this light preserves like amber encases flies. You defile this place with such narrow ideas and exclusionary tactics. Can't you see I'm trying to *fix* you?"

Stiles, one of the freshman linemen leaned toward Biggs and whispered, "What's an *exclusionary tactic*?" but Biggs wasn't listening. Biggs' head cut toward me violently.

"Fix *us*?" he asked in disbelief, his words hissing through gritted teeth. "Fix *us*? The guy who says he *hears in colors*? The guy who talks about dead people and universes in his sleep? The guy who took a loaded van and tried to kill..." He didn't finish that last thought though because Thomas Hicks Rambo had placed a hand on his forearm as if trying to sooth a distracted creature. Biggs buried his square chin into his broad pectorals, all silent and sullen.

"Well, Biggs," I said. "Glad to know you're talking to me again, because I really do love you. Since you brought it up, I can tell you that your angry words are the color of an overripe beefsteak tomato, which means they match the color of your face at the moment." I looked at all of them, threw my hands in the air and said, "Look, I'm sorry if I've made you all mad, but don't you remember, Hicksie, how both you and Biggs referred to Rampage as "*the nigger*" when he first joined the team, and now through common experiences, shared battles on the field, and the passage of seasons together you both would walk into oncoming traffic for him, which is as it should be? All I'm trying to do is speed up things by foisting a gay Mexican upon you so that the same process takes hold. I know you are each the perfection of your-selves, but there are other versions of you running around, other yous created by pivotal choices you might have made but didn't. Each of you is trapped in a bunch of junk marble and there's a beautiful thing trying to come out. I'm just a guy standing here with a chisel trying to make you beautiful. If you only knew how the sound of that glorious thing trying to claw its way out breaks my heart... Listen, I tell you what, let's all huddle up at the Alpha Alpha party tonight and talk things out. I'm about to embark on a big adventure, and one of you has a ticket for a seat on that plane. What do you say, my meat-headed buddies?"

They didn't say anything. Thomas Hicks Rambo was hanging his head with Biggs in shame, and Rampage was looking incredulously from one downcast face to another with a fierce look on his beautiful dark face.

I retrieved my shoebox, shrugged and made my way up the spine of tables to Santana Montana Ordóñez. Even so, I could hear Rampage clearly.

"Called me what?" I heard him say in disbelief. His voice sounded as coiled-and-spring-ready as his thickset frame, and I nodded a little in agreement with the righteousness of his rising anger. "Called me what?" he demanded louder.

6

The rest of my experience that morning was pleasant. I sat on Santana Montana Ordóñez's side of the table and we both read. He was reading through his extensive notes for Dr. Watson's exam, and I'd grabbed a copy of Berry's *The Angry Farmer Poems* and the collected short stories of Breece D'J Pancake. I'd also pulled a few books off the shelves that had to do with quantum physics and general science, mostly textbooks that I felt spoke the language of my impending adventure. I pretended to smoke a cigarette and read paragraphs here and there from each, feeling the mixing of their pieces would tell one story—a story that would be more complete than any one could tell on its own.

Big glass panels flanked Santana Montana Ordóñez and me. We sat looking out over the bright span of the library and I felt we were defiantly facing the entire world together. Every few minutes Santana Montana Ordóñez would lift his nose from his notes to glance at the stairwell and it was very much as if he was expecting something awful to come slithering up. He was dead silent, too. Maybe it was because we had Dr. Watson's exam tomorrow. Maybe it was because when he did speak, he employed a formality of speech to compensate for his accent that was immediately ridiculous. Regardless, he'd never asked me a single question, and I was waiting for him to do it because I knew it would mean he trusted me and that he felt comfortable.

He'd been in my canoeing elective at the beginning of the year. When our poor, doomed instructor, a free spirit former lifeguard we all just called Gary, took us on a trip to the James River and left the class behind to paddle out and test the conditions, the Alpha Alphas started picking on Santana Montana Ordóñez. He tried to ignore them by standing there and scribbling in his notebook but they wouldn't lay off. A group of girls might have been unintentionally elevating the degree of torment, and the boys crowded around him. Crampton, the big racist bastard, was there. Riley and Redmon, who were among the AAs I liked, had told me once that Crampton hated me because he was in love with Emmy. I'd told them that everyone was in love with Emmy and that hating me was irrational. Well, Crampton, you see, started pretending to speak in Spanish and kind of bumping Santana Montana Ordóñez around. A number of the folks hung back, and to be fair a few of the AAs did, too. I suppose they wanted to hide the fact that they were uncomfortable with what was going on, but did not want to crawl out on that suspect social limb to stop it.

I was off a ways contemplating a pale yellow butterfly asleep on a dark tree. Something in the composition called to mind bedtime lullabies and the comforting sounds parents make in the downstairs kitchen when little boys are supposed to be asleep in darkness above but aren't. So I wasn't aware of the brutality occurring on the sand right away, and, in truth, it might have looked like good-natured stuff because Santana Montana Ordóñez had closed his notebook and was sort of laughing along with them like he was in on it, too. But when I glanced over, even at my distance I could see the tightness of his mouth. His eyes were begging for it to be over. When Crampton *accidentally* bumped him, Santana Montana's notebook went flapping up into the air as he went over in a heap at the water's edge. I'd seen enough and came down to insert myself into the situation.

"There you are, you freaking nut," I'd said as I walked over to Santana Montana Ordóñez, grabbed him up, and slung my arm around him. I turned him to face Crampton and the AAs and I said, "You found him, you brilliant klatch of handsome bastards. Many thanks."

And off the hell we went, quick as an insult hurled from a passing car, back up the little spit of quarry sand.

Later on that afternoon, once I sat with my new friend in a canoe on the James and we were out of earshot, I leaned into him and said, "I've got this strange feeling like we've never met before."

"We have not."

"Jesus," I said, giving his knee a slap, "that was close on the beach, wasn't it?" He didn't say a word, and I laughed out loud. It felt safe out there and I thought of Huckleberry Finn and Jim and how continual movement was the only way to be safe. Gary was way up ahead, paddling furiously and leaving the rest of us behind. None of us ever got credit for that course. With two classes remaining, Gary Shuttlesworth hung himself with a belt from a rafter in his modest off-campus apartment. I guess he had his reasons.

Anyway, it was pretty soon after the intervention at the river, that I started sitting with Santana Montana Ordóñez in Estes Dining Hall all the time exactly because no one liked him and he sat alone. The o-line got to feeling unsettled by my absence at their table on account of Coach's rule that they sit with me at all times to really engrain the idea of constant protection. They stayed silent, though, no doubt waiting for my shenanigans to play out and for me to return to the status quo, as it were.

But I sat over with Santana Montana Ordóñez whenever possible. Students would give us the eye, but I'd give them the what-the-hell-are-you-staring-at face. Maybe I just thought they were giving us the eye, but then I spied Anne Marie, Emmy's short but luscious roommate, approaching.

I nudged him.

"Say hello," I said.

"I don't know," he said. "Her father owns Umbro."

"Say it, you glorious bespectacled bastard. Your grandfather stared down the fiercest bulls in Spain and was idolized by Hemingway!"

"Hello, Anne Marie," he said breathlessly as she drew near.

"Oh, god," Anne Marie said. Her lip curled unpleasantly and her pretty orbs rolled in her head.

"Go on, Anne Marie Wentworth, you gorgeous vixen!" I yelled over the crowded dining hall as she walked away. "You're at the top of the social ladder, you delicate creature, way up in rarefied air, but Santana Montana Ordóñez and I are up where ladders don't matter. We're outside the system!" I hung my arm around Santana Montana Ordóñez and looked over at the table of gawking freshmen beside us.

"What the heavenly fuck are you looking at?" I demanded.

And now here we were, Santana Montana Ordóñez and myself, sitting together in this bright library with the cocoon and the shoebox and books and notes strewn before us, and summer looming larger than Christmas to little children. I hadn't even seen the o-line leave, but they were gone. Santana Montana Ordóñez sat hunched over his composition book containing notes written in pastel purple ink from Dr. Watson's class. He kept his face only a few inches from the paper, but I could see enough of the writing to appreciate the elegant curves of his penmanship, and though I couldn't be sure, I suspected the entire notebook was filled from front to back and top to bottom with it.

I tried to leave the poor bastard alone to study but I was finding it difficult to read. God, did I want the exams done and the term over. I felt that if I didn't get going on my big adventure, I might explode before all could be made whole. I knew life was a narrow stream of streetlight and death the constricting darkness on either side. I knew that no one else understood it just

23

so.

A few hours later I was in a room full of anxious people. While we labored on his exam, Dr. Kwell sat up front behind a large black laboratory bench. There was a sink in it with the tall narrow tap rising and curving like the neck of some slender chrome serpent. On the bench were a pair of protective lab glasses, a few neat stacks of papers, and a steaming mug of coffee. The rest of the room expanding from the bench was an unfinished painting—a few empty cabinets and bookshelves giving way to pale, bare walls that faded in turn to the empty outskirts of the canvas.

The air in the room was tense with churning minds and the flare of heat rising from rigid anxious bodies, but there was silence, too. Beneath that silence I could hear a sudsing of foam, the bubbling of other universes, the hum of the machinery of it all. Emmy sat working intently a few spots away. I studied her as I listened to the secret music and found myself appreciating the familiar, well-loved, yellow tinge of her body. Those first few months we were dating, the sight of Emmy would inexplicably bring to my nose the scent of suntan lotion and flannel fresh and warm from the dryer.

Dr. Kwell's exam was full of short formulas that needed completion and word problems necessitating a great deal of math. I swear I tried, but I could not force myself to address such little things, so I wrote about light being both a wave and a particle and the concept of one particle being in many different places at once. Math proved that the only thing that could change the rule was someone observing the electron—then it had to pick a location which was a very curious thing.

It had to do with the double-slit experiment and Schrodinger's Cat, of course, and I mentioned them in my essay, for that was what I chose to do instead of the exam Kwell had provided. I wrote that I felt bad for that damn cat, being both dead and alive until Schrodinger looked in on it and what not. I suggested that Schrodinger should have just left that poor cat alone altogether. If he'd never looked in on it, I argued, it could be both alive and dead, and that sure the hell was better than risking being dead for certain.

That wasn't it, though, as I wanted to try and do more on my essay. In me was a desire to astound Dr. Kwell, to save him from his pessimism and sarcasm and show him something beautiful—which is the cure for such character traits. And I started to. I could sense that the discordance between the physics of large objects and the physics of particles could be solved and that the answer, if I could arrive at it, would be so ridiculously simple that it had to be true. I started writing toward that answer, but soon my head began to tighten. So I gave up and closed the booklet. When I glanced up, I caught Emmy looking at me with concern, but she returned her focus to the exam on her desk so quickly that I wondered whether I had imagined it.

I remembered telling Emmy that first night we met I thought I was great. I didn't mean it in any egotistical way but just as an observation. It was at that big party December before last at the Pineapple House. Emmy's drop dead gorgeous, no doubt about it. She's a year older and as tall as me. My chest got all water-logged and filled with sparkles when I saw her and I ran up to her because I'm weird, and that's just how I am. Anyway, the snow was falling outside, big silver dollar flakes coming down slow, and we were sitting on the couch yelling into each other's face because of the band, and when I told her I was great, she'd asked, "So you think that anyone would fall in love with you?"

I told her, "That's right. If they got to know me."

That one threw her, but later on, after we'd been hanging out for a few weeks, she said, "You know, Lightly. I think you might be right," which meant she loved me. It was true and I was right, but that doesn't mean I'm big-headed. I mean I'm smart and athletic, and I won a scholarship for my brain, and on the field my arm is pure gold. I know most would think I'm an egomaniac, but I swear to god, I'm not. All these things are just true, and I don't feel one way or the other about them.

I looked over at Emmy, feeling a little wistful about her but also wary. I knew special people like Emmy had the ability to derail a person's pursuit of his dream.

I flipped my exam booklet over on my desk. On the back I wrote down the official web address for the Large Hadron Collider at Cern and my mother's recipe for chocolate chip cookies along with a note that said, "Dr. Kwell, I encourage you to have some cookies and check out recent discoveries of the LHC. They will no doubt fill you with a longing that only a mother's cookies could quell." I knew Dr. Kwell would grimace or moan when he encountered that awful last word and that knowledge gave lightness to my spirit.

As I approached Dr. Kwell's lab bench at the front, he glanced up and rubbed his beard into his hand. He was a massive bear of a man, and he gave me one of those *Oh, for heaven's sake, what is it now?* looks, which seemed to intimidate other students but I found endearing in a way that was also a little sad. He looked at the shoebox I held and shook his head as if very tired.

I put the blue exam booklet down on the floor and stood on top of it.

"Look, Dr. Kwell," I whispered. "This exam is beneath me. Get it?"

His hand moved up and rubbed over the skin of his bald dome.

I picked it up and put it on his desk and smiled at him warmly. He glanced at the wall clock and then leaned across his desk at me and whispered, "This is a two hour exam, Lightly."

"God, I know it," I said. "It's a monster."

"Yes, I know that it is a monster," he said. "Which is why I'm confused as to how you could finish it in twenty-five minutes."

"You ever felt like you've done something before?"

"You mean you think you've taken this same test before?"

"No, I mean I've quit taking it after twenty-five minutes before and I want to be consistent." He put the cap on his pen and stuck it in his breast pocket.

"Did you answer any of the questions this time?" he asked quietly.

"Well, no," I whispered. "I wrote about particle-wave duality in light and how if you send a single photon particle through one of two slits, something like a wave goes through the other slit any damn way and then interferes with the light on the other side. I also tried to put forth a theory that could explain how the physics of the small and the physics of the large are actually the same physics because only in their difference can all things work in a successful and unified way. Sadly, though, I got a cramp in my pumpkin and had to stop."

Kwell leaned over his wide elbows at me so that our faces were very close.

"You know," he said in a low voice. "I was forgiving when you pulled this on the midterm. I won't be this time."

"I trust your judgment, Dr. Kwell," I said.

Dr. Kwell sighed heavily. A few of the students up front were inexpertly pretending not to watch us.

"You do know that failing this course jeopardizes your football eligibility."

Despite the dull throb in my head I smiled at him and gave him a wink to assure him that I was on his side in the matter. He studied me. The exam with my shoe prints lay on the desk between us.

"Fine," he said, giving a dismissive wave.

As I made for the door, I said, "Boy, do I love you, sir, and wish you all the best." Then I was off, much closer to my adventure now and being pulled down the hallway toward the glass double doors, through which I could already see how the leaves on the oaks were agitated by that nameless thing. The angle of the sun was such that the floor tiles shimmered brilliantly with the dual qualities of light. For a moment I had the feeling I was about to enter the sanctity of some bright, flooded place. But as the point of observation, which was me, drew closer to that celestial door, all the angles—of sunlight, tile, glass, and eyes—changed, so that I took the last few steps over plain, gritty tiles, which were chipped and imperfect.

When I get to where I'm going, I'll send Dr. Kwell a postcard. It will begin, *You are an angsty teenage son and the universe a mother waiting for you to grow up and realize the unmatched glory of the love she bears you.* It will end, *Don't you think the 11-dimensional folds of M-theory's structure of the universe look suspiciously similar to the folds of a human brain?*

All Things Await

7

That afternoon, back at the Moreland Dorm, I sat at the little desk in my room continuing my research on the good old computer. There was already loud music echoing through the hallway as the students drank in preparation for the drinking to follow at night, but I ignored it. Earlier, I'd narrowed my search down to Central America, and I pored over thousands of images from places all over it as I tried to zero in on the spot where my vision would appear. I had a sense of what the scene might look like—the background of the event, I mean.

After an hour of searching, I hit on a string of images in a shared, online travel album of the coast along Central America. My breath caught a little and there was sort of a rush inside me, if you know what I mean. When I began clicking on pictures in an album titled "Coastal Costa Rica," an electric tingle pulsated up and down my spine.

Ten minutes later I'd found *the* place. That was it. I'd known I was very close, but I was still surprised at how easy it was. The photo I found in the album was of a wide, crescent beach, with a dark exposed reef on the left jetting into the water. Curving palms leaned into the photo at either edge, the boughs bushy and rugged, tousled like the hair of my little nieces when they first crawl from their beds. I knew immediately I'd found the place.

I stared at it. I wanted to swallow it whole, but I also wanted to dissect it to find out what it was about the collection of elements in the photo that could produce my singular and profound feeling of certainty. Judging from the photo, there even appeared to be good surf there and that was fortunate.

Although it was true I'd never tried to stand up on a short board, I wasn't bad at all on a longer board. Pop had given me a board for my tenth birthday, an eight-foot, six-inch WRV fun shape, which I still kept with my mom's Dextra Classic at the beach house over on Hatteras Island.

I printed out two color copies. Gently, I sniffed the ink of the beach. I had the feeling that the vision had been waiting there for someone like me since before the place even existed, that its flowering intensity had made water and land form around it and on the land trees, and above the water sky and so on and so on. I looked at the printout closely. There was a fuzzy wumpling just above the horizon line and I studied it. Was the vision wrapped inside another dimension and so close but closed off to all but me? Would the vision grow from there or emerge in my mind as something like veils fell away? I didn't know. All I knew was that I'd found the place, and that when I actually saw it in person, with all its parts moving, folding in upon themselves and coiling, it would speak to me. It would tell me things, and I would be part of the thing being told.

I don't know how long I sat at the computer staring at the beach and ruminating before I noticed Biggs had entered the room. He was standing just inside the door looking me over, as if somehow surprised to find me there.

"Hey there, Biggs, old buddy," I said, twisting from the table to lean over the chair back at him. "What's shaking?"

"Nothing," he said somewhat reluctantly.

"Are you going to the Alpha Alpha party tonight?" I asked.

He glanced back out into the hallway. His dry down-turning mouth annoyed me.

"What's wrong Biggs," I asked. "You gone shy on me or something?" He was frozen there on the spot wanting to leave but not knowing if he should. Biggs' grandfather had been an oilman in Texas. He'd made his money with his hands, and a combination of hard work and dumb luck. I'd met the family a number of times, let them take me to dinner on a few occasions when they came up to visit Biggs, and I knew their love of manly silence, and their aversion to new ideas and fear of introspection, which had double-helixed its way into my roommate's persona. It occurred to me that the gray matter behind Biggs' dull brown eyes might not know why it hesitated just inside the threshold, why it wasn't sure what to do next.

I found that thought funny and the laughter I let loose was genuine and filled our little room.

"Jeez, Biggs," I said when I could. "I love you, you big, muscle-bound fool. And I know how you feel. I mean, on the one hand you're mad as hell because I stopped sitting with the o-line as coach instructed and then you got angrier when I returned and brought Santana Montana Ordóñez to sit with us, and now you're bordering on rage simply because I spoke the truth about the racist words you used as bricks to build a stupid wall between you and Rampage. But on the other hand you've been conditioned for a few years now to protect my hide at all costs, we've formed a good bond with one another going to battle on the gridiron and being roommates and all, perhaps its starting to dawn on you that I attack the bad parts of you because I love other parts of you, too."

I'd noticed the redness spreading on his face as I talked, but thought it was due to the embarrassment any man might feel to hear himself explained so accurately with such ease, or perhaps from hearing the word *love* come out of another man's mouth in his direction. But the barely suppressed anger in his response was so sharp, it gave a tremulous quality to his voice.

"Bad enough to stop being a teammate," he said, taking a half stride toward me then stopping as if uncertain of himself. "But you have to start hanging out with that Mexican fairy. Some wanted to write you off right then, but Rampage and Thomas Hicks Rambo said you'd come around, that this was just like the thing last year. Remember how that ended, with you wrecking a loaded van and your head all split open?" The tone of his words filled the air with pointy orange and red triangles. "I said that too, you know," he continued. "But then you go and bring that damn weirdo over to the table to sit with us at lunch. You make Rampage hate us, and you sit here with that stupid cocoon in a shoebox. And how you can laugh like that... And how someone like you, with your shit can think you can fix anyone…" There was more to say but I don't think Biggs could organize it. So his mouth clamped shut to keep it in, something which I saw now was more hurt than anything, and the embryo of another complaint died in his throat.

I gave him my most serious look until the glare in his eyes faded and then asked him if he knew what it meant to long for something.

He sighed, his meaty arms hung limp now from his shoulders.

"Sure," he said tiredly. "I long for food when I'm hungry."

"Sometimes, like in that desolate *Look Homeward, Angel* book you've never read, being hungry is a sign of the longing I'm talking about, but something tells me that's not the case for you. What other things have you longed for?"

He turned his head slowly from side to side as if the answer lay hidden somewhere on the cluttered floor. "I guess I long for Emmy's roommate—what's her name?—Anne Marie Wentworth. I long to win the ODAC next year. I long-"

"That is not what I'm talking about, Biggs, goddamn it. I'm talking about an overpowering yearning, something that your entire being is moved by and drawn toward."

He shifted his weight uneasily as if he needed to pee and fixed me with a

31

look of bewilderment, which seemed threaded somehow with an uncharacteristic openness.

"Are you," he began hesitantly. "Are you telling me you have gay longings?"

"Jesus, Biggs," I said. "I'm trying to tell you what is happening, why I'm behaving the way I am. What I'm referring to is something at the very core of what it means to be a human being. Listen, Biggs," I said, keeping my voice even. "I don't mean to upset your narrow view of the world. Often folks aren't conscious of the type of thing I'm talking about. Let's chat again at the party tonight—you, me, Rampage, and the rest of the o-line. I didn't want to be specific in front of the others in the library, but I have enough money to buy four extra tickets and I'd like you to take the first one. We'll hammer out the details. There are only two big parties left, after all. I'll bring a bottle of Jack Daniels and we'll sit on those stupid couches in front of Alpha Alpha with Redmon and that handsome bastard Riley and strike an accord."

Biggs sighed heavily. Outside the punctual whistle sounded and the train came down the tracks with a roar that shook the window.

"No one says *strike an accord*," he said quietly. "And I ain't going to be at no fucking party." He fixed his dark exhausted eyes on me. "Hicksie and I called a meeting with Coach tonight."

The air particles around me burst into microscopic splinters.

"Don't you do that, goddamn it," I snarled. "You know who he'll call, and there'll be no season next year. Worse yet no quest if she's fast enough!" But Biggs was already walking back down the hall. I leaned into the hallway. "My health is not part of Sanford's job description!" I yelled out after him.

He paused at the big door, through which I could see light leaving the sky like water draining from a punctured bottle.

"Right," he said. "It's part of mine, remember?"

Lately, I've been thinking a lot about god and death, and I've got my theories.

8

They were the top dog fraternity, the Alpha Alphas, and their end of the year party was always big. There was a whole ridiculous social system at play, and the Alpha Alphas were at the top. They were rich and the handsomest bunch, as I've said. What that meant was the best girls went there to party, which meant all the guys wanted to be there. Which was precisely why I didn't want to be there—especially since my o-line, who normally partied there, would be away with Coach Sanford completing the mutiny they'd no doubt hashed out in the library.

So, around ten o'clock I called up Santana Montana and Rampage and they came over. Rampage brought over a twelve pack of Budweiser. He was always gracious with his things like letting folks borrow his car, or copy off his notes, or sharing his food on those long bus rides home from away games. He offered me a beer, but I was already working on the Jack.

I loved Thelonious "Rampage" Monk. I loved how he was good at math and terrible at basketball. He loved horses, John Coltrane, and painting empty landscapes with acrylics. On the football field he lusted after violent collisions and had a tendency to enter upon what I called a berserker's rage, but I knew our opponents would be surprised if they were able to study his noble face and the bright intelligence of his brown, gold-stippled eyes.

Rampage sat on the bed drinking in silence, and I knew why but didn't say a word.

"You okay, Rampage?"

"Yeah," he said, his voice taking on its characteristic color of sliced liverwurst. "Why?"

"Just because. Hey, you need to speak in tropes more frequently. Don't respond. Think it over." I winked at him. He shook his head, lifted the beer. I knew coming over meant he wasn't angry with me, and I figured he'd talk about what happened at the library when he was ready. Santana Montana Ordóñez had brought a book that, judging by the cover, had to do with ecology or some similar subject and he kept jotting notes from it into his notebook. Santana Montana was sharp as a tack, and if he had his spectacles with him he could identify any tree just by looking at a leaf or inspecting the bark.

Since they were so silent, I told them I wanted to play a game. I told them I'd try and explain their childhoods—what growing up was like for them—and even outline a few of the more memorable events that had shaped them, and then they could tell me how close I was to their actual experiences. They sat back—Santana Montana on Biggs' bed and Rampage on mine—and I spent a half hour doing so. I paced as I talked, sipping occasionally from my bottle of Jack Daniels, as outside, the late evening began to fold itself down into night.

At the end, I asked them if I was close. Santana Montana Ordóñez said that he was sorry but that none of the things I'd said had happened to him. Rampage, though, nodded and said the particulars were different but some of the events I described rang true.

Maybe it was the silence of the room that followed or the unexpected turn my education of the o-line had taken, but I suddenly felt the need to see Emmy's face, to be close enough to her to see those tiny freckles across the bridge of her nose. I knew freckles were an imperfection of the skin and loved how perceived imperfections could make a face perfect. Such things proved truths others couldn't see and made me want to wink knowingly at someone but there was no one else who knew. I stood up and said, "We're going over to Emmy's. Let's roll."

Rampage shrugged. He stood up. He was short, maybe five-foot-seven in cleats, but built like a bomb shelter. He killed the rest of his fourth Budweiser, then crushed it in his hands and threw it violently against the wall.

"Okay," he said calmly. "I'm ready." Santana Montana Ordóñez tried to back out, saying he needed to study for Dr. Watson's English exam.

"You've studied all day," I said. "Let's roll." But we didn't roll. At least not straight away.

Halfway down the hall Rampage gave me a nudge. I looked up and saw it was about a dozen of them. All brand new Theta sisters, judging from their good looks.

"Oh, jeez, give me a break," I said under my breath to Rampage, but he put his arm behind me and pushed me forward. A cute little brunette was at the front of the girls. She had a little spray of freckles from cheek to cheek that looked like the speckles on a shell. She sported what looked to be an expensive, trendy haircut, but I couldn't be sure about such things.

"Hi, boys," she said, bringing her group to a halt.

"Let me guess," Rampage said smiling. "The annual hottie list." I didn't moan, but I wanted to. The hottie list was a rite of passage for recently pledged freshmen sorority girls. Basically they were given a list by their sorority of the ten hottest guys on campus and then, in order to become full-fledged sorority members, they had to track them down, introduce them-selves, and get signatures. Freshman year, it had been fun to be on the list, but it had gotten old last year. Now, it felt downright painful.

"You bet," the brunette said to Rampage enthusiastically. You could tell by the emphatic nod as she spoke that she was the energetic type, as were the five or six beaming beauties right behind her. The girls sort of clung to each other in a nervous, yet flirtatious sort of way. The tallest of them, a blonde sunbeam of a girl wearing a tight blue tee shirt that had *Yes!* written on it in white lettering, brought her face really close to mine. "Wow," she said. "You really do have insanely gorgeous blue eyes."

"With the key word there being *insane*," Rampage said with a laugh. I shook my head at him. God did I hate the hottie list, but the presence of beauty always made me smile like a moron. So I was smiling when I thanked her. Personally, though, I would be more likely to identify with the two or three standing in the back. They looked like the hottie list was an irritant and degrading somehow, and I agreed. I know I felt degraded.

"Would you like the hottie to sign it for you?" Rampage asked.

"That'd be awesome," the brunette said.

Rampage looked back down the hall past me to where Santana Montana had wandered off a ways. He winked at me and before I could stop him yelled, "It's the hottie list, Santana. Stop being shy and come up here and sign for these nice girls!" Santana Montana didn't even look at us. He turned away and leaned his shoulder into the wall.

The poor brunette looked a bit flustered. "I'm sorry," she said. She looked at the other girls for a moment and then back to us. "No. I'm sorry. Not him. We need Lightly's signature."

"Oh damn, Santana!" Rampage yelled. "Did you hear that?" He had him-self a good laugh. He was still laughing as I signed the paper and handed the clipboard back to the blushing brunette. I felt like saying, *You oughtn't to have done that*, to Rampage, but I didn't want him telling me how no one used *oughtn't* any more.

We stepped out of the Moreland Dorm into the warm, overcast night. Orbs of mist had awakened and fluttered up like moths to encircle each source of light. Small stains of streetlight spread across the sidewalk as we made our way across campus. I told Rampage and Santana Montana that each patch of light was a sunny tropical island and that the darkness between them was the sea. I leapt across the darkness from bright island to bright island.

The bottle of Jack was in my hand and I was a little tipsy, but only pleasurably so. I could hear Rampage laughing as he leapt along behind me, and it filled me with joy in a way that his laughter at the expense of Santana Montana had not.

When I turned to look at them, I saw that even Santana Montana, who was following the lights behind Rampage, was smiling shyly. They stopped to look at me. We were all perched on our little islands separated by dark water and I said, "I know the location of my big adventure, and I want you to know I'll be buying tickets for both of you." They looked like they were about to say something, but I held up my hand. "This adventure will be the most important thing that you ever do and I don't want to say another word on the matter tonight." I smiled and turned back to leap across another stretch of dark.

When we got to the sorority house that gorgeous vixen Anne Marie Wentworth, Emmy's roommate, said Emmy was gone. She stood in the doorway flanked by all those perfectly ordered black picture frames from floor to ceiling. She made sure to let me know what she thought of me bringing Rampage and Santana Montana into the radiance of her sorority by putting the worst look on her face I'd seen on a pretty girl in a while.

"Sweet, Jesus, Anne Marie," I said, not wanting to let it pass. Maybe it was wrong to rake her over the coals. I remembered lying naked with Emmy under her fresh sheets one night when the conversation drifted to Anne Marie, and Emmy had told me Anne Marie had a crush on me and had since the day she saw me. Emmy had said Anne Marie was wired to be dismissive of boys she liked for some unfathomable reason. But that hadn't softened me toward her, so I cocked my head at Anne Marie and asked, "Do you have the gases or something?"

She blinked and her hands shot up to her hips as if under the power of some great magnet. The air was sweet from the purple and yellow irises on the coffee table behind her.

"What do you mean?" she asked.

"The horrific look that just came across your face like someone punched your bowels." Anne Marie's wince was almost imperceptible, but I saw it clear as could be.

She didn't give me another second but said, in a voice the color of a beaver's pelt, "Emmy's at the AA party," and tried to shut the door. I put my foot against it and searched for something to say.

"What?" she demanded. "I've got to get ready to go, too."

"Nothing," I said. I didn't feel guilty, but felt that perhaps I should so I said, "Emmy tells me you're spending the summer amongst the beaches of the Outer Banks."

Anne Marie wasn't having any of it. She told me that no one said *amongst* and then she said something really odd. She looked me up and down and said, "It doesn't matter how good you look, Lightly. You can't get away with wearing the same shirt and pants for four days." I moved my foot and she slammed the door in my face. I wanted to laugh, but I didn't. I felt sorry for Anne Marie Wentworth because I knew then that she really did love me.

"Uh-oh," Rampage said once we were back outside.

"What?"

"Nothing. Maybe Emerald is going to stop slumming is all. Trade up for an AA guy." I laughed out loud.

"I love you, Rampage, you honest rascal. Your noble spirit is slumming just by being at a school like this, and I agree that Emmy is slumming with me no doubt, but I don't think she'd run off with one of those AA boys."

"Why not?" asked Santana Montana. Being that Santana Montana Ordóñez had never asked me a question, I momentarily couldn't figure out who had asked it. Then I smiled, feeling more certain than ever that I was saving him somehow, and said, "Because, my genius plump friend, I wouldn't mind if she did."

That one got them quiet, and I was glad they didn't ask me to explain because all I knew was that it was true. I didn't know why.

As we neared the Alpha Alpha house the mist changed and seemed to fatten and clog the lights. The resulting hazy glow might have made the well-lit place look tranquil and quaint except that the frat house air spun with blasts of music and raucous bragging and laughter. *Do it Again, Baby!* with its mind-jarring baseline blared. The end of the year party was in full swing inside and no doubt the rooms would be so packed you couldn't even stand without touching three people.

The brothers had pulled couches right outside the entrance like always, and were drinking, yelling to one another above the ear-splitting music. Santana Montana didn't turn up the walk to the house but held back.

"What is it, Santana Montana?" I asked.

"Nothing," he said. "I think that I will just wait out here is all." They were not a bad bunch all in all, the AAs. Not all of them were racist, but enough to make a visit uncomfortable for folks like him. I didn't like that Santana Montana felt uncomfortable about coming, but I didn't want to push it. After all, it was about midnight now, and they'd all be drunk as hell.

"You suit yourself, Santana Montana." I gave his fleshy shoulder a squeeze and it was like squeezing on an overripe cantaloupe.

"Ouch," he said. "That feels bad."

"Back in two shakes of the ugly stick," I told him.

"If it starts to rain," Santana Montana Ordóñez called behind us, "I will go back to your room and await you there."

I nodded, loving him a little for how he'd said *await*. Rampage and I went up the walk toward the house.

As we approached the couches I saw it was Crampton sitting there. He had what looked to be a bottle of bourbon in his hand, and his face was all red. It would have been bad for Santana Montana to encounter him again in this condition and I was embarrassed by how glad I was he'd not come along. The other faces, at least the few I could make out, I didn't know and didn't care to.

"Shit," I said, sensing we were going for trouble. Crampton was the worst. You could tolerate him when he was sober, but when he was drunk it was bad.

He hopped up off the couch quickly when he saw Rampage beside me.

"Hey!" he shouted coming up to stand in our way.

"Hello, there Crampton, old buddy," I said. "What's shaking?"

He drew himself up as best he could to be authoritative. Just the motion, the sad attempt at superiority, made me hate him. "Whoa there," he said, holding out his big paw to stop us. In his other hand he held a half-full bottle of Wild Turkey. "Where do you think you're going, Lightly?" he demanded. His voice was the same color I saw in the voices of other lowbrow racists, which was that of a half-eaten sachertorte left to sun for an hour on the table of a café in Oostende. Even a few feet away I could smell the liquor on his breath. Crampton glanced at the shadowy AAs who were gathered behind him. He was a big old bastard, a nasty defenseman on the lacrosse team and from all reports, one of the dirtiest players in the conference.

"I'm going lightly into this goddamn frat house, Cramps," I said.

"Not with him you're not," he said.

"Not with that what?" I said. My blood bubbled and I snarled, "You fucking…" I swung at him over Rampage's shoulder, but Rampage had already given him a vicious shove. Being so drunk, Crampton staggered back and couldn't catch his balance. Instead, the couch caught his knees and he went over it backwards in a heap.

He yelled something from behind the couch and the dark horde moved toward us.

"You racist shits!" I yelled. "I'm coming for you Cramps, you buffoon, you fucking racist dolt!" I surged into them but they were on us. Rampage had a group on him and then I didn't see him again. I only saw fists and shoes striking out from the dark. "Jesus!" I yelled, when one caught my face square. "That one hurt." I swung and clawed, thinking how one of the fuckers was snarling like a wolverine—primitive and guttural. I yelled, "This one's for Santana Montana Ordóñez!" and threw a right hook, and someone got caught by it. It sounded like a slap.

They shrieked and stumbled off.

There were two big thuds on my back. "Ouch, you sons of bitches!" I yelled, whirling to face the culprits. Someone hit me good but I didn't feel it. In me was something big now, something flickering to life, gathering and ready to explode on the world. I took a kid down with a vicious headbutt and giggled for I felt the something pumping through my veins. I was becoming something, some force that feels nothing but does what is right in full power and glory. I swung a huge haymaker in a full circle around me hitting nothing but knowing it was over for them now, that I would win. I tilted my head back and loosed a barbaric yawp. Not like the snarling, but like the gathering thing was surfacing, coming out to swallow the world or become it.

Then, just before the thing burst forth, something cold exploded on the back of my head.

9

When the dead visit me in my dreams they're always withdrawn, preoccupied, worried—not at all like the bright, lovely people they were when they lived. I don't dream of Dad all that much anymore, but of Margaret I've never stopped dreaming, never stopped hearing the champagne sparkle of that lost little voice.

If Margaret were alive, I'd make a bet with her.

I'd bet her that if—on that long ago night of sand, meteors, and stars—someone had warned Dad that the next time he stood would be the last time he ever did so under his own power, Dad still would have carelessly tossed that awful, mustard-colored Redskins' playbook on the floor and come out for a walk on the beach with Lance and me.

Of course July nights on the Outer Banks were always warm, but this one felt like a familiar blanket around us. As we walked the dark beach along the rough Atlantic, our house became nothing but a speck of light in the dunes. I was thrilled my dad was home because he wasn't much, and so I started dancing around Lance and Dad and singing nonsense songs, which always made Dad laugh. I sang the words into colors, wrapped them lovingly around my brother and father. At sixteen, Lance had become too mature to join in. He'd not been enthusiastic about the walk and in those days it was some sort of victory in the house if you could get him to smile. It'd been two years since Margaret had last drawn breath in the world.

The night sky was so clear that soon Lance, Dad and I decided to have us a rest. We reclined on our backs in the soft sand for a long time. We listened to the lapping waves become the in and out of the Earth breathing, but we were focused on the stars. By pure dumb luck there was a meteor shower that night, and we lay there in silent awe of the sparkly goings-on above us. That was the first time I became aware of the movement, of the hurtling of the Earth through space—a movement which the streaking meteors turned into a type of stomach-churning hyperspace. I lay there not knowing whether it was the fifteen pounds per square inch of gravity's pressure or the force of our hurtling that made me feel so firmly pressed into the sand.

Anyway, that was the night with Lance and Dad among the sand, meteors, and stars. When the celestial show was over, Lance and I got up but Dad did not, and so it also became the last night Dad ever stood up on his own. Lance shook him a number of times. Each shake rougher than the preceding one. Then he took off sprinting for the house without a word. How cool and superior Lance's shrug had been when he'd half-heartedly agreed to set out on our walk, but how his strides had thrummed with sadness and naked fear as they'd frantically stabbed the sand to return him home.

Was it fifteen minutes I was alone with my father? Twenty? His breathing slow and shallow, his eyes clear and bright but nothing behind them except maybe all those stars reflected in them. He lay in the strandline, and his head rested in the shadowy curve of it among the rays and bands of butterfly and scallop shells, among the black, horned tangles of mermaid purses.

What were those things I'd whispered in his ear? I could remember if I wanted to, and if I close my eyes, I could even imagine Lance clutching Mom's arm and tearing her from the little world she was incubating on the page of yet another romance novel. I could remember the hysteria in the slope of Mom's shoulder as she drove us to the hospital; sitting in back with my dad's head in my lap, his face framed by my bony, hairless arms; Lance up front crying; men lifting my father to the hospital bed; Gus McGovern going to pieces and Mom going down on the floor like some character from her books when the doctor gave us the news and so on. But then other memories would rise, too, crowding up as ghosts sensing the slab of a long sealed mass tomb beginning to open: Margaret all blood-drained with her delicate neck thrown back, her skin the color of ash.

I suppose I'm glad that when the dead visit me they hang back sullenly, unwilling to call out or step from the shadows that half obscure them. Oh I know that memories without tongues still have their demands, but I also know we don't owe them anything. And I'm not interested in excavating the past, in disinterring the dead. I'm bent on destroying the walls people build each day, on either swallowing tomorrow whole or having it swallow me.

10

There was no music playing when I came to. It was still dark, of course, but through the saturated air I could see two versions of Emmy's lovely face above me. They seemed to swim toward each other and then away. I didn't know which one to focus on, which was real and which was a trick of my eyes. Then, reluctantly, the two images merged, becoming one.

"I found the place," I said.

"What?"

"I said my head is in your lap."

"Yeah," she said. "What in the world were you doing?"

"Coming to find you. Where is Rampage?" I asked.

"Rampage is fine. Riley just walked him down to the infirmary to get some ice for his eye. Riley said Rampage gave worse than he got. The whole party stopped when you got knocked out. No one seems to know who did it, and as soon as I called for an ambulance everybody scattered knowing the cops would come.

I smiled and nestled my head against her warm thighs.

"This is the best case you realize," I said. "I could have come to and seen anything, but instead I wake up and you are holding me and glowing even in the absence of light. I just wish I could see your freckles, which are archipelagos, constellations." She looked ill just then. I gave her a little wink and tried to lean up on an elbow but got all swimmy. The slick grass had made the hair on the back of my head all damp and matted.

"Lie down, you idiot," Emmy said very quietly. "You had a bottle slammed on your head. Probably on top of your scar. Your head is going to fall off if you don't take better care of it."

I noticed I was nearer the road than the house and figured I must have been driven back during the attack. A glance toward the house showed the yard stood empty and quiet except for what appeared to be an obese figure sitting dejectedly on one of the couches. I smiled at that outline.

I rolled over on my stomach and pushed up to my hands and knees. I waited a moment, letting things steady out, and then rose to my feet.

"Wait," said Emmy. "Stay here. You've done enough. Wait for the ambulance. Someone should check your head in the light."

"Right, Emmy, darling," I said. I was unsteady on my legs. I felt like I was trying to stand still on the deck of some storm-tossed vessel. "But that looks like the outline of Santana Montana over there and I need to make sure he's okay."

I'd taken about three unsteady steps when Emmy blurted out, "I cheated on you." That gave me pause. "Tonight," she clarified. "I sort of made out with Riley. We didn't do it or anything, but I made out with him." I gave my battered brain another moment to make sense of her words. Riley was one of those fraternity lifers, of sorts, a tall handsome bastard entering his sixth year of college. I liked him a great deal.

I turned to look at her. God, she was beautiful standing there on the black grass. The weak light of the frat house had dissipated to such an extent before touching her that she looked to be made up of billions of little grains. She looked like someone who'd be wringing her hands but she wasn't. It seemed like she wanted to say, *Lightly, if you'd just…*or *Lightly, if you'd only*, but she didn't say a thing.

I'd woken in her lap in darkness with a ringing head and the glow of what kindness one person is capable of toward another radiating from her. I was humbled that anyone would put their love in me like that. It was painful, not what she'd said but to see her standing there looking lost somehow, looking like those billions of grains that miraculously gave her life might scatter into the abyss never to reassemble in such a glorious way again. But she seemed somehow resolute, too, and strong to have said such a thing at such a time. I felt pride swelling for her.

"Of course you did, you sweet beautiful person—you perfect, beaming thing," I said. "Your affection is yours, of course, and it's an affection that has a power you should never undervalue." I came over and put my arms around her and gave her a big hug. She didn't hug me back though, so I let go and said, "I want to see what's what with Santana Montana." I stood there until she turned slowly and walked off, then I stumbled away knowing I should be hurt by what she'd said, and that it upset her that I wasn't. It wasn't that I didn't love her or that I didn't feel things; it was that I was working under a different set of assumptions and filled with the knowledge that a new vision quivered on my horizon.

I stopped in front of the squat, frumpy form sitting on the couch.

"Santana Montana Ordóñez, is that you?"

"Yes," he said, remaining obscured in the dark. "I am sorry. I went to stand in the road as I said and—" He broke off. "Here." He held out something and I felt the cool neck of a glass bottle in my hand. I lifted it and turned it toward the light. It was a half-full bottle of Wild Turkey. The top was screwed on tight. With a movement of my wrist I sent the liquid inside spinning and little golden highlights flickered in the weak light. His head sagged dejectedly.

"I saw the confrontation," he said hesitantly, as if it pained him to speak. "It was Crampton." He glanced behind him. "I was scared," he added quietly.

"Listen," I said. "Don't worry about that."

He looked on the verge of tears, though. I didn't want him feeling bad, so I said, "Listen, I wouldn't have jumped in that bullring either, buddy. But tell me, Santana Montana Ordóñez, are you sure it was Crampton who hit me?"

"Yes," he said. "I am sure." He was breathing deep, but evenly, like something was balanced on his head. "My forefathers," he said, "stared down the fiercest bulls in Spain, yet I could not move to aid a friend." He rose suddenly and jogged off, moving awkwardly with a slow, pounding tread.

I would have called out or followed him but my head hurt with the sharpness of scissors snipping canvas and there were blue lights riding the wings of sirens to the crest of College Hill. I had every right to stay and bring the weight of the law on Crampton. "It's assault," I said, "plain and simple," but then there was the fact that I was underage, drunk, probably bleeding, and holding a fifth of Wild Turkey.

"Jesus," I said. I cradled the bottle and sprinted across the road to the parking lot opposite Alpha Alpha. I nestled down behind a black Land Rover as the townie cop screeched to a stop and then blubbered across AA's yard to bang authoritatively on the door.

I let go a heavy breath, unscrewed the top, and took a contemplative swig of the Wild Turkey. And though I considered the pleasures of going over and speaking to him only in the future anterior—*what he will have found out when the case ended* and whatnot—I decided instead to replace the cap and amble off.

I'd set off thinking to go back and lie down in my room but I'd kept going. My head hurt, but not like it surely would the next day. The Jack and Turkey had me feeling warm and numb, but I felt sure now that my hair was not wet with dew but with blood. It felt like it was working its way down the middle of my back slowly like a serpent on its belly. I figured vaguely I should stop in and see someone at the infirmary—perhaps Rampage would still be there—so I headed down campus.

I was intrigued, as I walked, by how everything I looked at seemed to be the slightly askew transposition of the same image. I took stock of the blurred buildings as I passed them in the dark and felt appreciative of the stately way they all seemed to stand at rigid attention as if guarding, even at night, all the frail bodies that came and went beneath their ever-watchful eyes.

When I got way the hell down to the Old Chapel, a small brick and stained glass building that seemed to bloom like a flower out of all the hollies and magnolias and mature plants that obscured its walls, I could see another police car parked outside the infirmary. While I stood there pondering my next move, the sky decided to just go ahead and rain. An out-and-out downpour ensued.

"You are a tricky rascal, clouds," I said. I squinted up at them, remembering a long time ago, in one of many elsewheres, when Margie had taken my hands at our parting and said, "Look up in the rain with eyes wide and I will do the same." When I'd asked her why, she said, "Because inside each drop, is an entire universe, and we'll see each other in some of them."

A breeze pushed the rain sideways for a moment and down the sidewalk. I imagined her moving forward, a lumpy trash bag held out in front of her. I wiped my wet eyes and when I looked again, she was gone.

I took a big pull from the Wild Turkey to finish it off and went over and crawled inside the green and bronze pagoda of an elderly magnolia. I leaned my back against the thick bole. The landscaping crew must have just worked the grounds over because the peaceful air bloomed with little florets of smells: opened soil, darkening trunks, vegetation exhaling. I breathed deep of the vapor and took it in like a cure. I knew scent could take firm hold on the brain, for I couldn't smell coffee or fresh bagels without Uluwehi and the Hui Nalu canoe club looming up in my mind's eye to send the pain prickling around my ventricles.

The rain pinged off the leaves like they were made of tin as I played out the fight in my mind. I saw Crampton flailing and going over the couch in a heap. I remembered Santana Montana going over the log by the river in a way so similar I was suspicious that the two were the same image somehow. Without opening my eyes I became aware of Crampton's presence beside me. If not him in the flesh, then the idea of him, which is just as real. He too was held inside the flesh of leaves, floating gently in a collection of vapor thick as amniotic fluid. I looked over to find his eyes, white as the eggs of spiders, on me. He winked at me then. He winked right at me knowingly—like a brother.

Maybe I passed out from the blood loss or maybe from the Jack and Turkey. Maybe I just went to sleep. Regardless, right before I sensed the structure giving way beneath me and felt myself plummeting to sweet unconscious shadows, I realized who the last member of my big adventure had to be. Not only that, I knew exactly how to force the awful bastard to go.

Inside the magnolia, my sleep was fitful and I awoke often, but I never entertained getting up. It seemed like a good opportunity to have poignant or telling dreams and perhaps I did, but each time I awoke and reached for the memory of it there was nothing but the residue of sound or image. For example, a handsome boy with blue eyes chasing wild rabbits through meadows; a pale, beautiful girl—a frail, freckled thing—standing in a yard with her bony arms clutched to her tiny chest; my mother's voice calling me home, the sound of her crying in a big, empty room.

These were just flashes though. The only dream I remembered was of Gary Shuttlesworth, my canoe instructor. In it he stood naked a ways off at the water's edge. A belt was around his stricken neck and he was shivering with lips the color of a rained on blue jay's wing. I wanted to ask him about that day on the James when he'd paddled so furiously without warning and whether he'd been furiously paddling toward something or away from something.

I wanted to go to him and, for reasons I couldn't make sense of upon waking, tell him that our galaxy has 200 billion planets in it and that there are at least 400 billion other galaxies—and those are just in the *observable* universe. That's at least, what? An eight followed by twenty-two zeros. That's how many planets. Our galaxy is small, I'd tell him, our solar system smaller, and Earth is but a speck on a speck of sand on the ocean floor. What luck it is to be alive, to draw breath and, most of all, to have been born from the ash of stars, from the very materials of which the universe is made, and yet to have consciousness—the miracle of man!

But, in the dream I neither moved toward him nor called out. It was a soundless dream. My mouth opened and shut without utterance and my feet wouldn't work.

11

I woke up in the dirt and mulch because a man was peering into my tree.

"Good Lord, almighty," I moaned. "Get your own damn tree." I rolled on my side away from him.

The peeping tom gasped. "You're bleeding," he said. His words were soft and thin.

I sat up slowly, propped up on an elbow and turned to look at the face sticking through the leaves. It was a kind face, nearly hairless save for a stubble of silver above the ears that went back below his otherwise bald dome. His eyes were blue and kind. Judging from the wrinkles around them I guessed him to be nearly fifty.

"I'm alright," I said. "This is a camping trip." I tried to smile but I was sure it came out as a grimace. My head hurt like hell, but my neck ached worse. "Ugh," I groaned. "I feel like shit."

"I'll call an ambulance," he said.

"No, no, this is nothing," I said, gently touching the back of my head and wondering if it was. "Just got jumped by a couple of thugs." There were dried clumps of blood in my hair, but none of it seemed fresh. "Step on back for a minute, you kind-faced, middle-aged buddy," I said. "I'm coming out." His face disappeared as the leaves he'd been holding came down like a curtain. I grabbed the empty bottle of Wild Turkey and crawled out of the magnolia on my hands and knees like some wild wood sprite being born.

The peeping tom had retreated to the sidewalk. I stood up. Above me the sky was all cloud, but it glowed with a terrible brightness. All around the deserted campus the birds were calling for the morning to open up. Here and there the stately oaks spread their arms and drew themselves up to dwarf the old brick buildings. I was wet and filthy and my head hurt something fierce. I sipped the cool morning air like a fine wine and looked at my new acquaintance. There was honest concern on his face, which had an arylide yellow sheen to it. In one hand he held a cell phone; the other was in the pocket of his black slacks. He wore a matching black jacket and there was a white collar circling his thin, but healthy-looking throat.

"You're the chaplain," I told him.

49

"Yes," he said. "But the students call me Greg." He motioned toward the Old Chapel. "My office," he explained.

"I'm going to call you Padre Johnson," I said. "That is, unless you find it insulting."

"My last name is not Johnson," he said, "but I've been called worse."

"Damn, but I like you already. I can tell by the way you stand and your word color that you are that rare type of religious person that I wouldn't find insufferable. What time is it?"

He looked at me a moment as if my question hadn't registered, then checked his cell phone. "Uh, it's ten 'til eight," he said. He looked at the bottle in my hand. He looked at me. I felt certain that within the grey matter between his ears some sort of calculation was being carried out and, inexplicably, I felt little charged particles of joy take to my blood stream.

Despite my pain, I smiled. I gave the bottle a little shake and motioned with it toward the tree behind me. "Leaving it in there would be littering," I said. "That's far worse in my opinion than leaving a bad impression on a new acquaintance. Truth is, I go camping like this all the time. Spring break freshman year, for example, I was supposed to fly with this new buddy of mine up to Connecticut to do some sailing on his father's boat. The kid bragged about it, said it'd be a week I'd always remember. Said his daddy's boat was an incredible custom Aprea Mare. His dad was to fly his private plane to pick us up but he never showed up. Can you believe it, Padre Johnson? What a bastard. I didn't care at all, but my buddy sat beside me on the bench at that private airstrip where we'd been dropped off and I could just feel him getting more and more humiliated. I'm sure he'd have cried were I not there. We didn't know each other all that well and he'd talked it up so big. He wanted to impress me, you see, because of how popular and amazing I am and all—which is true but I don't think about it much. Anyway, neither of us had a car and the students were long gone, having skedaddled to all these sunny spring break places, so do you know what we did?"

Padre Johnson said he didn't know, and so I told him how we'd walked about a quarter of a mile back to the Food Lion Super Grocery we'd passed on the way up. A big strip mall was opposite the Food Lion. A vast sea of parking spaces, mostly deserted, spanned the distance between them. But behind Food Lion, there was a patch, roughly circular, of big hardwoods, which in turn was flanked by the noisy Route 1 highway. The chaplain said he knew the place I meant.

"Jesus, Padre Johnson," I said. "We lived in the middle of that tiny wooded island for all of spring break. We got beer and food from the grocery. Slept under the stars. Thelonious—that was my new buddy's name—said it was one of the best times he'd ever had in his life. On the last night we built a little fire back there and drank Pabst Blue Ribbon, roasted marshmallows, and filled that speck of forest with laughter and talk of big plans. Been good friends ever since."

I wasn't sure why I'd told poor Padre Johnson that story. Maybe as a way of waging a little war against him or to test him. Maybe something else. I had noted that he hadn't flinched with the way I'd used Jesus' name. And to his credit he didn't get uncomfortable during my story but had listened patiently and then asked, "Why did you tell me that?"

"Because of what I told my buddy that last night."

The chaplain was sharp. He smiled at my obvious setup and asked, "Which was?"

I stepped closer to him, bits of mulch falling off me. He didn't step away so I put my hand on his shoulder. In a hushed voice I told him how I'd told my buddy that we don't remember in terms of weeks, not even in terms of days. We remember only moments. Striking, vicious, joyful moments. Little verdant patches of green in otherwise sterile, concrete landscapes. A speck of oasis on the tip of the yawning desert's tongue.

He did not smile. He nodded slowly.

"If you're not going to go to a hospital," he said, "why not come inside and let me look at your head? You can explain to me what you mean, because I'm not sure I understand. We can talk more comfortably there."

"Ah," I said, stepping back to fix him with a smile. "You're a cagey chaplain, Padre Johnson. I'll bet you've coaxed many to the Lord with your subtle and friendly brilliance. And I would like to chat with you, true enough. I'd like to tell you about quantum teleportation—the particles of light, which were, in fact, teleported six hundred meters under the River Danube from one side to the other and, more recently, the use of entanglement to teleport qubits inside a tiny chip in Zurich *und so weiter*. But I can't, Padre Johnson. I have Dr. Watson's exam at 8:30 and then I am off to pursue a moment so rare as to have never before occurred in the history of man and cannot afford to tarry."

He nodded. He held up his cell phone somewhat guiltily, and told me that he'd called campus security when he saw my feet protruding from the base of his beloved magnolia.

"I'll make a deal with you, though," he said. "If you'll agree to get your head looked at today, and to come and chat with me first thing at the start of next term, then I'll tell the security folks to hoof it on back to their little office."

I laughed heartily. It was a funny device for a chaplain to employ, and I wasn't sure but that his phrase about getting my head checked held a double meaning. "You've got yourself a deal," I said, having no intention of doing either.

"What is your name?" he asked.

"Lightly," I said, sticking out my hand.

"Ah," he said, shaking it. "I guess I'm Padre Johnson."

When I get to where I'm going, I'll send Padre Johnson a postcard. It will begin, *Religion was the rocket fuel for mankind, but I'm a big believer in humanity's sameness and the absence of god.* It will end, *In two hundred years, when we begin spreading ourselves through the universe, we'll jettison god like a used up rocket booster.* I'll write, *P. S. The sticker on the shuttles will read, THANKS FOR HELPING US THROUGH OUR IGNORANCE, LORD, BUT WE CAN HANDLE IT FROM HERE.*

12

As I walked slowly toward Moreland, my wet tee shirt and khakis made little sucking sounds against my skin. I'd been mostly sheltered inside the magnolia, but through the long night the drips had added up. I figured I had just about enough time to change my clothes, put on a hat, and hoof it up campus before Dr. Watson locked the door to his exam.

All around me the trees were awakening one by one to the scent of mist and last night's rain. It didn't smell at all like Washington, D.C. had after rain. Up there it had been a full smell of fumes, wet leaves, and concrete. We were up there a lot when Pop was with the Skins. Now he just was skin, I suppose.

A few underclassmen passed by and waved at me, but I just rubbed my neck. I was prepared for the savage pain in my head, but the neck was a different thing altogether. I tested my head by moving it around a little. I felt dizzy, like I was going to be sick, so I stopped.

Soundlessly the wind stirred a heap of cherry blossoms and sent them dancing around my feet. I was bothered by the feeling that someone had set out for me not long ago and that at any moment I might feel a finger tapping my shoulder.

When I reached the dorm and looked at Biggs' alarm clock, I saw I had only ten minutes to get to Watson's exam. There was a folded note on my bed with my name printed on the flap in Biggs' characteristic messy, virtually disabled script, but I didn't pick it up. I would have said to Biggs, "God, you are a card," but he was snoring away on his back, his massive body unclothed and uncovered. His gray, flaccid penis lay against his hairy, bulging thigh. It reminded me of some sad, lonely creature that lived in a vast, underground warren.

I crept around the room looking through piles of trash for something to wear that wasn't filthy. I put on a pair of jeans that were stained with paint, but I couldn't find a shirt that didn't stink. Finally, I gave up and took my high school football jersey from the closet—the only article of clothing I possessed that was on a hanger. I slipped it over my battered head gently. Since I didn't have time for a shower, I took a stocking cap from Biggs' drawer.

"Somebody came by for you," Biggs said. His eyes were closed but he'd stopped snoring.

"Who?" I asked, "and for god sakes cover up your penis."

"Dean Andrews," he said, kicking the blanket further down the bed. "He was fucking serious about it. Said you had to come to his office like right away." Biggs rubbed his eyes. "You didn't do something even more fucking stupid last night did you?"

"Why?" I asked. "What did he say?"

"Nothing. He asked for your car keys, though."

"What? That is literally unbelievable. Naturally, you didn't give them to him."

"Yeah, I did," he said. "I handed them right over. Best thing for you."

That pissed me off, so I put on his stocking cap and said, "Tell me, Biggs old buddy, did you stand there naked while Dean Andrews looked so serious and you handed over my keys?"

"Real funny," he said. One eye was opened a little. I knew he cared deeply for me but wished just as deeply that he didn't. "Are you okay?"

"Right as rain," I said.

"Yeah, well, you don't look it."

"And what do I look like?"

"Like someone who needs help," he said, turning away.

I thought about asking him how the meeting went with Thomas Hicks and Coach Sanford, but I knew I didn't need to. I knew I could write a script for the meeting that would be nearly word for word what was said. In the end Coach would come away thinking my mind was simmering again. He might even call my mother if she'd not already called him, partly out of concern for me, partly out of concern about losing his star player, and partly out of respect for my father who had also given his life to football as much or more than Coach Sanford had.

I grabbed the Nike shoebox and stepped quietly into the hall.

13

Unlike Dr. Kwell's final, I was one of the last working on Dr. Watson's exam.

Under Biggs' stocking cap my head felt pricked and itchy, but I let it be. I was in desperate need of a shower. Worse, though, I hadn't shaken that nervous feeling that someone was coming for me, someone I didn't want finding me. Simple logic told me that Dean Andrews had come by to speak about the fight. My logic was based on facts. At a school as small as Thomas Jefferson, the deans had many responsibilities. Dean Andrews, for example, was a professor and my advisor. He'd often said I was an asset to the school because I'd garnered a lot of regional news coverage through my exploits on the field. But I felt uneasy. The Dean coming for my keys, the vision of the girl in the rain with her bag of mysteries—I sensed something akin to an assemblage of conspirators, linked by invisible threads, closing in on me like some net closing around an unsuspecting creature.

I looked out the window. There was nothing out there but the rest of my *lives* and a sky attending to the business of clearing up. I took the cue and attended to the business of finishing my last exam.

When it was finally done, I wrote down the number of my barber, Mr. Peters, on the last page of the exam with a note suggesting Dr. Watson might like him. Only Santana Montana Ordóñez was still working as I grabbed the shoebox and took the blue book up front. He didn't glance up, so I stopped. Whether he was lost in thought or still agonizing about not helping me, I didn't know. I knew it might be a while before he finished because Santana Montana was a perfectionist and would write in his bold purple cursive until Dr. Watson pried the exam from him.

He looked up slowly, as if coming out of a dream, and put his big, brown eyes in me. God, but he looked like some adorable puppy dog, even with the little scraggly mustache sprouting above his full pink upper lip. Sure he was fleshy and short—frumpy and rotund, too—but what of it? What was it about people that made them hate him? It made you ill to think on it.

"Stop moping, Santana Montana Ordóñez." I placed the printout of the secret beach before him. "The past is a corpse," I hissed, "and our adventure is at hand. Meet in the library anon."

"No one says *anon*," he said breathlessly and glanced up front at Dr. Watson, who had his feet resting on his desk and his nose buried in a severely tattered book. He grabbed my wrist—it was the first time he'd ever voluntarily touched me—and said, "Someone is looking for you. Be careful."

I was going to ask him who, but just then Dr. Watson cleared his throat. The book was in his lap now, and he gave us a friendly but significant look to remind us we were, in fact, taking an exam. Normally, I'd have asked anyway, but I loved Dr. Watson so I shrugged. I went and put my exam on his desk, and gave him a wink. Dr. Watson smiled. He stood up and followed me into the hallway.

"Dean Andrews came by earlier," he rasped, pulling the door closed behind him. "I'm to tell you to report to his office directly." He was a thin man who always stood in an open relaxed way with his arms sort of dangling at his sides. He had perpetually flushed cheeks and a ruddy, handsome face. He always looked like he'd just been leaning against a wall trying to remember something amusing he'd once read. That was the type of person he was. He seemed amused then by what he'd been asked to say, but it was clear by his tone that he was prejudiced in my favor.

"Okay," I told him. "Kinda weird, isn't it?"

"Really weird. Let me know if I can put a word in for you. I've enjoyed having you in my last few classes."

"And I've loved your classes," I said. "I especially like how you get so worked up about literature you curse at least once a class. My favorite was when you'd say, 'Goddamn it!' at the end of some comment, with your face all red. It's kept me on the edge of my seat, I swear."

"I never got a chance to congratulate you on your performance at the Hampden-Sydney game. My wife is the football guru in the family," he admitted, "and she told me it was the only perfect performance that she's ever seen in the sport."

I told him how I'd sought perfection in each game and that the Hampden-Sydney game had come closest to it. In the game, I'd completed all twenty-seven passes—an ODAC record. I hit slants. I hit posts. I hit to the right, left, and middle. Threaded into double, triple coverage. Hit five-yard outs, twenty-yard comebacks. I could have closed my eyes and thrown left-handed—it didn't matter. It wasn't that I was standing back there untouched all day either. I got sacked nine times—a school record—and broke a rib. But I told

Dr. Watson that I was in that place athletes go, that *zone* where every element blends together in a sort of mystical unity of which you are both constitutive part, as they say, and singular master.

Dr. Watson listened attentively, then said, "You know, Hemingway thought Santana's grandfather was the most perfect bullfighter he'd ever seen. I suppose men seek perfection through many different mediums, but I do believe they are all pursuing the same thing."

I told him I agreed and asked by way of parting if he thought I was a Byronic Hero, but he said he didn't know me well enough to say.

"Keep it up, though," he whispered, glancing through the door at Santana Montana. "I think it's great seeing someone so popular take someone so unpopular under his wing without a care about what others think."

I told him he was right. It *was* great.

When I get to where I'm going, I'll send Dr. Watson a postcard. It will begin, *I hope when you're retired you'll have a nice garden to sit and drink bourbon in while you listen to Milton's crystalline spheres.* It will end, *Your goodness is quiet jazz playing in a little tropical bay bistro overlooking the sea at sunset in Los Gigantes.*

All Things Await

14

I shuffled toward the library feeling uneasy but, at the same time, ecstatic that my exams were now completed. I loved how all around me the birds were calling, twittering as if in response to the still clearing sky. I remembered being little and telling my mother that when the birds returned to spring trees they brought the leaves with them one by one. She'd just look at me, smile and say, "My Lightly." She was different then.

She had warm hands, my mother. She still smiles radiantly at me from old photos, walking Waikiki Beach, beside the snaking river Shannon in Ireland, flanked by a string of fishing boats in Belize. They hang in the hall of the farmhouse and seem creepy to think about like nosing through the photos of some long-dead stranger.

We traveled all the time before Margaret and Dad cast the shadow of tragedy on mom's smooth face. It was, to be sure, a strange form of dementia in which she dwelled: One that had proved powerful enough to wedge me from her, to make even the briefest of interactions with her destabilizing for me. If I wanted, it could all come back to me—mom's laugh, her eyes bright with love—but that was long ago and not worth thinking on. The pretty lady in those photos had flown the coop, and I wasn't that little boy holding her hand or standing fuzzily in the background of old photos. Hell, I wasn't even the young man standing in the farmhouse hallway studying them. And since it was not me, the memories were not mine. I let them go, pushed them right out.

I had other things to think on anyway. I knew, for example, that I had good reason to be uneasy. The o-line meeting with Coach, Dean Andrews absconding with my keys and forcing me to come to his office and meet someone to get them back, Santana Montana's cryptic warning—*Someone's looking for you,* he'd said. *Be careful*—the big net was behind me, moving up either side, and the aperture was closing quickly before me, being drawn closed by the force of many hands. My own fingers tingled and I looked at them.

I could throw a football forty yards on a frozen rope, and make a girl believe I loved her with a touch. In a perfect world, you wouldn't have to fight to be left the hell alone.

The dean was expecting me, but first I headed to the library and went straight for the computer lab. I sat down at an open computer between two girls.

"You have gorgeous hair," I said to the diminutive Korean girl sitting to my left. She smiled at me. It was a smile that meant she forgave me for saying such a weird thing and that she wanted to get back to work. I laughed and the fat girl on my right sighed heavily. She was wearing a TJC sweatshirt and had the hood up, so I couldn't see her face. She smelled really nice, but I didn't tell her.

I leaned back pretending to yawn and discreetly gave the Korean girl's hair a few light strokes, then logged on and bought five tickets bound for San Jose. I emailed Biggs and Rampage to tell them about the tickets. I attached the confirmation information with the flight number and so on. I told them to bring their passports, that I'd see them on the plane, and then added some bits to ensure they'd come.

To Biggs I wrote, *If you get on that flight, good buddy, then I promise not to bring Santana Montana to our table next year.* To ensure his compliance, I added, *P.S. I've taken pictures of you sleeping naked & I'll post them on the web if you refuse. I love you and am not joking at all.*

To Rampage, I wrote, *Do you remember spring break behind the Food Lion Super Grocery, Thelonious? Pabst Blue Ribbons, roasted marshmallows, light & laughter in that speck of forest—how I took the pain & embarrassment your father's negligence caused & turned it into one of the most memorable, precious, positive events of your life? How you were on the outside of Tommy Jeffs before that. How you've been on the inside—where you belong—ever after? Well, get on the fucking plane, you muscular artist, & return the favor.*

My last email was for Crampton. The genius of it was the way I told him Santana Montana Ordóñez had seen him stave my head in with the Wild Turkey. I had spoken to the police about pressing assault charges, I lied. They'd said it seemed like an open and shut case. I mentioned the element of race could bring bad press and concluded by writing that I was sure he'd do the right thing for his fraternity and for himself by simply getting on the goddamn plane in DC. *Go to San Jose,* I wrote, *or go to jail.* I signed off with, *Your friend who has your well-being in mind, Lightly.*

The flight I'd booked for them left from Dulles International in Washington, DC and flew direct to San Jose, Costa Rica. The secret though was that Santana Montana and I had different tickets. Unbeknownst to them, we were to leave from Dulles much earlier.

I didn't want them knowing any of that. I wanted them thinking we were coming with them. It'd be too late once they'd stowed their carryons and looked around the plane. My plan was to meet them at the San Jose airport. I'd always wanted to be one of those people in far away airports, standing on the other side of the railing holding up the name of some stranger they're about to whisk away to a new, secret place. I figured our head start would allow Santana Montana and me to locate the beach before they arrived. I didn't want to drag them all over looking for it.

The fat girl in the hoodie had said something to me.

"What?" I asked.

"I said, would you mind not breathing so loudly, and whispering to yourself," she said. "Maybe if you closed your mouth and tried breathing through your nose," she offered.

I could see now she had a lovely, big face, soft skin alive with color and the perfect angle for a female nose. Her blue eyes were not especially pretty but firm and intelligent.

"You smell really nice," I said sincerely. "And I like how you're being sort of rude to me. Of course, this is just my opinion, but I believe you are going to go far. What is your name?"

"We met once before in Estes," she said, her words coming out in orange arrowheads. "I told you my brother Bryan had broken his collarbone in that van you wrecked in Florida. You kept calling me 'Hoodie', remember?"

"Oh, yes, Hoodie," I said, "I do remember, but I can't talk now. You see I'm embarking on a big adventure but there are those that would see it stopped."

"Okay," she said. "Whatever. You're not funny."

I was so overjoyed to see Santana Montana Ordóñez step into the lab that I jumped up and hugged him.

We were done now with the exams, and I held him close. He was roundish to the touch, and there was a good deal of give to his flesh as I squeezed him. His head domed off just beneath my chin and I inhaled deeply of his hair, the scent of which was a curious mixture of Benadryl and chicken curry.

"Why didn't you tell me you were going to grow a mustache?" I asked, holding him close. He didn't return the hug, but he didn't pull away either. "We've got to talk about these things. I might've been able to undertake it with you."

"I am being squeezed too tight, please," he said.

I released him and said, "Glad you're here. I've just emailed Biggs, Rampage, and that awful Crampton bastard to invite them to join us on our adventure."

Santana Montana didn't say a thing, but I saw right away that he was horrified by the thought of Crampton joining us. There was also something in his stance that seemed a little defeated and frail somehow. His lower lip quivered slightly.

"Don't give me that look, buddy, goddamn it," I said. "You and I have to show him the way."

"Okay," Santana Montana said, and then, unexpectedly, he began to cry. It was a very quiet cry. He cried for a full a minute without making a sound. I watched him closely because it was very curious to me. Every time a tear appeared, he'd wipe it away before it could cut loose down his cheek.

When he was done, he dragged the oatmeal sleeve of his frumpy sweater under his nose from elbow to wrist.

He steadied himself visibly and asked, "Would you like for me to elaborate about my earlier warning in Dr. Watson's exam?" His words were varying shades of pink and they teetered on the edge of a great precipice.

"Oh," I said gently. "Yes, I do want to know. Tell me, why do I need to be careful? Who is it that's come looking for me?"

"A man. A doctor," he said. "He came to my room. He wore a blue jacket and red tie."

"How new did his jacket look? His tie? Did they look elegant and too new, almost unnaturally new?"

He looked down at his pudgy hands, then back at me. "Yes," he said. "That is fair to say."

"He was tall? Lean?"

"Yes."

"Okay," I said. "That's not good. Please continue."

"That is all. He asked if we were friends and if I knew where you were and I told him yes but that I did not."

"You are a trusted ally," I said. "He got here a lot faster than I thought. My mother must be really worried. Poor lady. I was hoping to be long gone before she freaked again."

"A friend?" he asked.

"No," I said. "He's a stepfather of sorts. Mine—but not really. He's a doctor, too, though he's not *my* doctor. Not really. Well," I said, "that is unfortunate. My guess is that Coach Sanford called my mother after the little chat with Biggs and Thomas Hicks Rambo last night. And now the dean is involved...ah, damn it! It's best if I speak to them straight away and see what's what. They are like dots. We need to connect them, see what picture emerges. I'm not ready to run, Santana Montana Ordóñez, but we may have to."

Santana Montana Ordóñez didn't look worried, but I told him not to worry just in case he was pretending to be brave for my benefit. He seemed fine now. Well, pretty much fine except that he was trembling a little and looked as if the wrong word from me at that moment could crush him forever. Personally, I've never been one to believe that people had hidden depths. I don't believe it because I think that all people are is depth—depth upon depth and so on, though they hardly know it. I may not have been able to understand simple things like reality television, popular music, how to find small objects in a big house, but I understood that. And I knew one thing: Crampton had nothing to do with why Santana Montana Ordóñez was overcome.

"Let's walk to the fountain and develop our strategy."

"Okay," he said. He didn't need to thank me for not asking what the hell he was just crying about. I could see the relief open itself on his beautiful olive face.

We walked over toward one of the benches facing the fountain. The water frothed and bubbled in the center of the courtyard, but it wasn't a pleasant sound. It was a confusion of continual motion, like a million feet sprinting down a corridor that was as wide as forever is long. The birds were busier than ever, but their calls seemed frantic, discordant in a way I'd not heard before. We sat down and I put the shoebox between us.

The photo of our secret beach was clutched tightly in his pudgy fingers, as if the dream of it might be snatched from him at any moment.

"Listen," I said, "you don't need to tell me what's going on—I mean I hate hearing about people's past. Just tell me if you want to come with me."

"Yes," he said. "Please." The note of pleading in his voice became a perfume of longing in the air which, though the color of halayà úbe, thankfully didn't smell like it.

"Okay," I said, rubbing my temples. "We haven't much time. Do you have a car?"

"No."

"No worries," I said, "Hey! I bet you know about Lexapro, since you want to be a pharmacist."

"What?"

"Lexapro."

"It is an SSRI that affects unbalanced chemicals in the brain that cause depression."

"Right," I said. "It's a disaster to give it to really happy people."

"People on such antidepressants are three times more likely to commit suicide than people who are not on it."

"You are my type of pharmacist exactly," I said. I nodded at a row of trees along the admissions office.

"What trees are those?" I asked.

"Willow oaks," he said. "You can tell by the narrow leaves. There are some who call it a pin oak." God, did I love Santana Montana Ordóñez. He was a genius. I didn't understand why he wanted to be a pharmacist when he knew so much about nature. "You speak in non sequiturs," he said. "Did you know?"

"We need a plan," I said. I took a few full breaths and noted that the air had changed. Above us, I saw that things had not, in fact, cleared up. It wasn't cloudy, but the edges of the sky were bruised purple. A boneless wind slithered through the trees.

"You are worried about the doctor," he said after a moment. I appreciated that he'd waited to bring it up. I assumed he was trying to return the favor I'd done for him when I'd not asked him why he was crying in the computer lab. I told him about the keys and Dr. Watson's message.

"I think we may be facing involuntary commitment," I said. "They can do that short-term. I've not looked into it, but I do know Virginia changed the law after that moron shot all those students at Virginia Tech. Bet you didn't know that."

"They think you are a danger?"

"Ha! I may very well be the least dangerous person in the world. Dean Andrews knows that, but he's going to cover his ass just the same, and I can't blame him. My mom is a nut, and she's got Dr. Crispin—the man in the suit and red tie—on her side. All you need in Virginia to get someone committed is a hysterical parent, a prior incident that might suggest dangerous behavior, and a healthcare professional willing to agree in writing."

"Dr. Crispin is the professional?"

"Jeez, you are sharp Santana Montana Ordóñez," I said. "He's the professional and more. And I've got the other two criteria checked off, as well. It's a really fucked up situation." It really was unbelievable. The whole thing was so ridiculous that it made you want to kick something. I didn't though, for my mind was already running ahead of them. There was a wumpling of an idea in the air.

"I am sorry things are not better with your mother," Santana Montana said. "A good mother should be everyone's right when they are born. My mother is...I mean to say, my mother was always—" He didn't finish the thought, but went sort of rigid all of a sudden. I glanced at his tight lips, which were pulled thin with the corners trembling almost imperceptibly. He seemed to be trying to keep in some little creature that wanted to crawl up his throat and escape.

I wondered if he hadn't grown a little in love with me. Either that or his mother had died recently.

All Things Await

15

The plan didn't take an hour or even five minutes.

I suppose fear was a motivating factor. That and being so close now to entering that bright, flooded place somewhere along a remote peninsula in Costa Rica. Regardless, the whole plan bloomed suddenly, fully formed in the air between us like it had for that professor bastard in that novel by Willa something-or-other. I reckon it took about four minutes to lay it all out for Santana Montana Ordóñez.

When I was done whispering it in his ear, he said, "That is the plan?"

I slapped him on the shoulder and gave him a gentle shake the way Coach Sanford would always shake me when he'd take me by the back of my neck with that big sandpaper hand of his. Coach was in on it, of course. I could see him shaking his big crew cut in disappointment, and it truly did make me sad. He was probably chewing his nails, wondering if all this meant next season was ruined for him, but that was his problem.

"It's the only plan we've got, good buddy," I said.

"I don't know," he said doubtfully. "What if she says no?"

"She won't. Look, it'll work if you do it right. I'll go speak to Emmy and that'll flush her right out the front door. Just make sure you're there waiting. It would kill me to have to leave without you."

"Okay," he said. "But isn't the dean expecting you now?"

"It won't kill them to wait a little longer," I said. "Besides I'm going to take two people into that meeting with me." We were looking across the fountain and down campus all the way to the science building. My eyesight felt incredibly acute, like I could count every needle on a white pine climbing the blue sky above my parents' farm.

As I made my way over to the Theta house to see Emmy, I gently drummed the lid of the shoebox with my fingers.

Emmy would be leaving for Jennifer's lake house in a few days. John Allen was coming for Penelope and that said something to Emmy about my not coming. After that it was another summer in Georgia helping her parents in the flower gardens and playing the piano for their friends. Dusk meant iced tea, crossword puzzles, and light reading on the veranda while evening breezes fought against the wet southern heat to lift thin curtains into the bedrooms of her parent's cavernous home. And then?

She would graduate now after all. What path would spill out from beneath her feet? I didn't know, but I knew her path would be brightly lit, bordered by endless rows of bursting blooms, and that whoever she pulled down that path with her, it would not be me. That knowledge felt the opposite of alright but it had to be. I knew that sometimes—if you wanted to gain everything—you had to give up something that was nearly equal to it.

I looked at the sky as I walked, but I felt nothing. Even with my heightened senses the leaves weren't filling me with longing, weren't urging me on toward my goal as they should. I watched them move in the treetops like scraps of paper, but there were no entries written on them this time.

16

I knocked on Emmy's door. Anne Marie Wentworth opened it. She put her hand on her hip as soon as she saw it was me. There was a big green duffle bag at her feet.

"Greetings, Anne Marie," I said breathlessly. "You look really beautiful today." She looked confused but then seemed to tense up as if some hurtful comment was about to follow. Emmy was on the couch in a white tank top and powder blue shorts. She had one of those long gorgeous legs crossed over the other and there was a magazine in her lap. She leaned over to see around Anne Marie.

"Hello, Lightly," Emmy said. "Why are you here? Did you see a doctor?" She seemed genuinely surprised to see me.

"I came by to talk, Emmy darling," I said. "I'm leaving soon and there are things that need saying, if you know what I mean."

Anne Marie glanced at Emmy and then at the ceiling. She sighed. "Right. I'm going to put this last bag in the car and take a longish walk then," she said.

As she stepped by into the hall, I said, "Don't you go too far, kitten."

She stopped. She looked at my orange shoebox and rolled her eyes. "Ugh," she said. "Whatever."

I closed the door behind her and turned to look at Emmy.

"You shouldn't do that to her," Emmy whispered. "It's really mean. You know she likes you."

I held my hand up to shush her. I put the shoebox on the floor and started getting undressed.

"What are you doing?" she asked.

I slipped my jersey over my head. "Do you want to take a shower?"

"What!" she exclaimed, as if insulted. We'd been *together*, as they say, often. Obviously. But she always wanted it virtually dark and most of the time I was only half sober.

"Come on, sweet pea," I said, kicking off one flip-flop and then the other. "I need to clean up and wash the dried blood from my shattered head. I was hoping you'd take a look at it, let me know if it requires stitches." I stripped bare and stood before her. "Look," I said. "I know it's kinda gross what with my head and all, but you're all I've got, you radiant angel you. Please."

We stepped into the tiny bathroom Emmy and Anne Marie shared with the two girls on the other side of them, and Emmy locked both doors. She tried not to giggle as she got undressed but she never was much good at hiding how she felt. Her blush, clear and wide against her pale, soft cheeks revealed it all anyway. Her blush was so wonderfully red that the freckles seemed to disappear like planets being devoured by a red giant sun. It made me wish we'd been together this way more—completely sober, middle of the day, every possible light on and the like.

We stood at the shower door together holding our hands under the water. The water pressure in her shower was even better than it was in the Moreland Dorm, which was saying something. She put her arm around me.

"You're warm," she said. "You're always so warm."

We got the water as hot as we could stand it and then got in. As always, I stood there a moment looking up into the water, eyes wide.

"What are you doing?" Emmy asked.

"Looking for someone," I said.

"Who?"

"No one. Someone in another universe, I suppose."

Emmy shook her head at me and moved me in front of her. She applied a generous amount of soap to her long, well-loved fingers, rubbing them until they were frothy white. She didn't start with washing my head, though. She squatted behind me. Each of her long legs folded, the sharp points of her knees visible on either side of me. She began to scrub my feet and calves, her soft, slick cheek occasionally brushing against my thigh.

She worked her way on up, stopping only to rinse away the soap or to apply more of it to her gifted hands. She scrubbed in a way that was not particularly romantic and perhaps only vaguely sexual—if at all. She distributed the soap slowly over my skin in a thorough, almost clinical way. True, I was leaving and would not be coming back, but it was also true that I loved Emmy very much, that I felt a little guilty that I'd never let her know me at all, and that I wanted to rectify that even if it was in front of strangers. I owed her the tenderest of goodbyes.

As her hands approached my upper thighs, she stood and leaned into me, her small breasts pressing into my back with great warmth. In the same practical, methodical way she applied soap liberally as she worked her way up from my thighs, never lingering anywhere longer than was necessary no matter how I responded. She was standing behind me now with her whole lean body pressed snug against mine. I looked down and watched her pale soapy fingers move across my dark torso, applying a constant pleasant pressure to everything they explored.

Many times I'd studied Emmy's fingers. It wasn't just their length or softness I'd admired, but their grace and agility. Countless times I'd sat studying with her as she'd thoughtfully turned the pages of her textbooks with those lean fingers, or listened, slightly drunk, as she played the piano—not expertly, but with enthusiasm—in the lounge of the sorority house. It was silly, but I suppose I'd fantasized a whole separate life for those fingers, an entire identity of their own that was somehow separate from the girl they belonged to.

In the warm water, and under a spell cast by those glorious hands, I let every muscle in my body uncoil. I did so one by one until my shoulders were completely slack and my head hung to the side in absolute surrender. I let those fingers clean everything, remove every stain and imperfection, to the point that even memories began to fall. As they worked, those hands swept away football—first the practices, then each game, then each play memorized from Sanford's playbook. Each touchdown and each big hit I took were wiped away, too, cleansed forever from my mind. Emmy soaped her hands again and when they returned to my shoulders it was to wipe away each night of heavy drinking, each drug from my body. With them went the memories, half-remembered images of laughing faces in smoke-filled rooms, people puking off of balconies.

One by one little patches of memory fell until the only ones left were of Emmy—snow falling outside the Pineapple House, for example, as we talked on the couch that first night; a picnic basket on a blanket we'd spread in the field off Independence Road; the night we snuck up a ladder and stumbled drunkenly over the Ashland rooftops; the time we climbed the Clifton water tower under midnight rain; our first kiss in the Garth House with her parents away, her sisters downstairs eating breakfast, and so on.

And then those memories, too. Emmy's fingers moved with an intelligence all their own. Stroke by stroke I felt them washing Emmy from me. Across my back, down my arms, each movement gently obliterating another trace of her.

I wasn't sad to lose them, truth be told. Not really. Where I was going there was no place for memories. There was only now and the future that would grow from that moment—that *now*—where all was to be made whole.

Anyway, by the time we stepped from the shower, I was positive that if anyone asked me, I would not have been able to tell them her name.

After the shower, I felt like I couldn't or didn't want to speak and so I didn't at first. Emmy had said my scalp was split but not bad enough to require stitches. We went back into her room. It felt cold and too well-ordered, what with her perfectly arranged desk and picture frames. I sat on the couch and watched her get dressed. She was a tall, skinny thing and pale. Something in the hunched way she crossed her arms over her breasts and shivered after dropping her towel forced me to see her as the little girl she once was, which was not all that long ago.

The air was sweet with the flowers that she constantly replenished in the vase on the coffee table—now yellow roses. Through the window everything was saturated with a weak light, and I had the feeling the whole world had taken a deep breath and that I'd been listening for it to let it out, but it wasn't doing it.

Once she was dressed she took out a medicine kit from her closet and dug through it. She stood over me and said, "Lean forward."

I did and she squeezed some medicine from a tube on the back of my head. It felt cold and sickly in the wound.

"There," she said. "Much better."

I stood up and went over to my little pile of filthy clothes by the door and stared down at them.

"Don't you dare put that back on," Emmy said. "You've oozed blood on the back of that shirt. You know, my mother always says you can tell how rough a person lives by how they treat their clothes." She went over to her closet and, after a moment, pulled out a tee shirt and jeans but didn't hand them to me. "You ruined my skirt." I looked at her. "When your head was in my lap," she explained. "I got back here and there was blood on it."

She handed me the clothes and I started pulling them on.

"You've left a lot of things over here," she said, watching me. "You'd be surprised. You can have your pants back, but I've been sleeping in your shirt and want it back. And not," she said firmly, "because it smells like you, but because I like it. It's soft."

"Okay," I said, "but can we take a walk? I'd like for you to sit in on something with me before I go."

"Okay, Lightly," she said. "If you'd like to. Just let me blow dry my hair first." She stepped into the little bathroom and a moment later the sound of her hairdryer echoed noisily against the tiles. I squatted down and took the lid from the shoebox and stood up. I looked at the cocoon inside and breathed deeply of Emmy's room, of everything that was her—the tropical scent of her shampoo, the sickly sweet perfume of fresh flowers.

Emmy. I said her name two more times in my head and thought, *She is peace as much as October is the scent of burning leaves. She is night rain pouring down while inside you sleep deeply.*

I took the cocoon from the shoebox, holding it by the fragile poplar twig it was spun to. It hung horizontally from the twig. The sides neat and flat. I'd not noticed before how it was the same color and had the same texture as Santana Montana's favorite sweater. I took it over to the spikes of yellow roses and very gently slid it in among them.

Emmy. A name the wind scatters through the air.

All Things Await

17

When we got down to the Old Chapel, Emmy stopped outside the door.

"Who do you want to meet here?" she asked.

"Just wait."

I pushed on the big wooden doors and they groaned as they swung inward. There was a little bulletin board just inside and I checked it for the chaplain's room number. He was listed. It wasn't lost on me that this was the first time I'd been inside the Old Chapel since freshman year when I'd taken ecstasy and gone to bob for apples with a group of comely female drama students. I never had learned why the Drama Club had met in that room above the Chapel, and I didn't plan on ever finding out.

Anyway, I went to the end of the hall and down a little half-flight of stairs and turned into the chaplain's office. His door stood open. He looked up from his desk.

"Well," he said. "It's the magnolia dweller."

"I didn't know if you'd be here," I said.

He leaned back in his chair. "I'm the chaplain at a tiny college with huge parties. I'm always here and always free. I wasn't expecting you so quickly, though. Did you get your head looked at?"

"Boy, did I ever," I said. His faded blue eyes were just as friendly as they had been earlier. His smile was just as sincere. "Well, Padre Johnson," I said. "I'd love to have our talk now, but I'm afraid I can't. There's this really awkward conversation that is about to take place and I'd love having you there with me. You seem like a really fair chaplain, which I'm totally surprised by since *fair chaplain* seems like an oxymoron of sorts. I don't want your guidance or anything like that on account of how I know everything that is important to me and have no problems. There are those who think I have problems, though, and think they know what is important for me. Anyway, I'd really appreciate it if you could come along, if not as a spiritual advisor, then perhaps as a spiritual presence."

"Well," Padre Johnson said. He looked at the papers before him on his desk for a moment. "I do have some paperwork to attend to." He pushed the papers away decidedly and said, "But we did agree to a conversation, didn't we?"

"Good," I said. "I'm grateful and can't help but feel slightly indebted to you in a way that defies articulation."

He laughed at what I suppose he considered an odd phrase. "Don't mention it," he said, getting to his feet. "I'm glad to be part of the conversation, even though I don't know what it's about."

"Time reveals to us what was, though unseen, always true," I said, pulling at a hangnail. He stood in the doorway looking up at me, a small man, resigned to a body that seemed sunken in on itself. Looking at him made me acutely aware—and a little guilty—of the strong, agile body on which my brain so heavily relied. Involuntarily I moved my shoulders and felt the play of muscles across my back.

He gave me a funny look, as if he knew I was thinking something.

"Shall we go?" he asked.

"Yes," I said. "But, just the same, it'd mean a lot to me if I could come by tomorrow morning and talk god with you. I'm in some need of the Lord's strength."

"Talk god," he said. "I've not heard it put that way. That'd be fine, though."

"It's really important that I talk to you about it tomorrow. I think my life may depend on it."

He searched my eyes. "Okay," he said quietly. "Okay."

When the chaplain stepped out of the Old Chapel with me, Emmy was clearly confused.

"Hello," the chaplain said, giving Emmy a quizzical look and holding out his hand, which she took hesitantly.

"Hi," she said. She opened her mouth as if to say something else but seemed to think better of it. They both looked at me.

"Alright," I said. Emmy squinted at me. "Oh," I said. "No, this is not who I wanted you to meet. It's just up here a ways."

We made our way back up campus for the meeting with Dean Andrews and Dr. Crispin. Of course, they no doubt thought I was coming alone, but then I'd never agreed to that and, anyway, I'd never been one to save odd experiences for just myself. There'd be enough awkwardness to go around. No need to hoard it up. Besides, perhaps I owed it to Emmy in a way.

Emmy walked along beside me. We passed by Mary Branch dorm. Here and there some of the bricks seemed to glow and then fade as if there were some logical sequence, some sort of message trying to emerge. There were a few workmen attending to the dorm's exterior. It was being updated—mostly cosmetic stuff from the look of it—and I could hear the whine of several saws, the scraping of a ladder over concrete. Padre Johnson, perhaps sensing by Emmy's confusion that his presence needed explanation, slagged behind.

"And how do you know the chaplain?" Emmy asked in a hushed voice. "What was it you called him?"

I smiled. "We're both shepherds, of course, responsible for leading our flock to the monk's pasture, as they say, where everything is full of life and enterprise and whatnot but that's not how I know him. You know that big magnolia tree right outside the chapel?"

"Yes."

"I know him from there."

"I don't understand," she said.

"I know," I said.

Emmy was noticeably more rigid than when we'd set out, and she asked nervously, "Lightly, just where is it you are taking us?"

"You'll see," I said. "You'll see." I glanced back at Padre Johnson. He was about fifteen yards behind, but keeping our exact pace and humming pleasantly. "Look how he hangs back just far enough for us to be able to chat, but not too far so as to make us think he's not interested in coming along." I shook my head with admiration. "He really is very bright and very perceptive. I can see why he'd be easy to talk to." I'd never much cared for who people were and what had shaped them and so on unless I was speculating on it as a type of intelligence game. After all, I knew the past was a dead, useless thing, and even a little dangerous if not treated as such. But Padre Johnson had my interest. For a moment I allowed myself to wonder, as I rarely ever did, what his story was.

Of course, everybody had a story and that was exactly the problem in my opinion.

I knew too many people used their personal story as an excuse or as a reason not to try harder. There were drastic examples, such as parents who abused their children and explained their behavior by pointing to their own abuse and so on. But there were seemingly innocuous ones, too. These generally went unnoticed. Crampton's family were racists, so he had to be racist. Biggs' family couldn't talk about anything unmanly or intangible, so Biggs found it impossible and uncomfortable to do so. Emmy's mother loved colorful parties with everyone dressed up nicely and fresh flowers in colossal southern-style houses and so Emmy loved those things, too. If people weren't careful the past could be something they found themselves needlessly shackled to.

I remember when Dr. Watson had encouraged me to write and submit a fiction story to the little literary magazine our school put out. He said that though my creativity and the liberties I'd taken with facts had backfired on some of my papers and essays, they might come in handy in the form of fiction. Out of respect for him, I began writing a story one afternoon and stayed up well beyond midnight to finish it.

The story was about this boy. He was scrawny but strong and perpetually tan on account of his distant Cherokee heritage. He had eyes so blue that women couldn't resist cupping his smooth face in their hands and gazing into them. By the time this boy was twelve he could chase down the family's German Shepherd in open pastures. He could master any sport within a matter of weeks, but couldn't hold on to a line of thought to save his life. He had trouble following very simple commands or locating small items he was asked to find. The boy had to be forced to change his clothes and shower because it never occurred to him to do so.

I gave him two really odd character traits. The first was that it had never occurred to the boy that he was a separate entity from the people and the objects around him; they were extensions of himself and he of them. The second was that the boy could not be taught; everything the boy ever knew he knew because he felt it intuitively.

But the story I wrote for Dr. Watson wasn't really about the boy. The boy had a twin sister who was very pale and perpetually ill. She was beautiful, too. She had glossy brown hair that seemed to be drifting about her face like a spider web that'd just been cut in half. She was always thinking. From the time she could understand words, she was deeply worried about everything. The simplest questions could furrow her little brow and draw her into a silence that ended in tears. She never ran and she never seemed happy. The boy loved his twin sister very much. Their father loved her, too, and most likely it was his deep concern that accounted for the sound of his footsteps in the hall at night.

So, near the end of the story the boy, now thirteen, becomes the youngest person to ever be brought up to play on the high school junior varsity basketball team. He still has so much energy after the grueling practices that he comes home and stalks the sprawling woods surrounding the farm. He chases a monster into the deepest parts of the forest, but he doesn't catch it, though he comes pretty goddamn close. Anyway, his sister is afraid of the woods. She's always tapping her chin with fingers as thin and brittle as toothpicks and saying that something is out there. When she does walk, she sticks close to the house and ghosts through the yard with her frail shoulders hunched, arms folded and pressed against her as if caught in a perpetual shiver. She's so smart it causes problems for her because she can follow a line of thought forever until it ends in darkness. Sometimes the boy feels he can see through her to the background beyond.

I'll tell you what happened to these characters toward the conclusion of my story. The girl ends her worrying on a Tuesday night after crying at the dinner table. Cuts her wrists. Classic suicide. She's been dead a while before the boy stumbles across her in the bathroom, only he's still mostly asleep, you see, so he lies down in the morning dark beside her. He's not upset or afraid or anything. It does not occur to him that she is dead, and it does not bother him that the floor is wet and sticky. He puts his arms around his sister's cold form with the thought of warming her and drifts into a deep and very peaceful sleep. The mother wakes up and comes in a few hours later. She sees them lying there in that mess and screams louder than a train whistle. She screams so loud, in fact, that something in her head dislodges and she's never quite the same.

Well, that was the story I wrote and submitted. Not upbeat, I'll admit, except that at the very end I mentioned that a few years later the boy actually did catch that big monster. He chases it deep into the old pine forest along the southern edge of the property to where it gets sort of boxed in by these rocky cliffs. He climbs a tree and that big creature walks under it. He leaps on its bright back, wrestles it to the ground by its stag-like horns and then simply and happily lets it go.

The Creative Writing teacher, Mrs. Skulton—who Dr. Watson said edited the little magazine—did not like the story at all. She was a bony, middle-aged poet with a number of publications in literary magazines and shadowy eyes sunk deeply in brittle sockets. She sent me a really nice letter explaining she couldn't accept it because the grammar and spelling were bad and because the story was kind of unsettling for a little college magazine, but most of all because it was implausible.

I wasn't mad at all. I knew exactly what she meant.

18

To have really done the meeting up correctly, I would've needed to bring Santana Montana Ordóñez along in a suit and tie. I would have combed his hair to the side and plastered it down with gel. He would initially protest, of course, but I'd be able to convince him. I'd mention that I'd seen him cry like a baby and not said a word, so he owed me. Anyway, he already had the mustache, but I'd need to dig out my aluminum briefcase from under my bed.

I wasn't crazy or anything, obviously. It was just that the idea of having him dressed like that and referring to him, as I chatted with Dean Andrews, as *my attorney* was nearly impossible to pass up despite the recent troubling developments. I knew, though, that the job I'd given him was too important to entrust to anyone else.

As we passed by her, Dean Andrews' secretary seemed about to object to my guests, but she decided to let it go, and we went on in. Dean Andrews was standing at the big window behind his desk. I'd always liked Dean Andrews' office. It was done up in dark wood with built-in bookcases, which were filled with the colorful, uncreased spines of hardcover books. The big window behind his impressive desk looked out over the courtyard and the fountain with its ancient and well-placed oaks and the birds fluttering hither and thither. Dean Andrews had been my advisor since freshman year. I'd even taken the course he taught: The Bible: Old Testament. God, was it terrible.

"Hey there, Lightly," he said, as he came around his desk to shake my hand. "We were expecting you an hour ago." He was short, rotund, and bearded with curly flames of red and yellow hair and wore little, round wire glasses. And a bowtie, always.

"And I was expecting not to come at all," I told him. "It's a compromise." He raised his eyebrows in a good-natured, way. "Greg, Emerald," he said nodding to each in turn. "Lightly, are you sure you wouldn't prefer to talk privately?" he asked.

"No," I said. "This meeting is sort of a violation of privacy, if you know what I mean, but, then again, even if you don't. I'd like nothing more than for us all to get moving and go about our lives, doing the things we want and so on. Believe me, having to be here makes me downright claustrophobic. But if

I have to endure this, I'd like to have Emmy and Padre Johnson with me just the same." I kept my tone light, but there was anger sniffing around the edges of my words. I kicked it away. I didn't want to explode or get defensive—I sure the hell didn't want to mention the vision and the quest. In all honesty, I just did not want to seem crazy. I knew, of course, that I wasn't. There was a fine line between brilliant and crazy. I just didn't trust Dr. Crispin or the dean to know the difference.

There was a polite knock at the door and Dr. Crispin stepped coolly into the room. "Hello, Lightly," he said. He didn't move forward but stood there in that infuriatingly patient way of his. He was tall, thin, and vaguely handsome in a reserved, stately sense. As usual, his suit and red tie looked so new and spotless that unless he moved, you'd think you were looking at a mannequin. He introduced himself to my companions and we all shuffled over to the coffee table with its cheerful magazines and settled on the bench and into chairs upholstered in stripes of crème and red. He unbuttoned his jacket and when he leaned forward to sit down, it opened momentarily to reveal a small yellow square on the inside just above the pocket.

Dr. Crispin didn't waste time but went on and told me with calm directness, and in a voice the exact color of wild corn poppies, that if I did not agree to come home, get back on my medicine, devote myself to getting better and meeting with a shrink regularly, my mother—with Dr. Crispin's support—would seek to have me involuntarily committed. He said it was something my mother had discussed with him after my unauthorized adventure to Disney World and recent erratic behavior.

It was true, of course, that—if I was remembering it correctly—it had been my idea to escape the awful Orlandoian tourists by making haste to the Keys and renting a fast boat, but I'd not forced everyone to climb into that van with me. And I sure to god was not the only one who'd taken ecstasy once the bourbon had dried up. I knew that for a fact. If fearing tourists, drinking liquor, and taking a few drugs in college meant you were crazy, then I suppose everyone must be insane. And anyway, what the hell kind of mother would force her son to see a psychiatrist—one, as it turned out, she happened to be fucking—because she believed her son wrecked a loaded van going ninety *on purpose*?

Well now, I had to admit that I knew the answer to that one: a mother whose personal tragedies—a lost husband, dead daughter, estranged sons—had made her neurotic. She was the one who hadn't left the house in two years and yet she feared *I* was the one who'd never dealt with difficult psychological-type things, that *I* was the one who needed help. It wasn't just her, though. Coach had called the dean to say I'd been off the medication and was planning another adventure, and that was enough to convince the dean to go and collect my keys. I didn't say a thing because the truth was I hadn't been taking the meds for a long time. I mean, what did they think would happen when they gave a naturally upbeat, happy person drugs to improve *their* attitude? That was the point. They didn't know, of course. I did, though. I started obsessively tidying and sweeping the room I shared with Biggs and watching reruns of *The View*.

Jesus, but I was the least depressed person I had ever met. No joke. I was pure irrepressible enthusiasm. Could I help it if my mother was idiotically trying to cure herself by treating me or rather focusing on me to avoid seeing her own condition clearly? It was all a mess and so ridiculous I nearly convinced myself it couldn't be happening. But it was happening and I listened as the doc reminded me of promises I'd made in sessions with him after the crash and all. He didn't uncross his legs or lean forward or anything as he spoke. His hands continued to lie peacefully, almost preternaturally peacefully, in his lap.

"You are exceptionally smart, Lightly," he said. "And convincing. You've convinced yourself that you're fine. It's a coping strategy. Think. Consider the van wreck alongside the incident the summer before you enrolled here, the family history of mental illness."

I smiled at him. He was a sweet man and doing the best he could. Unlike the others, I could see beneath his cool exterior to the desperate creature that huddled wet and whimpering at his core. I knew the calm control he exerted over the movements of his body and the inflections in his voice belied in direct proportion the lack of calm and control that he must have truly felt. I didn't know what fiery traumas had forged his personality, but I could guess, and I would never have tried to rob him of those mechanisms he'd built to cope with them.

"Stella made it clear to me," he went on, "that she's exploring involuntary commitment only if you refuse to come back to the farm. From there we can get treatment and consider the appropriate course of action." He added that my mother would be stopping the automatic transfer of my allowance and cutting off my credit card and that he hoped I'd see it for what it was: a way to get me home.

"She's worried about *me* getting treatment?" I asked. "Tell me, Doc, has she shared her delusion with you?"

"Which one?"

"Which *one*?" I repeated. "Jesus. I mean the big one. Tell these nice folks about the new book she's writing, Doc. And, hey, could you open your jacket for me."

"What?"

"Your jacket."

He opened his jacket to reveal the yellow sticky note.

"Well," I asked, "what's it say, Doc?"

He pulled it from the lining and looked at it. "It says, 'wear this suit'," he explained, then presents an argument for why this suit was the best choice.

"Good lord," I said, looking around at everyone as if this explained everything, which it did, but they just looked at me like mannequins in various positions of repose.

"This isn't about your mother, Lightly. This is about *you*."

"But it doesn't make sense," I said. "If we're all her characters, then why send you to bring me home? Know what I mean? Why not just write that I came home?" I applied pressure to my temples. "It's freaking crazy."

"Stella is suffering, too, Lightly," he said, delicately folding up my mother's note. "She has her way of coping—just like you. I don't think she'd dispute that. But she's working on it. She wants you to come home and work on it, too."

"Oh, you think having me around my delusional mother is going to help keep me sane—that it, Doc? She can have her coping mechanism, but I can't have mine?"

"You'd be working with me or a doctor of your choice. Your mom is just worried. She's already lost a lot. You both have."

I looked at Emmy. She was looking at me like she didn't know me. I leaned back in the chair, stuck my hands deep in my pockets, and looked at those divine fingers of hers but they'd formed themselves into two fists in her lap.

"When I was fourteen," I told her, "my sister committed suicide. Mom went off her rocker, started micromanaging us but really infecting us with her own phobias and illness. So there's just my brother Lance and me. Before you look shocked or anything, consider that parents—especially bright ones—get increasingly neurotic, and that a million people commit suicide each year. That's about three thousand people a day, so a couple while we've been sitting here. Half a person has died in the last fifteen seconds—that's a joke, but you get the idea. In my opinion, and as long as we're pointlessly hashing it out, all the weird stuff happened later. A year after Margaret's death, Dad's head popped during a meteor shower over the Outer Banks." I pointed to the back of my head. "Aneurism—probably induced by guilt—and a year after that Mom understandably started seeing a psychiatrist. She's a romance novelist—yes, *that* super popular romance novelist, sorry I lied to you about that —and what with a dead daughter and having to kind of take care of Dad after what he did, she was burning both ends of the candle. He's in full-time care now and she's sort of married to that certain psychiatrist," I said, eyeing Dr. Crispin, "but not really since it's not legal seeing as how she isn't well enough to divorce my father. She can't leave the house anymore."

I watched as my words played themselves out predictably across Emmy's face and found myself wishing I was a painter so that I could get Emmy just right on paper. Well, not me, I thought, since she was gone from my memory now, but somebody ought to. As I looked at her it really was like she was a stranger and I was seeing her for the first time. Her freckles were a map of galaxies, her pale green eyes the color of bedroom walls inside old beach houses. *Poor Emmy*, I thought, who hadn't known my dear mother was a nut job, and who believed my father was just plain dead, and all my siblings happily alive.

Emmy twisted slightly in the chair. She looked pained. She looked like she wanted to put her arms around me. "I don't—" she said, then glanced at Dr. Crispin. She leaned toward me. "What did he mean about the summer before you came here?"

I laughed. "Out of all that, that's what you ask? The *incident?* Well, don't be sorry—it's a big misunderstanding, but I'll tell you if you want to hear. Lance was back at the farm from college and we took this walk and did some climbing up this big ridge of cliffs that are way the hell out in the woods. Lance and I went up there lots as little kids. Hell, this one time we went up there to read the Bible one Sunday and got attacked by a swarm of yellow jackets but that's a whole other story. Anyway, Lance kept trekking once we'd climbed to the top, but I was looking back across a sea of pine tree tips that stabbed up from the forest floor below. They were lovely, pointed, sloping like cathedral spires and the scent of pine was dreamy like the smell of a mother that hugs your face into her comforting bosom. I really, truly thought that if I ran fast enough I could jump the gap between the cliff and those pines and put a bear hug on one of those big pine tops, you see, and climb it on down. I've always been physically gifted, and I knew in my bones it could be done."

"Good lord," I said, "but did I ever misjudge the distance." I winked at Padre Johnson. "I didn't get anywhere near the damn bole. I went through a lot of limbs on the way down, which was good as it turned out, because I reckon it was a seventy-foot drop. Well, the unfortunate thing was that when Lance got to me, he misconstrued something that I said and told Mom I'd tried to off myself. Jesus, but I was only half conscious after that fall—I could have been saying all sorts of nonsense. But Margaret had offed herself just recently, so Mom couldn't be told different. Emmy, I know I said it was a separated shoulder that made me miss part of my freshman football season, but it was the fall—mostly lingering pain in my throwing shoulder."

Instinctually, I began rubbing my right shoulder, squeezing it and rolling the muscle like a hose in a rubber bag.

Dr. Crispin cleared his throat and leaned forward in his chair.

"Lightly," he said softly, "the guilt you all feel is normal. But you've got to work through it. It's not your fault. You were just a kid."

"So was she."

"I know. You all were."

I glanced at Emmy. The worry on her face smelled like a potato—as worry sometimes did—but her sadness like confederate jasmine. The others just looked plain confused.

I leaned toward Crispin with my elbows on my knees.

"I don't need help," I said. "Margaret needed help. My brother needs help. My mom—good lord, my mother needs help. What I need is to set out. I'm full of joy, Doc, not misery. When the sunlight is still golden in September and the dogwoods get red and the tulip poplar leaves turn yellow and start to twist down slowly in sweet driftwood colored breezes, its so beautiful I can hardly take it. I am not depressed. There's something beautiful and glorious out there waiting for me—not something horrible and dangerous. You and Mom make the world sound so dirty and awful and broken, but what I see—everywhere—is beauty. A world that is clean and wonderful and whole. And you'd rather keep me here mired in family trauma? In what it did to all of us rather than let me go out there into the comforting arms of such wonders?"

I looked around at them. They were all looking at me like they couldn't tell a truth from a lie. I knew I could go on and tell them why they had it all wrong, defend myself. It'd be easy, but they'd still not see it even if I talked forever. So, I shut up. And, anyway, the thing I didn't like about *troubled* folks was that the more they told people their story, the more they were shackled to it. The more their past defined and continued to define them. It killed me that they didn't see that. If Emmy had known about my sister and father and that my mother stupidly thought I was suicidal, I would have been able to feel Emmy's pity and concern every time those wonderful fingers of hers touched me. Each touch and look from all those that knew would become nothing but reminders that I should be shattered and that I might shatter until I took their opinion as my truth.

That was the problem. I wasn't fragile, and I could not be shattered.

Margaret was dead, my brother depressed, my dad was brain dead, and my mom was a complete delusional disaster, but I was perfectly fine. I wasn't sick. I wasn't disturbed. I wasn't crying myself to sleep. I wasn't angry at god. In fact, my curiosity and robust joy at the mysteries of existence were irrepressible and genuine, even bordering on rapturous excitement, what with the impending adventure and all. I knew, though, that this was what all the business with my mother and Dr. Crispin was really about. It wasn't that I was quirky and, admittedly, a bit different—I'd been that way since I'd first drawn breath in the world. It sure wasn't that I was *a danger*.

The problem was that I was fine and there were those who thought I shouldn't be.

But how could the truth matter when everyone else believed you needed help? That you were too weird and crazy to possibly be as happy as you seemed? I could see it in their faces. What could I do when confronted with so much genuine concern?

I caved, of course. I let my gaze fall and said, "You know what? I've been a fool. I think maybe I do need help." I tried my damnedest to make it sound sincere.

What else could I do? I had no car, apparently no more money, and no other options but to head on back home to my mother, to the farmhouse with its opened windows through which the crickets sang their ageless songs all summer long, and determine a course of action. Dr. Crispin would give me a ride back to the farm. He'd said as much. In fact, he wanted to get going right away, but I told him I had to pack up my things and I wanted to honor the meeting I'd agreed to with the chaplain tomorrow morning. I thought maybe talking god—"takin' it to the man," as Biggs liked to say—would be helpful, and the chaplain was quick to agree, as I'd known he would.

Finally, when it was all agreed and everything about my departure was squared away, I stood up and slunk out of the room.

When I get to where I'm going, I'll send Dr. Crispin a postcard. It will begin, *If Mama Stella makes you be quiet when you have sex with her in the house, remind her that he can't hear you—my father, I mean.* It will end, *You're a good psychiatrist and you can make whatever you want out of my attitude, words, gestures, possessions, but in the end I'll still be here—resistant, present, and unknowable—to mock whatever meaning you ascribe to me.*

19

I stepped outside and felt a breezy rush among the buildings, which tickled over the flowerbeds, curled in eddies around the trunks of trees. I stepped wide leaving my friends and foes behind in the deanery, and eating up the distance to the Theta house in great joyous strides.

I passed by a few underclassmen. They waved and said my name, but I was thinking of Dr. Kwell's exam where I'd written that a particle of light could be simultaneously anywhere in the universe at any given time. I knew that although folks couldn't understand much beyond what they could see, invisible phenomena—such as on the quantum level—were playing out all around them just the same. Anyway, I'd written how the only way you could stop a particle from being magnificently everywhere was to observe it and measure it, which would result in what scientists called its collapse. I didn't know why I was thinking on Kwell's exam but maybe it had something to do with potential and the collapse of potential.

After all, I couldn't stick around to be poked and prodded, observed and so forth because all my life I'd heard this urgent voice telling me, "Go, go, go!" And then, finally, from far, far off—so far, in fact, that I could not hear it for the longest time—a voice had been calling in reply. "Here, here, here!" it said. "Come, come, come!"

I rounded the corner of the Theta house and saw Santana Montana Ordóñez standing awkwardly beside Anne Marie Wentworth in the parking lot. He still held his notebook and the rolled up photo of the beach in his soft brown hands, but he looked so horribly uncomfortable I thought he might melt into a puddle on the asphalt.

"Is what he saying true?" Anne Marie asked even before I was close enough to hear her clearly. She was leaning against a blue Volvo station wagon with her hand placed defiantly on her hip and chewing the hell out of a piece of gum. She raised her other hand up to her eyes to shield them from the sun. "I'm only waiting here because I want to tell you that I know it's not and that it's not funny at all."

I stopped in front of her and smiled.

"Hell, yes," I said. "It's like Santana Montana says. I just thought we could ride to Hatteras Island together and talk it over. I'm sure Emmy's confided in you how we sort of ended things."

"Right," she said. "And you expect me to believe your friend here? That you broke things off with her because of me?"

"Anne Marie," I said, bringing up my palm to gently cup her smooth cheek. "You don't give yourself enough credit."

She'd stopped chewing her gum. I let my hand linger a moment on her warm cheek then let it fall away. Anne Marie shifted her stance a little. Something about her didn't seem so defiant anymore. When she spoke, in fact, she sounded sort of uncomfortable, nervous. "My backseat is all full of bags," she said. She cast a doubtful look toward Santana Montana.

"Look," I said, holding out my hands. "I haven't got a thing in the world, and Santana Montana is portly but he's very flexible and can fit back there under and among a few bags no problem. Let's just get in the car and go the hell on. It's not like we don't have a lot to talk about now is it, Anne Marie?"

Her mouth was hung open a little and I smiled at her. All around us the heart of the afternoon had opened and there was a glow from each thing I beheld: Anne Marie's flushed cheek and the copper-ochre of Santana Montana's fat hands, the Volvo with its silver hubcaps gleaming in the sun, the green stretch of grass beyond the asphalt, and the high white-washed walls of the Theta house all pulsating as if their very brightness fed off the eyes that perceived them.

"Okay then, Lightly," Anne Marie said. She seemed at once confused and pleased, shaking her head as she went around to get in behind the wheel. I put my arm around Santana Montana Ordóñez. His back was damp against my forearm.

"Let's go my friend," I whispered, "the magnificent everywhere has spread its arms in embrace."

Anne Marie didn't waste any damn time, but ran two yellow lights and pulled a Hollywood through a stop sign on the way to the interstate. Once we hit I-64 she smoothed the Volvo out and put on some traveling music. I watched her sway to the rhythm and it was odd to see her look so happy.

"Anne Marie," I said, "I know something's kind of hanging in the air between us, but I think we should talk about other stuff first, to make it all seem more natural even though it won't be at all, which is kind of funny."

"Okay, Lightly," she said. The sweet way she said it made her voice unrecognizable. It was like another girl was talking out of Anne Marie's mouth and that filled me with a gentle and confused curiosity. We talked about all sorts of things as we sped on. She spilled the beans on her long-standing crush, but then talked about it so long and with such emotion that it soon strayed into psycho territory. I was enormously relieved when she mentioned that she loved reading books because I steered the conversation in that direction. I told her I was aces on the subject on account of my mother and Dr. Watson, but Anne Marie said, "Nobody says *aces* anymore."

I laughed when she said that—not because it was funny, but because the wind in my hair was summer. This light was summer, too. It was heating up the edges of all I could see, but there was more. We were hell-bent for the beach, Santana Montana was safe in a blanket of luggage, and Anne Marie was going a dozen miles over the speed limit. Each rotation of the Volvo's tires reeled in the Outer Banks with its swaying sea oats along the crests of scraggy dunes, its rough and stormy waters. I lay my head back and took a deep breath because *it* was happening. I was on my way and it all was there before me, the whole of everything looming, unstable, explosive and true. I'd sprung the trap behind me and stepped away before the steel jaws clamped shut.

"You know, Lightly," Anne Marie whispered. "When he told me about your feelings for me, I thought about leaving without you anyway."

"I know it, Anne Marie Wentworth," I said. "Emmy is your friend and what not. I can understand the guilt but you can't let anyone get in the way of what you want."

"I don't feel guilty," she said. "Like, maybe I will later. I mean I was a little worried to get involved with you because I remembered how upset Emerald was about the thing last year. But, I have to say that you seem really nice and normal and sweet."

"What can I tell you Anne Marie?" I said. "I've been misrepresented and misunderstood. I'm just different that's all."

"Why are you going to the Outer Banks?" she asked. "I mean, it's not *just* to talk to me is it?"

"Anne Marie, sweetheart," I said, "there's a surfboard tucked away in a tool room with my name on it. It's all part of my big adventure."

She asked me if my parents had taught me how to surf, and I told her, "Heavens, no. My mother's a romance novelist, and my father's a washed up athlete."

"Mary Jo said your mom was Stella Steele. I asked Emmy but Emmy didn't seem sure."

"That's because I told Emerald that she wasn't Stella Steele—it's a pen name anyway, you know, so I wasn't really lying. Our name is Higgs, but Mom thought Steele might sell a few more books," I said. "I want to deal truly with you, Anne Marie. That's why I'm telling you my mother is a certified artist with the written word as it pertains to emotion, flesh, desire, unrealistic plot twists and very poorly rendered exotic locales."

"She's written like five-hundred romance novels."

"I guess," I said, "but what of it? You Wentworths have more money than most small countries."

"I know," she said. "It's just I've read her books because my stepmother has like every one of them. I knew she must be your mother because of your name, but I didn't say anything to Emmy. Lightly was the main character in the *Thrushes* series, right?"

"You got it," I said. "That series put her on the map, as they say, but boy is it creepy that she named me after that glistening horn-dog."

"But he was attractive—Lightly was. He came back to right a terrible wrong." She gave me a sweet smile and added, "And he gets the girl in the end, and a few more along the way."

"Hell, don't I know it," I said. "But it smacks of ludicrous situations and unworkable extremes, and how he can have his brain splinter to pieces when he's shot in his melon and dumped into the Blue Hole off the coast of Belize and still be handsome once he wakes up from his coma in the sand is beyond the laws that govern physical objects in our universe."

"Did you really go to all those places where her stories happened?"

"Yes, indeed. Each summer was some new crazy place. For *Thrushes* we stayed right there on the coast of Belize. Damn, but it must have been three weeks or more with Pop god knows where and me following Lance around the *cabina* with a load in my diaper and a Spanish speaking nanny trying to coax me out from under the table or get me to play Legos. Those were heady times, but then even when we weren't abroad we were on the move—the beach house, the farm. We even kept an apartment in DC. We went up there bunches and god did I hate it. My little sister used to say about the farm that in winter she could hear the clover screaming under blankets of snow, but I felt that way in the city. Thinking on all that land entombed beneath seas of concrete. Did you know seventy percent of the Earth is underwater? I wonder how much of what is left is destined to be under concrete."

"Emerald never said you had a sister."

"Well, I do," I said. "A sweet little thing. Can you believe she has the exact same birthday as me? I mean think of the odds—it's crazy."

I must've gotten a little loud for she shushed me and gave a nod toward the back. I twisted in the seat and saw that Santana Montana had gone to sleep among the towering bags. The soft golden bulb of his head lay on Anne Marie's fat green duffle bag. His mouth was open, his eyes were shut, and he was breathing rapidly. A speck of drool had formed on the bag. It sparkled in the light.

"Why is he your friend?" Anne Marie whispered. "It's driving me crazy." There was something conspiratorial in the way she asked it. There wasn't any implied judgment, though, just genuine bafflement.

"Santana Montana?" I laughed. "He is awesome. Just look at him back there pretending to sleep. The kid is a genius and I'm not joking at all. Did you know he can identify any tree or plant and that he knows a lot about wildlife?"

"No," Anne Marie said flatly.

"It's true," I said. "His grandfather was a bullfighter in Spain who Ernest Hemingway greatly admired. No one knows how, why, or when his family moved from Spain to Mexico, but he's made it here to the most racist school in the state. He's also an asthmatic with pharmacist aspirations."

"Why are you listing things?"

"Oh, there's so much more, Anne Marie, and I could go on and on about him but essentially he is the most amazing person at our college—myself included."

"But," she said, seeming truly confused. "He's really weird, though, and, well, ugly." I thought about mentioning mating practices and herd acceptance and how if an animal sensed something different or off about another animal it was genetically predisposed to either kill or avoid that animal but I didn't. I decided against it because I didn't think Anne Marie could grasp the reprimand behind it, so instead I said, "Anne Marie, one thing you'll learn is that every single person is interesting if you get to know them. Santana Montana is special, but this is a difficult time for him. He is a very sensitive sort and he's in love with me."

"Oh," she whispered. "I didn't know he was a fag." There wasn't exactly compassion in her voice, but maybe something coming close, which was odd on account of how she'd just used a slur and didn't seem to know. But the first awkward steps in a bigot's ham-fisted attempt to move beyond an infantile closed-mindedness were never pretty.

"Gay," I corrected, "and neither do I. He hasn't told me yet, and that's undeniably part of his mysterious greatness."

"Aren't you going to ask him?" she said.

"Hell no," I said. "What for?"

Anne Marie said she didn't know but she looked pleased for some reason, maybe knowing about the book, the origin of my name, made her feel she was already closer than Emmy and I had been, since Emmy had not really known. Or perhaps she felt she was on the saintly path by trying to understand Santana Montana though he obviously wasn't worth her time.

Anyway, she shook her head in a playful sort of way and kept her eyes on the road. She put another piece of gum in her mouth and started crushing it repeatedly with her teeth, which made the masseter muscles ripple in her jaw. She'd put her window down a bit and pulled her hair back into a tight ponytail. Some strands had wriggled free to snap like silk scarves on a clothesline in a storm.

She was wearing a black skirt that only covered half her thigh and I swear to god I wasn't looking, but I caught a glimpse of her legs. Her coloring was such that she seemed to have a perpetual tan, which was different from Emmy who was kind of a tall, pale beauty.

"I like your coloring," I told her. "You look like you were born at the beach."

She laughed. "Thanks, Lightly," she said. "I like you, too."

"Aw shucks," I told her. "Now we're friends."

20

Before the night of sand, meteors, and stars, my best memories of the Outer Banks involved Pop. One of my favorite things about him was that he left you alone when he was with you, unlike Mother who was always in your business.

Pop's distance made you want to tell him things, though you didn't know why and he was too wonderfully simple-minded to understand them. I remember one day during the summer I turned ten, Pop and I were silently packing up that stupid Astro van we used to clown around in. We were leaving the Outer Banks to head up to DC. in advance of the Redskin's OTAs. The summer was over for us and that meant it'd be forever until I could collect shells again, and I was down as hell.

Anyway, after a while Pop stopped packing, and he hugged me against his big leg and said, "Don't you wish you could stay in a place without having outside things make you leave?" I remember it really well because it might have been the most philosophical thing he ever uttered in his life.

I gave his leg a vicious hug and asked him why he'd said it, and he told me it was because I looked so sad.

"I'm not sad," I said, "but kind of angry."

He made the mistake of asking me why, so I told him how for the past year I'd had the feeling that every time he and Mom had made me leave one place for another, a version of me stayed behind to live out the life I'd have led had I not left.

Jesus, but I thought I'd broken Pop's brain or something. His face got all screwed up like he had the cramps, so I said, "When we leave here, Pop, a little boy that looks just like me gets to stay behind. He walks the beach and gets all the best shells and his skin will get so golden brown with light that a cold, dark winter won't take his tan away and that makes me mad. Did you know boa constrictors absorb a great deal of heat during the summer so that they can survive the winter? What? It's true."

Pop had put his hand on me. He loved playing all sorts of sports with me —basketball in the driveway, golf clubs on the beach, the pigskin spiraling between us, batting practice at the cage and so on. Many times he said I had a future in any of them if I wanted, but he often looked uncomfortable when we'd talk about stuff other than sports. Anyway, on that long ago, bright, lost day at the Outer Banks, he'd patted my back awkwardly and said, "Son, I wouldn't go around telling people that. It's not healthy."

I told him, "Okay," and maybe I even gave him a thumbs up—I don't remember. Truth was, it was often uncomfortable to talk to him, too, on account of how he used sports clichés—*coach talk*, Lance was fond of calling it. "One game at a time," "It is what it is," "Keep your eye on the ball," "Give one hundred and ten percent," and so on, which was fine when talking sports but got under your skin when applied to education, finances, literature, government, alternate universes and whatnot.

But I told him, "Okay" and, except for one small slipup, I stuck to my word and didn't tell a soul about it, but I've never stopped thinking it. Each time we left the Outer Banks, or DC, or the farm, or we left those crazy places Mother went to research her pointless romance novels—Ireland, Spain, Belize, even O'ahu, the goddamn Azores—I continued to suspect, and perhaps desperately wanted to believe—that a version of me lived on there totally autonomous but just as real.

Sometimes Pop returns to me uninvited. Not in dreams, but when I'm in that vulnerable place between sleep and wakefulness. I hear, for example, someone call his name and there he is: on a football field in those tight coaching shorts, or snoring in the beach house bed beside Mother, leading me by the hand through the Newport News coalfields, packing his luggage in a trunk or taking his luggage out, sitting on the couch with sunlight on the floor beneath him, or mucking out the horse stalls at the farm, or creeping down the hallway at night and so on. The strangeness of a fond memory when weighed against the unforgivable.

All these little fragments like floaters in the eye. Blood on tiles, Uluwehi's bright eyes, Pop limp in the cool, pitted sand—frail specks of memory winging themselves feebly across the dark coliseum of death.

21

Anne Marie and I chatted on and off until Santana Montana Ordóñez was awake.

"Santana Montana," I said. "Would you mind speaking Spanish from here on out? I want to learn and that's the best way I know how."

"I would prefer not to," he replied.

With Santana Montana Ordóñez awake, Anne Marie became less willing to talk and her growing tolerance of him evaporated. We drove in silence for a good ways, and I noticed how she held herself more erect now and let out occasional annoyed sighs through her nostrils.

I told Santana Montana it would have been less awkward for everybody if he'd just slept—or pretended to sleep—the whole damn way. He said he'd considered it but couldn't do it for so long, and I told him I knew what he meant. So, I told them both about the Newport News coalfields we'd soon be passing by and how we'd stop there often because Gus, who had played high school ball with my dad at Hampton Roads, worked there and they'd stayed close.

Gus was a huge bastard, I explained, and he'd come straight to the hospital to see dad. Gus had grown fat in his old age, with a thick mustache and dark stains on his hands and coal under his nails. I didn't know him well, but at the hospital he wrapped me in a bear hug as if to console me but then he just broke the hell down. He'd buried his wide, rough face in my frail shoulder and cried. He kept saying, "Not him. Sweet Jesus, not him." His hair had smelled like coal dust and engine grease and his breath—I would identify later—of Old Milwaukee's Best.

Hell, I was just a kid at the time. I didn't know what to say to him, so I patted his ursine back, as they say, and started repeating something, too. It's something that, to this day, I still don't understand. "There, there, Gus," I'd said. "We'll arrange something." Anyway, it worked I guess because he quieted down and just listened. He went limp against me—all bent down on me as he was—but after a minute or so he straightened, wiped his eyes, and said, "You'll make him proud, son."

I've never forgiven him for saying that.

Anyway, that was long ago and Gus was a floater now. Gus McGovern who loved fishing and was on his third or fourth wife, and who adored his only child, a daughter who was pretty despite the genetic disadvantage. I'd seen her once ages ago when we'd stopped there, from a distance, picking along the shoreline in mismatched socks, long coils of blonde hair on her shoulders and most likely humming something heartbreaking to herself. Anyway, one could go on and on about such things but why bother. Besides I'd heard through Mother that Gus had moved to Mississippi a few years back to be near his daughter. Only the coalfields remained, and with them those memories—stupid, useless images flitting in your large mind. Floaters in the eye. Little dead things that cloud your vision.

When we drew near the coalfields, Anne Marie insisted on seeing them. I guessed my story had taken on some weird significance for her. At first I said no but finally gave up with a shrug and said we could.

The gravel grated as Anne Marie addled the car up between two big green dumpsters a little off from the main gate. No one around, she cut the car and we looked out silently at the scene before us. Beyond the high chain fence, giant pyramids of coal twisted into the sky. Skinny metal towers rose between the pyramids supporting massive hoses, which sprayed the mounds to keep the dust down and the coal from combusting.

"Best not to light a cigarette," I said. "This whole place could go."

We looked out over the coal yard. One of the hoses had caught a rainbow in its mist.

"Damn," I said. "Mom would stay in the car. Pop would take us into the fields and Gus would walk us around and show us the cannon sprays or the West Virginia soft coal that'd come in on the rails. If a ship was in, he'd take us aboard to watch the coal dumpers load them up for shipment up and down the coast."

I looked at Anne Marie. She was looking at me. Her eyes had an invitation in them, if you know what I mean. I thought maybe I was seeing things, but then she deliberately touched her upper lip with the tip of her tongue and ran it slowly across. I knew it was time to give her the bad news.

"Santana Montana," I said. "If you walk out to the water's edge over yonder you might be able to find a place to sit down and study the adjacent Navy shipyard for a minute. There's fish along the rocks—white perch and shad. There are cormorants and herons and perhaps you'll spot one of those, too."

"I prefer not to," Santana Montana said. I tried rephrasing my request.

"Santana Montana," I said. "Could you take a little walk so that Anne Marie and I can talk about special relationship type things, which would be awkward for you to have to listen to?"

"I will," he said, but it took him a long time to maneuver through the luggage. Finally he did, and we watched him walk slowly and unsteadily toward the water's edge. He seemed downright morose as he plopped down among the rocks.

"What a geek," Anne Marie said.

"Anne Marie," I said. "Have you ever seen lights moving along bedroom walls? If so, did you think they were the souls of the dead or some sort of neurological phenomena?" Anne Marie shook her head and leaned in to kiss me. It was a big, sort of deep kiss, if you know what I mean, with a lot of passion and whatnot in it.

I realized the spot between the dumpsters had been a tactical choice. I felt sad for Anne Marie, for how she didn't know I would not be spending even one more day of my summer with her at the Outer Banks. Maybe that's why, rather than following through on my instinct to push her away, I put my hand around the back of her delicate neck and pulled her to me. There was no flavor of the gum she'd been chewing, but I could find hints of chocolate on her tongue if I sought them out, and though her kisses were slobberingly invasive, as they say, I convinced myself they were also warm and alive, each one with its own little pounding heart.

I heard myself say, "Anne Marie, darling, I am wild for you."

Without taking her lips from mine, she climbed over the gearshift and into my lap. She was a small girl but she worked vigorously—with more persistent force than grace—to get my jeans down to my knees. She pulled her panties aside, and brought me into her and then I didn't think of her anymore but of the promise of summer, even as she crushed my face into her chest and worked me over.

It wasn't like me to have sex because I wasn't big on it, but there was something about the school and football and the people being behind me and something about the freedom of my impending adventure that urged me onward in a direction I was normally loath to go. Anne Marie put her hand down there to touch herself because she was experienced, and as she shuddered in my lap, I felt as if I'd made love to the coming adventure, to some looming promise I was only beginning to make mine.

Afterwards, we sat in our seats getting readjusted to the nature of things.

Anne Marie peeked around and then started to get her clothing repositioned. She laughed.

"What?" I asked.

"Nothing," she said. "Did you know that until you started dating Emmy all the sororities thought you were gay?"

I told her I did, but that I could never be gay because I was a nut about women. I told her how I could just see a girl cross the street and something in the shape of her legs, the way she walked, her clothes or the way the tip of her ear peeked out of her hair would make me fall utterly in love.

"I don't know if that makes sense to you," I said. "I don't know why I'm like that, but I am. I'll fall in love with a pretty girl even before she's turned around or opened her mouth. Unfortunately, I'll fall out of love just as quick, and you should know that. I guess I've hurt a few girls that way, falling so crazy for them and then just turning off so quick. That's just how I am. I can't help it."

"Is that what happened with Emmy?" she asked.

"What? Falling out of love?" I looked out over the water beyond Santana Montana's form, which was slumped dejectedly among the rocks—the same rocks Gus McGovern's daughter had picked along, humming. A loose pack of gulls was crossing way up in the air. They turned from purple to bright white as they dipped one wing and then the other in a muscular twisting through the sky. People with the right eyes could see how they left elongating tendrils of disturbed air in their wake like the vapor trails of aircraft bound for distant cities where people were—even now—waking or sleeping, sifting through papers or squeezing the fruit for ripeness in the cluttered market at the corner of Fifth and *wherever*.

"No," I said. "Emmy was something else. You see, I'm seeking something perfect and when Emmy's around it's easy to mistake her for the thing I seek even though I know she's not. No, I love Emmy so much that she's the greatest threat. I know that doesn't make sense, but neither does the behavior of matter on the quantum level. True is true no matter how weird it seems."

I popped on out of the car and walked over and gently placed my hand on Santana Montana's fleshy shoulder and he looked up at me. His notebook lay open in his lap and the purple ink was smeared in blotches on the pages. He had an iphone in his hand and his lovely brown cheeks were streaked with tears.

"Jesus, Santana Montana, what is wrong?"

He wiped at his face with his sleeve.

"I am sad," he said.

"I know," I said, patting his shoulder gently. "I know." What with dumb asses like Anne Marie calling him ugly, the football team's constant resentment, and his desire for me eating at his insides, I was sure these were hard times. I looked off across the headwaters all speckled with light—little riffles and rills along the shoreline. Here and there ships broke the horizon. I knew Anne Marie was boring a hole in my back with her love-struck eyes. I felt bad for her and hoped that she didn't really like me all that much, but I guessed she was gone on me. I was full of mystery and promise. The air of romance swirled around me and maybe for Anne Marie we'd become characters in a romance novel. She saw my shirtless likeness painted on the cover of our story crushing her passionately against my bronze, chiseled torso. I was sorry for that—extremely sorry.

I got my arms around Santana Montana and hoisted him up. He was struggling mightily and I aimed to support him without being intrusive. I knew that sometimes the greatest kindness you could offer was to be with someone while leaving them the hell alone.

"May I see your phone?" I asked gently. He placed it my hand and I turned and slung it as far as I could. It helicoptered out over the bay and then disappeared with a distant *plunk*. "Do you trust me?" I asked him.

"My phone," he said.

"Shush. We'll need to disappear entirely to see ourselves clearly." I turned toward the dumpsters.

"Come on," I encouraged him, but he just stood there looking out over the water.

22

After the coalfields, back on the road, the conversation with Anne Marie went bad quickly. It wasn't just the natural awkwardness that exists after two people who don't know each other all that well engage in vigorous lovemaking. My guess was it had to do with how she'd asked me how soon I could get down to her house on Ocracoke Island, and I'd told her I wasn't staying at the Outer Banks at all.

"I'm bound for a beach," I'd told her. "But for a remote, Central American beach—not Ocracoke Island, you poor, love-drunk, driver of my getaway car."

It'd be fair to say that things deteriorated after that. She stayed rigid in her seat and was quiet for a long time. After a while she said, "But your friend said you wanted us to talk things out and that you were really into me. I thought coming to the beach for the summer *was* your big adventure."

"Good lord, Anne Marie," I said. "I am. We've got a lot of work to do with you. You're cute—especially when you're smiling—and you make love like you chew gum, but you're a racist and an elitist of sorts and that needs some fixing. I think we've made a good start on things and I'm looking forward to you and I maybe picking up where we left off once we're back at Tommy Jeffs. Maybe not."

Apparently, that was not what Anne Marie Wentworth had wanted to hear at all. Perhaps that was why, when she dropped me off at the beach house in Hatteras Village, she leaned in for a grumpy hug and bumped into my hand that I had extended for a shake.

Quickly, I hugged her and said, "Anne Marie, darling, this is awkward, I know, but it's only awkward if you let it be and I still think you're great. I certainly do wish you all the best during the coming summer here at the Outer Banks."

She looked miserable, and it truly upset me to see her so. I didn't like beating around the bush or playing games so I said, "I can tell you want something from me but you've got to understand I've got this big adventure I've got to go on, and I cannot afford to tarry."

"Nobody says *tarry* anymore, Lightly," she said. She said it without amusement. Then she asked me to get out of her car.

"Well, all right then, Anne Marie," I said, and I got out.

I leaned in the open window and asked, "What's your address on Ocracoke?"

"Why?" she asked.

When I get to where I'm going I'll send a postcard to Anne Marie. It will say, *Anne Marie Wentworth you are a beautiful creature and should trust yourself more. The contrast of those inky coal pyramids and the foreground of your throat when you threw your head back atop me is still powerful. It is an image that will never leave me. Stop being a goddamn bigot and remember that no one will take you seriously, if you do not.* I will sign it, *Someone who takes you seriously.*

23

I sent Santana Montana on down to the Dancing Turtle for coffee and sandwiches and then retrieved the key from behind the power box and went in the house. I pulled the board from the wall and lay it on the floor. It was an eight-foot-six-inch WRV fun shape. Fun shapes are a cross between long boards and short boards, and god did I love them.

I used the wax comb to shave off the old wax, and discovered a hole in the board the size of a thumbprint.

"Shit," I said and looked over at mom's 1960 Dextra Classic. It was as tall as my board but three times thicker and heavy as a kitchen table. "Goddamn it," I said to the ceiling, "I'll be like Jesus when he had to lug that cross and all."

There was nothing to be done about it, so I switched boards and wrapped the ancient behemoth in some bubble tape Mom had saved and then bagged the board. When I was all done, I called the Billy Mitchell Airport to make arrangements with the owner of a little plane. Then I went upstairs and looked out over the beach that Pop had never risen from and all those blue bands of water and sky stacked upon themselves.

After Santana Montana and I had finished our sandwiches, I called a taxi. While we waited for the taxi, I went to my mother's office.

I should have known better.

Built-in bookcases wrapped around the room and were full of novels, poetry and criticism that she had ordered—not by genre or author's name, as one would expect, but by the size of the book and the color of their spines. Her romance novels took up six whole shelves. But that's not what jumped out at you. It was the overwhelming preponderance of sticky notes. They were on the books, in the books, on the bookcase itself, on the front and sides and top of the desk, the back of the door from top to bottom and the walls, too, all the way to the ceiling. Each yellow, curling note bore line after line of small, thin cursive script—endless notes to self, ideas, suggestions, critiques. To read them was to court madness. And in truth it looked like an exhibit dreamed up by some mad artist—an office made entirely from sticky notes.

I went over and sat down at her desk, shaking my head at the muted crunch and crinkle of notes beneath my ass. I opened the drawer, admiring the way its contents beneath the notes were perfectly arranged—the sharpened pencils in perfect rows, the red pens and black pens held together by their own rubber band, envelopes in little stacks according to size, stamps clipped together not according to value but by color. I could envision Mom sitting at the desk, as she used to do, biting her bottom lip anxiously while her husband sat in the porch swing where, with the aid of the live-in nurse, she'd placed him hours before. The swing overlooked the dunes, beach and ocean, and Dad would sit on it motionless, his breathing peaceful and rhythmic like the swells lifting the water, driving toward the shore beneath the gathering clouds.

This was before she'd read his confession in the hidden journal that Maida, the house keeper, had discovered and given her before my mother had stabbed his motionless body and called the police, before the darkness and guilt picked up our scent and came loping and snarling after us. He'd been in the care facility since then, my father, I mean, and, needless to say, none of us had visited him. Of course, Mom couldn't have anyway, and she had a bit of a brush up with the police after the attack. Once they'd read the journal, too, they let the charges against Mom sort of fade. After the discovery of the journal and the trauma of the investigation, she'd retreated to the farmhouse. Hadn't set foot off the property since. No wonder, the poor, mad lady.

Santana Montana was standing at the door, looking in quiet awe at the room.

"What do you think?" I said, leaning back and gesturing at it all.

He gently moved his hand over a stretch of curled notes on the wall.

"It looks like festoons of Monarch butterflies in the Oyamel fir forests microclime."

"Oh, that's right," I said. "They light out for that place to survive the harsh winter."

"Yes," he said. "They do."

"*Festoons*!" I screamed suddenly, slamming my fist on the desk in joy and startling him. "What a word choice! You're a freaking genius!"

When I get to where I'm going, I'll send Mom a postcard. It will begin, *Mom, old darling, you should have never named me after the main character in one of your romance novels, as it still creeps me out.* It will end, *I hope you never come to see that the more we try to label, annotate, and control, the more we reveal the depth of our powerlessness.* PS, I'll add, *I'll forgive you for that stunt you pulled with the good doctor so long as you leave me to my adventure this summer you dear, broken, gorgeous lady.*

24

The taxi came and the cab driver helped us tie the massive board bag to the roof. His name was—I swear to god—Elvis, and he spoke of, with great affection, a flat-coated retriever named Ms. B that awaited his return in the little three-room apartment over on Bay Street. I put my hand on his shoulder as he drove to the tiny Billy Mitchell Airport and said, "I like you, Elvis, and feel as if I've known Ms. B my whole life."

"You're a fine young man," Elvis said. "I wish my son was as mature as you."

"Let's give him some time, Elvis," I said.

"I will," he said. "I will."

Guess where we flew to from the Outer Banks?

Charlottesville, Virginia, that's where. Karen and Lance lived there in a townhouse with the girls. Lance was too damn young to have kids and a wife already, but I knew why he'd done it. He was seeking to fix the past through recreating it in the present.

Lance had just started his program at the University of Virginia School of Law and Karen—who was four years older than him—was finishing up her PhD in Neuroscience, which I understood had something to do with the brain.

Anyway, my brother Lance was very smart, super responsible, and legally deaf in one ear. I called him when we landed and he picked us up that afternoon at the Albemarle airport. We shook hands awkwardly, and I introduced him to Santana Montana, then we struggled to get my board on his roof. The sky was darkening. Clouds gathered shoulder to shoulder above us.

Lance took several long lengths of thick, yellow, nylon rope from the trunk to tie the board down.

On the way to the house I told him I was going to take a little trip and he said, "Mom is going to fall to pieces."

"She's in pieces already," I said. "Did you know about the stunt with the doc?"

"No, but nothing would surprise me. She needs us," he said. "And we need to stay away." I knew what he meant. He and I were both estranged from Mom and ever since our disagreement over my leap we'd been distant from each other. I could feel some sharp edges to our reunion, so I told him not to worry about it and then shared with him how I'd befriended Santana Montana at the river.

"Are you sure you're okay?" he asked.

"I'm as right as rain, big brother," I told him.

"You stopped with the meds," he said.

"Don't be a moron, Lance. I don't need medication."

"Sure," he said.

"You're the one carrying lengths of nylon rope in your trunk."

25

We went into their townhouse right off of JPJ and Karen gave me a great big hug and stood back.

"Damn, you just keep getting taller," she said, her voice, as always, the same cosmic latte color as Napoleon Bonaparte's favorite trousers.

"I know," I said. "And the taller I get, the handsomer I am."

She laughed. "And your ego grows with it," she said, reaching up to tousle my hair. She'd had a sisterly affection for me from the beginning and whereas I baffled Lance, I had a strong suspicion that Karen got me.

While she and Lance made dinner in the kitchen, I sat in the little family room, toys littered all around me, and wrestled with the twins—Louise and Adelaide. The twins were twenty-three months and still talking gibberish. They seemed frightened of Santana Montana—maybe because of the way he sat hunched and awkward in the rocking chair like a bulbous pervert. Luckily gibberish was a language I was fluent in, so I relaxed the girls by gibbering right back at them as they climbed all over me on the floor and belly laughed. I tickled their little bird necks and growled comically.

Karen came in wiping her hands on a dishtowel. She smiled and said, "I don't know what it is about you that gets them all worked up, Lightly."

"Well Karen, my sister, I guess it's just that I never grew up at all, and I'm still a little snot-nosed kid myself."

"Are you calling my children snot-nosed?" she asked feigning anger.

"Sweet Christ in his kingdom above, Karen," I said. "I can't slip a thing by you."

"What's that?" Lance asked from the kitchen. There was something sizzling on the stove and he couldn't hear us. He came in and stood beside Karen.

"Your brother just called his nieces snot-nosed," she said, severely.

Lance looked extremely worried, and I felt bad. I didn't want my little trip putting anyone out, but poor Lance was tighter than a banjo string.

"I was telling Karen," I said. "How I have this effect on women, always have." Louise squealed and fell across my legs. Adelaide stumbled toward me from the toy box like a drunken pirate. "They just climb all over me. It's just natural, in the genes, you know?"

"What's that?" Lance asked. He turned his good ear toward me and took the dish towel from Karen to wipe his hands.

Karen winked at me.

"I guess Lance here missed those genes," she said.

"God, yes, Karen," I said. "Poor Lance here missed the train on everything except success and dependability."

Karen laughed and put her arms around her husband, squeezing him to her. I knew she loved him and he was damn lucky for it. The twins were laughing too. They were at my shoes now trying to pry them off.

"You know," I said. "You two have a beautiful thing here. These little angels of yours are more joy than one has a right to dream of." I waved off Karen. "Oh, I know you're both so young and nothing was planned, and I know there's tough times juggling your grad school work or in the supermarket and what not with both of them screaming with loads in their diapers, but it's a beautiful life. I mean that, everything is so cool and comfortable like a great pool of blue, blue water."

Karen smiled at me, but Lance still looked outright sad. I wondered if he remembered all those exotic places we'd spent time at, how he felt about them.

"Do you remember the summer on O'ahu?" I asked.

"You mean the *Warm-Hearted Ice Sculptor* summer?"

"He's named them, you know," Karen said. "You might be the only family that has titles for its summers. Hey," she said, turning to Lance. "Isn't that the one when Lightly got his heart broken?"

Lance didn't answer; he had inherited mom's tendency to nibble at his lower lip when he was worried, and he was practically gnawing at it now. I bet he'd do it in the courtroom, too, if he thought he was losing.

"You know," he said. "Karen and I were talking just the other day about coming over to Ashland to watch your season opener against Emory next year."

"We were?" Karen asked, leaning back to look at him.

"Of course we were," Lance said, squeezing her and giving her a look.

Karen hesitated. "Oh," she said. She looked at me.

I laughed, but I did not look at them. It had started raining. I could hear it on the roof, like the sound of November gusts skittering hoards of dead leaves along gravel drives. I looked out the window at the blading of silver rain and said, "Listen, big brother. I'm just going on an adventure. It's not like I'm going into space or off the edge of the world."

Lance kept his arm around Karen.

"It's not like I don't have reason to worry. You know," he said, looking very unnatural, "that I...that I love you, right?"

I looked at Karen.

"Oh my god," I said. "Look how awkward this is for him."

Karen and I shared a big laugh. Then Karen said, "He's being very sweet, Lightly."

When I could manage it, I said, "I love you, too, big brother."

26

The twins slept on opposite sides of the only other bedroom in the cramped condo, but Karen had put them in the same bed so one of us could have the only other bed in the house. We were going to crash on the floor in the living room, but the twins had made such a hysterical fuss about letting us share their room that ultimately Karen had relented. I was on the floor in Lance's old green sleeping bag. Everything else in the room was either pink or white. The beds had matching pink fairy sheets and pillowcases and matching mosquito netting, which hung fancifully down to encase them.

Santana Montana had fallen asleep immediately in the fairy bed, which I'd forced him to take, and I lay there on the floor listening to his irregular wheezing, which smelled like the opening to a dank cavern where hay bale-sized meatballs lay among fields of chartreuse-streaked, wedgewood thyme.

I was nearly asleep when I heard footsteps in the hallway and then felt the presence of someone in the room. I continued breathing deep and evenly, but through my eye slits I watched Lance tiptoe over and gently nudge Santana Montana awake. Santana Montana sat up. Inside the netting, he looked like some morosely obese mosquito that'd eaten the person inside and was now too hopelessly fat to get out again. He blinked at Lance. My brother held a finger to his own lips and motioned for Santana Montana to come with him. He held the netting open and Santana Montana slowly and ungracefully climbed out of the bed and padded from the room in his sagging white athletic socks.

I waited until I heard the chairs scrape on the kitchen floor to get up and go over to the door where I heard Lance make what sounded like a muffled apology and Santana Montana grunt in reply. I inched closer to the hall.

"Do you know where my brother's going?" I heard Lance whisper.

"Yes," Santana Montana replied, clearing his throat quietly.

"And you will be going with him?"

"Yes."

"Good. Listen, I'm not saying you should tell me where you're going—I mean, you should probably tell me—but if you haven't figured it out already, you should know that Lightly is...well, mentally he's...."

I found myself rooting for my brother to find the right word.

"I mean," he said, giving up, "you have noticed that he's different?" I wished I could see the look on Santana Montana's face or which way his head might be shaking, but I could see nothing.

"I have noticed he is smart. Eccentric."

"Right. Well it's just that for all his physical prowess and all his, at times, brilliance, my little brother is very naïve and vulnerable. He's had problems, we've all had problems, I guess, but I'm worried that this trip—whatever it is —I'm worried that he'll get hurt. He has no support. I've got Karen and the kids, but I can't be around my mother or even Lightly for very long. I just can't. I wish—did he happen to tell you about our sister?"

"No."

I listened as Lance tried to explain what had happened to our little sister. I listened quite intently for I'd never known it could be explained at all.

For a long time, Santana Montana was silent. So long that I thought maybe he'd fallen asleep at the table. After a while, though, I heard him say, "I did not know that. It is awfully sad." Another bubble of silence expanded in the air, then he said, "Is it that you want me to stop him from going?"

"No. Nothing but death or prison could stop him from going once he gets obsessed like this. Here," he said, "just take this. If things look bad, just promise that you'll contact me. I don't want him to be far away and all alone if things go sideways again. I mean, you know he sees things, right? Colors, visions, and so forth."

"In a fashion." *In a fashion*—such brilliance!

"So you know what I'm telling you?"

"You are either telling me he can see things the rest of us cannot, or he sees things that are not there."

"Yes."

To my great surprise, Santana Montana asked, "Which do you believe is the case?" I leaned my head toward the silence in the kitchen. A car passed by outside. Behind me the girls lay motionless in the dark, each the mirror image of the other. Their minds entangled in dreams of beauty and magic, their mouths breathing out beds of sweet alyssum.

27

The next morning Santana Montana surprised everyone by getting up very early and making a fine breakfast of toast and cheesy eggs. They sat at the table and the twins ate every last bite of it. Karen marveled at Santana Montana's culinary skills.

"I can never get them to eat anything in the mornings," she said.

"That's true," Lance confirmed.

I put my arm around Santana Montana and told them that he was a true to god genius. "Anyone who doesn't believe that," I said, "should not be allowed to propagate the species." His cheeks went bright red and he tried to turn away but I held him firm, so he foraged in his pocket and took a puff from a little red inhaler.

Lance was looking at me like I'd just spoken in Latin.

"It is a compliment utilizing Darwinian logic," Santana Montana explained quietly, but I don't think that helped my brother all that much.

At the airport Lance and I untied the board and set it on the pavement. He shook hands with Santana Montana. Awkwardly, he hugged me for the first time in years. He apologized for not coming to my games and said he was proud of me. He said again how he was going to come to the Emory game next year. He wouldn't let go of me until I agreed to look for him in the stands.

"Sweet, lord, Lance," I said. "Alright, alright, put it on the calendar. Just let me go now, okay?"

He stood back. He took the first full breath I'd seen since my arrival. I knew it was because I was leaving—that was why he could breathe easy. It was sad, but it was true—we both needed to be free of our family to breathe properly.

"I know you don't like when I say it, Lightly, but you're so innocent in a way," he warned. "People aren't always as bright and great as you say. Where's your cell phone? Have you lost it again?"

"Nah," I said, waving him off. "I punted it."

"You what?"

"I dropkicked it into the forest ages ago."

117

"Can't you tell me where to go look in case you don't come back?"

"No can do, big brother," I said, glancing at Santana Montana. "Remember the Canary Islands—Tenerife? The lights moving on the wall? The most precious things should not be shared."

"The lights? Lightly, that was so long ago. I was worried about you. And you were scaring her."

"Right. Exactly like now."

"I don't mean Mother," he said. "I mean *her*."

"Margaret—why don't you ever say her name?"

"Fine," he said. "Margaret. Now promise me you'll be careful."

"Promise me you'll loosen up," I said.

"I'm serious, Lightly."

"You're such a lovely weirdo, Lance," I said.

"I know it's been hard on you," he said.

"Me?" I said. "You're in counseling up to your neck and it looks like a drug dealer is renting out the vanity mirror in your hall bathroom. I wasn't snooping," I explained, "just looking for floss."

"We're all trying in our own way," he said. "You shouldn't be too mad at Mom, though."

"Shouldn't I?"

"I know, Lightly. I mean, she named us after characters in her romance books. I *know*. What kind of mother names her kid after a character that she's created sex scenes for? And *Lance*—might as well've named me *Shaft* or *Penis*."

"It's not that bad," I said though I suspected it was worse. After all, Lance L'Orgone had been the horniest of mom's protagonists—not even gender or species could get in the way of his passions.

"So of course I'm in counseling. I feel like a big phallus walking around all the time. *Lance*," he said again in quiet dismay. He rubbed his chin, looked from Santana Montana to me. It was the most I'd spoken to my brother since Margaret's death. "But, little brother, the point is I'm working on that in my sessions. Not carrying around anger or guilt. That's what I'm trying to say here."

"I know, big bro. I know." I scraped at a piece of gum fossilized to the sidewalk with the tip of my shoe. "It's okay, Lance," I said, but I wanted him to tell me that. He watched me.

"Did you really see her, Lightly? Margaret, I mean. Do you *really*?"

"On occasion."

"How does she look?"

"She looks well," I lied. "Really healthy and as lovely as she was in life."

"Well," he said looking pained again. "At least she didn't do that with Margaret's name. At least Margie was spared that one little indignity." His chin wrinkled up suddenly and his lips worked to keep the sob in his throat from escaping. He covered his mouth. This is why he was estranged, of course. It was pure survival. He took out his wallet, counted a few bills, and held them out to me. They were crisp one hundred dollar bills.

"Shit, what's all that for?" I asked, not taking it.

"For your adventure," he said. "A lot of it's from Mom anyway, so there's some irony in that."

"I'm fine," I said.

"You're not fine," he said. "I lied earlier. I did know about Crispin. I told Mom it was a bad idea. I told her *she* needed more therapy *and* a different therapist." I looked at him. I looked at the money in his hand and took it without a word. It was a relief to know that Santana Montana would not have to float the entire bill for our trip.

"Jesus," he said looking through the glass doors at the people standing in lines at the counters. "I'm going to do it right with the girls, how it should be done. It's my shot to clean the slate. To leave everything from that old life behind and be the father a child deserves. It wouldn't be so bad if he hadn't been such a good father in every other way."

The engines of a big plane started up on the other side of the building. Everything to this point had seemed like the actions of a play, and I found myself hesitating under the weight of the decision. The deafening, vascular drumming of the engines filled my ears and for no reason at all a vision of coalfields in Newport News sprang to mind. All of the hoses and cannon sprays had been turned off and the big pyramids were simmering, simmering, simmering—beginning to smoke under the unyielding heat.

Lance climbed back into the car and started to pull away but caught the look on my face. He stopped, glanced at Santana Montana, and leaned out the window and added, "You know that if anything happens to you, Mom will never forgive me, right?"

"I know, Lance," I said. I knew this was going to be hard on him. It'd be harder on Mom, but I'd made my decision.

28

It was the summer I turned eight, that one we spent in Tenerife, that I began to see lights moving along the bedroom walls at night. I didn't tell anyone at first, not because I was worried or embarrassed, but because I enjoyed the lights and wanted to keep them for myself. They moved horizontally, two bright yellow dots, from left to right. They were my secret because they were a gift and because they glowed so gently and warmly, as love would glow if it glowed at all. Love doesn't glow, but letters do. I don't know why that's so, but it is.

Were those lights the souls of the dead? I didn't believe in ghosts. Was I going mad? Hell, I hardly knew what mad was but I'm sure that even then—as now—I knew I was strong and that madness was for the weak.

I shared a room with Lance and Margaret. Eventually, I told them of my secret. Lance had made fun of me but the idea scared and thrilled Margaret. She climbed in bed with me that very night to see if she could glimpse them, too, and we clung together like each was the other's emergency flotation device and we were far out at sea or some similar formulation—you get the idea.

And do you know what happened?

Sure as anything, the lights appeared and ghosted across the walls in pairs. I kept pointing them out, but that little monkey never did see them.

The next morning Lance betrayed me and told my secret to Mother and she got very worried. She was so worried that, after her morning writing time, she called a doctor or somebody. They told her I needed to see a retinal specialist for my retina was surely detaching. She was all set to take me, too, but the next morning I lied and told her the lights were gone. She asked me the next morning and the next, and I kept telling her they were gone time and time again. I had to lie to Margaret and Lance, too, for you can never trust anyone with your greatest treasures and that is something even an eight year old could tell you.

Anyway, I saw those lovely lights for the last time in early August, a few days before we left Tenerife. When I'd told Mother they were gone for good, she had said I was incredibly lucky. Now that they really were, though, I was devastated. I felt abandoned, like some gift had been stripped away, and I wished I'd known that last time they'd ghosted over the wall together that it really was the last time. Then I would have *really* watched them, *really* committed every detail of their bright, regal cantering to memory.

I guess what I learned was if you say something isn't true enough times, then, even if it is true, it'll stop being true.

I thought about my mother while we waited to board our flight to DC, about how it was thanks to her that I am haunted by the names of foreign places: Los Gigantes, Bocas Del Toro, Makiki, the coastal towns of Portugal, Greece, the Azores. Sometimes I can close my eyes and see Mother in one of her white bathing suits or in her gauzy beach cover with her hair tied back, always with the big round sunglasses on her face and that beautiful jawline of hers I'd inherited. I'd gotten my strength and incredible physical gifts from Pop, but all my beauty came from her, though she was never as comfortable with it as I am.

Anyway, when I close my eyes and see her all those years ago, she's always sitting on some seafront deck punching the keys on the electric typewriter—a blue Super Coronet 12—while the brown forearm of some foreign baby sitter keeps gently holding the three of us from her.

So what if I travel? It makes sense as I've always been on the move. Movement and change and cycles within cycles—planets spinning and orbiting within entire collections of galaxies themselves in motion above and below.

Hell, Mother had said in an interview somewhere that all her love stories came to her complete and that she only had to go write in a real background to her story, and so we traveled only to collect backgrounds and not so we could learn or be enriched or whatever the good reasons for traveling are. Damn, but she hated traveling, and I'm not surprised at all that now she can't even bring herself to step foot from the property lines of the farm. And maybe that's all Costa Rica was for me: a background into which my already finished story would be pressed, the geographical space where my vision would unpack itself from a small disruption of sky.

29

Our plane was a frail little thing, only two seats on either side of the aisle. Santana Montana and I sat near the back. I watched a man in a blue jumpsuit on the tarmac drag away the wheel blocks. We jolted a little as the plane started to move, and I thought of how when we used to sit down to dinner the air around Margaret's empty seat always seemed denser and warmer than elsewhere in the room.

During the first few weeks following her death, I'd sometimes say something to the thick, heated air, and I suppose I'd forget for a moment that she was dead. For a long time after I'd wake up wondering, hoping. Then my mind would untangle itself from the dragnets of sleep and the horror of it would settle on me anew.

We hurtled down the runway and I felt us lift.

"Don't be nervous," I told Santana Montana.

"Okay," he said. He was reading his guide to Costa Rica and didn't look up. There was a library tag on it.

A few minutes more and everything was so small beneath us. I thought how one true thing about losing someone you love is how their absence is a presence and, at the same time, their presence is an absence.

Through the window, I spied the bright bellies of clouds moving as if they'd somewhere to go, and I remembered that long gone November evening when Margaret had said, "Running cedar binds spirits to the forest floor" and then shyly turned away.

Sometimes loud music or voices in the Moreland dorm corridor would coax me from the depths of sleep, and I'd find myself thinking of Margaret. How she'd ask me to brush the sand from her legs at the Outer Banks, or insist, at the farm, that I hold her hand before she'd enter the green and violet trees along the field's pale sleeve.

There are things in life that reveal to us the loneliness and fragility of it all. Margaret was that thing for me.

We made our connection in DC without incident. Halfway through our flight to San Jose I got up to visit the restroom and passed by a lovely girl about my age sitting at a window seat. Beside her, an old man with richly tan skin was dead to the world; his black and silver head thrown back, mouth open—the whole deal—like he was pantomiming sleep. Anyway, the girl's lips were a striking shade of natural pink, and her hair was so brilliantly, lustrously black that it seemed to shimmer in the air around her. She was tan as hell and there was something gorgeous in the shape of her lean shoulders. There wasn't a speck of makeup on her but she was so beautiful that it hurt me to look at her, if you know what I mean.

Naturally on my way back from the restroom, I studied her as I came down the aisle. She was wearing a faded tee shirt, which, in white lettering, read, *Now's Not The Time To Catch On*. She glanced up as I passed and I got all nervous and fluttery and hustled on back to my seat.

Santana Montana studied his Costa Rica book, but my insides were like a stick of butter in a red-hot saucepan. I tried to wrestle it all out of my head but the thing about her that had really gotten its hooks in me was that when she'd glanced up I'd caught that her eyes were different colors. Whereas one was a bright, speckled brown, the other was a striking mixture of pale green and hazel. And her shirt! I laughed out loud like a fool. God, did I love that message. It meant if you didn't get it by now, then you should just forget it and be stupid. It meant being stupid is easier on folks and damn if it wasn't true.

"I'll be right back, Santana Montana," I said. I thought of something funny and leaned over and whispered, "And when I return, I'll be disguised as an elderly gentleman with sleep in my eyes. You'll know it's really me when I pretend not to know you at all."

Before he could respond, I stood and went back up toward the girl with mismatched eyes admiring as I did the mousey way her delicate ear peeked from all that midnight hair. Anyway, I tapped the old man beside her on the shoulder. He came reluctantly out of a dream with brown eyes only half there.

"Hello, sir," I said. "Hello. Listen, I sure to god hate to wake you from your slumber, but I'm wondering if you'd mind switching seats with me so that I can sit with my sister here." I nodded toward her and gave a friendly wink. She didn't smile at all but just watched me in a relaxed, easy way. The old man straightened himself up a bit. "What?" he asked. He cleared his throat. "What did you say?"

"My sister there," I said. "The truth is I've just seen a girl I'm so in love with that I think I'm going to die, and I'd like to get my sister's advice on how to proceed. My seat is just right back there and it's an aisle seat so there's the same leg room and you'd be sitting with a genius from Mexico whose grandfather was the bullfighter in some book by that Hemingway fellow. Did you know his mother used to dress him as a girl and call him Ernestine? Hemingway, I mean, not the genius from Mexico. You'll have to work to get him talking, but he'll regale you with fascinating tales of heroism, adversity, the foraging habits of flying squirrels." The old man just sort of stared at me a moment. It was a hard look, if you know what I mean.

"Listen, young man," he said, not unkindly but firm. "It would be very odd if this was your sister, since she happens to be my daughter."

"Oh," I said. Truth be told, I had considered it, but their appearances had made it seem unlikely. He was broad at the shoulder and his face—and nose for that matter—was wide and strong. I'd concluded he'd not be able to have a slender, graceful daughter because of the genetics of it all. "Well," I said, "I suppose that either makes you my father or me a well-intentioned scammer, of sorts."

"I'm not your father," he said carelessly. "So why don't you go back to your seat and spend the rest of the flight reliving this embarrassing moment in your head and feeling sheepish." I noted his accent, which suggested he was originally from Central or South America, but that he had lived in the States for some time.

"You are great, sir," I said. "I like how you think, and even though you are not my father, I wouldn't mind if you were on account of how funny and true what you just said to me is. But I won't feel sheepish if you don't mind, sir, on account of knowing that if I'd not tried to sit beside your daughter I would have regretted it for the rest of my life, which would've been longer and worse." Though he didn't exactly smile, some of the hardness left his face. He looked at his daughter. "Well, Indi?" he asked. "The young man says he'll regret it forever."

There was something quiet and reserved yet pleasant in the way she took me in. Her face was clean and smooth with skin the color of an avocado nut with hints of gold. The lips above the neat little point of her chin were not the color pink after all, but the color of misted raspberries. But her eyes held me most. Not just the comfortable intelligence in them, but how the hazel in her green eye formed exactly the shape of a star around her iris and how one point of the star seemed to continue on into the razor thin, delicate curve of a scar—a barely perceptible wound—that went from temple to eyebrow in a fine flourish of cursive.

"I don't know, Papá," she said to him. "What do you think?"

He laughed. "The test?"

"Certainly not," she said.

"My daughter's very smart," he said to me. "I always give little intelligence tests to boys that bother her."

"Papá," she said, as if reprimanding him. She placed her hand on his arm. "You don't have to answer," she said to me. "Papá is a physicist and loves belittling people."

"A physicist!" I exclaimed a bit louder than I intended. A stewardess cleared her throat and I had to step away to let her by. She slid past and I said, "I can't believe my luck. Finally, someone who can talk sense." I took a knee and leaned toward him in a way I hoped was more friendly than overly zealous and whispered, "Listen, I'd like to get your opinion on something because I'm a fan of the multiverse, you see? People used to believe the Earth was the center of the solar system, right? Then they believed the solar system was the center of the galaxy. Surely you know that until the 1920s people thought our galaxy was the only one and was surrounded by an infinite void. It's no different, is it, sir, than thinking we're the only universe? Isn't that just the next step in our wrong thinking? It's obvious to me that we're not, but I lack the tools to prove it."

The old physicist looked genuinely surprised.

"Ha! You pass," he said, creaking up to his feet.

"¡Espera! ¿Qué?" his daughter exclaimed in a mixture of humor and genuine disbelief.

"I'll sit with your friend for ten minutes," the physicist said. "Just ten minutes, Indi," he told her patting her head.

I pointed back toward my seat.

"Be careful," he said, so that she could hear him. "My daughter is lovely and much smarter than you. She will toy with your brain."

"You're unbelievable," she said to him. She was shaking her head but she'd said it in a gentle way that showed the playful connection between the two. She winked at her father and he winked back.

"Good lord," I said. "You two are a pair."

He went down the aisle slowly and I sat down beside Star Eye. "You know," I said, "it just occurred to me that your father didn't respond to my questions about the multiverse."

"You're not meant to realize he's told you nothing until he's gone."

"That's brilliant," I said.

"It gets old."

"I want to ask you about your eye," I said, "but I realize that might not be an appropriate question, seeing as how we are meeting for the first time right at this moment, so, instead, I'll ask you why you are bound for Costa Rica."

"I come back a lot, but the reasons are sort of complicated."

"I can handle complicated," I said.

"Can you?"

"Yes."

"What if I were to tell you I'm going there on a missions trip of sorts?" There was something distant, yet playful in her eyes when she said it, and I felt very distinctly that I was being toyed with exactly as her father had said.

I didn't care, though. I wanted to join her in the toying, if in fact, she was engaged in one, so I said, "I want to play a game because you make me feel jittery, and I've never felt that way around a girl before and it's thrilling and worrisome all at the same time. How the game works is, I'll tell you all about your past and how you grew up and maybe throw in a few of the bigger events in your life that shaped you and then you can tell me how close I was. If I'm right on the big stuff, though, I'd like to have your shirt—I mean, once you've changed, of course—because that is the coolest shirt I have ever seen."

"What is your name?" she asked. I noticed her voice was purple and velvety. There was nothing erotic in the feel of her voice, but it was pleasing, like the caress of a gentle breeze.

"My name is Lightly," I said.

"Ligeramente."

"What? I don't speak Spanish."

"That is one way to say your name—Ligeramente."

I said "Wow" like a love-struck moron because her name for me sounded more familiar than the English version. I started my game and told her then all about her life, what with the international household replete with a Costa Rican physicist for a father and a Canadian housekeeper and whatnot and how her exotic accent told me that.

"Damn, you loved that Canadian nanny," I said. "She used to be a flight attendant and was cheeky, sure, but she had always been there for you and you were crushed when she left your father on his own to run off and marry a man from a distant country. You sat on a swing beneath a purple sky with the hermit crabs foraging about and wondered how your father would ever run a household when he always had his head poking up through the clouds." She sat comfortably and listened exactly as a girl would sit on the couch with her legs curled under her, with jazz drifting down from the upstairs bedroom and rain coming down at an angle outside like billons of blue strings. There was a patient but pleasant look on her face that might have been called gently mocking though maybe not.

I didn't have any bead on her mother and I said as much. "Your mother is a non-entity of sorts. It's not like I know what the hell that means, but I sense it's true just the same." I told her about how she had run track—how the *toneness* of her long arms meant she was an athlete—and explained how she was going to Costa Rica to see friends and do her missionary work. I told her about the formation of the solar system from swirling dust and the accretion of it into planetary bodies and so on. I said, "I don't know how you could be a missionary what with your father being a physicist and all, but you are and even though I think it's silly to dwell upon such superstitious beliefs, I commend you for the bravery it takes to embrace such ridiculous religious ideas in the face of overwhelming logic suggesting otherwise."

"You like the stars, the planets, don't you?"

"Of course," I said, "you heard me blabbering to your father."

"To play devil's advocate," she said, "I might say that you love them, but that you don't seem to appreciate how perfectly set up for life things are. In a chaotic universe, do you really think it is pure luck that we are alive and not design? Did you know that if the Earth were even a fraction closer to the Sun that we'd burn up? A little further and we'd freeze? Aren't we too perfectly situated for it to be chance?"

"Jesus, I love you a little just for, among other things, thinking on that larger scale, but I don't think you should stop with such little things as the Earth and the Sun. If, for example, you increase the nuclear force in nature, then stars burn up too fast to allow for life. If you decrease it then the stars never catch fire at all. If you increase gravity then our universe gets crushed together, but if you decrease it then we spread out too fast and everything turns to ice. Some thoughtful people believe in god because things are too perfectly set up for life, but my theory is that if things weren't so perfectly set up there wouldn't be any life. We're both appreciative but they'd rather give thanks to a bearded man riding a cloud across the sky like that George Washington bastard rode that little boat across the Hudson, but not me. God loves us—right?—and he wanted to make us and you believe that. I'm more appreciative of life though because the universe didn't *want* to make us and yet we grew out of the natural processes of the universe and that to me is so stunning, so fragilely beautiful and fortunate for us that it makes me want to cry, but I won't."

"Really?" she asked. "And why won't you cry, Ligeramente?"

I had a little something in my throat from her calling me that, so I went on ahead and swallowed it down. Then I told her how I wouldn't cry on account of how I was too damn tough and manly and all that to cry.

"The captain of the football team," I explained, "doesn't cry unless it's when the star running back, who also happens to be his best friend and has a rough family history, severely breaks his leg in a freak accident right before the state title game that might have secured a scholarship for him. The captain sheds like one solitary tear and all and maybe he puts his hand on his good buddy's shoulder and says, 'We're gonna win this one for you, Emmit' or something equally cheesy and then goes out and quarterbacks his team to victory and everyone's cheering and carrying him off the field after he's tossed the game winner, you see, but he tells them to put him down and runs instead into the stands to find his handicapped buddy who's in a wheelchair at this point and they hug and cry.

"Then music comes from nowhere and they both look around uneasily because the band's not playing and they're wondering where the music is coming from. To their dismay, they see credits start to roll—written across the gray sky, the green field, the bleachers with peeling blue paint, their own skin—the names of strangers, of set designers, stunt coordinators, of fashion consultants named Sebastian so and so, with the casting done by the Dana Lane Agency and on and on with them just standing there bewildered, clutching each other in fright, but neither of them having sense enough to search the credits for a good baby name, which is too bad, because it's always good to think ahead.

"Anyway, that's the only time I cry, you see—when the dramatic moment demands that I do, rather than, for example, when the presence of an actual emotion compels me to. But, regardless, I think you'd agree that if we were talking right now at Five Points in South Carolina or a bus stop in San Jose instead of on a plane it'd be appropriate for me to say something like, 'It's too damn hot to cry or to think about such silly things' and to ask you something

like, 'What do you say we hoof it on down the road to the ice cream shop and
see if Beckwith—or some similarly named individual—will give us some ice
creams if we agree to sweep out the restaurant floor and wash a few dishes.'"

Her laugh sent electricity through my veins but I didn't die from her
smile. It was a sweet, blue-green laugh that made me feel like I was walking
in fields of clover along the water's edge.

"But if you asked me that," she said, "it would be a way of asking me on
a date without actually having to ask me."

"My god," I said breathlessly. "You nailed me. What are you, some sort of
genius?"

"I'm a *tica*," she said.

"Isn't that a patio torch?"

"No."

"Say something mind-blowing."

"How do you know for sure that you're not at a costume party right now."

"Good lord," I said, looking around. I didn't know these people. They all
seemed so ridiculous, strange, improbable. And I didn't know her. Was she
saying she wasn't who I thought she was? Was I not who I thought I was?
Maybe I was in costume and as soon as I could unravel the costume I'd recognize my true self. "How do you say 'Star Eyes' in Spanish?"

"My name is Indigo."

"But how do you say it?"

"*Ojos estrellados*," she said.

"That's too complicated," I said. "My focus is scattered about like chaff in
the wind, shattered like a billion shards of glass through which one moon is
reflected a billion times over. I'll never remember all that."

I could have spent a week sitting there beside the pretty girl with the
magic eyes, but it was not to be. I felt her father's hand on my shoulder soon
after.

"Time's up," he said.

I stood aside and her father sat down without a word and only then did it
occur to me that maybe she'd got me to talking so that she didn't have to. I
hadn't really learned a thing about her but had blabbed on like a moron because she was so gorgeous and calm it had made me nervous.

I knew I was unlikely to see her again, so I asked if I could have her address so that I might send her a postcard. She'd shrugged those lovely shoulders—shoulders that flower petals should rest on, that could stick something

through the heart of a man from across a room—and took a pen from her father's shirt pocket. I didn't have any paper so I held out my hand and she wrote down her address on my palm while her touch sent volts of electricity up and down my arm that only a stroke victim could identify with.

"Thank you, sir," I said. "I hope to ask you next time about the Big Bang just being stuff coming into a new black hole which is our universe and the beauty of there being black holes inside the black hole we're inside of and all that." To Indigo I said, "Good luck on your travels. I'm so glad to have met you, to have been able to talk to someone who could so expertly allow me to learn nothing about them in such a pleasant way." I wanted to say something like, *I shan't forget you,* but I didn't want her to tell me how no one said *shan't* anymore.

She brushed a dark strand of hair from her face and gave a bright smile.

"Goodbye, Ligeramente," she said kindly. "Perhaps if nuclear forces hold even and gravity remains in balance, we'll see one another again."

"I'd like that," I said like a breathless buffoon. "I'd like it very, very much."

When I get to where I'm going, there will be no need to send the girl with mismatched eyes a postcard.

30

Our descent into San Jose took about an hour, but soon we were on the ground and then we were all standing there to deplane. People were jostling each other, and tourists were noisy at their overhead compartments and whatnot. The hurried, stressed, self-important way people always went about deplaning filled me with great despair for humanity.

I wasn't thinking on that, though, because I found myself straining to see Indigo and her father. I watched them gather their things, not in the hurried way of the other passengers, but slowly, calmly, giving the ignorant folks who bumped them a sympathetic smile. Why was she so peaceful? I had seen it in her eyes, too. She was quiet and still, so much different from my wild bumblings. Had I been toyed with? God, I hoped so. I smiled with joy when she stood up because of the way she unfolded her lean body from her seat and because I saw how she was taller than the passengers around her.

I kept waiting for her to glance at me so that I could wave, but also because I knew that if she did, it meant she was interested in me, but she didn't. They left quickly and when we exited the ramp into the body of the airport, they were nowhere to be seen.

We made our way through the airport and there was a sparkling of sadness in my lungs as I breathed deeply and said, "Costa Rica" three times because I knew it was not so much a country as it was a stepping stone bridge that had sprung, millions and millions of years ago, from volcanic activity on the ocean's floor. At least that's what Santana Montana had told me on the plane.

"Call it Chepe—its secret name," Santana Montana said tiredly.

"Okay, but what of that?" I said to Santana Montana as we went through customs. "Did you know that the movement of the earth's plates has formed and destroyed entire oceans, assembled and split apart supercontinents?"

Santana Montana said he did know it so I told him, "Fair enough. Then you know some continents have wandered such vast distances that they've changed latitude, climate. My god," I'd said looking beyond him and out the window. "How do we live on this ever changing ball of collapsed dust with its cycles within cycles within cycles?"

"I do not know," he said absently. "I do not know how to live anymore." I squinted at him suspiciously. With his ridiculous knowledge about trees, insects, the social behavior of hammerhead sharks, I knew that if anyone alive had a theory about such a thing it would be this plump, wondrous genius with his thick glasses, sprouting mustache, and kind, olive eyes.

The outside of the airport was a humid concrete confusion of tourists, locals, and taxi lights. I waved off a dozen cabbies before I found one that looked trustworthy. He was thin and frail through the shoulders with the face of a fifty-year-old man and a plaid shirt tucked into his jeans. His legs were bowed as if he'd been riding horses his whole life.

"This one," I said to Santana Montana. "Yes, yes," I shouted at the cabber. "You're our man."

He said his name was Nico, but maybe I misheard him. It was getting dark as we hefted the Dextra Classic to his roof under a pale, moonless sky. I opened the door and nudged Santana Montana in.

"He says, 'Where to?'" Santana Montana translated. His words were slow, as if it took great effort to utter them.

"What's a *tica*?"

"A Costa Rican girl," he said. "Boys call themselves *ticos*. Where to? His meter is running."

"Who cares?" I said fondly. "A nice part of the city, for tomorrow we're off to the coast."

On the way to the hotel, Santana Montana had a little cry and then fell asleep against the window, and that is when I knew for a fact he was depressed. I was worried—not about Santana Montana directly but that perhaps his pain was deeper than I'd suspected and the fixing would require much more of my time, energy, and focus than I'd allowed for. With Crampton, Rampage, and Biggs soon to join us, that was a problem.

"He's tired, Nico," I explained to the cabber, who then—without any prompting or discernable reason—asked me a series of bizarre questions in Spanish, the import of which I could hardly grasp. I was able to discern his first question had to do with whether I liked the color green or the color white.

"Hell," I said. "I don't know. White, I suppose. *Blanco*, you called it? Hell, *blanco* then."

Then it seemed he was asking me about girls. I missed nearly everything he was saying, and my usual prowess of immediately discerning what people meant was weakened due to all the traveling and my current lack of interest in the man. I kept saying "Sí" repeatedly, for I did not yet know how some cab drivers in Chepe held the keys to the gates of Hades.

Finally I said, "Hell, yes, I like girls. Who doesn't?" But the cabber wanted to know if I liked girls that were young or girls that were old, though I could have been wrong. Hell, I liked the elderly fine, but I preferred the company of women my age, so I said, "Very much the young, goddamn it," for I was growing angry and anxious. "Look," I added. "You should know that I consider my inability to speak Spanish a great shortcoming on my part, but I don't want to talk with you anymore because my friend is sleeping and because we can't communicate well and, to be honest, when things don't make sense to me I get this claustrophobic feeling. Now, don't get upset or anything, my friend, I think you're still our man, but let's be quiet the rest of the way if you don't mind. No more talk. You and I. Friends. No talk."

He smiled sadly and nodded. I looked out the window. The lights from cars and houses were moving toward and by us and it seemed as if our car were stationary, the whole landscape a blanket being dragged beneath us.

We took the long sloping rise at a healthy pace and, as we rose, I beheld the hidden lines of Chepe—a vast city sparkling like lights off water in the flat gut of the land, coursing away in bright splashes down valley stretches that, here and there, sprinkled up on the sides of the big ridges which rose into the night. The right eyes could see how all those randomly twinkling lights were actually twinkling in a vast and complicated sequence. It was too immense and mysterious to decode and my head wasn't right for it yet, but it was another glimpse, another promise of the vision, which, even now was approaching that beach out there somewhere in the savage Costa Rican night. I smiled out at the dark's mangy snout enormously glad to see it had not lost its fangs in this country.

The cabber took us to a little hotel in Santa Ana, which was a suburb of Chepe. There was a fancy, dark wooden fence around the hotel that must've been twelve feet tall and you had to stop at a huge gate and press a button before they'd let you in.

Anyway, we pulled up in front of the lobby which had a wall of glass that was on fire with lights, and I woke Santana Montana by shaking him and singing gently over and over, "Santana Montana is in Santa Ana," until he groaned and moved heavily out of the cab. The cabber rolled down his window. He gave us his business card, and I saw his name was not Nico at all.

He said something to Santana Montana. Then he drove off and we were standing alone in the bright light lean of the Hotel Luisiana with Santana Montana looking confused.

"What did he say?" I asked.

"He will return with the things you asked for."

"Jesus," I said. "What did I ask for?"

"Listen," Santana Montana said sadly.

"What? I hear nothing."

"Over there. In those trees." He pointed. "A *yiguirro*—the official bird of Costa Rica."

"Where? I see nothing."

He sighed heavily. "It is said that the *yiquirro's* call coaxes in the winter rains."

I gave Santana Montana a little shove just then—perhaps harder then I'd intended—for he was on the verge of depression and I didn't want him tumbling in. He stumbled forward, but there was something so sad, so defeated in the slope of his shoulders that he reminded me of those suicidal bridge leapers you read about. Only he seemed like he'd lack the strength to leap to his death and would instead just sort of go over tiredly—like, say, from the Golden Gate Bridge, for example, as if falling asleep on a couch and with just one weary sigh.

The Hotel Luisiana was a gorgeous little place. We entered the reception area under black iron chandeliers and beheld white walls, a floor of brown, uniquely cut stones, and original, colorful artwork by various talented artists. Some Bob Dylan song was playing but damn if I knew which one on account of how I hated music and all. Hell, it might not have been Bob Dylan at all come to think of it.

The owner, a blonde Italian woman in her late thirties named Mrs. Elena checked us in. I noted how she pronounced the area as San-Tana when she welcomed us and I decided to call it the same. She wore a white blouse with short sleeves and tight jeans to accent her firm and shapely posterior and was by far the most attractive hotelier I'd ever met. She was my height, so six feet tall, and thick without an ounce of fat. There was a muscular physicality to her even though she was unmistakably feminine, and I believed her husband must've thought himself in heaven on the nights he could convince her to wrestle naked with him in a shallow pool of oil. God, but the prospect would have filled me more with fear than lust.

Elena said that all she had available was the *Sweetheart's Jacuzzi Room* with one king bed, so Santana Montana gave her his card and she gave us our room key.

"You are attractive," I told her, "but what's really impressive is the tasteful, artful décor of this place, what with the white leather couches, stacks of ancient art books, and ceiling to floor curtains, etcetera. I also love those high-stabbing stalks in the tall glass vases you've stuck in each corner. There's a library in Virginia that could use your touch. Sometimes I just know things, Mrs. Elena," I told her, "and I know you decorated this place for it has the same feel as you do."

"I did," she said.

"I know," I told her. "That's what I said."

31

We'd been in the room an hour or so when Elena called from reception."Your man from taxi," she said. "He has returned."

"What does he want, Mrs. Elena?" I asked.

"He is saying he has things for you."

"Okay, Mrs. Elena," I said. "Send him up and the mystery will be solved."

But the mystery was to thicken before it was solved, for our cabber came in with his daughter and half a sandwich bag of cocaine. I wasn't one to be easily offended, but his daughter's tight "Hello Kitty" halter top and skimpy shorts made me immediately uncomfortable.

My brother Lance has always claimed that I am dangerously naïve and maybe he was right to a certain extent. However, any naïveté that I might have had about the situation evaporated immediately, for I sensed instantly what was going on.

"What gives, my friend?" I demanded of the cabber, so angrily it surprised me. "I mean, what in god's name is the meaning of this?" He spoke rapidly and nervously to Santana Montana who could not hide the horror on his face. The whole thing was making me crazy as if my head might explode.

"What! What does he say, Santana Montana?" I demanded. I took off my shoe and threw it at the wall. "Jesus, we've not even unpacked our bags!"

Hesitantly, for it seemed he hardly believed it, Santana Montana explained that I had ordered cocaine and an underage prostitute in the few minutes he'd been asleep in the cab.

"Santana Montana," I said, taking a step away. "I never. My word to god, I never did. You know me, my friend." He said he did and speaking together in English we figured out where I'd gone wrong. The whole time the cabber was getting extremely agitated, and he looked like there was some violence on his face or fear for his own life or suspicions of us.

"And this girl," I was saying to Santana Montana. "She can't be a day over fifteen at most. You don't really mean-" but I let the rest of the sentence dangle there. Santana Montana knew what I meant and said it was indeed so. The cabber could tell, of course, that things were horribly wrong for him and he started demanding something of Santana Montana.

"Where's he going, Santana Montana?" I asked, for he had the dear little girl by the arm, though in a bizarrely tender way, and I was suddenly fearful of his departure but unsure why. Certainly my system had suffered a great shock and the way the little girl's exposed thighs were as thin as her hairless calves made me think of sleepovers and pool parties, balloons and chestnut ponies with shaggy blonde manes, but not of the awful things evil men might do to her.

Santana Montana was explaining our position, no doubt, and he was more heated than I'd ever seen him before. His cheeks were red and mottled like the poison frogs of Bastimentos Island. The cabber made for the door suddenly.

"No, no, wait, Santana Montana. Wait!" I blurted out. "He'll just take her off to some awful pedophile. No, no, tell him we'll pay." I held up the handful of hundreds Lance had given me and waved them crazily in the air, for I was desperate. "Tell him we'd like her to stay. Jesus, Santana Montana, please. Please don't look at me like that. We've got to do something."

32

We spent a few hours with the girl whose name, we learned, was Rosa. At first the cabber, who I had so horribly misjudged, was reluctant to let her stay. In fact, he outright refused and was out the door until I had started waving that money.

The financial aspect proved too much for him and thankfully he decided to risk it and left Rosa there—though at a significantly higher price than if we'd only wanted to have sex with her. I figured this was to cover some of what he thought he'd make on the cocaine, which, obviously, we were *not* buying.

It was enough—the transaction and the girl—to send you scurrying for the nearest peak to leap from, and, to be sure, I already felt in a free fall of sorts. It was the worst possible beginning to our time in Costa Rica and had immediately summoned from the crypt of memory Hawai'i and the Na'Pali coast because my heart had first been broken there and because I had pursued a golden beach but found in its place something shocking and terrible.

I went over and sat down on the bed beside Rosa, but the plush comforter felt decadent, obscene. So I popped up suddenly and went over to sit at the little desk beside the door. We bought dinner for Rosa, which was sent up from the hotel's kitchen.

The whole time my head was swimming and I couldn't get my feet beneath me. I figured if I could understand about her, I could move beyond my awful sense of unease. Santana Montana translated as I asked her questions about her life.

She was very candid and unashamed about her circumstances. She said various things had happened in Nicaragua so that she was forced to live with her uncle and her uncle's wife in San Jose, where they had come just the year before. The uncle had apparently started abusing her right off, though she used the term "training" which made me want to cry. She said it was okay, though, because he didn't do it to pleasure himself but to get her prepared to work. She said that when he was teaching her he'd never had an orgasm and he'd given her a needle and told her she could jab him with it in the arm if he hurt her. He apologized a lot, she said, and at least twice he cried.

"He was gentle," she said through Santana Montana. "He showed me what to do and how to act during. Since I have been working he has not touched me, so I know his heart was in the right place. He said that hopefully if I can make good money then my little sister won't have to do the same. I don't mind it so much, but I don't think it would be good for my little sister. She is so sensitive."

As she talked something curious happened. All of my guts were removed from my stomach by a pair of disembodied hands and placed in a freezer bag. Then the bag went into the icebox. After a long while, the hands removed it and allowed it to thaw. Finally, the hands shook the bag firmly and poured the soggy contents back into my stomach. The problem was that the items had suffered a terrible shock and that nothing had been put back in the right place.

"Jesus," I said. "If I wasn't broken—if I was normal in my head—I would just sob right now, but I'm not, so my anguish is great what with there being no way to release it from me. I want to kill someone, Santana Montana, to bite their throat, slam my knee into their cranium." I spread my fingers against the warm span of my pectorals, pressed them gently there. "Santana Montana, tell her I feel each letter of the words she spoke right here. They have gone in me and will not leave. Tell her it feels terrible. That it's killing me." He told her, and it must have been pretty goddamn funny to her because she studied me for a moment and then giggled at my silliness. I asked if she'd ever stuck her uncle with that needle and she said that she had many times.

It occurred to me then that it might be better to allow her some time not to dwell on her misfortunes, so we all three lay on our bellies on the bed and shared the microwavable popcorn we'd found in the mini fridge. We watched two episodes of her favorite Spanish soap opera.

"The thing I can't figure out," I said to Rosa, "is why all these actors look so passionate and emotional the whole show through. I mean, it would be exhausting to always be on an emotional high." Santana Montana seemed to know the soap for he and Rosa exchanged comments occasionally and gestured at the television when certain characters appeared. It seemed to me that there was something husky in my friend's voice that I'd not heard before, something tender and breakable.

It all ended too soon, though, and our time was up for her uncle returned. I was so disoriented that I just watched as she stood up and ran her brown hand over the bristles of hair on Santana Montana's head. She touched my shoulder lightly, then gave my bewildered face a single soft stroke before disappearing through the doorway with her shifty-eyed uncle.

The door shut quietly, and I buried my face in the muscles of my forearms and breathed heavily. Santana Montana did not say a word, and I wondered if he was as distraught as I.

"Oh hell," I said, not bothering to lift my head. "The bones in her hand have yet to stop growing." I felt sick for I kept imagining thick hair on pasty, scaly forearms, pudgy fingers with gold rings tightening around Rosa's slender throat, squeezing out her giggles and dumping them—still dewy-eyed and wriggling—into cardboard boxes addressed to grandfathers in distant, snow-covered cities. I looked to Santana Montana for commiseration, but he was staring dejectedly at a spot in the air.

"*Esto lo confirma*," he said so quietly I could scarcely hear. "*Todo es tuna mierda. Todo.*"

"*Mierda?* What's '*mierda*' mean?" I asked.

"Shit," he said.

I watched him. There was an unpleasant odor uncoiling in the air.

As soon as I could manage to stand, which was a long time coming, I went over and filled up the tiled Jacuzzi for Santana Montana. I got the water as hot as I believed he could stand it, which was much cooler than I'd have it, but I knew Santana Montana was the sensitive sort. I came out and he was still sitting at the foot of the bed, which had a striking painting of a blue woman sunk to the shoulders in blue water hanging above it. It made me miss Rampage, the painting I mean, for he was not only a violent hitter on the field but an excellent artist at the easel. Rampage preferred acrylics, though, and the blue woman looked to be done in chalky pastels, but the truth was that I knew less about painting than I did about music, and, anyway, how could I care about such things when I was on the verge of throwing up.

I squatted down and took off Santana Montana's shoes for him. They must have been from Mexico for I'd never heard of the brand. I liked them, though, because they had one Velcro strap instead of laces. I stood up, ignoring the rank stench that issued forth from them and tossed them over my shoulder.

"When I come back," I told him, "I want you to be in that tub for I must go out and sniff the rumpus of Chepe, if you know what I mean. I can tell there's something wrong with you, my dear friend, something that goes beyond even the horror this evening has already produced. I want to give you space to relax and figure it out on your own, because talking about past sadnesses is a poor use of time. Even so, if you're the type that needs to talk it out then, I guess, we can upon my return. Thus is the degree of my love for you. Now stand up, Santana Montana, and raise your arms."

Slowly he stood and raised his short, fat arms and I was shocked to see that they were so stubby that his wrists only barely cleared the top of his head —though this had more to do with him not being able to lift his arms very high than it did their actual length. The water rushed and thrummed into the Jacuzzi as I pulled and tugged at the sweater and was greeted, as it came free, with the heavy odor of Santana Montana, which was that of warm skin lotion, stale potato chips, and the nervous stink of travel.

"Jesus, Santana Montana, but you can handle the rest, can't you?" I asked and wondered if he could.

I put the key in my pocket and stepped out with Santana Montana just standing there shirtless and despondent in the center of the room, his soft, hairless nipples the color of a rabbit's nose and the fleshy bag of his golden stomach sagging softly over the belt of his khaki trousers. I tied his sweater around my waist and made for the hotel gate, thinking of how his belly was round as the globe in my mother's office at the beach house, which had always seemed so swollen with the names of foreign countries, distant cities.

33

Evening in San-Tana, Costa Rica.

I couldn't get enough of the air, and I walked away from the Hotel Luisiana and back toward the little town that bastard cabber had brought us through. I wanted to clear my mind of everything, so I focused with great intensity on the things before me. On the street I beheld women in untucked, collared shirts with thick plastic name tags pinned to them hustling from their places of employment, trying to arrive home before evening turned to late night, their heels click, click, clicking against badly cracked pavement.

Santana Montana had read that San Jose could be a dangerous place and told me as much on the plane. I believed him, for sure, because every single house had a wall or fence and most had coils of razor wire along the tops, too. I passed by closed up shops and through the windows I spied mostly ceramics, but in one I saw a carved wooden mask like the Kanaloa masks I'd seen in Waikiki. In another I glimpsed black iron gates and big black iron chandeliers like the ones in the Hotel Luisiana.

I went into several bars not to try to forget about Rosa at all, but rather to familiarize myself with the main local beers and discovered there were essentially two: Imperial and Pilsen. I tried one in each bar. Imperial came in a yellow and red can with a black dragon on it with his wings spread wide. The Pilsen can was white with a red rectangle in which Pilsen was written in white lettering. I lingered in the shadowy corners of these places. They stank of sawdust, wood oil and burnt leaves. The humidity of the city rubbed its red palms against me to coax out moisture from my secret places.

It was by pure accident that I came upon the center of San-Tana, which was a good-sized stone church. It sat on a square patch of grass and among some lovely plantings and big trees behind the waist-high stone and iron fence surrounding it. There was a road on each of the four sides, and you could see how the entire town had sprung up years and years ago before Chepe had snaked out like a boa of concrete and wires and swallowed it whole. I'd stepped into a little store to buy a sixer of Imperial and a pair of orange-handled scissors and the church was just right there before me as I stepped out. It was lit up with its high arching doors swung open.

So, I walked over and went inside the church to get a feel for the spirituality of the place. It sure the hell was a pretty church. The thing that bothered me, though, was the two life-sized Jesuses I discovered inside. No one was there save for me and the Jesus behind the pulpit and the Jesus against the side entrance, so I took out a beer and opened it as quietly as I could out of respect for the holy place and all.

I sat down on a pew and used my newly acquired scissors to snip away the sleeves from Santana Montana's sweater. I didn't want him overheating in this humidity.

The trick was to cut a ways down from the seam so that the damn thing wouldn't start unraveling on him. I held them up and saw the snail trail of snot down the length of one sleeve from where my friend had wiped his nose in the computer lab. I folded the sleeves neatly and placed them on the pew. I stood up and used the scissors to cut my jeans just above the knee. I pulled the legs off over my flip-flops. I put the fabric on the pew and put the sweater over my shoulder.

I took a sip and eyeballed Pulpit Jesus, but he was up too high to see very well, so I went over to study Side Entrance Jesus.

Hell, but they'd put that poor bastard behind glass. Side Entrance Jesus' mouth hung open with exhaustion, and he was bleeding from the head, because of the thorns and all. His robes were shiny red and white. He looked so sad, brilliant, tired and compassionate at the same time. I took a sip of beer and felt nothing happening inside my chest or head at all.

"Don't look at me like that, Jesus," I told him. "I know it's hard and I'm sorry as hell they've trapped you in there, but what can I do about it, anyway, being just one right-thinking man on a planet full of idiots? Hell, but I was born two hundred and thirty-seven years too early, my friend."

I gave the Imperial another little shake and sent the contents swirling. A stray dog appeared in the doorway. A young, little brown and black mangy thing. It occurred to me that it might be beautiful if it'd not suffered so horribly from its life on the streets. I whistled to her but she just sniffed the air tentatively and gave me the stink eye before slinking off.

"Jesus," I said, "I should be out among the stars. I should've come along after everyone realized we are just Earth, goddamn it, and that all these factions—all this sectarianism, as they call it—is nothing but the product of frail minds. No, no, I'm not blaming you. You're all right with me, and I suppose we need to nearly wipe ourselves out before we get it. Either way it's rotten luck to live during these trying times, Lord, where we're capable enough to destroy humanity but too dumb to see humanity is all we are. Do me a favor, Jesus. If Mother or Emmy or Padre Johnson or some world leader with a stockpile of weapons speak to you tonight, please don't tell them you're not real, 'cause I don't think they could handle it at all."

I got up and went to the door and called out for that poor, little brown dog who had no doubt suffered mightily. I called for her loudly but with sweetness and resolved to name her *Ms. Bingly* if she would only come. She didn't come, though, for she had returned to the night, to the brutal days which awaited her.

"I've lost my chance," I said. "I might have saved her."

On my way back to the hotel I noted how the clouds, underlit by the light of Chepe, had pulled themselves up over the mountains now and were bringing the rain with them. For no particular reason at all I thought of an article I'd read in one of my physics journals about this NIF facility with a hundred and ninety-two lasers that was bigger than several football fields put together. The lasers all concentrated on this point to create nuclear fusion or whatnot and those mad scientists were using it to simulate the interiors of giant planets, stars, and supernovae—it was things like that got me to feeling that we were all still cavemen basically.

I don't know how long I'd been walking in it, but I realized then that it was drizzling. I looked up into the Pepto sky to see it coming down and lost my footing crossing a bridge under a big Budget Rent-a-Car billboard and nearly went over into a deep ravine.

I balled up my fist to keep her address dry, and braced myself for walking the whole way in the rain, but then a car horn tooted behind me.

I heard someone whistle.

All Things Await

34

A few hours later a group of girls dropped me off at the hotel's gate. Elena was behind the glass desk when I came stumbling in and a big storm was doing a number on Santa Ana. The painting behind her was of a nude woman lying full-length on her side.

"Some storm, Mrs. Elena," I said. "When do you sleep?" I looked at her arms for the slightest indication of baby oil but found none.

"Your friend and you don't come back," she was saying. "After you leave."

I pointed up to the iron chandelier above us.

"You bought that at a place in town, Mrs. Elena," I said. "I walked right by it."

"I know that little girl was not really only little girl," she said. "I should call police."

"You've got it all wrong, Mrs. Elena," I said.

"Then your friend ask where he can get gun. Then he go and then he come back. If he have gun up there, I am mad."

"Please calm down, Mrs. Elena," I urged. "Santana Montana does not have a gun. The girl was a misunderstanding." I could see Mrs. Elena was not the forgiving type. She crossed those well-defined arms at me. "Alright," I said. "You win." I would have tried to make my case, but I knew I was drunk, slightly stoned, ridiculous in my friend's de-sleeved sweater, and very tired, so I moped on out dejectedly.

If I'd had a tail instead of the coccyx, which is the remnant of a tail, it would have been tucked between my legs.

I wished Indigo had a tail—it would be a clean, shining, bristly one. I wondered if it would wag if she saw me again.

I knew that it would.

When I came back to the room, Santana Montana was no longer in the Sweetheart's Jacuzzi but face down asleep on the bed, and why not, after all, as it was nearly two in the morning. I really had meant to come straight back from the church and leave enough time for him to share whatever burden he was suffering under. What had delayed me was not my desire to avoid such an unpleasant subject as Santana Montana's past, but, instead, a group of Costa Rican girls crammed into a green Yaris. Twenty yards past my near fall at the Budget sign, they'd beeped at me and whistled playfully out the window as they'd passed and then stopped altogether on the road and waited for me to catch up.

I'd leaned in their window, a little wet in the light rain, and smiled and they were ogling me like no tomorrow on account of my blue eyes and good looks, of course, and who could blame them for their gentle, shy flirtations?

Anyway, I'd made a night of it with them, riding around here and there without understanding a word. They passed my face around to admire my eyes, which was a little awkward, but also touching for their fingers were made of cotton and collectively they smelled of gardenias and of lemon balm right before you crush it into your palm.

We had a grand old time while the rain beat hell on the roof of the Yaris with all of us happy and laughing and confused together and not at all heartbroken or fearful. Much happened, much that could be told, such as our unauthorized visit to a ceramics shop and the hour we spent smoking pot and kicking balls at a San-Tana indoor soccer field, which was cleverly disguised as a fruit processing plant, for it was an adventure in miniature, but what of it? It didn't involve Santana Montana and so it was not part of the story proper, as it were.

Anyway, at the end we were all tired and ready for oblivion, as everyone is in the end. I had the name of the hotel and that proved enough for them to get me back. And, indeed, I was back, standing over Santana Montana while the gods moved their furniture around in their cloud house above the city, and Santana Montana was sleeping face down, as I'd said, and very much as if he'd tried to kill himself. I placed my hand gently on his fat, golden, fleshy back just to make sure he was breathing and was glad and a little surprised to find that he was. I gently turned his head to the side so he could get air and he didn't stir at all, but began breathing very rapidly. I feared he was hyperventilating and so I shook him a little until his eyes opened.

"Are you well?" I asked.

"No," he said. He was looking up at me. He said he suffered from something called *sleep paralysis* and said he used to breathe rapidly to signal his mother to shake him vigorously for people with sleep paralysis, I learned, really were paralyzed except for their breathing. I asked him if he'd been awake when I came in the room.

"Yes," he whispered.

I asked him if he could not move and if the rapid breathing I'd heard when I'd unplugged his beloved face from the pillow was a signal of sorts that he needed a violent shaking.

"Yes." He explained how once he was shaken roughly he could immediately regain control of his visceral frame.

"Were you sending such a signal when you were asleep in the back of Anne Marie's car?"

"Yes."

"And no one helped you."

"No."

"What can I do to help ease your suffering?" I asked

"Do not shake me," he said. Then he rolled on his side and went quiet.

I sat there for a long time brooding over him, over how to save him, but after a while, the rain knocked the power out, and so I kicked off my shoes and lay on my back in the pitch black. Santana Montana's breathing was normal now. I stuck a pillow under my feet for they were terribly swollen, and started counting the clicks in his breathing. It is a strange fact of my existence that whenever my feet are swollen and I'm sitting down, and half drunk, and feeling exhausted, many regrets come uninvited into my thoughts. And so they did now, for I regretted suddenly not coming back to speak with Santana Montana, as I'd said I would. And I regretted, for example, not taking a bath and how I'd left Jesus in that glass prison, and how I never had asked Pop why he was always creeping in the hallway at night because now I never could. And I fiercely regretted Indigo—how I'd blabbed on and learned nothing about her.

The thing I did not regret was Rosa, for you can't regret something you cannot change.

All Things Await

35

In the dream, Margaret and I had stripped to our underwear, left our clothes in a little pile, and gone down a bank lined with peeling river birches, their citrine catkins stirring in the breeze, to a little shaded pool and sank in.

Her pale shoulders rose from the dark water like the crowning of iridescent moons. Dragonflies sped past. Water striders drew circles on the surface and I was telling her about how all the gold in the world came from stars exploding.

"I'm just a kid, you know?" she said.

"Well, hell," I said, "we all are. But it's nice to have someone to share this brain with."

"Do you sense them, too?" she said.

"What?"

"Our other selves. All of them. Just on the other side of what's visible."

"Maybe. Your brain has always been more powerful than mine."

"Do you ever think of going?" she said.

"I wouldn't know how."

"I do," she said shyly. "Each drop of rain is a universe unto itself, a little bubble, and versions of us are spread throughout. You've jumped from them before."

"Hey," I said, looking around inside the dream. "Isn't this the place you found that trash bag?"

She just shrugged and tilted her head back as if to offer her lovely face to the day.

After a while, she said, "Keep your eyes wide, look up into the rain, and you will find me in the drops."

"Really? What else?" But there was nothing else. Just the sound of water. The scent of the creek. The sun a locomotive of light on its arcing track in the sky blah blah blah. And butterflies. Little blue ones winging at her shoulders, landing and lifting and landing again.

36

I awoke to a stab of tropical sunlight, the drumbeat of a hangover, and Santana Montana sitting in a chair beside the window holding a small silver pistol to his head.

"Is it raining?" I asked him, but I was telling myself to be calm. The scent of the farm creek was still in my nose, but the sight of the gun was a shock. I wanted to avoid mentioning it right off because, I suppose, I was afraid if I said the word gun, it might go off.

"No," he said, not lowering the gun.

"Do you know where Santa Teresa is? It's on our peninsula. I bet the only way to get there is by plane." *Get him talking*, I thought.

"No. There is a ferry that can convey you."

"Damn it," I said, sitting up. "You are a genius for how you just used the word *convey* there. No one else I know would have used that word there. You are unique, special, the only one of your kind." I pressed my feet into the carpet, wiggled my toes. "We are closer to the vision than ever before. Where is your guidebook? I need to read up on Santa Teresa."

"By the dresser." The gun flashed in the sun as he gestured with it toward the dresser, and I watched him. He didn't return the gun to his temple, but placed it in his lap.

"Santana Montana," I said as casually as I could. "I'm wondering if you intend to shoot yourself." He waited a little before answering, and I understood he was giving the question some thought.

"I do not know," he said finally. "I am vacillating."

"Out with it all, Santana Montana," I said, laying my head back into the pillows and bracing myself for that awful tightness I felt whenever someone reminisced over things from their past that had impacted them greatly. "I wanted to do you the courtesy of not prying, but it is now unavoidable, so spill it."

He said softly that he was miserable.

"Why are you miserable?" I asked. "Santana Montana, is it because you are in love with me?"

He said he wasn't, but that his mother had died.

"Damn. I expected it was one or the other. Oh, my poor friend, Santana Montana," I said for I was thinking now not only of how others teased him, which they did, but of all those burdens under which he toiled. All that suffering of his which was done about the midsection, about those short arms he could hardly lift.

I won't recount the details of his story fully. I've always been aware that talking about the past allows it to lay claim to you precisely because it reenergizes events which no longer hold any real influence.

In short, though, I learned how his parents had divorced and he'd split his time unevenly between Puerto Vallarta—where he spent most of his time—and, occasionally, Mexico City. You know the story, I'm sure. His tough, street savvy father never approved of his sensitivity or even his intelligence, while his mother fostered those things even as she fussed about his weight and took him repeatedly to the little museum in the botanical gardens on La Isla de Rio Cuale. There was a lecture in English everyday in the gardens beside the museum for the tourists on Mesoamerican history and art, and the aging director of the museum—who loved Santana Montana's mother greatly—often asked Santana Montana to give it when he was around. It wasn't hard to imagine him standing on a little stool and giving that talk with the carpenter bees and butterflies busy about the bursting blooms and the hills beyond sloping and curving down to Puerto Vallarta like the ridged tail of some slumbering green dragon.

Anyway, Santana Montana's mother had indirectly suggested numerous times that the reason for her and his father's separation was that his father might have been involved with the high-end drug scene and whatnot. His mother had died on a Tuesday and Santana Montana was soon after in possession of her estate. According to tradition, Santana Montana was to go now to live with his father, who had called Santana Montana and very forcefully ordered him to return to Mexico City. Santana Montana claimed his father loved only money and power and neither loved nor approved of him and so on. I asked him why his father would want him to come stay with him then, and Santana Montana said it was precisely because his mother had told his father that her son was an intellectual—not a ruffian—and she would never again allow his father to hold sway over Santana Montana.

When he finished, I went over and kneeled before him. He stared at the floor. Beyond him, through the window, I caught the morning trying to accrue sneakily in the tops of a few visible trees. The stress of contemplating self-slaughter had coated his face in an anxious film of grease. His glasses had slid down his nose. I leaned over and pushed them back up gently with my thumb and considered him.

I was running toward something. Santana Montana was running away from something and perhaps it was just that we were running in the same direction. Maybe for him, like me, there simply never was a chance of going back. Maybe there was. Some might say that time would tell but not me. If time could ever tell anything, it would only tell a shushing sound, like the kind a mother makes when the baby in her arms is crying in hysterics. I sat before him on the carpet.

"You're considering offing yourself because of your mother?" I asked.

"Yes."

"And how you despise your father?"

"Yes."

"And your treatment at Tommy Jeffs?"

"Yes."

"And other things?"

"Yes."

"And you'll give me that little pistol now?"

"No."

I sighed heavily and told him all the things he had to live for—our friendship, possible reconcilement with his father, our quest and so on—but he said his father would not change and that the quest was what I had to live for, not him. So, I told him if he shot himself, then I would kill myself, too, for I suspected he loved me and would not wish me harm. "Really?" he asked. He was looking at me with those big almond eyes of his, through which I beheld—quite easily—all his deep pain and vast intelligence. I knew if he'd been dumb and in pain, then he'd be better off. It was a terrible burden to be so homely and unloved when one was also intelligent enough to see the hardships and misfortunes so accurately.

"No," I said. "I cannot lie to you, my friend." He slumped, gently traced the barrel of the gun with the tip of a pudgy finger. I nibbled at my lip. Maybe he needed to be slapped from his malaise.

"Consider the goddamn limpet!" I exclaimed, startling him. "That old, tricky, soft-bodied invertebrate lives along the rocks on the seashore, which runs in cycles with the tides, and in a twelve-hour cycle that poor limpet is exposed alternatively to air, wind, heat from the sun, then gets a nice pounding from the sea for its trouble. As you know, life can mean extreme exposure to broad ranging cycles within cycles. Hell, but it's full of suffering, Santana Montana, and disappointments, awful parents, sleep paralysis, stress-induced bruxism. It is also full of beauty and joy but that's nothing new either. What is new is the fact that in three billion years the Andromeda Galaxy will cannibalize our Milky Way and what will it all matter then? Nothing, unless we can colonize elsewheres or tear a hole in space and follow gravity in its escape from one universe to another."

"Is this your attempt to cheer me?"

"Oh, I don't know, my friend, but I will say this: you can't do anything about your father or your mother. You cannot do anything about the face you were born with—which I love dearly mind you—but ask yourself this my rotund genius of a friend: Is there anything significantly weighing on you that you *can*—that you truly *might*—do something about?" Whatever ready-made reply he was about to utter died on his lips. Wheels spun in his irises, rolling back his lids so that his eyes got bigger and bigger until they were unbelievably wide. It was as if I'd shown him some miraculous possibility that he'd never dared imagine was possible. He turned in the chair to stare out the window, and I believed, though I could not be sure, that his wonderful brain was churning feverishly in that lovely dome of his as it gave full consideration to the question I'd challenged him with.

I left my suffering friend to his thoughts and put on my pants and went over and picked up the guidebook, and then fell on the bed to read about Santa Teresa.

Santana Montana had been right and there was a ferry. We would need to catch a bus to Puntarenas and then board the ferry there, which would take us —and the bus—across the Gulf of Nicoya to Paquera on the Nicoyan Peninsula. It was remote. The god-awful lame tourists would never venture there— only the sturdiest of travelers would backpack to a place so far off the beaten trail and that gave me hope.

I tossed the book aside and imagined Indigo walking toward me in a bikini under the coastline trees—the feminine swing of her arms and movement of her legs in the dappled light, all that dark hair hanging halfway down her back. I sighed sweetly, shut my eyes, and made a kissing sound.

Santana Montana stood up so suddenly and resolutely that he knocked the chair over as he rose.

I looked up at him.

"Give me his card!" he snarled, threateningly, holding out his pudgy hand palm up.

"What? But Santa Teresa," I said. "The book says there's a bus leaving from the Coca Cola bus stop in three hours."

"The taxi driver," he said. "Give me his card."

Something in his stance unsettled me, and for a moment I wavered. Then I realized, of course, that I'd rather Santana Montana shoot the cab driver than himself.

"I'll visit you in prison," I told him sadly and handed over the card.

All Things Await

37

After Santana Montana had rushed out, caught up in his own designs, whatever those designs were, I could not bear to be in the room alone, so I walked out and ate breakfast at a little dive and drank a coffee.

I sat there watching the traffic of old cars and scooters come and go. *There are so many people*, I thought. *Just so many of them.* I kept thinking of the girl with the star in her eye, imagining her in a white dress with her black hair done up in a blue ribbon. I wanted to ask her to a dance, to touch her slender waist and turn together under the lights with my fingers resting lightly on the nape of her smooth neck, but she was gone.

Everyone was gone but me. I felt disoriented, off-kilter.

After breakfast, I trudged back over to the hotel and checked the room to see if Santana Montana had returned.

He hadn't. He'd left in such violent haste that he'd forgotten his little bag. I collected it and went down and checked out. I sat at a place across the street from the hotel so that I could watch for my friend's return. Moving the Dextra around by myself was a bitch, so I ordered an Imperial to restore my spirits and stared bleakly at the road. Some schoolgirls ran by in their blue blazers and plaid skirts. A few workers were cleaning up debris in the street. After a while, a tired looking woman in a blue dress wandered up holding a cigarette and sat beside me.

She asked something in a smoky, gravelly voice.

"Shush," I said. "Listen—the *yuigurro* calls winter into the hearts of men."

She watched me for a moment, her head rocking slightly on her frail neck, then she got up and walked off unsteadily.

When it was time to leave and I'd still not spied my friend, my heart was broken.

"I've lost you, and I am alone," I said. I figured I'd see something of his exploits in the papers, but there was nothing I could do now for him. Heavy was my heart. I knew his path was his and that mine awaited me. I knew my path had not changed, even with Santana Montana gone. Except, perhaps, it'd just become much lonelier than I'd ever expected it to be.

Maybe it was Santana Montana's actions, but I found myself thinking on death as I labored in the direction of the bus stop.

I've been aware of that cliff we're all racing toward since the day we buried Margie, but it had never created a crisis for me. I am happy to bud and bloom and wilt and fall just as all other things in nature, and who the hell would want to do it all over anyway or stay the same age forever like in all those teenage vampires in the books the kids were reading these days? Emmy loved those angsty, horny vampires and whatnot but not me. Hell, I wouldn't want to be a vampire because I don't like touching people—much less biting them—and I wouldn't want to do it all over even though I haven't even done it all yet. It just makes you really tired to think on living again.

In no rush to die, in no rush to keep on living past my time, I simply lumbered forth, navigating the perilously crowded San Jose streets as scooters and old, rusted motorcycles scraped here and there through lanes of taxis and buses.

They were all bound for that cliff, too. Tooting their little horns along the way.

When I arrived at the Coca Cola bus stop, I just put the board down wearily and stood there feeling heavy and despondent.

I heard someone say, "There you are," and I looked over at the people sitting on the bench and right into the upturned face of Santana Montana. My surprise was so great that I threw my arms around him and yanked him up from that old rusty, paint-flecked bench and stooped to bury my face in the crook of his neck. I made such a fuss the band of stray dogs that'd been lounging lazily under the benches became wary and commenced to barking at us.

"Please," Santana Montana said. Some strange emotion had made him hoarse. "Please. Your grip on me is unnecessarily firm."

I released him and stepped back.

"My friend, my friend!"

"It is fine," he said.

"Truly?"

"Yes." I took off his glasses and cleaned them with the front of my shirt.

"And your desire to shoot yourself?"

"It has passed." I gently returned the glasses to his face.

"What has restored your spirits?" I asked him.

"Your question," he said. He looked away, and I followed his glance to the bench where I noticed the girl sitting there. Her thin little legs moved as she scraped the toes of her shoes at a piece of fossilized gum on the sidewalk exactly as I had outside the Albemarle airport. She was leaning over and her hair was in her face. Even so, I knew it was Rosa.

"Well I'll be goddamned," I said. Rosa looked up then and saw me. A smile opened on her smooth, lovely face, and my heart rose and softened at the same time. She skipped over and latched onto me with a scrawny hug. I thought of Margaret, how frail she was, how vulnerable. I hugged Rosa to me tightly. If I could have spoken Spanish, I'd have told her to stand on the tops of my feet for I sure the hell felt as if I was about to dance like a lunatic, such was the depth and breadth of this unexpected joy upon expected joy.

Santana Montana put his hands on my shoulders and fixed me with a serious look.

"Now," he said, his voice trembling with grateful passion, "let us go find your vision."

38

We got my board stowed below in the baggage compartment and then climbed on the bus. Santana Montana paid the sixty-six hundred colones apiece tab, and we moved down the center of the bus and settled into our seats under the smell of stale, musty air.

From my vantage point near the rear I glimpsed tan leg after long tan leg stretching up the aisle as the other riders, most of them seeming to be surfers, settled in for the long ride to Puntarenas and the ferry that awaited our arrival. Soon we were bumping along over potholes, and it was curvy as hell taking the rise from San Jose up into the Meseta Central with people trying to hold themselves into the seat to sleep.

"This is the type of trip where you *behold* things," I said to Santana Montana. He was one seat up, for Rosa had pushed him away to sit beside me. They shared a glance, and I wondered what they had discussed and what had caused Rosa to come along. In fact, I was dying to know, but I also didn't want to push things with Santana Montana. There would be time to sort out whether he'd shot that old cabber once I was sure he was truly beyond depression's cold grip. I wanted first to draw his thoughts into other happy things.

We motored on, stopping occasionally to pick up and drop off passengers. We lumbered past a gas station and headed west on the Pan American Highway, and I beheld three attendants in red polo shirts with white trim standing glumly in the shade of the store. It must have been their similar attire that called to mind how not even evolution—beautiful and true as a groundbreaking equation—could explain mimicry in butterflies or the presence of certain instincts in the newly born.

"Well," he said, "actually…"

"Santana Montana," I said, reaching up to touch his shoulder, "surely you have heard of how small animals respond to the mere shadow of a predatory bird they've never seen."

He said that he had and explained how a butterfly could be the same color of a tree with even the random holes bored by beetles being gloriously reproduced.

"There is something inexplicable in knowledge being encoded into genes and passed on," I told him, "that even Darwin—with his brilliance and morbid earthworm fascination—couldn't account for." But, tell me, who could think of that when the face of another Jesus was staring them down?

This Jesus had been etched into the glass divide between the driver of the bus and his passengers. It just leapt out at you suddenly like he does from the fake wood paneling on mobile home walls in Arkansas trailer parks, Mississippi doublewides, or in all those broken down RVs behind motels in Bellevue, North Carolina.

This Jesus looked as if he'd just stepped from his cycle after finishing that stage of the Tour de France that goes through the Pyrenees, which are named, I know, after some poor girl who was raped, abandoned, then eaten by wolves. Now *that* is suffering, but I suppose this Jesus suffered, too, because his head was angled down, slightly to the side, mouth gaped open—the whole deal. I was pretty sure he was looking at me. And if I'd had a beer I would have held it up to him and said, "I know how you feel, Jesus—exactly—but remember that Greek girl and be grateful."

The bus slowed and Rosa snuggled against me and shut her doe-like eyes which had seemed wet with youth when I'd first beheld them. I wanted very much to kiss the top of Rosa's head but didn't. I sighed deeply for I was rich with happiness just then, but it was not to last.

I'll tell why I say that.

Because a few stops later some inebriated, globetrotting bastard hopped on the bus. He had a towering backpack with running shoes and a baby rattle swinging from it and he held a Pilsen in his hand. He came down the aisle like a block of stone in a huge raincoat, and his squarish face was heavily pockmarked, which might have been the result of acne as a youngster or some strange Central American disease against which he'd not been immunized.

He was so wide that he needed to turn to the side to avoid knocking into people in the aisle seats. Of course, he didn't turn to the side at all but came on straight, stepping on toes, kicking against naked legs and knocking—with elbows or the edges of his backpack—the hell out of old women, the heads of sleeping children. People swore in his wake and children cried, but it didn't make a damn to him.

He was drunk, too, for I could smell beer on him, liquor, too. I could smell it precisely because he'd stopped at my seat to stare down at me or at

Rosa. I couldn't tell because of the sunglasses in which I beheld Rosa and myself dimly reflected.

"Anit," a man called authoritatively, "*Siéntate, Anit!*"

He sat down right behind us but soon started singing in a mix of Spanish and English. Except for the repeated word "kill," I couldn't make out any of the other lyrics, but he shook his head terribly and the lyrics seemed to be about death, rape, torture or about the trials and tribulations of being, I believed, a Honduran gang member though I might have well been wrong.

The thing that happened, though, was this: he started touching Rosa's hair and apologizing immediately as if it were unintentional. Each time he did it the old woman who had the misfortune of being stuck in the seat beside him yelled, "*Deja que la niña sola!*" and slapped at his knees and a big *tico* across from us would shout at him, too. It was the same man who had gotten him to sit down, and when he laid into Anit the rational woman beside him, most likely his wife, would try to calm him down. It was enough to get Anit to leave Rosa alone for a song or two but then he'd do it again.

"Goddamn it," I said to Santana Montana after yet another drunken apology, "but if he touches Rosa again, I don't know what I'll do." I was burning up to protect Rosa, to ensure she not suffer as poor Pyrene had all those gaggles of centuries ago.

"Please," Santana Montana said. "Remain calm."

"Why?" I asked. "Will we be there soon, Santana Montana? "He looked at the guidebook, which was open in his lap, the sun sharp and bright on its pages.

"No," he said. "We will not."

"Okay then," I said. "But only because of the love and respect I bear you."

Naturally, he touched her again, and I was going to keep my word to Santana Montana—honest to god—but Rosa had the furrowed brow and fearful eyes, and when she fished out the little needle her uncle had given her, it was simply more than my heart could stand.

I spun to go over the seatback at Anit, but the big *tico* beat me to it for he was already up and screaming and soon they were tangling violently in the aisle. It was only then, as they tangled, that I noticed Anit's physique. At some point he'd removed the raincoat and the shirt underneath had the sleeves torn out to show off his heavily muscled arms, which were covered with the faded tattoos of women and children.

The veins that roped up Anit's inked forearms and biceps pulsed and bulged as he grappled with the man. The *tico* threw a punch but Anit shifted so that the punch thudded harmlessly against his shoulder, which was not a shoulder at all, but a bag of concrete mix.

Anit's rattle swung wildly as they tussled and the air was filled with the sound of old seeds shaking in a dry gourd. It ended poorly for the aging *tico* —who was in the right, of course—for he fell unconscious across my lap.

The driver stopped the bus. He came down the aisle yelling at Anit and pointing to indicate he wished him to leave. But, I noticed, he stayed a good distance away. Several men on the bus were standing now and yelling at Anit, but he shook his head and kept singing.

As they slowly backed him toward the rear of the bus with loud voices and animated gestures, there was no concern at all on Anit's face.

The driver yelled something to everyone on the bus. He yelled it again several times and it seemed he was begging for calm. Then he pushed his way back up front and got the bus moving very swiftly. The passengers stopped yelling but stayed on their feet glowering at Anit. Two men lifted the unconscious *tico* from my lap and I realized, as they did, I'd been stroking his hair and telling him how brave and kind he'd been. They placed him back in his seat, and several women fussed with gentle fingers about the poor man's face, which was already swelling and purple at the left eye.

In no time at all, though, we approached the outskirts of Puntarenas and the driver pulled over at a police station. He leapt from the bus and disappeared inside. He came out with a ragtag klatch of officers.

Apparently, the *policia* were familiar with Anit because they stood before him—nervous about the knees—in their white polo shirts tucked into royal navy shorts and kept saying "Anit" this and "Anit" that in a cajoling almost pleading way.

In the end, it took all six members of the *policia* to pull him off the bus. Anit didn't swing at them, just refused to aid in his own removal. He kept holding onto things and singing his kill songs, even grinding his hips ever so slightly, but finally they got him off. Everyone was standing. We watched as they took Anit into the little white *policia* station.

When the driver got back on the bus and we started moving again, the entire bus erupted in cheers. A few *ticos* gathered around me to pat my back and Rosa clung to me adoringly.

"They say 'good,'" Santana Montana translated. "They saw you meant to attack him. They are saying you are a good, good foreigner." My heart went all swollen just then and my eyesight got blurred like as if I was coming down with something.

"But I did nothing," I protested softly, sort of patting back at them but really trying to push them gently away. Sometimes we save things only because of the things we did not save. The sad thing is how that means there's no joy in saving, since the original thing always remains lost.

39

Even if you're one of the good foreigners, apparently, the bus driver gives you a ticket when you reach the Puntarenas ferry, then kicks you off the bus, so you have to walk onto the ferry yourself and you can't climb back on the bus until the ferry has reached the other side of the gulf.

We stepped from the bus and were greeted with the stink of rotten food and dead fish. There was a long line of vehicles in various states of decay waiting to drive onto the ferry. We crossed a graveled lot to the wooden bridge and then stepped over the ferry apron and onto the ratty vessel itself. Whatever normal tourists had been on the bus were evidently staying in Puntarenas, for only locals and hardcore travelers—mostly bearded, wild-eyed backpackers—came aboard. A grim-looking man in a blue uniform directed the stream of *ticos* around the vehicles that were beginning to fill up the double-ended deck. I pointed out the awful condition of the vehicles and Santana Montana said these were all locals heading to visit family on the distant peninsula because of some holiday or such. That made me happy because we were now beyond the reach of the Disneyland tourists.

We climbed a narrow stair to find blue benches, gross toilets, and a tasty little snack shop. I bought two beers at the snack shop for I needed a few after the distressing business on the bus. I sat down on one of the starboard benches, and Santana Montana and Rosa slid in beside me.

"Would you like a beer?" I asked Santana Montana.

"Okay," he said.

"Well, you'd better hurry," I said, gesturing with one of my Imperials at the snack shack. "A line is forming."

"Never mind," he said. Rosa leaned toward him, spoke quietly, and Santana Montana replied firmly.

"What does she say?"

"She asked to have a beer, but I told her no."

"That's right. Don't make me look any worse than I already do," I said and wondered what I meant. I gulped down the entire beer in big mouthfuls and stared down at a Fruver World truck that had pulled up on the deck below and at the childish painting of the Earth on the side of it. Something in the way the painter had gotten the continents all wrong upset me, but I cheered myself by thinking how, with the movements of the plates and whatnot, perhaps the continents might look exactly so in a few million years.

"He's a visionary," I said aloud. As I opened the other can, a sleek Land Cruiser with a bevy of surfboards lashed to the top pulled onto the deck between the visionary's truck and rusted Isuzu Trooper. A golden and undeniably handsome guy with spiky hair stepped from it. He wore a crisp tee shirt, fashionable board shorts that went past his knees, and no shoes. To my surprise, Indigo appeared from the passenger side and slid her gorgeous arm around him.

"Oop," I gabbled. "That's...that's not right."

He put his arm around her, too, and it was a handsome, sun-drenched arm. Prettier than mine—the kind you see on Olympic swimmers or guys who grow up on the beach and surf competitively.

When they came up the stairs they were not arm in arm because of the crowd, but close together in single file. I sat up expectantly, but she didn't see me. They pressed through past the snack shop and went up another set of stairs to the top deck.

Santana Montana and Rosa were still murmuring and fidgeting like water in a kettle on a hot eye.

"What is it now?" I demanded.

"She wants to go in where the air conditioning is." Then he added, "She is smart. Not educated, but smart. I should warn you, though, she is smitten."

"What? With me? Hell, that's just what I need." I spat a piece of something off my tongue, scratched my rib, and gave Santana Montana's face a good running over. "You know, if you killed that poor, awful taxi driver—I mean at some point we need to...aw, hell," I said. I squinted at the stairs to the top deck. *Could be a brother*, I thought, but I knew that was wrong. Perhaps they're only casually dating. That was plausible.

It could have been the beer, but I felt stirred, anxious, rushed. It was competition. When had I ever shied from that? I looked at the faded address on my hand.

"What's that?" Santana Montana asked, nodding toward my palm.

"Nothing." I shut it into a fist and squeezed protectively like I was holding something very small and precious. "Why don't you two go on in that cabin. I think I'll stay here and admire the scenery, for, look-a-yonder," I said, pointing portside, "at the distant layering of mountains in front of mountains and how they look like purple paper ridges in a popup book."

I hummed pleasantly as I watched Rosa and Santana Montana shamble toward the amidships. As soon as they disappeared through the double doors, I sprang up and pushed my way past the throng of locals to the stairs.

The top floor had rows of the same blue benches stretching from the stairwell to the superstructure. Music drifted from the aft. It was all open save for tarps that had been strung up high to block the sun. It was a ship that had seen better days, too, and here and there some of the tarps had frayed on one end at the laces and had fallen to hang like shower curtains between the rows.

I was ushered along by the stream of passengers to the stern and felt the ferry move and heard it groan, and then we were off. The movement kicked up a welcomed breeze that rustled over the sweaty crowd and my eyes roamed over the faces. A little Costa Rican boy, four or five years old, was climbing the steps to the Captain's platform and then sliding down the white, rust-flecked railing.

I rounded the superstructure and headed aft in the direction of the music looking for Indigo and feeling no less confident about my prospects. We were moving three-wide down the aisle when I passed one of the hanging tarps and glanced over to find Indigo and my comely competition at the end of a bench with their backs to the tarp.

I turned and pushed back against the crowd and into the row directly behind them. The bench was full, but right about where I guessed Indigo was on the other side of the curtain, an obese local woman in a purple floral dress had her matching purse on the bench beside her. I went over and gestured to the purse with my Imperial. She lifted it up, hugged it protectively, and I sat down.

"You have no idea," I told her happily, though I hardly knew what I meant. She had a sweet, grandmotherly face. I wouldn't have been surprised to learn that her name was Helen and that she was exceedingly popular with her eight grand children, but she might have owned thirty cats, had no grand-children, and drank warm beer in a plastic baby pool for all I knew.

"Doesn't matter," I said. I held my finger to my lips and leaned back to get my ear against the weathered sheeting.

Muffled as it was, the color and velvety feel of Indigo's voice was unmistakable.

"*Sólo tengo un mes*," she said. "*¿Vas a estar enojado todo el tiempo?*"

"*No me bastaría,*" the handsome bastard responded passionately. "*Tú no amas más. Ya lo sé.*"

"Of course I love you, Perry."

"Doesn't mean it's final," I whispered at Helen dismissively.

"*Siempre te amaré,*" Indigo went on, "*pero las cosas son diferentes. Yo soy diferente.* "

"*Ha cambiado,*" Perry said quietly.

"Perry," she said sternly. "You are my first kiss. My first love. I will always love you. Nothing will change that. "

"Well that's final," I said sinking into the bench.

I listened a little longer but the next song on the speakers was a bit louder. I couldn't hear as well, and, anyway, what I could hear amounted to childhood loves reminiscing about experiences shared growing up together in a little fishing village. I put my elbows on my knees and my head in my hands because I did not need to listen—I could see them. Sun-drenched children chasing iguanas with fishing net lassos, walking a dirt road hand in hand to a little whitewashed school, both of them more golden and beautiful than you could believe. Their history was a maze cave of breccia and water traps, of dripstone passages and collapsed tunnels, and I was on the outside of it. I felt like a common vandal prying his way into the sacred chamber of a pharaoh's tomb, and my heart shriveled in my broad chest to a cold and lonesome *raisinette.*

I'd felt nearly as bad once before, when I'd said goodbye to Uluwehi at the Duke Kahanamoku statue on Waikiki Beach, and walked away all bleary-eyed because my fledgling heart had fluttered from its nest to die on the ground at her feet.

That feeling had foretold the onset of a period my mother had termed, "a fairly normal depression." I shut my eyes for a moment, for I felt so tired and hopeless and *fairly normally depressed* all of a sudden.

"Oh, Helen," I said quietly to the sweet old *tica* beside me, "I am uncoupled from my shoring, alone in all the world."

"*No estés triste,*" she said, not unkindly. "*Él es sólo un amigo.*"

"You seem really wise," I told her as I stood up. "I wish I could understand you."

40

The summer after Margaret's death, but before the night of meteors, sand, and stars, my family lived in an apartment in Waikiki, two streets from the beach with its imported sand and statue of Duke K, which I told Pop not to confuse with Coach K from Duke but he didn't understand it was a joke. Anyway, Mother brought us there to get away from the despair of Margaret's passing but also so she might absorb the Hawaiian background for yet another romance novel. I was happier for the Hawaiian climate, especially after having spent a cold, rainy time in Ireland for her previous book, *A Peninsula of Passion*. The one in Hawai'i was titled *The Warm-Hearted Ice Sculptor*.

Oh, that poor sculptor bastard! I would have to tell Santana Montana all about it—how the hotter his heart was for her the more she melted away from him, for he had shaped her with his demands and expectations as surely as he had shaped ice in his cold locker with his sharp saws and cruel chisels. Jesus, but it was a brilliant conceit on Mother's part, because it was how he warmed to his creation that ensured her heart-wrenching destruction at the end.

It was a dull time for me, too, though. Pop took Lance and me to Kaua'i and we hiked that goddamn Na'Pali Coast Trail out there, which, if you don't know, is a totally remote eleven mile hike along the shoreline cliffs, a thousand or so feet up. I was thirteen and overripe with energy and hormones. Dad was quiet, as remote as the trail itself and heavy as always with the knowledge of how far he was from the heights of his athletic fame. So, I sang my crazy songs to get him laughing, but Lance stayed sullen the whole way.

The hike ended at a golden sand beach with waterfalls falling and signs warning of *leptospirosis* in the water, or some such thing. There were tents scattered here and there among the palms and people were showering or brushing their teeth in the falls. It's true, I swear, you can go there yourself and see, but I'd advise against it.

I'd advise against it because even though there was a picturesque secluded golden sand beach there, there was also a bunch of middle-aged hippy-ish bastards who'd decided to set up a nudist colony without telling a goddamn soul, posting signs, or filing out the necessary application forms to be nude in public, as hippy-ish people seldom seem to do. It would have been fine if they were Kauaians, or at least lovely, golden people but they weren't. They were aging folk, the type you see either teaching at European universities—dressed in black, smoking cigarettes against the backdrop of a crumbling fountain—or lounging on wicker furniture on the early morning porches of houses in DC suburbs, wearing slippers and robes, and reading the newspaper or drinking coffee or both or neither. Hell, they could have been Cubans or Kiwis, though, for how could I tell being only a young teen and so absorbed with myself that I'd sometimes caress my own arm fondly for minutes at a time?

Anyway, Pop had been so annoyed with the lack of fitness on display that he made us turn around and walk the whole damn eleven miles back. So, instead of a tent on a golden beach, we slept on a Kauaian mountain side pullover in our rental car—a tiny, blue Dodge Neon that stank wetly of gas fumes, body odor, and cigarette smoke. We awoke, cramped and aching, to the scratch and crow of feral chickens on the roof and a view over that green, vernal island that could break a grown man's heart.

That very day we flew back to O'ahu, and I went to work at Kimo Bagelman's in downtown Honolulu just to get the hell out of the house. Mother's friend owned it and allowed me to work there despite my young age. It was a thankless job—the bagel place, I mean. I had to wear a brown Kimo Bagelman's hat and apron. What was that logo of theirs, a mustachioed Hawaiian chasing a roll-away bagel? I'd sit out front on my short lunch break with a copy of Dante's *Inferno* to improve my brain, but really I was just pretending to read because I didn't get a bit of it at all with its rings of hell and people suffering and crying out from lakes of fire and whatnot.

More than anything, though, I'll remember that summer on O'ahu for all those creepy, older, well-dressed ladies who came down for bagels from their high-rise offices and asked for my phone number, and for how I fell in love with Uluwehi, that lovely eighteen year old Hawaiian surfing goddess who said she liked me and that if I were even two years older I'd be in "trouble." Lord, how I longed that whole summer to make trouble to Uluwehi, to have Uluwehi make trouble to me, but it just was not so.

41

On my way back down the ferry steps, I stopped to lean over the railing. We were passing two little islands of rock and far beyond them the mainland ridges twisted into a threateningly dark and purple sky.

Two grey pelicans came planing over the gulf. The water itself was silent about its business beneath our boat, so wrinkled and dark and smooth all at once, and I remembered telling my mother in the Greek Isles that if a person would just go out to sea and look at the water—I mean really study its movements, its fickle, complex beauty—they might get *truly* changed for the better. I'd always known how people needed to be more humble, more appreciative, and more sure of themselves all at once and I'd always believed that studying far-out deep waters could teach you just that. The dock at Paquera was a primitive structure of wood and rope. We came over the apron and shuffled across it with the rest of the crowd. Not much to see. The dilapidated Puerto Paquera Restaurante y Soda. A modest fan of beach just off to the left. Four slender fishing boats pulled up on the sand like bread knives on a cutting board.

We sat down on a log beside the rutted road to wait for the bus. Vehicles came streaming over the hog slats and set the buttresses and weathered pilings to groaning in complaint. We covered our mouths against the dust.

There were three strangler figs across the way shielding off the little beach and they had all those vines hanging from them. I told Santana Montana that they looked like the hanging moss you see in trees on Hilton Head Island, but Santana Montana is a genius and so he said they looked more like synapses in the brain, or dendrites, or basal ganglia—I can't remember which.

While he translated for Rosa I turned away and covered my face because I caught the flash of the sporty Land Cruiser approaching among the disembarking cars and trucks. I found myself staring at a well-dressed Costa Rican in a cowboy hat who stood beside me with bags of apples in his arms.

He looked at me, but a truck pulled to a stop right beside us, and then he wasn't looking at me anymore.

"*Que chica más linda,*" the apple monger said. I heard the muted hum of the window motor through the door panel

"What are you doing here?" Indigo asked.

Santana Montana elbowed me sharply in the ribs. I took my hands from my face and looked up into their car and at Indigo's bright, smooth face.

"Adventuring," I said.

"Where are you headed?" she asked. Perry strained forward to see us.

"Uh-"

"Santa Teresa," Santana Montana interjected helpfully. Indigo looked from him to me.

"Santa Teresa? But how come you didn't mention that when you saw my address?"

I rubbed my palm, and Santana Montana eyed me suspiciously.

"*Le dijiste dónde vives?*" Perry snapped.

One of the cars behind them blew their horn and then another.

"*Tenemos que ir,*" Perry said roughly. He was a good-looking guy, but his eyes were too close together to suit me.

"Would you like to ride with us?" Indigo asked. She looked at my friends. and made a motion with her hand for us to join them. Her hair had been tucked neatly behind her ear, but the gesture sent it spilling out in abundance over her shoulder. My chest throbbed. Why torture myself? Santana Montana was trying to struggle up from the log, but I pulled him down by the shoulder.

"No thank you," I said. "But thanks all the same."

Horns split the air. Indigo looked like she wanted to say something else.

"*Le dijiste dónde vives!*" Perry said gruffly and then sped off. His tires had spun in the gravel and lifted a haze of dust. It drifted like woodsmoke in the air.

42

The bus lumbered and creaked up the road as it climbed the hill above Paquera. The dark clouds had moved on or burned off and we crested the rise to find rich, green mountains sunning their spines in the distance beneath the heat-weight of a pure blue sky.

Santana Montana was looking at me.

"What?" I asked him.

"You know what. I sat with her father on the plane."

"Happenstance," I said.

"Show me your hand."

"No."

"Show it to me."

"I'd rather not."

"Show me."

"Okay." I opened it. He had to lean close to make it out.

"Indigo. Mrs. Engdahl's," he read. "Santa Teresa. Peninsula de Nicoya."

"So?" I demanded. He sat up.

"You are off course."

"Nonsense. I told you the vision awaited me on the peninsula."

"Which vision?"

"Drop it."

"Her or the other?"

"I don't want to talk about it." He might not have let it drop, but then Rosa said casually, "*¿Quién era esa puta?*" It must have meant something awful because they were soon in an argument over it.

43

As we neared the coast, the mountains gave way to foothills and we came shuddering over the washboard roads to cross little streams in the low places until, at last, we turned right onto the beach road at Playa Carmen—just north of Mal Pais.

We passed by a couple of small medical centers and by newish blue buildings of surf stores, coffee shops, lunch dives, even a seafood boutique. We rumbled on and I caught glimpses of the sea through the tree boles. There were quads kicking up dust and dark shirtless folks lounging with their boards in the run down sodas that dotted the road.

The bus pulled into the shade of an ancient mango tree beside Soda Taunos, which looked like nothing more than a leaning shack with fronds for a roof. I collected the Dextra Classic and we set off walking toward the campsite Santana Montana and I had picked out on the bus.

I had liked the idea of pitching a tent right beside the endless drumming of the surf because I knew my vision awaited me on one of the beaches. Santana Montana had stipulated that we each have our own tent because it would make his study of plants and wildlife easier having his own quiet space.

We thought we had it all settled but we were wrong. As we hoofed it on down the hard, dusty road, Santana Montana conveyed our plans to Rosa, and she became animated in her refusal to sleep outside.

Santana Montana translated Rosa's fears of the outdoors and disdain for leaving one hostile environment of sorts for another. I don't know what he said back to her, but suddenly Rosa was yelling. She cursed heavily, and I was surprised by the foulness of her language, particularly because I felt—as offensive as I sensed it might be—that Santana Montana was toning it down for me in his translation. So we stood in the street halfway to the campground and tried to resolve the matter with the little stripling that was our charge. She was very defiant about it all and wanted to stay at a backpacker's hovel known as Brunela's. My golden arm was asleep from holding the Dextra and I was bored and agitated all at once. I could hear the call of the waves through the trees, through the walls of massive nylon tarps attached to wooden posts meant, I guessed, to keep the dust kicked up by vehicles from set-

181

tling on the little seafront shacks and cabanas from drifting into wall-less houses and settling into rustic cups and dishes and the collars of hand-washed shirts that hung drying on stretches of coarse, fraying rope.

And I was hot as hell, because the sun was once more pressing its fiery stamp on all it touched. After making several failed arguments, I finally directed Santana Montana to ask Rosa if there was anything that could make her agree.

Santana Montana listened to her response, which I instantly noticed had lost its edge and became shy or playful and then he sighed—what seemed to me—a weary or sad or annoyed exhalation. "She says if she could share a tent with you..." He coughed into his fist and wouldn't look at me. "Just the two of you," he added.

"But what of your sleep paralysis?" I asked. "Who will shake you roughly?" He just looked at me blankly. "Ah, hell. Fine," I said, for I knew how even the most skittish creatures had always crept hesitantly toward me in the end. Jeez, I had the touch with scared and shattered creatures. The skin and bone fox cub, the fawn Pop had bush-hogged a leg off of, the bat babies and the little crow that had fallen out of its nest—all these things I'd nursed back to health and earned, in reward, their slowly dying devotion for my kindness. Well, at least as much as could be expected—for hadn't Foxy, BuckBuck, the three-legged deer, and Jim Bob, the crow, returned frequently through the years to yip for me in the yard, nuzzle me at the salt block, or light on my shoulder and cackle lovingly in my ear?

Hell, yes, they had. They had needed me just as Santana Montana and Rosa needed me and I had enough in me to heal them all.

We hoofed it on down the blazing strip of dirt road. Ancient SUVs creaked and groaned by and cherry red quads tore down the road, the swimsuit-clad drivers nearly always cradling their surfboards across their laps. Each time something passed us the dust took to the air. Some of the bicyclists—also awkwardly toting surfboards—wore bandanas over their mouths.

"There's been research done," Santana Montana said from behind me. He was carrying the other end of the surfboard. "People are becoming sick from breathing the dust." He translated for Rosa.

"Maybe we should get bandanas, too," I said.

"It would be wise," he said.

Finally we saw the sign for the campsite and were able to leave that dusty sun-burnt main road and took the campsite road, which curved away in a sandy swath through the trees. Santana Montana identified the trees for Rosa —*pachote, almendro, brasil, ceibo* and so on—and I listened in with great interest. Rosa seemed interested, too, and I believed—I hoped—that Santana Montana's knowledge of such things could open up the world a little for her.

I left Santana Montana and Rosa at the campsite office. No one was manning it, so I asked them to wait and made straight for the beach. The big trees, to which Santana Montana had given names, rose all around—*almendros* and *brasils* and *pachotes* with their armor of thorns.

An iguana sat motionless on an old log in the dappled light, shoulders up, head raised. "You will come to know me," I yelled to him. "You will eat from my hand and croak outside my tent to be held!" He scurried off indignantly. I laughed and kicked my shoes off against the base of a palm at the edge of the beach so that I could feel the sand beneath my feet, let the history of the land enter through my soles.

Playa Santa Teresa was shaped like a crescent moon. I shut my eyes, filled my nostrils with it all. Behind me I could feel the old trees looming and I was comforted at how their canopy darkened the sand floor where iguanas slept, and hunted, and bathed their scales in little pools of renegade light.

I opened my eyes and looked south and saw, about three miles off, how the headlands beyond Mal Pais bookended the beach with a rocky escarpment. To the north I could just see the cusp-shaped projection of the coast, where the sand gave way to a black reef that everyday, I guessed, must be covered and uncovered by the tide.

There were a dozen surfers out, the distant outline of their dark heads bobbing far out over the swells like a raft of sea birds. And the waves—my god —they were monsters, but beautiful monsters. Eight to fourteen feet in height, consistent and clean with a long break. I watched a big breaker roll in and its crest curled over pockets of air and the sunlight shimmered and played in the smooth uprush.

I set out along the the debris line with its limbs and twigs and green nuts and parts of wooden boats and fishing ropes and plastic bottle tops. I picked up a narrow, pale green nylon fishing rope from a pile of sticks. It was sunburnt and sea-soiled. I sniffed it. It smelled of the water and sand and, using my teeth, I tied it around my left wrist, saying that it would be my charm.

I wasn't sure this was the place. Not yet. But I wasn't sure that it wasn't.

There was a good, lovely breeze coming off the water—not at all like the stillness of the air along the brutally burnt main road—and I set off down the beach with my whole being open to the place—to every constitutive part—and drank deeply and continuously of how the sand felt beneath my feet, the breeze against my skin, of all the smells and sounds, which found me ready and welcoming. They rushed into me frantically and it was very much as if they'd been waiting eons for someone to notice them, for just the right person to appear and *really, truly* apprehend them.

"Easy now," I told those shifty, constitutive parts. "We have time and there's plenty of room for everyone."

After my walk, I cut back up toward the campsite feeling tired and ready for a meal and a good night's sleep in my tent. Strange birds whirred and clicked at me from somewhere in the leafy canopy. I went back over to where I'd left my flip-flops. They were no longer there.

44

Santana Montana had rented two tents and he and Rosa had got them up whilst I was on my beach walk. They were not particularly in good shape. One was brown and green and terribly frayed about the edging with tape holding together the window netting in places. The other was red and, though also worn and edged, in obvious better repair than the other.

"I'll take the red one," I said. Santana Montana looked at me. "It's because of Rosa," I explained. "Naturally, she should have the best."

He didn't argue but glanced at Rosa where she'd slumped against a log beside a pile of sticks they'd collected for firewood.

"What's wrong?" I whispered.

"Rosa," he said.

"Are you having regrets?"

"No, but things will get worse before they get better. Much worse."

We went out to eat that night at Pizza Tomate, which was at the end of a little row of well-lit, rustic stores that included the Kina Surf Shop and an internet café. The restaurant had a roof of palm fronds and a little walled-in kitchen surrounded by an open platform with wooden tables and chairs. It was dilapidated in all the right ways and filled with people, which I took to be a good sign of the edibility of the food.

Our waitress came by. She was a tan, thickset gal. She wore a short black thing that looked more like a beach cover than a dress. I suggested we let Rosa order for us, but our waitress had trouble understanding her.

"She's from Russia," Santana Montana explained as Rosa gestured at the menu. I noticed she had bracelets around her ankles and a string of tiny bells that jingled when she moved. She wore no shoes of any kind. When she took the menu from Rosa, I asked her if I could call her Anklebells, if I saw her again.

"My name is Anechka, but a cutie like you can call me whatever," she said and laughed.

She jangled away with our order, and was soon back with a big, steaming, mushroom and cheese pizza on a tray and paper plates under her arm. She didn't leave right away for Rosa and Santana Montana spoke quietly with her.

It was dark now, but the string-lights of Pizza Tomate coaxed up a muted saffron incandescence from the people there: shirtless surfers in swimsuits, their dreads pulled back and lovely, sun-kissed girls born on the beach, an Italian couple and their three small daughters running amok with pizza-stained faces. Here and there friendly dogs drowsed beneath the tables as foreign utterances filled the air with colors I'd not seen before. I was happy to be someplace new. I felt alive—settled and unsettled at the same time—which was rare and good.

I stopped looking around at things precisely because Santana Montana and Rosa were arguing. Santana Montana spoke calmly but insistently to her, but Rosa was getting louder and more vehement about whatever the issue was. People were looking at us. The pizza-stained Italian children stared from the aisle, their eyes blue and bright, their mouths slightly open.

While everyone watched, and with Santana Montana's cheeks flushed bright red, Rosa stood up and slapped the table three times very hard, cursing heartily and then stalked away and threw herself into an aluminum chair at the rear of the restaurant. Her toes barely touched the floor and she crossed her little arms and glowered at us.

Santana Montana leaned over the table in embarrassment and awkwardly picked up a slice of pizza.

I leaned in, too, and whispered, "Santana Montana—what in *the hell* was that?"

He finished his bite of pizza and told me that Rosa had been asking after parties or places to party. The waitress had said there would be a big party at Mrs. Engdahl's house which was right on the ocean across the street.

"Engdahl's?" I glanced across the dusty road to the big wooden gates closing off the path on the other side, which, it was to be assumed, led to Mrs. Engdahl's place. I sniffed gently for the scent of Indigo, but there was only dust on the air.

"Yes, Engdahl's," Santana Montana said, "which is fine and good for you, but not for Rosa."

"But why is she upset? Because she is jealous?"

"No. Because I forbade her to go," he said quietly.

"You *forbade*?"

He still didn't meet my eyes, but he curled his hand on the table into a tight fist.

"Can you even fathom," he began, his voice still low, trembling with emotion, "how her life has damaged her?"

"No," I admitted, for her life and the damage done to it were, in fact, *fathomless.*

"She needs direction," he said. "She needs exposure to good things. She is very smart," he said, his voice quivering. "She's very smart and..." He stopped short, though, of whatever he was going to say. My eyes drifted to the wooden gates. How long dare I tarry? Indigo was likely somewhere beyond the gate and fencing, beyond sight, beyond reach.

On the way home we walked along the moonlit road, cratered and pale beneath the little clouds of chalk our feet kicked up, the stars fanning above us, the sky clear, the air tinged with the lingering mugginess of the day. Crabs kept scuttling underfoot, arms raised, claws open, and disappearing into the undergrowth.

"Orange legs and purple claws," I said.

"And blackish carapace. *Gecarcinus quadratus*—Halloween crabs," Santana Montana said. "Very active in the rainy season."

Rosa trailed about twenty yards behind us, still obviously sulking about Santana Montana's decree. We stopped to wait for her twice, but she would stop, too, cross her arms and glower at us. If one of those cute little crabs came scuttling out Rosa would stomp at it.

"Jesus," I said, after the sickening crunch of a few crabs had got me feeling sort of bothered. "Let's not stop again." It was vaguely disturbing, though, this ghosting about behind us, so we ducked into the Super Olas Tres for a few groceries. I wanted to pick up mostly snackish type items, but also a bottle of vodka and a sixer of warm beer. It was just a little concrete building consisting of two rooms. There was an iron gate swung open that they must have locked up at night. An old man sat on a bucket in the dust beside the entrance. He was drunk or tired or both. He'd lean over until I thought he was going to go off his bucket but then he'd catch himself.

I told Santana Montana that I'd thought of a new saying—*He's gone off the bucket*—but Santana Montana just rolled his eyes.

Back at the camp, the fire we built was warm in the cool of the night. I gently scooped away a few hermit crabs and sat with a warm beer against the Dextra Classic, which I'd sat on edge and leaned against an *almendro.* I watched Rosa and Santana Montana.

"Do you want me to translate?" Santana Montana asked.

"Hell no," I said.

"And you will be going to Mrs. Engdahl's tonight?"

"Hell no. There is nothing there for me." I leaned back into the embrace of the Imperial and thought of Jay Gatsby moping along the silent streets of Louisville. I thought of him and then there came Jordan with her tan arms and Daisy with her whispered hush. There came Nick Carraway who I liked and then hated and then just plain old felt sorry for. Other things, too.

I thought of my throw at the end of the Hampden-Sydney game—scrambling for my life and firing a pass forty yards on a frozen rope all the way back across the field to the distant corner of the end zone. It was the kind of throw a quarterback should never make. Coach Sanford said afterwards that he doubted six quarterbacks in division one could make that throw. He was right.

45

I awoke in the tent that night to Rosa spooning me from behind. I lifted my head to protest but she whimpered pitifully and shivered to make it known that she only sought warmth. It was true, for I knew from the comments of past lovers that my body produced an inordinate amount of heat. So, I relented to her tiny embrace, put my head back down to go to sleep and thought of how the moon sends sunlight fluting to our upturned eyes, for fluting was the word exactly for that lunar reflection. I didn't think long, though, for Rosa's fingers had found the zipper of my pants.

If I'd had time to think it through, I would not have reacted as I did. I would not have slapped so viciously at her little hands or turned to scream indignantly at her small, dark frame, which, as she had bolted upright, was silhouetted against the tent fabric that seemed to possess a pale red radiance in the blanched moonlight.

But I didn't have time and I reacted with an anger whose source I could not pinpoint. There was a moment of stunned, tense silence. The air inside the tent had felt rough, splintered. Then, a small rustling sound, as if someone was looking through a pile of clothes, followed by a sharp, painful sting in my forearm, like the sting of a yellow jacket. Then the tent zipper ripped open and the little shadow went dashing out.

I listened to the retreating crunch of her footfalls in the leaves and held my arm cradled to me. I held my tongue, too, and did not call out, for what could I have said?

I rubbed the stinging spot on my arm. There was nothing there, but I was sure I'd been stabbed with that needle—the one she'd stabbed her uncle with and possibly other out-of-line customers, the kind that got too rough and so on. I sat there feeling guilty and slightly nauseous, as if the red tent were bobbing and moving sickeningly way up in the night sky.

Rosa had left the tent flap agape when she'd fled, and I leaned out just to make sure I wasn't inside some stomach-churning balloon. What I looked out upon was the moon. It hung like a sheet in the sky, and the light that shone from it was not *fluting* at all but ghostly, and oddly discordant.

On and off, I listened out for Rosa through the remainder of the night, but the only sound that came to my ears was that of distant music, the obdurate murmur of waves, and the gentle whickering of dead, restless *almendro* leaves. Once I awoke to rapid breathing and bolted outside. I unzipped Santana Montana's tent and shook him viciously.

"Please stop," he croaked.

"Are you okay?"

"Yes."

"Can you breathe?"

"Yes. I wasn't having one."

"I'm watching over you," I said. "I always will be."

"*Tengo que ir pronto,*" he mumbled. "*¿Quién te protegerá a ti?*" He rolled on his side. I liked hearing him speak Spanish. It opened up that whole other side of his life that I could only guess at—his life as a child on a little island of flowers, museums, and heartbreak.

I put my hand gently on his big, fleshy hip and told him I was proud of the way he was trying to help Rosa.

"You're brave," I said. "She'll have to wade through seas of anger in order to reach the other side of what's happened to her." I thought about telling him how Rosa had run off, but Santana Montana was already snoring gently.

46

The morning opened damp and bright. I crawled from the tent and stood up. Santana Montana was still sleeping. There was no sign of Rosa, but maybe she was on the beach.

I stretched and then walked through the mizzle with the sunlight catching in the mist and droplets. It was like walking through sparks. On the beach I saw how the purple clouds retreated over the wet headlands beyond Mal Pais and how the shadows deepened as the mist burned off. I walked up the beach looking for Rosa. It would not have surprised me to find her washed up and blue, lovely with wet hair, naked and youthful as a merchild who'd drowned in the air.

I didn't know whether it was conscious or not, but I realized I was making my way up the beach in the direction of Mrs. Engdahl's. It was about a fifteen-minute walk and I suppose I was thinking it might be a place that Rosa would have gone to. I passed by a few beachfront houses, none of them massive or offensive, but small and elegant, mostly open structures with exposed and treated tree boles for posts and big, tiled porches.

I passed by a public access and came to a house set off the beach a ways. What caught my eye about it was that whereas the other houses were all surrounded by big trees and sand, this particular house had a big grassy yard and —save for a thin row of *almendros* along the beach, no trees in front of it. Also catching my eye, were the large number of colorful hammocks hanging in the trees and the number of people sleeping in the yard itself. There were a few trim girls doing Tai Chi in the side yard. I didn't know what Tai Chi was, but I guessed it would look a hell of a lot like what these girls were up to.

It looked like the aftermath of a party, so I went up to the house searching the hammocks stealthily for Rosa. As I crossed over the grass, I saw a few forms sitting at a table on the raised, open porch. Since they'd seen me sneaking around, peaking into hammocks, I felt compelled to go up and explain.

I came up the steps and saw it was Indigo and Perry sitting with two blonde girls. They were flanked by a half-dozen shirtless surfers—all locals—who looked to be lounging in an opium den. I recognized Anklebells from our dinner at Pizza Tomate. The other had her dreads tied up with a white bandana. She sat beside Perry and there was a green bong in her hands. The table they lounged around was littered with beer cans and fruit rinds. A few lines of cocaine were still noticeably at the edge of the table. In front of Indigo was a white plate with waffles and a chipped blue bowl with slices of mango and banana.

Perry said something under his breath. White Bandana said, "But I think he's cute."

"Don't be rude," Indigo said quietly to Perry.

"Hello," I said to him. "I'm Lightly. It's nice to meet you."

Perry just looked at my hand and then at Indigo. I couldn't catch what he said to her—it was in Spanish—but it was accusatory, edged with anger.

"Perry," she said soothingly. "Please."

Perry stood up. He was just in his board shorts. He went to lean against one of the porch posts and looked down his long elegant nose at me. He was taller than I was by more than a few inches, and he was leaner and more graceful in his build. He didn't have the broad, muscular frame that I had in my shoulders and chest. I didn't mean to be measuring him up as an opponent, but I realized that was just what I was doing.

I looked at Indigo. "Why is he mad at me?" I asked her.

"He's being sulky," she said. She turned to him. "*Que grosero,*" she said sharply.

White Bandana came over and stood behind Perry. She put her hand on his hip and stood on her tiptoes to whisper in his ear.

"Tell him he's got a lovely male body," I said to Indigo, "just as lovely as my own, and that I wish him well and do not want to tangle." I told her I wasn't there to chat, that I was just looking for the little girl who rode the bus with Santana Montana Ordóñez and myself.

"Lost your girlfriend?" Perry asked. "That's what you tourists do to children down here." I ignored him. I didn't like how his words were red-tipped spears or that he'd pretended he couldn't speak English, but I bit my tongue. Maybe I didn't like that I'd thought he couldn't.

"The girl at dinner with you last night?" Anklebells asked.

"Yes. Have you seen her?"

"No," Anklebells said.

"Do you want us to come get you if she comes by?" Indigo asked helpfully. "Where are you staying?"

I told her and said goodbye. I would've said goodbye to Perry, but the air

192

around him was full of splinters.

I trekked back toward the beach stopping only to join the Tai Chi group of girls. I guessed that they had been at the party and were purging the excesses of the night before. I tried to follow their slow, arching movements, wondering, as I did, whether Indigo was watching from the porch, but it was too difficult. A couple of them smiled at me and one cheeky blonde winked sweetly but I gave up. It was like they were moving in cursive, and all I knew how to do was print.

I reached the campsite feeling bewildered and depressed to find a shoeless youngster stealing the Dextra Classic. He was a lithe chap and the board was so goddamn heavy that he hadn't been able to pick it up and so he was dragging it ever so slowly away. I walked over until I'd caught up to him and picked up the dragging end of the board.

"Jesus," I said. "That was the worst attempt at thievery I've ever seen." I'd not said it unkindly, but he let go of the board and hightailed it through a stand of *pachotes*.

Strange birds made questioning sounds in the canopy. I watched the boy until he reached the road and disappeared into the dust at a dead sprint.

I went over and put the board down and looked at it. Perry and Indigo drifted through my mind like swansdown. Her tan arms, her smooth, soft cheek. I felt the brush of her against my palm and shuddered. She loved someone else, but I had followed. What was I doing? I decided immediately to go back to sleep, but I was greatly surprised to find that Rosa had crawled into the tent while I was away and was sound asleep.

I leaned over her to make sure she was breathing. There were little blossoms in her oily hair and she was shivering like she'd slept all night on the ground with only the stars for a blanket. She'd curled into a ball with her palms together and pressed between her knees. I removed my shirt and draped it over her. I went outside, sat down on the log, and looked at the ashes in the little fire pit Santana Montana and Rosa had built.

In the distance the ocean called to me, singing its song along the shore, scatter-sparkling the early light through the still sleeping trees. I wished sincerely that I had asked Indigo for a bowl of fruit and I hoped, just as sincerely that I might never see her again. When a person got tangled up with a couple of childhood sweethearts it was always the outsider who ended up with the rope around his neck.

Later that morning, Rosa stumbled from the tent bleary-eyed and—it seemed—hung over. She went into the woods and vomited. Santana Montana looked at her a moment and then went on writing in his notebook. I went over to her. She'd dropped my shirt and I picked it up and handed it to her. She wiped her little chin and then held my shirt out to me and stared off into the trees.

I looked at her thin brown legs, the little wings of her frail shoulder blades and the scrawny shoulders protruding from the spaghetti straps of her pink halter top, which was slack and twisted on her torso, so that I could see the brown upper edge of a nipple on her flat chest. I hurt for her, for the way her slender, hairless arm held the shirt out to me like an apology and felt my knees threatening to give out. I took the shirt from her. I straightened her shirt and then pulled her smooth cheek into my naked chest. She was skinny and brittle against my muscled frame. I buried my nose in her dark, greasy hair and breathed deeply of Rosa—the acrid stench of vomit, but also the scent of leaves and stale beer, of wet sand, forgotten hopes, lovely, irretrievable things and campfire smoke and faintly, very faintly, of almond blossoms.

"It's okay, honey," I said. "Everything is okay, my little one. It will take forever to fix, but the fixing has begun."

She didn't move at first, but stood there, grudgingly allowing herself to be held. Then her little arms encircled my waist and she began to shake, choking and sobbing into my skin. I rocked slowly from one foot to the other, leaned down to rest my chin on the top of her head. I hummed a wistful tune and looked over at Santana Montana, perhaps for some sort of commiseration—I don't know. He pretended to busy himself with writing in his notebook.

Of course, Rosa wanted to come with me, but I made it known through a reluctant Santana Montana that she must go with him. She protested, but I was firm. I told her I must be alone or the vision would not come and in the end she agreed, though she crossed her arms and squinted hatefully at him as he gathered his items and announced they would be setting out to see what ecological curiosities could be found along the cuspate foreland.

I didn't ask him to explain, for they set off with Santana Montana leading the way and Rosa moping behind him and casting longful glances back at me.

47

I spent most of the day on the beach looking for the place where my vision would occur. I walked as far south as the headlands and as far north as the reef, before it occurred to me that maybe I just needed to wait. I went over and sat on a washed up log and looked around the beach: a few locals, girls in straw hats, surfers paddling out into the teeth of massive waves. The water beckoned me with its foamy backwash, but I was too anxious about the vision to paddle out on the Dextra.

I wanted my scar to tingle but it wouldn't. Still, though, I felt the electric thing move inside for there was the straggle of palms, the tines of the playa trees, the low pale skyline over all that expanse of water. This was the general area for it was all there: the scatter of light from the infinite sand mirrors, the brilliance of living and dead things, all that warm air at the edges foreshadowing the day's white heat, the hermit crabs with their diagonal sailing over sea sand, the troupe of howler monkeys moving through a stand of *brasil* trees and everything shining back into my face from the ground up.

I left the beach when I got to starving and cut back over to the track of dust that ran through the town. There were so many flattened crabs in the road that they seemed a decorative part of it—the black bodies, purple arms, orange legs forming a ceramic mosaic.

I walked south along the road covering my mouth and nose whenever a truck or quad or twenty-year old SUV came bumping and creaking along to send the choking dust spiraling up in streamers. The dust fought to suffocate everything, but pockets of odors drifted or curled beneath it. I could smell the sea, and a person with the right nose could smell the jungle that cascaded over the big, steep hills to the east—a dark, damp, leafy heat-stink of soil and rotting plants, of the animals that moved through it stealthily, their fur, the warmth of their bodies, their breath. I could smell fruit, too, and beer from the little sodas—Alma, Luz de Luna, the Ginger Café with its stand of yucca plants, Soda El Jardin, Platin-Ta with its shaggy roof and chipped blue tiles, Otra Lado and Meli Melo. The air was pungent with the scent of *casados*, of rice and tomatoes and eggs, refried beans, coffee.

I was going to stop at Pizza Tomate, but I spied Indigo lounging in the shade on the little terrace with Perry and a group of friends. She called out to me as I passed, but I ignored her and scurried on as if I was none the wiser, which, in truth, I wasn't.

Farther down, I discovered a little shit-hole shack across from the town's rundown soccer field. The place was called Burger Rancho and it was staffed —almost exclusively—with friendly Belgians. It had no walls and was right on the road. Everything was coated in dust. I sat down and drank an Imperial and struck up a conversation with two men—a scrawny Israeli man named Danny and Aldo, a young, ruggedly handsome Belgian who I initially mistook for an Italian—at the table beside me

There were only eight little tables in the place, all rickety and surrounded by mismatched chairs. There was a little TV, though, that hung from the ceiling in a little box. The whole hour I was there Danny and Aldo sat at the center table smoking joints and watching soccer. They spoke to each other mostly in English. I can't remember how it happened, but at some point in our chat they said if I'd come sweep the floor and hose down the dust in front of Burger Rancho, then they'd pay me with an ice cream or beer.

I went ahead and swept the place and hosed down the road and Aldo gave me another beer. Danny was gone and Aldo put his hand on my shoulder and said I seemed to be the good kind of American. He asked if I'd like to see his house.

We crossed the street and went up the hill a sandy block or two and he showed me the little two-story house.

"The whole staff lives here," he said. "We sleep on the floor and in hammocks. Even now Martijn and Massimo are experimenting with bagel recipes." He took me inside and introduced me to Martijn and Massimo— both friendly and curly-haired Belgians. I sat in the kitchen and they tried out their different bagel sprinklings on me. I ate five or six bagels with different toppings straight from the little oven and gave out grades.

"Poppy seed is my favorite," I said, my mouth full of it.

Aldo slapped my back fairly hard and laughed. "You must see my vegetables!"

He opened two beers and went into the yard and pointed out all the different things he'd planted. Whenever he came to something that wasn't doing well, he'd bitch about how the spot his *jardinero* had picked for the raised beds was too much in the shade. A blonde, topless girl was sunning herself in a lawn chair just beyond the garden.

"That is my girlfriend, Océane," he said. "But you should see my spinach."

He pointed to a row of leafy plants that looked yellow and blighted.

"These seeds I smuggle from Belgium in my shoe," he said. He rolled a joint and offered it to me. "You try? Is no problem."

"No thanks," I said appreciatively.

He laughed and said, "Because you are high on life. I get it!"

"No, no," I said. "I've come here for a vision."

"This will give you visions, my friend."

I waved him off. "I must be clear-headed, Aldo, for this vision will come and go in an instant."

"Okay," he said, "but men come here for one of two reasons: the waves or a girl. You are sure of this vision?"

I thought of Indigo. I didn't want to, but I did. The color of her lips, the delicate bridge of her nose, the shimmer of her fine hair.

48

When I returned to camp that afternoon, Rosa was gone and Santana Montana was breaking scavenged limbs into firewood.

"Where is Rosa?" I asked.

"I gave her money for groceries."

"Do you think that is wise?"

"We must give her trust and responsibilities. Come and look at this." He went over and retrieved his notebook and sat on the log. I sat beside him and he showed me all the work he and Rosa had done throughout the day.

The notebook contained sketches of tree bark, blossoms, nuts, and plants with the names written below them. They'd done the same with the wildlife —an iguana, a troupe of howler monkeys moaning in the trees, some white-faced capuchins, even a coati, a boa, and a deadly bushmaster. And they'd pressed leaves and flowers in the notebook, too, and surrounded them with notes.

"That's not your elegant handwriting," I said. "Looks like an elephant tried to write in Spanish." He raised his eyebrows reproachfully.

"Rosa is helping," he said. I put my arm around him because I was touched. It was very much as if he were some intrepid ecologist and she his little assistant—though, truth be told, she was much more of a natural leader than he was. I told him as much but he seemed more bothered by my comment than pleased.

"What's wrong?" I asked.

"I am perplexed." He told me that stray dogs had followed Rosa around and licked at her fingers. This confused him. They didn't do this to him. I laughed and said it was because she was so lovely, so sweet. He seemed to get uncomfortable and I thought, though I might have been wrong, that he was blushing.

"Yes, well," he said. "She kicks at them and tries to pinch their ears."

"And still they follow?"

"Still," he said. Then he asked me if I was thinking of her.

"Who?"

"The tall girl with heterochromic eyes. You know who I mean."

"Yes," I said.

He said that he and Rosa had seen her on the shore and that she and her male friend from the ferry at Paquera had helped them identify a tree that wasn't in their book. "It was a *pau-brasil*," Santana Montana said. "They have smaller thorns than the *pachote*. She said the whole of Brazil is named for this tree. It's invasive here. That is why it was not in my book." He rubbed his arm. "Rare," he said.

"What?"

"Such a mixture of beauty and intelligence."

"That's great," I said. I pinched my nose and sighed heavily. Santana Montana studied my face. He looked off toward the beach.

"You should stop thinking about her," he said. "She and her friend appear to be a couple."

"I know," I told him, "but that doesn't help anything, does it?"

"No," he said. "Not with a girl such as that." A little breeze brought the scent of ocean to us and stirred the leaves and in the distance we heard the call of geckos and dogs barking.

"The problem," I said. "Is that down deep, she is like me."

"I'm sorry," he said. "No one is like you."

That evening back at camp would have been pleasant with the sound of waves in the distance, sparks flitting up from the heat like fireflies, and Santana Montana reading through his notes as darkness descended on our remote peninsula like a heavy curtain, except for the fact that Rosa had never returned. It was nearly amusing, the way Santana Montana was growing slowly and quietly enraged.

By the time she returned, I'd fallen the hell asleep with my head on the Dextra. What woke me was Rosa yelling, "*Dictador gordo!*" at Santana Montana.

I sat up and spied them a ways off in the ghostly, flickering trees. Santana Montana made gestures as if he was demanding something of her or pleading with her. It wasn't until they'd come into the firelight that I saw how wild and bloodshot Rosa's eyes were. The center of them shone like the skin of blackberries and there were streaks of dust on her face where her tears had dried.

She held a surf shop boutique bag that overflowed with clothes and kept shoving Santana Montana away with her free hand.

"*El demonio me perseguía!*" she yelled at him. I heard Anit's name and asked Santana Montana what had happened.

"She is saying the man from the bus was pursuing her," Santana Montana said. "She had to run up into the *colinas*. But she is drunk. I can smell it. And she has bought all of these clothes with our grocery money." At the mention of Anit, I looked out into the dark trees and around the little fires at the other campsites. I half expected him to be standing silently at the edge of our campfire. Either Santana Montana did not buy her story or, perhaps he felt it necessary to confront Rosa on the dangerous situation she had put herself in. In any event, Rosa did not like what Santana Montana was saying and it wasn't long before Rosa was screaming at him.

Santana Montana was holding his arms out in front of Rosa as if he were explaining his position, pleading for Rosa to comprehend the logic in it.

"*Fue estúpido,*" he said pointing to his temple, "*y peligroso.*"

I turned my back to them to give them some privacy and that's when it happened. I heard a loud slap and turned to see Rosa making for our tent and Santana Montana holding his fleshy cheek in pain. I'd never seen him look so furious.

49

I emerged from my tent in the morning to find the campfire dead and black on the ground with Santana Montana sitting sullenly on one side of it and Rosa in a crisp moss green beach cover-up on the other.

I shrugged and went over and sat beside Rosa on the log. A tag hung from the sleeve of her shirt. Without a word she leaned all her little frame against me, so I put my arm around her and whispered, "It's okay, little Rosa. I know. I know all about it, honey." I hummed an improvised tune.

"Rosa," I whispered. I pointed across the fire pit at Santana Montana. She looked at him impassively. "Rosa, he likes you. He cares for you. Do you understand? He only wants to help you, honey." I stood up slowly. I stretched, reaching toward the sky. I felt my muscles stretching in my arms; my hips felt thin and springy. I slumped my arms and looked down at her broad nose, the little point of her chin. "Go and make up with him," I said quietly, nodding in Santana Montana's direction. "Go on, little monkey. It's the right thing to do, isn't it? Go little honey. I know all about it. Go on." She shook her head at me but it was not a resolute response. It seemed more to me that she knew I was right.

I realized, of course, that she didn't know what I was saying, but I knew she knew what I meant. I knew she was sweet because dogs followed her where she went, and dogs are the best readers of people. But she was wounded. We all were, but Rosa's wounds showed how silly ours were. I offered her my hand, gave her my hound dog eyes. "Please, Rosa?" I begged. "Please, honey?"

Reluctantly she put her small hand in mine and allowed me to pull her up. She weighed nothing and her small fingers felt like the brittle ribcage of a wounded fox cub. Great sadness moved through me, but also hope. Great hope. I sat back down on the log and watched Rosa go silently to Santana Montana, watched him set his book aside and speak to her as she settled down beside him. They looked at the ground as they spoke quietly, their heads slightly inclined toward one another.

The breeze stirred in the gray *almendros* above. Here and there I caught the movement of Halloween crabs against the pale, ghostly sand, their colors strange, exotic, as they made one last scavenge before the heat drove them into shadows.

There are so few things that are touching—that are *really* touching.

I shut my eyes. Morning was opening herself in the treetops now and somewhere a hot air balloon was floating like a jellyfish in the sky. Somewhere two people had just missed each other. Somewhere a radio had been left on. You could hear the music clearly from the right terrace in Italy, if you were there. You were not there, of course. Neither was I, but still it played.

50

Santana Montana went into town to buy some supplies and Rosa and I went down to see what the tide had brought in. We collected limpet shells in the strand line debris and slid them on a length of twine. By far the most prevalent trash was bottlecaps, and I suggested we collect those, too. A big piece of ship hull had washed up and I dragged it back toward our camp with Rosa sitting on top until I saw something glinting and went over to it. It was a child's watch half-buried in the sand. There was water in it and the face of it was a cartoon of Sponge Bob Squarepants. I gave it to Rosa and she put it on her wrist and smiled at me.

"It's nothing," I told her. "There's so much I wish I could do for you."

A stretch of pelicans rustled overhead and the shimmering water blinked from dark to light as they passed under the bright sun. Then, the water lay as it had before.

When we got back, Santana Montana had returned with food and colored pens. He said that Rosa would set out with him to make sketches and collect specimens down near the channels. I told him I planned on walking the beach.

He looked at the Dextra.

"What about your board?"

"It'll be fine," I said. "Besides, if someone steals it, I'll just follow the drag marks in the sand to their doorstep."

We made plans to meet for dinner at Meli Melo, and then I watched them fondly as they ambled off through the *ceibos*.

I leaned the hull against one of the *ceibos* and piled the bottlecaps beside it. I pulled the board over so that it was between our tents and then walked off down the beach in the opposite direction to search for that spot where my vision would unfold, but I saw nothing. Of course, it'd only been a day, but I was a little worried. Playa Santa Teresa was not like the beach in the photo we carried. Yet I felt some pull to stay, to give the area just a bit more time.

Later in the day, the heat drove me up into the shoreline shade in a stand of *almendros* and I watched the surfers. They were small, dark forms on the face of waves twice their height. I heard the call of a familiar voice and looked over to see Indigo and Perry jogging down the beach with their short-boards tucked under their arms. Perry knelt to wax his board and Indigo ran past him, leapt over a little breaker in the wash up, and went paddling out swiftly into the teeth of those curling monsters.

I noticed Perry had paused mid-stroke with his wax to watch her. He watched until she was through the breakwater and had duck-dived cleanly through the big sets.

I had meant to get back to camp, but I found myself transfixed by Indigo as she dropped in on wave after wave. I appreciated the clean and efficient lines she cut along the face of the wave and admired how adeptly she navigated the watery violence in the paddle back.

Two hours had passed by the time she came skimming in on one of the little breakers, her body drenched and the light turning the beads of sea water on her tan shoulders and the backs of her long legs into flecks of pure, brilliant gold. She emerged from the water to whistles and calls from a group of local men smoking pot beneath a copse of playa palms. She didn't acknowledge them but turned and walked back up the beach. There was something silent and reserved about the way she carried herself, something regal, dignified.

51

Meli Melo Restaurante was a red house right set back from the dusty main road. Santana Montana and Rosa had not arrived, so I ordered a beer and drank it slowly. The owners were French and had their newborn daughter in a little swing beside the door to the kitchen.

As the mother cooked, she sang to the little imp from the open kitchen.

"*La queue dans la poussière,*" she cooed sweetly, "*Il s'en allait combattr' les éléphants-*"

Suddenly Rosa came skipping up excitedly from the road with Santana Montana bumbling along awkwardly behind. She rushed over and crushed my head against her in a hug and then began speaking excitedly. She used wild hand gestures. She made a face like a monster and bared her teeth as Santana Montana came up to the table wheezing slightly and sweating like a cold jug of milk left out on a countertop.

"*Era cocodrilo grande,*" Rosa exclaimed, "*y pensé que estaba muerto!*" She pointed to Santana Montana and smiled such a sweet smile I thought I would die. She patted his shoulder. Santana Montana rolled his eyes and sighed heavily as he slouched into the chair across from me.

"For the love of god, Santana Montana," I said, thrilled to see Rosa so excited about something, "tell me what the little angel is saying!" So he told me how he and Rosa had walked south along the shore to identify and sketch birds down at one of the tidal channels where a creek cut across the beach to the sea and Rosa had lost her footing and tumbled down on a sandbar at the edge of a freshwater bowl and came face to face with a big croc that was sunning itself there.

"Jesus," I said amazed.

"Rosa sketched an excellent boat-billed heron," he said.

"*Corrió hacia él,*" Rosa said excitedly and pointed at Santana Montana, who kept his face impassive, "*el grande monstro!*" She had sat down, too, but her whole body seemed to writhe with agitation.

"Yes," Santana Montana said soothingly, "but I was not so brave to chase it away. It was a caiman," he explained. "Not a croc." He looked at Rosa. "*Se trataba de un caiman.*"

"What's the difference?" I asked.

"*Caiman* will run from people," he said. "Crocs will eat them."

"That's it?" I asked. "You mean you jumped down there without knowing which it was?"

"It was just a *caiman*," he said with the slightest note of pleading in his voice.

52

I was shocked the next morning to step from my tent and see Indigo standing just outside. There were beads of water on her and she was holding the short board horizontally with her arms stretched behind her to press the board gently against her slender back. All her weight was on her right leg like she'd been waiting a while. She was wearing a white bikini and her sea-tangled hair hung over her shoulders in a lustrous mane. She looked like a wild, untamed girl who had never suffered under a brush or been tortured into a dress.

"Hey," she whispered. She peered past me to Rosa who was curled up in the center of the tent. Rosa snored lightly in little clicks and whirs.

I glanced at Rosa and then back at Indigo. I lowered the tent flap and we walked to the fire pit.

"What are you going to do with that girl?" she asked.

"I don't know."

"Where did you find her?"

"Don't ask," I said. "I'm not sure how it all happened."

"Is she…"

"She's an angel," I said. "I'm going to protect her. Santana Montana and I are and no one is going to bother her ever again. Not ever."

"Okay," Indigo said. She searched my face.

"You wore a bikini on purpose," I said.

"I'm at the beach," she said. "I've been out surfing. It's best when no one is there."

"Isn't Perry usually there?"

"Yes," she said. "But sometimes I wish he wasn't. Things used to be different."

"I'm sorry," I said.

"It's okay. I came because I have a present for you."

"Where?" I asked.

"At the house," she said.

"Lead the way."

She nodded at the Dextra Classic. It looked like the carcass of a sea creature that'd washed up between our tents in the night.

"That yours?"

"Nope. No."

We walked up the beach. No one was out yet. We walked shoulder to shoulder. I felt troubled, confused. We didn't touch, but I felt like I was holding her hand. She turned to go up to Mrs. Engdahl's.

"This is your house?" I asked, rubbing my eyes.

"My mother's," she said. She laughed. She put her hands on my shoulders and turned me around. She looked me over and I felt myself flush. I glanced down at myself.

"What?" I asked.

"Will you come with me to the guesthouse?" she asked.

"Yes," I said, very seriously. "I will come with you to the guesthouse, Indigo."

The guesthouse was just beyond Mrs. Engdahl's main house and looked to be a converted garage. I followed Indigo in and saw straight off that the guesthouse was just a very large bedroom. She turned on a weak lamp beside the bed and the room was flooded with pale orange light and long, dark shadows. There was a blue tapestry with waves and a dolphin hanging over the bed. On the table I saw ribbons, a legal pad, and a coffee cup full of pens, pencils, and feathers.

I was finding it difficult to breathe properly. Indigo went over and opened a teak closet on the far wall. I couldn't see what she was doing behind the door and wouldn't have been surprised if she'd pulled out a pound of cocaine or a negligee. I waited there, rocking slightly on my bare feet and humming quietly. I was happy in that moment of not knowing, in that moment of enormous and gentle curiosity. She stepped from the closet and walked over holding swimming trunks in one hand and a folded shirt in the other.

"Here," she said. "My brother's about your size."

"Where is he?" I asked.

"San Jose. He's sick of all the tourists here and how the drug scene is getting. I heard some of the girls talking about the hot American on the beach who dressed like a bum. I thought I'd help you out."

"Help me out with what?" I asked, glancing down at my stained shirt and equally filthy jean shorts. I knew jean shorts were the least cool thing a guy could wear—especially cut offs—I just couldn't be bothered to worry over what was cool and what was not.

"With that," she said, pointing at my clothes.

"Oh my god," I said. "You feel sorry for me. For the way I'm dressed."

"Yes," she said. "You can't swim in cut off jeans. The humidity down here will soon rot them off."

I didn't say a word but stripped down. It was very kind of Indigo, and I wanted to show her I wasn't insulted by her honest appraisal of my attire.

"Oh," she said. "You're just going to do that here." She tossed the clothes at me and turned away. She stood there waiting with her hand holding the elbow of her other arm behind her back. I put on the spiffy surfing shorts. I shook the shirt loose and felt a lump form in my throat. It was her shirt from the plane, the *Catch On* shirt that I'd so desperately wanted. The shorts were a perfect fit but the shirt was very tight on me so that my biceps bulged from it and I could make out the muscles in my abdomen. When I was finished, I stood there studying her back, the long black hair still wet from the sea, the strong, yet supple shape of those smooth shoulders. I wanted to braid her long hair or come upon her washing her face in a stream or floating in it with her dark hair tendriling in the water and silently, humbly back away.

Finally, I said, "You turned from me."

"You mean while you dressed?" she asked. "Yes, well, I *am* a missionary. Didn't you say that?" She turned around then and met my gaze. The orange light made her eyes deep pools of brown and hazel and green—pools I longed to bathe in and so much more lovely than the rock pools I'd seen in Hawai'i and along the coasts of all those foreign places where romance novels are not written but take place.

"You're no missionary," I said. "But you are a prude. That means there's hope for you," though I didn't know at all what I meant.

"*Yo no creo en Dios*," she said. "I believe in the majestic improbability of it all, though I accept the scientific logic that is undoubtedly behind everything."

I felt something move in me, perhaps a tightening of the perceived intimate similarities that I believed existed between us.

"People say how we formed from dust and return to dust as if it's amazing, but the crazy thing," I told her, "is that our solar system formed from a rotating disc of gas, mainly of hydrogen and helium and what not, and the center of the disc was where the sun formed. You must know, of course, how planets formed from the remainder of the disc and in the inner part of the disc, grains of dust formed which had a mainly rocky composition, and the rocky dust gathered together to form larger bodies and eventually they combined to form the terrestrial planets and all and so forth. Amen."

She said she did and I told her how, in a sense, the whole universe came from dust and so, too, the solar system, and so, too, the Earth and from the Earth's dust came forth living things, which were all just outgrowths of the universe's natural processes as much as stars and planets. I'd used my hands a bit too energetically as I'd talked. I crossed my arms, worried she might laugh at me but she didn't.

"Yes," she said quietly. "One only has to look at the similar bone structures of the vertebrates."

"Exactly!" I exclaimed. "Fish fins are bird wings are the leg of a lamb, the hand of man!" Then I told her—not because she didn't know it, but because I was aching to articulate and confirm what I was sure was our shared understanding—how man came forth and looked back at all the *coming forth* and asked *how* and asked *why* and it was exactly the same as the universe asking itself *how am I, why am I, what am I?* There was no difference and it meant man was not alone because he is not set apart.

"Yes," she said. "Because we are an outgrowth just like all other naturally occurring things."

I longed to take her in my arms, to kiss her neck and drape her intellect over me like a cloak. I was thankful to find someone who understood that the improbable science and logic of everything was more original in its *mysticality* than anything that had come before.

"This shirt, though." I held up my arms. "Does this mean I was mostly right when I told you about your past on the plane?"

"Maybe," she said. She brushed sand from her stomach.

"You love Perry, don't you?" I asked.

She looked up. She looked into my eyes and there was surprise and pain in them. And memories, too.

"Yes," she said. "I do love him."

"I see," I said. I fumbled for something else to say but there was nothing.

"It is complicated. I suppose everything is. But tell me, why have you been avoiding me? I've called out to you but you pretend not to hear me."

What could I say—that I loved her but she loved another?

"I'm on a quest, which is driven by a longing of great intensity," I said. "I cannot afford to be waylaid by trivial matters." I'd not meant for it to sound bad, but I saw on her face that I'd offended her.

"Oh," she said, turning, "I see." She went over and shut the closet. There was nothing else that I could say except perhaps that I felt something for her that thrilled and scared me, so I stayed quiet. She came back over and met my gaze confidently. "The reason, actually, that I've been trying to get up with you is that Perry and I saw your friends yesterday. They said you spent the whole day alone, and I thought I could take you out and introduce you to some of my friends who have noticed you. They're all quite pretty."

"Noticed me where?"

"On the beach. Tai Chi maybe."

"And you'll be there?"

"Yes."

I felt bewildered. She'd seemed stung when I'd equated her calls to trivial matters and that meant—didn't it?—that she liked me. But she was taking me out to set me up with one of her friends and that was a very unsatisfactory thing.

She would be there, though, and I didn't think I could bear being rude to her a second time so I agreed to meet her friends. It seemed silly not to. She told me to come to the D&N around nine.

"It will get really crowded around ten when Niele plays," she said. "Anechka is behind the bar and can point you over to us."

"Anechka—is that Anklebells?"

"Yes. Your Anklebells."

53

I hoofed it on down with Rosa and Santana Montana to Burger Rancho for dinner. I'd told them about my date with Indigo and her friends, and Rosa had not been happy about it. We ordered *casados* from Océane for dinner. From the kitchen Martijn and Massimo waved and puffed at invisible joints in their mouths. I waved back.

"What's this?" Santana Montana asked.

"Nothing," I said. "Just Belgian chicanery." We ate our *casados* in silence. I ordered a beer and then we sat and watched four local children playing on the soccer field under a few sputtering lights. Rosa had her arms crossed like she had the cramps. I asked her if she wanted go and join the footballers.

Santana Montana hadn't even finished translating before the disdain was on Rosa's face.

"*Puedo jugar?*" she asked the air in a shrill, mocking voice.

"*Claro,*" she answered herself in a deep voice.

Again in the shrill sarcastic voice she exclaimed, "*Bueno!—Pásamela! O!*" she screamed, grabbing her little knee in agony. Everyone was looking at us. "*O, me duele!*"

She banged the table with her tiny fist and pointed at me. "*Yo no soy una niña estúpida!*" She crossed her little arms again and glowered at the faces in Burger Rancho until one by one they turned away except for Aldo. His mouth hung open and he was holding his joint in his hand, which had written its red calligraphy across his vacant eyes.

"Jesus, Santana Montana," I said. "What was that act about?" Santana Montana's jaw tightened and he did not look at me.

"She says she does not want to play the games of children," he translated quietly. "She says she is not a child." There was something delicate in Santana Montana's voice, something sad and lost. Aldo came over and asked if we were okay.

"Yes," I said. "I think so."

Santana Montana went up and paid the bill. When he came back I told him I was going to stay at Burger Rancho. It didn't make sense to walk back up to the campsite and then turn around and walk all the way back down to the D&N.

"Okay. Be safe," Santana Montana said. "The guidebook indicates frequent robberies on the beach at night. Return by way of the road." I told him not to worry.

"Look," I said, spreading my arms. "Look how muscular I am." Santana Montana eyed Indigo's shirt critically. "Too tight. It is unfashionable."

"Says the man in the sleeveless sweater. What do you know anyway?" I turned to Rosa. "How do I look, Rosa?"

"*Su novia es una puta,*" she snapped and got up from the table.

"What is wrong with her?" I asked.

"Isn't it obvious," he said, "why she wouldn't want to hear about your evening with other girls?" There was something uncharacteristically bitter in his voice. "Don't you know?"

"Because she loves me," I said. Santana Montana made a sound like a snort.

"It's a curse I have," I told him. "Please don't hate me for it."

54

In the end, I was very late getting to the D&N. I was late because Martijn and Massimo said they were going, too, and that I could ride with them if I waited until they were off, so I waited. Océane brought me a little plate of Belgian cookies and I drank another beer. Then two more for the road. Martijn and Massimo got off on time but then joined Aldo at the table for a toke and then another.

I didn't want to be rude, but it was getting late and the second hand smoke had dried my tongue and scrambled my thoughts. Finally I said, "Look, stay if you want, but I'm already going to be late. We've got to set out now for fuck's sake."

"I agree with the culturally insensitive American," Martijn said.

"Me, too," Massimo said.

"I remain firmly in opposition," Aldo said, "but then again, I am stoned and not going and why would I? Look at my girlfriend there." He waved to Océane across the tables. She was taking an order but wiggled her backside at him playfully. A stray dog with heavy teats sat expectantly at her heel. Aldo blew her a little kiss. Some sort of Brussels clubbing music drifted from a hidden speaker.

"Jesus," I demanded. "What does it all mean?"

It was a long drive all the way the hell down the road to Playa Carmen and the D&N. We turned through a pair of brick columns and drove down to the beach. There was a big crowd and the D&N was so close to the water that it looked as if the whole bar had been washed up on the back shore during a big storm. Everything was outside, too. The big bar area had a thatched roof, and the DJ tower was covered, but otherwise it was all just open under the stars and the elements.

Martijn and Massimo went off to find their friends, and I pushed through the crowd toward the bar. There was a big clock affixed to one of the ceiling beams above the bar and I saw that I was an hour late. Anklebells moved down the line taking orders and darting back to fill them. When she got to me, she smiled and said, "Hey there." She had to yell it so I could hear.

"Where's Indigo?" I yelled.

"Couldn't make it. Some sort of emergency. Chabelita and Aurelia stayed until half past and then figured you were not coming. They left for La Lora's. Niele is still here, though." She pointed out Niele to me through the crowded bar. There was a concrete platform for dancing flanked by the three-story tower where a DJ spun the music behind a big glass window. The dance floor was already packed and that's where I saw a bright yellow smear of a girl wave to us. She came over and sat on the barstool beside me. She was a petite, pretty girl with golden, sun-kissed hair, blonde eyelashes, blue eyes and bright red lips the color of a cardinal's breast.

"Did Neche tell you that it is just us?" she asked.

"Yes, she said there was an emergency. Is Indigo okay?"

"Oh, she is fine. Someone else and she go to help but don't worry—you are in good hands with me. *Aš gerai rūpintis jumis šį vakarą.*"

Niele really did her best to put me at ease. We did the obligatory chat about where we were from and how it was we'd come here. I learned that she was Lithuanian and had come for the surf and to teach yoga at Milarepa. We shouted into each other's ears over the music and the din of all the merrymaking.

"Hey," she exclaimed at one point, "you don't wear shoes, either!"

I told her how they'd been stolen and that's about when Anklebells started sneaking us shots. The first few tasted like rum but the fourth shot was dark.

"What is it?" I asked.

"Does it matter?" Anklebells asked. A group of guys were waving money from the other side of the bar trying to get her attention.

"Thanks, Neche," Niele said after she took her shot. She wiped her chin with the back of her hand then leaned over the bar and kissed Anechka on the lips. The people at the bar cheered. The man beside me slapped my back in a congratulatory way. Anechka winked at me and slid over to the guys who had been yelling for her. "We're roommates," Niele yelled into my cheek. "I love that girl. You've got to dance with me," she said. Anechka returned and invited me to come with them behind the toilets.

I thought it was a strange place to be invited, so I asked Niele what was back there.

"That's where the fun happens," Niele said. I shrugged. Anklebells tossed her little towel to the other girl behind the bar and came around and we went together to the little stand-alone toilets with Anklebells out front and Niele leading me by the hand beneath the stars and swirling music. The concrete was bumpy and cool beneath my feet, covered in a thin layer of sand.

There were a lot of people "making the fun happen" behind the toilets—well, a dozen or so. A couple of groups were passing joints around and Massimo waved to me.

"*¿Quieres tener una cortina de humo?*" he asked. He was waving a huge joint at me.

"No thanks, my friend." I was a little stoned already from their second-hand smoke. I told him how it made me laugh at phantoms and shadows, when what I was after was the absolute heart of the nature of reality. I watched his face go blank, but then Niele took my hand and pulled me over to where a group of girls in thin dresses were leaning over a little marble countertop affixed to the back of the bathroom wall. One of them was White Bandana, who'd been sitting beside Perry on the porch at Mrs. Engdahl's. She had her hand on the lean, muscular back of a tan, shirtless guy. Even though the guy was leaning over the little counter, I knew by the shape and color of his back and legs that it was Perry. It wasn't until I saw him that I realized I had been thinking that the emergency had something to do with him.

"*Yo uso de vez en cuando,*" Niele explained. "But I'll be straight for the show."

"Right," I said, giving her the thumbs up.

Perry straightened. He threw his head back, snorted loudly, then pinched his nose. White Bandana put her arms around his neck and kissed him hard and deep. Niele giggled and put her arm around me.

"If you do a line with me," she said, "our night will go better than you could imagine." Perry looked back at us. He looked at Niele and then at me again. His eyes all blurry and his hair a mess. I was too offended that he would cheat on someone like Indigo to say a word. He put his arm around White Bandana and laughed. I watched them make their way out to the crowded dance floor.

Though I wanted very much to leave, Niele insisted I dance with her. She led me through the people then turned and smiled at me with her eyes bright and mischievous, full of promises. She was a pretty girl, striking in fact, and her voice was the color of the same rue in bloom that poor, mad Ophelia had strewn about. Just the same, though, I didn't much care for dancing. But I'd had a few shots and felt that I owed Niele something though I didn't know why. So, I moved my legs and arms to the music and turned around and hopped up and down a bit with her in what I hoped—but only half-heartedly—was passable dancing. I even smiled, and that was big of me considering how I didn't like music or dancing and how I very much wanted to go on back to my tent. Part of the reason I was having a bad time was that I was crestfallen at Indigo's absence and unsettled by Perry's infidelity. Also my feet were getting scraped and stomped in the crowded space, and I kept worrying over Rosa, whether she was cold and lonely for me.

I suppose my feigned happiness was too convincing, though, for soon Niele's lovely, scrawny frame was rubbing up against me.

"*Bailas excelente,*" she said warmly into my ear. I wondered if she were subtly mocking me, but then she got her arms around my neck and got to squeezing my buttocks a bit more than was necessary. The very next song Anechka came from behind the bar to dance with us, and I was caught between them on the packed dance floor with all of us sweating and moving and the music rippling overtop of us like a snapping red flag while they writhed against me.

When the music stopped again, Anechka whispered in Niele's ear and Niele pulled me down and kissed my mouth. Then Anechka said, "I want to do that, too," and she turned and kissed me. Once more I felt strangers slapping my back and yelling encouragement.

"I've done nothing," I told them, but they didn't care.

"I'm up for my set," Niele said into my face. "Don't move your sexy ass from this spot!" That little tigress winked right at me, and I was positive just then that if she got me in a bed—if they both got me in bed—I'd be a broken man in the morning.

The brain-drubbing baseline of the dance music still echoed dully in my head as Niele made her way over to a stool that was on the edge of the dance floor. Some of the revelers made for the bar to get a beverage but most of them sat on the concrete before Niele as she tuned her guitar. She plugged in to a little amp as the DJ set up the microphone and then she was coaxing out haunting notes from her acoustic guitar with her small, delicate fingers.

Her songs were in her native language, so I didn't know what they were about but they were slow and quiet, crumbling in on themselves in a way that was like hearing long-dead girls talking in darkened corridors about the people they had dearly loved. Her playing had the exact opposite tone and feel to the high-energy, fast-talking girl from a moment before, and even the color of her voice mellowed. I was struck and pleased by the contrast and felt I knew then why Indigo might have thought Niele would be a good match, though she was still wrong to have thought it.

More people gathered at her feet as her guitar quieted the spirited Costa Rican air. I felt a hand on my arm.

It was Martjin. There was a joint in his mouth and a serious look on his face.

He put his lips to my ear. "Next week Massimo and I go to a meditation retreat in the high mountains. No roads. Must climb the mountain first. Rice only and no talking. Complete silence for nine days. You will come, yeah? It will change your life. Massimo will come round to collect you."

I opened my mouth to reply but he placed the joint in it, pushed my mouth gently shut with his thumb, and kissed me on the cheek. Anklebells came and put her arm around my waist and through the smoke in my eyes I watched Martjin move up front to sit with Massimo at Niele's feet.

"Niele likes you," Anklebells said, her Russian accent pulling the English words in strange directions. "Listen. She is talented, no? She thinks you are very sexy. I can tell. She will come to your tent tonight, if I say. She is attracted to you. Maybe I come, too?" She laughed. I didn't know if she was joking or not. I decided she wasn't. "Or," she went on, "you could come to disco night on Wednesday. Massimo and Martjin wear these incredible outfits. Belgians are the best. Very sexy. Great music and great crowd—more drugs and beautiful people than tonight."

"What does D&N mean?" I asked, passing her the joint.

"*Day and Night.*" She smiled at me and for no reason at all I could see the history of her entire country behind her eyes—the wars and the hardships, transitions, concrete slums jutting out of all that snow. I could see the people living and dying in big coats and those bulbous, golden buildings in Moscow that thin to sparkling spires—the ones you always see glimmering in the background of tourist's photos. I knew that she'd found the opposite of that life here, that she'd wanted exactly that.

"How many languages do you speak, Anklebells?"

"Four."

"You're a genius," I said.

"Maybe," she said shyly, "but I am also not so smart."

"I know exactly what you mean," I said.

Anklebells was called back to the bar and took the joint with her. Above me the stars were bright. Niele's haunting voice pulled threads taut in my heart, and I was suddenly tired, lost and ready for oblivion. I turned and walked quickly down to the beach, heading back in the direction of Santa Teresa. There were no quads or cars to kick up tornados of dust, but I covered my mouth with Indigo's shirt just to suffer what her scent did to me.

It must have been the fact that I was half stoned and drunk or moping about Indigo that made me forget Santana Montana's warning about the dangers of Nicoyan beaches at night. I walked along in the cool run-up oblivious, enjoying how the wash back tickled the foam over my toes. I didn't register the footfalls behind me until the board had cracked over the back of my head.

I was lying on my back in the sand. A dark figure blocked out the stars. His shoulders were bags of concrete mix. Hands patted down my clothes. I saw inky women and girls ghosting over the heavily muscled, outstretched arms. I heard the faint, dry shaking of a baby rattle, and then everything went black.

I must have fallen out of time for a while for I was lying in the wash-up but I was simultaneously walking through palm rows in Limón toward the Mercado Municipal. A string of red taxis along the park, ahead of me an open-air market full of cashews, leather items, silver jewelry, wooden boxes with hidden compartments. Two monstrous cruise ships made ridges of light in the distant skyline, and Santana Montana was telling me about the mating habits of the two-toed sloths that lived in the Parque Vargas trees. But how could that be, for wasn't Limón on the other side of the country? Yes, but I knew then that I was seeing through the eyes of another version of me. A *me* who had headed to the other coast. It was only through decoherence that I was cut off from all those me's. Was there no way to bridge the divide, to make all of me *whole, to make it all cohere*?

I don't remember waking from that vision, or going the rest of the way up the beach to our tent. I do remember rain and crawling in beside Rosa, but then all was dark again.

55

A downpour roused me in the night, and I felt Rosa's trembling embrace. Thunderclaps shook the tent. We were both wet.

"It's okay, Rosa," I whispered. "It will pass."

I stroked her head where she lay. There was a raw ache in my neck and a cold spot on the back of my scalp, but Rosa was a balm. Our scent mingled and hung in the heated damp of the tent. Water dripped through little runs in the tent fabric as the thunder trundled off to the south.

All Things Await

224

56

I awoke to Rosa's shrill scream and the tent aglow with morning light. She was still in my embrace, but sitting up and twisted at the hips to look at me. My first instinct was that the rain had driven a scorpion into the tent, but then I saw the blood.

Santana Montana tore through the flap and thrust his head in. Blood was on my arm. On Rosa's too. I thought of my mother. Of the pool of it she'd found Margie and me in.

"Don't scream," I said weakly, "or you'll never be the same."

57

It was high tide, so we had to make the walk south to Playa Carman along the road instead of the beach. My feet were bare and I had to pick my way gingerly. Santana Montana and Rosa walked on either side of me, as if at any moment I might stagger or go stumbling headfirst into the rocky ditch. And perhaps I would have.

I'd bled quite a bit. Much of it was on Rosa's shirt and skirt. My legs wobbled, and I pressed the hand towel Santana Montana had given me firmly to the back of my head, but I was not unhappy. The air was pungent with the scent of breakfast *casados* and coffee.

We passed the little concrete school and followed the rutted road where it split the old soccer field from Burger Rancho. The field stood empty. A troupe of howler monkeys moved through the canopy, sounding their primitive howls.

It took all of an hour for us to get to Dr. Jorge de Carlos Campos' office in Playa Carman. The blinds were drawn and the door was locked. There was a big sign with an arrow pointing to a doorbell. Rosa pushed the button. She kept her finger on it until the doctor himself appeared in the doorway.

He was a big *tico* with powerful shoulders and a gut that only alcohol could account for. He had a wide face, big prominent nose and wore a white t-shirt that was decidedly unclean. His meaty legs and arms were dotted with patches of white, dry skin and he wore old flip-flops that had nearly rotted off his big, coarse feet, which were, I saw, covered with corns and thick yellow calluses.

He gave our little band a slow going over with eyes that were shiny with alcohol. We must've appeared as a strange assortment, each of us in our type and degree of suffering. It wouldn't have surprised me if he'd just shut the door slowly in our faces, but he didn't.

He waved us in.

"Listen," I told him, but he held his finger to his mouth and motioned for me to turn around. As I turned, he moved my hand and peeled away the towel. He smelled lightly of sugarcane liquor, but it was not stale. The scent was crisp and fresh. He turned my head this way and that.

"Tut, tut," he cooed softly. While he examined me a little white poodle with bows in its hair came trotting out to sniff at me. He shooed it away. It skittered over to lick at Rosa's fingers, and I worried for a moment that she might send it sliding across the floor with a vicious kick, but she was too busy worriedly rubbing a hole in my back with the palm of her hand. She meant well.

"I wish I could speak Spanish," I said. "I would tell you that you are my kind of doctor exactly."

"Relax," he said. "I practice in Houston for thirteen years. As you know, I speak English, okay? So don't hurt yourself fumbling with Spanish. Take some lessons maybe." His voice was deep, decidedly local, but clear and he was obviously adept at English.

"Is it bad?"

"Not so bad. But I will need to suture you. No!" he yelled aiming a kick at Sparkles, who had been sniffing at the backs of my knees with her cold nose. "Sorry," he said. "I hit Sparkles because I want that Sparkles should be a better dog."

"I understand."

He muttered something unintelligible and pushed my head down again so that I stared at his desk. There were trilobite fossils on it and a Houston, Texas calendar. On the little staticky television behind it, Raphael Nadal was playing at Wimbledon.

We left Rosa and Santana Montana in the reception area, and he led me down a narrow hall into a back room. There was a little examination bed and I sat on it with my back to him.

He disappeared for a bit and then returned, wheeling a little tray before him.

"Okay," he said, "so pay attention." I turned. He was holding what looked like scissors. "This is the needle driver." He held his other hand up. "This is the suture needle."

"Why are your hands shaking so terribly?" I asked. He looked at them.

"Well, that is a problem," he said. "My assistant is asleep in back. She does the suturing but was up all night with a patient."

"You could wake her."

"I will not."

"I trust you, Dr. Jorge. I can tell about people and I know you are a good doctor. Sew away."

His trembling knuckles tap-danced on my skull as he knitted me up. Sparkles lay in the corner licking her groin. The needle didn't hurt at all.

"How did you come to be here?" I asked him.

"As to my family," he said, "they are nearby. I have *mi cama* in back and sleep back in there with Sparkles, but I am home every weekend. I live in Houston all those years while they stay on my *finca*. Better money, you know. Not as many patients."

"I don't want you to think poorly of me," I told him. "I wasn't being an obnoxious American or anything. I was jumped on the beach and knocked in the head."

"Many robberies on the beach these days," he said. "It will be six stitches or seven, but who struck you? How many were there?"

"Just one," I said. "He had tattoos up and down his arm. I think I know him. A man named Anit. I nearly tangled with him before."

"Ah yes," he said. "Anit. Bad news. On the beaches at night. I've seen his signature writ on the skulls of tourists and locals alike."

"He lives here?"

"He lives here, yes. In the jungle on the ridge above Florblanca, just there before the Witch's Hat."

"The what hat?"

"Never mind," he said. "We all know Anit. He is Nico, but his mother lives nearby. She is always sending him out on bus rides all over the country just to get peace. He has killed dogs along the beach. I have to watch Sparkles all the time. Mothers know to call their girls in when he is around. Years ago, they found a young one in the jungle. Her head bashed in. Everyone knew it was him. There's no *policia* here, so they had to send agents from San Jose. Even so, nothing could be proved."

"Ouch. You're hurting me."

"Be braver," he said.

"But that's not tissue; it's skull."

"Oh, yes. So it is." He said there were only three stitches left, but I deeply regretted that his assistant was asleep.

"What happened to the patient?" I asked.

"What?"

"Last night."

"Oh, very sad," he said. "A local wiped out on the rock platform at Mar Azul. Cervical vertebra. I would guess C5. Good man. My assistant stayed with him, kept him immobilized. I could do it, you see, but I was out and very drunk. He has two daughters and they came. Tears and all. I'm no good at that, but Indi stayed up with them until a transport could be arranged. Maybe he will walk. Maybe not."

"Indi? Indigo?"

"You too, eh?" He gave my back a rough slap. "Everyone Indi treats, they fall in love. Everyone I treat, not so. It's unfair, no?"

"She didn't treat me. We were supposed to meet last night. How do you know her?"

He laughed.

"Her father and I go to Colegio De La Salle in San Jose. LC returns a week or two in summers to teach. First and only Latin American astronaut. Can you believe it? We were both in the States, too. We got together some, but then he is so busy. He is at a big university and in business with his magnetic thermal thruster company or whatever the hell it is."

"Yes," I said. "For traveling efficiently in a vacuum."

"Don't be stupid," he said. "For traveling in space. Anyway, he lived here before all that when he was first married and they had Indigo."

"Is that why Indigo comes here?"

"That and the crazy senator's son. Oh, he is a mess. Drinking and drugging when she is gone. Drinking is a fine thing to do but you must do it seriously. Look at me. I have been drinking just now, but I am happy and have everything in my control—except my hands. She comes back and he sulks. It's a pity, but Indigo is not careless. Her mother was careless—loud and loose and ready to laugh. She was lovely, too."

"What happened to her?"

"They were on a DeHavilland Twin Otter. Five passengers and two pilots. It went down near Carara. Wind gusts. Ava had a broken supraorbital, broken mandible, broken teeth—lacerations. Bled to death. Indigo was nine or ten— I forget. She got Ava out of the seatbelt and on the ground. Tried to stop the bleeding. In the morning they found her."

"Jesus."

"What Jesus?" he spat. "Jesus was nowhere to be found." He was quiet for a while, then he said, "Best not to dwell among such ruin. Indi is here and beautiful, and I am happy to have her even if she fusses at my drinking. She is smart and will be a great doctor. No doubt you have seen how the air shimmers where she moves. You boys won't leave her alone. There. Now your head," he said, leaning away. "It will leak blood and pus. This is not a problem."

"How does it look?" I asked, but I was bothered.

"Not good. My hands shake as you have seen. But what is the difference? You have a mess of scars back here."

It was bad news, indeed, but I was not able to feel despair. True, I was haunted and disturbed by the image of Indigo as a child cradling the battered, bloodied face of her mother through the long Costa Rican night, but I also felt light-headed, strangely enlivened, and thrilled by the proximity of something incredible. She'd held the stiffening body of a loved one until that loved one had bled out cold. That had changed her in ways others couldn't understand. I understood. I hurt for her, but she was in medical school and that made me feel a cautious joy. I would need to think about that.

She'd spent the night before tending to a father who'd broken his neck, and I could see her with her hair pulled back leaning over the gurney in a white coat, using her forearms to keep the man's head still, and telling him all the while that everything would be okay. I knew she'd told her mother that same thing in her little, trembling voice. I knew it for a fact.

New dimensions swirled and flowered behind the star in her lovely eye, and I suspected the fine flourish of her scar was really a path that led to worlds where ripe discoveries hung from bursts of bright trees.

Rosa embraced me when I came out front. Santana Montana took out his wallet and paid the charge, but the doc was keeping his eye on the little television.

"Come on, Rafa, goddamn it!" he yelled suddenly at the television. He looked at me and said, "I yell at Rafa because I want Rafa to do well."

"I understand, Dr. Jorge," I said gently touching my wound. I longed to rush into the back of the office, gather Indigo in my arms, and tell her about Perry's infidelity, but I didn't. "You are very much my sort of physician, Dr. Jorge," I said. "I hope to meet you again. Perhaps we could grab a coffee at one of the shops some day."

"Ba!" he spat. "Coffee is poison. We can have beer or some guaro. I will bring Sparkles and she will lie on the table between us. Where do you live?"

I told him, and he said he'd be up that way tomorrow afternoon.

"I'll stop by the camp, and we will have a drink. I will check your stitches. Maybe they'll have flattened out. They won't have, but who knows? I have my little *finca*," he said. "We grow rice. You go on the ferry and then through some *ríos* that have lots of *crocodrilos* to get there. Foreigners are always impressed, but they know nothing. Costa Ricans are educated, peaceful. This is why we stay away from noisy tourists and jingoistic Americans with their Bibles and gun racks. But way out here, bad tourists get weeded out. This area wipes out the unfit and selfish and loathsome tourists. Only the right temperaments can survive this remote area. Maybe I will take you to my *finca*. My wife would be happy to have you visit. You would need to stay a few days."

An old fan oscillated haltingly on the floor, lifted a few papers tacked to the board behind him. Dr. Jorge seemed crazy and brilliant. He seemed like he would have turned Houston on its head all those years. That made me have confidence in him.

"I'd be honored to have a drink with you," I told him. I really meant it, too.

58

Indigo, Indigo, Indigo.

We walked the beach back up toward Santa Teresa and I slagged behind my friends. The tide had turned and was going down. A trail of pelicans swooped along the waterline of a wave crest then curved off over the swells away from the coast, their wings angling in glide, catching and losing the slants of light, but so what?

I'd taken Indigo's name and placed it in a hammock in my mind, and let it swing, swing, swing in the shade of shaggy palms: each "I" a sun-kissed yellow, the "N" like fresh oatmeal in a chipped bowl, the creamy "D" giving way to a rich rubbery tone surrounding "G," and finally the "O" at the end of her name, which glowed with the exact color of an ivory-backed hand mirror.

59

I was raw and subdued the next day. It was a hot one for the wind went lazy and didn't lift a finger to tickle at the leaves. The dense canopy barely moved at all and when it did, it reminded me of the big nets cast by those six fishing boats we saw twinkling just off the peninsula coast at night, how slowly those nets moved in the depths. The clouds stretched like soiled silk and the sun pulsed dimly behind it.

"Cloudy," I said to Rosa and pointed at the sky.

"*Nublado,*" she said and pointed also.

"New-bla-do," I said.

"Clow-dee," she said and smiled.

It was a humid, oppressive heat, so Santana Montana and Rosa and I went down at low tide to lounge in the tide pools. I watched them lounge in their separate tidal tubs—Rosa a delicate sea nymph the retreating water had abandoned there and Santana Montana with the expansive bulb of his soft gut rising from the water like the crowning of some unspeakably brilliant, big-headed child about to come forth into the unsuspecting world. Rosa splashed water across the rocks at him. Santana Montana turned his head, pinched his nose, and squeezed his eyes shut. He just sat there with stream after stream finding his face, and Rosa giggling like a cherub.

She'd been angry at Santana Montana a few times, and it made me happy to know she'd gotten over it. In fact, she was getting better all the time. The time with us had brought out an effulgence in her eyes and even in her skin—no more musty, dank rooms with enseamed beds and nasty styes. It was all sun and sand and salt air for her now. And she was responding to the lack of sexual abuse and the nourishing of her mind that, to be honest, Santana Montana was the sole provider of. I'd even heard him teaching her English, and seen for the first time that bloom of eagerness, a thirst for knowledge that made me feel so warm I wanted to hug myself.

She probably wasn't cleaner in the strictest sense, to be honest, for the traveling had made us stink and everyone's hair was matted and sticky with ocean. Truth be told, Santana Montana and I were both just really awful at personal hygiene, but I knew that bathing in the sea was not bathing at all.

"You know," I told Santana Montana as we walked back to camp a little later, "I've never had the necessary focus to keep up my appearance. But for you," I encouraged him, "there's something beautiful inside you that better hygiene will help reveal. If only the world could see you with my eyes instead of their own. Such beauty they would behold!"

To my surprise, my comment had not elicited his thanks. Instead he seemed angered by my remark and grew suddenly as quiet as a slow-moving cloud. Rosa had to repeat herself to get him to translate for her. He did and she did not laugh, either. Her look suggested gentle concern, if anything.

We walked along collecting plastic bottle caps. She and I had been affixing them to the hull I found to make trash art. Rosa scavenged the strand line, and I walked down at the edge of the runup picking up a few of the brightly colored cobbles that caught my eye. Rosa found a straw hat that had washed up and gave it to me as a gift. Crabs had pinched holes in the top of it but it was otherwise in good shape.

"*Me casaré contigo,*" she said, which I was sure was a comment on the gift.

"Yes. *Sí.* It'll serve me well," I told her. I gave her a hug and stuck the hat upon my head.

We spent an hour working on the plastic bottle top project back at camp, gluing on the tops we'd collected in the shape of a whale. We tired and stood back to look at it. Santana Montana came over and appraised it with us. Rosa had her arms crossed and squinted at our incomplete, multicolored whale on the ship hull, as if pondering the mysteries of some intricate work of post-modern art.

"*No me gusta,*" she said. "*Es una mierda.*"

"I know," I said. "It actually looks amazing."

Santana Montana coughed into his fist. "Well," he said quietly. "It is good to get trash off the beach."

"Wait a minute. Didn't you tell me that *mierda* meant poop or shit?"

He shrugged. His eyes moved subtly in their sockets from our whale to my new hat. A breeze moved through our camp and there was rain in it. Through the limbs I saw summer thunderheads moving up from the south.

We went down to Burger Rancho around lunchtime and visited with Aldo. He and Danny were sharing a *casado.* They were very stoned and watching a tennis match.

We sat down at the table beneath the TV. I asked Santana Montana if he was buying and he said he was, so I ordered a beer for myself and a coke for Rosa when Martijn came by.

Martijn asked Santana Montana if he wanted anything to drink.

"Do you have grape soda?" he asked.

"Massimo!" Martijn called to the other waiter in the kitchen. He asked him something in Belgian. The response came and Martijn said, "I'm sorry but no. Sadly."

"Then no," Santana Montana said. "*Agua, por favor.*"

I asked Santana Montana if he wanted to play the *Genius* game. I explained how you went back and forth with the combatants saying obscure and brilliant facts until somebody ran out of genius things to say.

"Okay," he said. He translated to Rosa and then said, "You will lose." His voice was sharp at the edges and he was sweating terribly. It rolled down his forehead in rivulets and his sweater was stained at the pits.

It was a difficult and tricky contest to be sure. I said that our solar system formed forty-six thousand million years ago.

"There are eight-hundred species of trees in the Amazonian Rainforest," Santana Montana countered.

"Over the span of your life, your skin will entirely replace itself nine hundred times," I said.

"There are three thousand species of butterflies in the Amazon," he said.

"Our solar system orbits the nuclear bulge every two hundred and forty million years."

"A cell is the smallest unit capable of independent existence."

"When hydrogen is converted into helium during nuclear fusion, matter coverts to energy. That is the sun's energy source, my friend."

"There are schools of fish living five miles deep in the ocean with literally tons of pressure bearing down on them."

We went back and forth for half an hour or so, even as we ate our lunch. A stray came over to rest beneath our table, and I rubbed the panting beast and looked at Danny and Aldo. I kept thinking we'd get a group of folks around us, choosing sides and cheering us on, but no one seemed to care at all. Halfway through, Rosa stretched out on the bench I'd sat down on and fell asleep with her head in my lap. Danny ordered another *casado* and Martijn played the Counting Crows yet again over the speakers.

"There's ten thousand times more water in Earth's atmosphere than Venus'," I said.

"Four hundred million years ago the first of our ancestors crawled from Earth's seas," he countered.

I yelled over to Aldo and Danny to see if they wanted to come and listen in, but they waved me off. "We must watch, as the winner of this match will play Rafa in the final, my friend," Aldo said. "Perhaps later."

Then Rosa said something without lifting her head and Santana Montana stiffened visibly. I glanced down at her and she had the sweetest smile on her soft little face. Her eyes were closed, and I wondered whether she was awake at all.

"What did she say, Santana Montana?" I asked.

His lips set, formed a tight line.

"She says that she loves us," he said as if struggling to make his mouth perform properly. "That she loves you and me very much." I believed that both of our chests seized up just then in the grip of some strange, yet shared, emotion.

I suggested that we agree to a draw. We walked back down the road in the unflinching heat and blinding dust. Just the three of us. Our little family.

60

Dr. Jorge came by in the afternoon on a scooter the color of a peach heart. Sparkles was in a little woven basket affixed loosely to the front of the machine. Her tongue was out. Her head lolled crazily and she was gasping like some tiny asthmatic.

"Why do I love such a lazy beast?" he asked. "Look at her tiring from a ride."

"She's probably stressed. How fast do you go with her in that basket? It looks loose."

Dr. Jorge took me to a little local soda up the hill a block that I'd not known existed. We sat down at an uneven table. I ordered an Imperial and Dr. Jorge ordered a glass of Cacique *guaro*.

We talked more of his *finca*. He offered again for me to come and stay for the weekend with his family. He'd brought me a great deal of rice in a paper bag. He placed it on the table and said, "Here. It is from my *finca*. Very good." I thanked him.

Dr. Jorge put Sparkles on our table exactly as he'd said he would. There were strays lying about and I suppose he wanted to keep Sparkles above the fray.

"Do you surf?" he asked.

"Yes, but not well."

"Good." He lay back in his chair and watched as one of the buses groaned down toward the big mango tree at Soda Tuanos with a fresh load of surfers and seekers from distant places.

"I told Indigo you asked after her," he said nonchalantly. "I take it you know each other well."

"No, not really." I felt like he was fishing for something. He studied my face as if he didn't believe me.

"But you like her," he said.

"I suppose," I said, as coolly as I could, but all I could think was how her lips were the color of a rained on raspberry. Not the kind you buy in the store, but the wild ones you come across sometimes on a farm that are swollen and ripe on the prickled stalks and so lush that when you sink your teeth into them their tangy-sweet juices explode on your tongue. "But she's with someone else."

"Only a fool would not like her," he said looking away. He took a long, deep drink of his *guaro*. He sat it aside and leaned across the table on his heavy forearms.

"I think she likes you anyway. I can tell these things. Ha!" He slammed his fist on the table startling Sparkles. "You young people with your secrets and goings on, but I know. Indi said you are smart and her friends come by to complain how you ran when they became sexual on you."

"Well, I…"

"I was in *mi cama* with Sparkles but not asleep. I hear it all and this made me favorable to you." He stroked Sparkles and she settled beneath his touch. "So, I've decided you should ask her out—not to some bar. Don't be stupid! She is smarter than you, but what does it matter? If you are dumb, it will fail. It may fail anyway."

I wasn't sure how to respond or even if I'd understood him.

"There's Perry, though," I said after a moment.

"Perry is ruined," he said. "She has ruined him, but it is not her fault. His father is a bastard. You let nannies and future ex-wives raise your son and this is what happens." Dr. Jorge pointed to his head and then to his heart. "Perry is weak in these places. He won't be happy unless Indigo is keeping his house and she is too smart for that and even then he would hold her intelligence against her. She is special. That is all."

"Aren't they together?" I asked.

"Did she tell you that? She told you I drink too much, I bet, and how I call her in emergencies. I do drink a little, but I am happy. My mind wanders, my hands shake, but in my heart I don't care."

"But I heard her say she loved Perry. I even asked and she said she did."

"Ha!" he said. "See? She does love him, of course. They grew up together. I remember them knocking iguanas from the trees with sticks and stealing my neighbor's horse to ride to the beach. I spent much time with her father, because he was good to drink and talk with. First in space and all. It's true. Perry was always there—this was after his mother had taken off. Later, the nanny would take him to bring Indigo fruit and flowers in the mornings, but he knew Indi would leave like her father."

"They're not together?" I said, but this time it was like I was testing the idea myself.

"Maybe you are not as smart as I thought," he said. "They are not together. Have you seen him? He is a mess because they are not together. It kills him. I knew his father well—a fool to run our great country. We have no army here—do you know this? Not like you Americans with your guns." A middle-aged *tica* came from around the counter and asked Dr. Jorge if he wanted another glass.

"I have a glass already, Estefania," he said, holding up his empty glass. "What I don't have is a bottle of Cacique *guaro* to fill it with." Estefania hurried off to retrieve a bottle for the doctor. He leaned back and watched her go. "Perry goes around with girls," he said. "Tries to get her jealous. It doesn't work. It breaks Indigo's heart—I see—but she is not jealous. I feel bad for him, but so what? I would feel worse for Indigo were she with such a mess of a man. I tell you this because when I spoke of you, I saw something on her face. It was what was on my face when I first fell for my wife who is on my *finca* and a very fine woman. I am lucky. She is better than I. Taste the rice she has sent and you will know."

"What should I do, Dr. Jorge?" I asked.

"I could come up with a plan that is very brilliant," he said. "When I was in Houston my secretary was in love with another doctor and I arranged things perfectly."

"And they married?"

"No. I don't know. You're not listening. Sparkles! Shut your mouth when you pant. Your breath is killing me. Anyway, I'll mention you want to learn to surf and ask her to give you a lesson. She used to instruct."

"But I've surfed before."

"Maybe you are dumb. Indigo said you impressed LC, so I thought you bright. I am telling you something brilliant and you are worrying over details of honesty." Estefania returned and placed a bottle on the table.

"Okay, Dr. Jorge," I said. "I'll wait and see if she says anything about a lesson, but I don't think she will." He shook his head.

"You young people are so dumb," he said dejectedly. "A few days and she'll be gone. She likes you; you like her." He stood up and so I did, too. He came around and put his big arm on my shoulder and we both stood there looking at the calluses on his wide, ashy feet and he said, "I like you, for what it is worth. I'd be happy to have you like a son." His calves were as thick as my quads, and I had good quads. "But Indi is like my *sobrina*. Hurt her and I will do terrible things. I was not always so kind as this."

241

Sparkles had rolled on her back to show us her spotted belly and her pink tongue hung out upside down. He looked at her contemplatively.

"Sparkles can sense evil," he said. "She likes you, though she is a coward and useless on my *finca*. Indigo needs to break from Perry. You're the timely man. Keep in mind that Perry may try to kill you. This is not unforeseeable."

61

If I'd known how my comments about hygiene would play out that evening, then maybe I would have kept my trap shut. Maybe I wouldn't have.

After I returned from my drink with the doctor, I wanted only to wait in the camp all day, for I felt optimistic and the air around me had a tremulous quality. However, I'd not even sat down before Rosa came up from the beach pulling Santana Montana by the wrist and rather forcefully marched us to the rustic shower area rear of the check-in building. Naturally, it was an outdoor shower—just a rusty pipe sticking out of the side of the building.

She told us to strip down to our skivvies. Santana Montana translated with growing alarm, such that I only caught some of what he translated, mostly about how she was always the one to bathe her little sister because she didn't want anyone else touching her, so she was very good at it. It was a somber thing to hear, no doubt, but there was humor to be found, too, for I don't think I'd ever laughed so hard as I did at Santana Montana's extraordinary discomfort at the idea of stripping down to his underwear in Rosa's presence. There was only four or five years, give or take, between them in age and just the idea of Rosa washing him had turned his cheeks the color of watermelon flesh. Rosa would not be easily denied, though, and she was soon practically wrestling his clothes off of him, for it was pretty clear that she thought we were in need of a major cleaning. Santana Montana was giving me a look as if to say, *Why the hell couldn't you have kept your trap shut?*

"Come on, Santana Montana!" I yelled enthusiastically between bursts of gut-wrenching laughter. "You're like a giant, golden, chunky baby genius, but lord, oh lord do you ever stink to high heaven!"

When he looked at me again, his face bore the stamp of anger, embarrassment and indignation, which only made the whole thing more comical.

"Let her wash you, for god sakes!" I screamed with joy.

But he wouldn't allow it and he scurried away—if a lad of such build might be said to *scurry*—sleeveless sweater in hand, clutching at his shorts, for Rosa was yanking viciously at the back of his pants.

When she finally came back through the green *ceibos* panting heavily and smiling a wild smile through that tangle of dark hair that hung in her face, I stopped giggling right off. She looked so sweet in that single moment, so much like the child she should have been, that my guts felt busted.

She said something to me—in Spanish, of course—and pointed at the gurgling old spigot that was our shower.

"God, you are glorious," I told her, holding up my hands like I was at gunpoint. "You won't get any fight from me." I stripped on down to my boxers and she led me by the hand to the shower. I saw then that she had a bar of soap waiting, though I could not fathom where the little imp had gotten it. She pulled me down, and I sat crossed-legged on the ground beneath the spigot and let that lovely little sprite soap up my back and clean my ears.

She made me raise my arms, so she could scrub my armpits and when she washed my feet, I laughed like I was once more a little boy in the tub with soapy fingers between my toes. As she bathed me, though, I got to thinking on how she'd said she always washed her little sister and—I don't know how exactly—but I was positive I could *feel* in her touch that she was washing me in exactly the same tender way that she had her. Of course, I'd thought about her little sister, wondered if we'd damned her to a worse hell by keeping Rosa with us, but I didn't wonder about it much. I pushed it from my brain each time because I couldn't think of Rosa's little sister without also thinking of little girls who died in wells.

I wondered about her then, though—wondered if Rosa missed her, worried over her. I knew that she did. That led me down a dark avenue of thought. A soap bubble—or something like it—swelled in my throat, and I suddenly *saw* Rosa in the tub of her uncle's rundown apartment in Chepe, saw, clear as day, her little sister there, too. How gently she cleaned her, how slowly she went about it as if to make that moment last longer than all those other moments that awaited her, that had already occurred in dim rooms.

Rosa was talking to me. I didn't know what she was saying, but I could guess.

"Am I crying?" I asked her. "Hell, yes, I'm crying," I said, though *sobbing* was the better word. "I am, Rosa, and I don't know if I'll ever stop."

That night Santana Montana went to bed without a word to Rosa, even though she called to him and teased him mercilessly. And I had stopped crying, because Dr. Jorge had conferred upon me a certain amount of cautious joy. After Rosa retired, I sat by the fire and stared into the flickering red and yellow flames until I heard Santana Montana saying my name in his sleep. I crawled into his tent and shook him gently.

"I am not asleep," he said.

"But you've been in here for hours."

"I know."

"Are you assailed by dark thoughts again?"

"No. Quite the opposite. I must leave," he said. "I was lost when I came, but something happened. I know now what I must do."

"Jeez," I said. "You're thinking of facing him, aren't you?" Santana Montana said nothing. "Forever grappling with the darkest thing in your life ensures entanglement rather than escape, my friend."

"That is only true," he said quietly, "if you do not win."

"You cannot leave," I told him, feeling stung by his words. "The vision approaches."

"What I cannot do," he said, "what *you* cannot do, is stay here forever."

"Right," I said. "You're getting antsy. But we have to go to San Jose and collect Rampage, Crampton, and Biggs in a couple of days, remember? Let's make a deal. If my vision hasn't shown up in two weeks, then we'll head elsewhere. Maybe I'll even come with you."

He sighed heavily, as if the traveling and tent dwelling was suddenly upon him, putting the screws into his overtaxed musculature and twisting them.

"No. I will need to leave. Soon. I am ready now to face what awaits me."

"But what of Rosa?" I asked, going right for the soft spot. He went quiet and I listened to his breathing. It was steady, familiar, comforting in the dark.

"Rosa and I will talk. We will negotiate. The only thing keeping me here is you. I worry over you," he said. "Rosa does, too. You need someone."

It was touching. Having kids like Santana Montana and Rosa worry over me, I mean. I was the one who was worrying over them. They were the ones who needed someone. They needed me. They did.

62

I crawled into my tent and lay down to sleep under the scent of Rosa's soap. Soon after, I felt her snuggle up behind to spoon me.

Her small quest for warmth—and just the thought of being without her—caused that old bubble to rise again in my throat. This time I managed to wrestle it down and couldn't help but gloat a little after such a terrible defeat to it beneath that spitting, cold water.

Not this time you tricky old emotions, I thought, then thought further, *and leave me the hell alone, anyway*.

Feeling clean, sad, and expectant, I fell into the deep, deep sleep of the patently exhausted.

All Things Await

63

That night Niele came to my tent under the cover of darkness. She must have stripped before entering because she lay down beside me naked. She smelled strongly of an exotic fruit cocktail and, half asleep, I imagined that when Niele wore her hair up all her songs were caught in it as in a net.

She put her lips to my ear and whispered, in her endearing accent, "It's okay. No one will know."

But she was wrong, for Rosa knew. She sprang up suddenly to shriek at Niele—who was shocked and surprised by Rosa's presence—and was driven from my tent forcefully.

After chasing Niele away, Rosa had come back to the tent and lay down beside me. She snorted and smoothed my hair a few times as if I'd been upset and she wanted to pacify me, which was odd and touching and a little sad in a way I could not explain. Then she lay very still and dozed off. I sighed deeply, somewhat confused but vaguely happy and drowsed.

64

Imagine how my respect for Dr. Jorge blossomed into unadulterated ado-ration when I spied Indigo sashaying toward the campsite under the low hang of the morning sun. I'd awoken and sat at the fire pit feeling guilty about not reciprocating Niele's advances. I was glad I hadn't, but I felt bad for her and hoped she'd not felt too painfully scorned. Watching Indigo pick through the *almendro* nuts on her bare feet filled me with joy and longing.

"You ready?" she asked, once she'd reached me.

"For what?" I asked breathlessly.

"For the lesson," she said. "Didn't you ask Jorge to talk to me about it?" I stood there mute as stone and swaying a little in the gentle morning breeze. My whole thought process was thrown off. Her hair was not pulled back neatly as I'd imagined it when I'd envisioned her stabilizing the neck of the injured man. It draped over her golden shoulders in dark curls that hung half way to her waist. "And I'm sorry about the D&N—for bailing on you. I heard Niele and Anechka made you uncomfortable."

"Well, yes, but no worries." I decided not to mention Niele's nocturnal visitation. "And," I added quickly, "I do understand about you missing it. Dr. Jorge explained about the emergency. You're multifaceted."

"Oh, no. I'm just helping. I don't start med school until the fall, so I don't really know what I'm doing." She put her hands on her hips. The leaves stirred and her eyes shone like a sun-spangled river.

"You want to be a doctor," I said. I sounded very much like a simpleton and knew it.

"Yes," she said. "But I'm still a long ways from it. Let me see your head."

I came over and turned and felt her fingers moving my hair gently.

"Oh, wow," she said. "This will heal in bumps. You really should let me take them out and redo it."

"No, thanks," I said, moving away. "I shall wear it like a badge of honor."

"Your call," she said. "Are you ready to go?"

"Yes," I said. "Very much, yes."

"Where's your board?"

I went over and retrieved the Dextra Classic. Indigo was shaking her head.

"Unbelievable," she said.

"No. It really isn't mine. It's Santana Montana's. Boy is it a piece of shit. I think for anyone it'd be really embarrassing to be seen with it on the beach or in the water. I mean, it's thicker at the center than my hips are wide and it's so goddamn heavy he has to roll it down to the beach in a *jardinero's* wheelbarrow."

I lifted the board vertically, screwing my face up in pain to demonstrate just how heavy it was, but admiring the way my muscles coiled and moved in my arms.

"You have the perfect legs for a boy," she said and then turned away.

It was slow going for us on Indigo's quad. She had her board across her lap and I was behind her with the Dextra across mine. A few locals pointed and laughed at my board as we weaved our way through the rutted road of the village center. I didn't care. I was happy because I felt raw, exposed. Indigo was in her bikini and every place my body touched her tingled and hummed with electricity.

Soon the village fell behind us, the road flattened and we motored north through the dust, ruts and crushed crabs and frogs until we were beyond Milarepa and Florblanca. It was farther than I'd walked, and I told her as much as we cut down a sandy swath to the beach.

We climbed off the quad. I stretched and looked around. Clouds obscured the sun, but they glowed with white light.

"Why such a deserted location?" I asked, hoping she'd say how she wanted to get us alone together, but she said she didn't want anyone else about on account of how my u-boat might kill a grommet if it rocketed out from under me.

I thanked her for her honesty, and we walked down out of the tree line and it was then that I beheld the Witch's Hat. It was a high-rising mountainous point of rock that stabbed a hundred feet or so up directly from the sand on the beach itself. Its base rose from a karst area, etched with clints and grykes and there was an ancient *pau-brasil* tree growing up beside it at a great height. From a distance the geological anomaly of rising, fissured and broken out rock looked exactly like the rising point of a witch hat.

"That's the Witch's Hat," I said to myself as much as to Indigo.

"Yes." She looked at it.

"Would you mind if we climbed it before our lesson?"

"Okay," she said.

The climb up was hard going. The winds that tore unchecked over the sea had sent saltwater pellets slamming into the structure for eons. As a result, there were many crevices for handholds, but I was very worried about snakes. Only the day before, Rosa and Santana Montana had come across—and run from—a surly, venomous bushmaster.

Indigo had climbed it before and led the way. After a rigorous fifteen-minute climb, we stood at the top and looked out over the sea and the blue and purple bands of horizon. The *pau-brasil* branches stirring near the summit, the trees flanking me green and sweeping. The cliffs slick and dark, inscribed over the eons with cracks, fissures, crevices, the breaking off of stony shelves over time. This was a place for full hearts, for remembering the source from which lives such as ours had crawled. It was a reminder, all of it: the sand, shells, and cobbles oscillating along the shore face and beyond the clear blue water bending and twisting and crinkling far out like aluminum foil and breaking the light into multidimensional shapes that disappeared and reappeared and disappeared again.

"Beautiful, isn't it?" she asked. Her dark hair trailed and rippled in the sea breeze.

"Yes," I said for I knew that people took such beauty in and, if they were capable of saying anything, said, *This is beauty and it feels good even as it makes me long for something I can't pin down*, but what they were really saying was, *This is the closest I can get to this thing I'm feeling, this joy which is beautiful, painful, wistful, full of yearning.*

I'd been looking for the small disruption of sky that would reveal all to me, that would make all constitutive elements merge into a working whole in my mind. But there was no disruption of sky, only a shimmering of air surrounding the girl with the star in her eye. She watched me. A gentle, curious expression on her lovely face. The wind played over us and we were smiling because it was like we had known each other a long time before.

True, the Witch's Hat was not the place in the photo, but maybe the photo was wrong. If the photo was wrong, then I'd not have to choose between being near Indigo and pursuing the vision. Maybe I didn't have to anyway.

We drew close and in the small space we kissed. Sparkling bursts rolled out in bright waves of red and gold to sizzle and pulse beneath my fingernails. I kissed the thin scar at her temple, where it curled delicately over the socket, and then I kissed the lid that covered the star in her eye.

"You have a magic eye," I said.

"I'm self-conscious about it," she said.

"It is the single most perfect thing about you." She turned away and looked off to where the strand hooked along the water and gave way to the distant headland. I thought of her as a girl curled protectively around her mother's cold head.

"What is it?" I asked.

"Nothing. Can we climb back down?"

After we'd reached the bottom we went to the water's edge and stood holding hands and our boards with our feet in the wash up. I said we should catch a few close ones in the secondary break, but she pointed way out to where the green monsters coiled and hissed.

"But my lessons," I protested. She gave me a playful look.

"Jorge told me you'd surfed before."

"Then why did you—" But she took a few steps and smoothly leapt with her board over the breakwater and skimmed right on out, duck diving under a few of the big waves and leaving me behind to get maytagged in the white-wash on my sea caddie.

When I finally got myself out, Indigo sat her board peaceful and happy. She hit me with a dazzling smile.

"What took you so long?" she asked.

"This is hard," I said. I held up my arms so she could see how roped and swollen they were with effort. I was naturally tan, but I was getting dark fast. My veins looked like they were about to burst from my golden arms. "This is why your arms and shoulders look so lovely," I told her. "Not running but all this paddling."

We sat our boards for a while so I could catch my breath and rest my arms. The clouds were breaking apart and the sun shone and flared over the water. Distant flocks of birds were moving inland over the peninsula and the Witch's Hat was a twisting seamount in the air. She drifted close to me. The water sent skeins of light dancing across her face.

It was quiet out. She said the good waves had died out two or three hours ago, so it was a good time for learners like me. Maybe they weren't big to her but there were waves. They came coiling and uncoiling beneath us. They slapped against our boards as they lifted, then dropped us, broke and re-formed, then carried forth to break again on the distant shore.

"Jesus," I said. "I've never ridden waves like this. I'm going to eat wax.

You're going to get me in trouble."

"You already are in trouble," she said.

"What does that mean?" I asked, but I knew exactly what it meant. I was in big trouble. She didn't answer but cupped her hands together in the water and squeezed. The spray hit my cheek.

"Hey!" I said. Her head was back as she laughed and the softness of her throat in the light and the way it caught the angle and delicacy of her sharp jawline summoned up music and colors around me. She met my eyes then and in them was something so intimate that I nearly died.

"Indigo?"

She didn't respond but just looked at me with that white smile and all that dark hair. I looked at the beaded water on the nose of my board and then back at her.

"I'm crazy for you. I would have told you right away except that I thought you were with Perry."

"I like you, too," she said, "and I'm not with Perry, but it's complicated. I must speak with him before we can..."

"Why?" I interrupted. "You have to ask his permission?"

"No," she said. "I don't have to ask permission." A set rolled under to lift and drop us. "When we were little our mothers would sit on the porch while we played naked along the shore. We would throw stones at the monkeys and steal fruit from the *jaqui* trees. Mom hoped we would marry." She looked off at the sky, which was reddening now. The cool of morning was still in it and I could feel it encircling us out on the water. She said, "I try to tell him my father has gone into space on his missions," but then stopped as if she could not explain it, or as if that very fact explained it all. "It would be rude for me not to tell him first. I owe him that. It's not just you," she said. "There were guys at college. It's silly for him to keep pretending and of me to keep putting it off."

"Putting off what?"

"What he already knows. That there are and will be other people. That I love him, but that it is not like what I feel for you."

"When will you talk to him? Maybe I should lay low."

"Tomorrow I go to Liberia to see my *abuela*. I will talk to him when I come back."

The waves had been lifting and dropping us, but I saw a big set approaching.

255

"Hold on," she yelled, "I'll be right back." She was already paddling at an angle toward the shore. I paddled toward the wave to get out of its break and rocketed up and then sunk in the trough outside. I turned and saw her drop. Then she disappeared. When I was able to see her again she was shooting on the line in the green water. Her dark hair shimmered above the foamy lip like volleys of black light in the red and gold of the sun.

We spent a few hours out in the waves and then caught the last one together until it gave out and then we skimmed in on our tummies through the whitewash. We dragged the boards up into the shade of the Witch's Hat and set out walking the strandline shoulder to shoulder and talking softly with our heads slightly inclined to one another. After a while, I turned back and went to sit in the shade of the sea rocks. We lay on our sides and kissed and held each other and kissed again. We rested in the sand and I was so happy and peaceful that I fell into a deep sleep.

I awoke to Indigo shaking me gently.

"Lightly," she said. "I've got to get back. I'm going to be late."

65

That night, even with Indigo away, I felt like a celebration was in order, and I set about convincing Santana Montana and Rosa to go out and do just that. We waited until dark to set out and it was hot like always, of course, and La Lora Amarillo was rocking and there we came over the hill, the three of us, with Rosa walking between and holding our hands. Every few steps, she'd swing our hands really high and laugh.

Jesus, I thought. How she could still laugh so innocently after all the shit was so much it made you grit your teeth, if you know what I mean. It almost made you realize how a person could spend a lifetime refusing to see pain, to acknowledge how it scaffolds about the heart.

We spent the evening at La Lora's, which was just a big warehouse with a concrete floor for dancing. There were a few disco balls hanging and a *tico* sitting up on a tiny stage in the rear who put the dancing music on. In Guanacaste, a lot of the *ticos* rode horses and wore cowboy hats. These were the type of good people that came to La Lora's. In contrast to the rustic building and floor, the bar was done up in teak wood polished to a high, dark chocolate shine. Liquor bottles gleamed and sparkled in the disco lights. I ordered two beers and we went to sit at a little wooden table whose legs were horribly uneven.

Before long Rosa started pestering us to dance, but Santana Montana was adamant about not dancing. The job fell to me and so we danced like crazy together. Hell, there were a lot of strange looks to be sure, but I felt the people here understood how we loved Rosa and cared for her the best we could.

After a while I was spent and called it quits on my dancing career. Rosa started in on Santana Montana, calling his name and pulling on his arm. He was deeply embarrassed I could tell, so, to help things along, I leaned toward him and said if he didn't go dance with her one of those men was going to latch on to her. It was a mean thing to say but it worked, appealing to his protective nature, I mean. The resentment was on his face as he turned and trudged off to join Rosa on the dance floor.

Of course, I was accosted here and there throughout the night. I was no stranger to that. Sweet local ladies, many of them looking to be in their late thirties kept dancing up to me and laughing, calling out to me in Spanish. A couple of times I even got *danced upon,* as they say, whilst minding my own business. One lady, for instance, rubbed her considerable rumpus playfully on my arm as she swayed to the rhythm in a pair of awfully tight jeans. Another time a motherly-sort-of-figured-lady rested her backside in my lap and smiled coyly.

It was a playful affair and they each laughed as they did it and it was all in great fun. They seemed thrilled by my unwillingness to stand up and I found that touching. It was very much like what happened to me at sorority houses and the like, what with being on the terrible "Hottie List" and all. Only here, at La Lora's, I didn't mind their attentions. This was their country, their province, their town and so on, and they did not hate me. I was humbled and thankful at their unwanted advances.

Also touching were how natural and comfortable Rosa and Santana Montana danced with each other. Doubtless, they'd formed an understanding from working together pressing flowers, identifying plants and the like, but I would have thought their dancing would be highlighted by overly dramatic and intentionally ridiculous moves—to ease the obvious awkwardness of the situation—but it was not so. On the contrary, Santana Montana carried himself with dignity as he danced as if he was very serious about doing a good job of it for Rosa. Rosa, for her part, did not laugh and tease him as I was sure she would, but seemed rather serious about the whole thing, too, even downright formal. I thought I recognized in their dancing that they respected each other and cared for each other very much, and I was quite grateful just then—and eager—to call them my best friends.

The browbeating baseline died away. There was silence a moment as the DJ on the stage flipped through a collection and picked one. Santana Montana had turned to come back over to our little table when the first chords came out slow and haunting, as if from deep in a well, and a melancholy Costa Rican love song unfolded its music above the crowd the way summer rain clouds bloom over the Outer Banks to send small touches of rain tickling over the dunes, over all those lonely, shingled beach houses nestled down among the sea oats, cordgrass, and scrub pines. Rosa caught his wrist to pull him back and he let himself be turned. She put her thin arms as far around his waist as she could and lay her cheek gently against the shelf of his gut.

Santana Montana stiffened.

Another matronly local lady materialized from the crowd and smiled mischievously. She moved past my chair and began dancing seductively behind me. I saw her form appearing and twisting slowly at the edges of my periphery. I felt her gut bump softly and playfully against the scar on the back of my head a few times as she writhed.

I kept my eyes on Santana Montana just then because, for a moment, it seemed as though he were deciding between two things, though I didn't know what those things were. Then he put his arms around Rosa and they rocked slowly to and fro—much like those fishing vessels on the horizon off the coast. Rising as some dark force came coiling towards them, gently falling as it rolled harmlessly away. He shut his eyes. There was anguish on his face. There was anguish but also tenderness. There was something else, too. Something. I couldn't quite take hold of what it was.

I pinched my nose, breathed heavily and warmly into the palm of my hand and thought of how when the wind stirred the dry leaves, they sounded like the prayers of children kneeling at their beds. I lay my head on the table and counted to twenty to keep from running outside for I was desperate to steal a quad and gather Indigo from her grandmother's house. I wanted to sink with her into the clean, blue ocean, to be part of that inscription the waves scrawled into the shore, so that we might be stirred, mixed—dissolved.

All Things Await

66

I spent the next morning on my sea caddie. I'd tossed and turned through the night in the tent and every image that floated into my mind had Indigo's glorious eyes transposed on it. I thought surfing would work out some of my nervousness and that I would walk down to the Witch's Hat later with a quieted heart.

It was a mistake, though. I'll tell why I say that.

Some old-timers gave me the thumbs up as I dragged the board toward the water. Others, Danny and Aldo chiefly among them, heckled me in a good-natured sort of way. The problem was that Perry was out there the whole time. Whenever he and I dropped in on the same wave, he would do a curious and vexing thing. He'd try and nose me with his board or cut me off. Twice he shoved me over as he sliced by. It was bad form to drop on a local's wave, and each time I tried to pull out, but my massive, half wooden flotation device was slow and lumbersome, what with it being produced as it was during a time when the mechanics of surfboard design were very poorly grasped. By contrast Perry's expensive short board flicked its tail like a gleaming minnow, slithered nimbly like a white snake across the wave's blue-green belly. And, to be fair, it seemed as though he were lying in wait for me.

After coming up on shore at the end of a few hours of it, I told Perry, "Jesus, you are really something on that quick little board." He was already smoking a bowl with a couple of the other surfers sitting in the treeline shade. White Bandana lay on her stomach on a towel beside him. "You're flipping all around and then you're carving and spraying or whatever the hell it's called," I told him. "Did you see how that big wave you wiggle-waggled under so nimbly knocked the heavenly fuck out of me and sent my sea caddie sky-high?"

"You're a speed bump," he said. "A kook."

I studied his beautiful golden face and smug eyes in the awkward silence, and I very much wanted to smite his fine-looking nose right off the table of his face.

But I didn't. I wanted to explain to him that he hated me only because of his own insecurities. But I didn't do that either. I knew that pointing out insecurities was the quickest way to ignite the fear and violence so tightly bound to them.

True, I wanted to hit him, but I wanted to tell him I was sorry, too. You'd have thought it'd feel good to know what Indigo would soon tell him but it didn't.

It felt terrible. I felt like an intruder, like someone who had come to Costa Rica, disrespected its history and taken the most precious thing I could find for myself.

In any event, back bent and feet moving like I was driving the tackling sled under Coach Sanford's watchful eye, I dragged my fat ancient whale of a board back to camp.

67

I had intended to walk all the way to the Witch's Hat, but I had not. I could feel an accusatory idea treading around the edges of my perception. I knew it had to do with my vision, with the fact that I'd pursued a girl, that I'd traded my pursuit of one vision for the pursuit of another. I kicked it away when I sensed it, for I didn't want to have to face such a thing and I was not all that convinced that I would need to make such a choice.

I told Santana Montana and Rosa about Perry's antics that afternoon back at the campsite and how I'd held back from retaliating. Santana Montana and Rosa had spent the morning collecting dead turtle fetuses. They'd removed them from the soft white shell, which was about the size of a golf ball, and put the little baby turtles on a log across from the tents so they lay there like tiny carvings of turtles only with the yellowish amniotic fluid ball still attached to their scaly, ill-formed tummies.

"It is big of you," Santana Montana said. "You are right to feel as you do." But Rosa said that I was afraid.

"I am afraid," I told them. "I am afraid of what I'll do to him. I know he has pretty muscles, but I have something terrible in me that I'd rather not release. It'd be a real shame, Santana Montana, were I to throttle him, for he is beautiful and one of the most graceful surfers I've ever seen."

"Okay," Santana Montana said. He then told me they'd be *turtling* late into the night. "There will be many of them that need our help getting to the sea. They are such small, helpless creatures, yet they are majestic. We will assist them."

"Yes!" exclaimed Rosa in her perfect Santana Montanaian accent. "We... will!"

"Jesus," I said, laughing a little despite my jittery mood. "What am I going to do with you two?" The question I kicked away was, what would I do without you two?

Rosa came over and touched my cheek and then she went around and hugged Santana Montana from behind where he sat on the log. Santana Montana froze and Rosa buried her nose in the top of his head and made a kissing sound. She giggled at his embarrassment and set off through the *ceibos* toward the beach singing a heartbreaking song the way Gus McGovern's daughter had years ago along the shore at the coalfields. Santana Montana was left to sit there with a mighty blush on his stony face.

"You should see your face," I told him. "It is so beautiful to see something like that on your face." He looked at me evenly.

"I am leaving tomorrow," he said.

"Just wait," I said. "Only a little longer now. The thing approaches. And after the vision, as I said, we'll need to pick our friends up at the airport."

"I do not think they will come."

"They'll come," I told him. "They need us. They need me."

68

That night I was agitated beyond compare. We'd built a little fire at dusk and Santana Montana and Rosa organized their supplies. I kept imagining Indigo's talk with Perry and playing out all the multiple variations that might occur during and after it.

Of course, Santana Montana and Rosa offered to let me go out *turtling* with them but I declined.

"It soothes the nerves," Santana Montana said, but I didn't agree.

"It's a worthy enterprise," I told them, "but the fetuses you two collect creep me the hell out. Look," I said, pointing to where they lay on the log like pilfered dragon embryos. "What kind of socially tone-deaf genius does things like that?"

"A scientist," he replied. "Someone who wishes to understand the world and the creatures in it in a highly intelligent way. Someone who..."

"You two *are* my baby turtles," I told them, "and I've carried you both to the water's edge. I see that now."

The fire flared and a breeze rushed the sparks over the contours of the cold, pitted sand.

69

I couldn't keep pacing around. I remembered Anklebells had said it was disco night at the D&N, so I took to the cratered and dusty road and made my way south. I thought the D&N would take my mind off things, but I also thought it'd be good if I were away from camp in case Perry came to kill me as Dr. Jorge had warned he might.

I put on my straw hat and hoofed on down the road lost in thought, luxuriating in the possibilities.

The D&N was packed and the deafening music hung densely over the crowded dance floor. The bar was pressed with hot bodies. I wedged in and waited for Anklebells. She slid a beer to the man beside me and tousled my hair. She yelled that Niele had told her about Rosa chasing her from my tent.

"I know," I hollered. "I should apologize to her." She nodded out at Massimo and Martijn who were spinning arm and arm with two local girls on the dance floor in their crazy disco attire.

"See your friends?" she asked, pointing at them. I nodded.

"I hope our multilayered global governance system, which will one day be in place, will wind up with mostly Belgians in power positions."

"No more of that," she said. "I have news."

It was Anklebells who told me Indigo and Perry were there and that Perry was in a rage. She leaned over the bar to put her mouth on my cheek and said excitedly, "Apparently, there's some other guy," she confided. "Can you believe it? She is so elegant and smart. I can't imagine who it could be, but I'd hate to be that guy. Perry is going to kill him."

"Jesus," I said. "I hope that's not true."

"Do you know who it is?"

"I am him," I told her. "I mean, it is me."

"Oh dear," she said. She looked at me with wide eyes and it was like she was seeing me for the first time. She looked worriedly into the crowd. I asked her if I should leave before Perry spied me and she said it was too late and to look toward the dance floor. Perry and Indigo were standing there with a semicircle of disco dancers just beyond them. I couldn't hear it over the music, but Perry was screaming at her. His face, normally so superior and beautiful, was red and ugly. His mouth moved violently and he was gesturing wildly and pulling at his hair. The hurt was in his teeth as he yelled and the spit that flew from his mouth. I had a flash vision of them as kids—all golden and lovely with their dark hair about their soft faces. They were cracking the washed up almond nuts with rocks and eating them together while the laundry lifted on the clothesline above in the warm Costa Rican breeze. Of course, that would have been long ago and this night Perry was grown, looking insanely drunk, but just as beautiful. There was something in his anguish that I recognized, and I was overcome by a wave of sympathy for him. I knew that his intense insecurities were an accurate measure of the degree of his pain, whatever the source of that pain might be.

He caught me watching.

"Uh-oh," Anklebells said. "You should leave—*NOW!*" I told her he couldn't possibly recognize me beneath my hat, but I was wrong. Perry strode across the stones in haste toward me with Indigo skittering behind, something desperate in her movements, her eyes slightly weary at the edges. Perry was there in a matter of seconds. He had me by the collar and was shaking me roughly. He seemed to be asking me many questions all at once, chiefly concerning how funny I thought *it* was and how long I'd been fucking his girlfriend.

I couldn't understand all of his slurred, anger-fueled questions, but his suffering I grasped immediately. I patted his shoulder gently as he viciously wrangled me off the barstool. "There, there, Perry," I said. "We'll arrange something." I considered telling him about the hardships of the limpet. I didn't though, for Perry was pulling me down to the cement slab that was the floor of the bar.

"No, no, Perry," I told him. "Let's not do that."

Indigo pulled at him. She was pleading with him. There were tears on her cheeks. Massimo and Martijn had come over and were trying to pry his arms from me. Mostly, though, the patrons looked on with mild curiosity and some even kept on dancing as I lay on my back with my arms out to the side, completely surrendered there in the dust and sand, with the cool press of spilled Imperial, Pilsen, and that mixed drink of rum and pineapple and lime that was so popular at D&N slowly dampening the back of my shirt and rear of my shorts, which were twisted uncomfortably now about my torso.

As they struggled to pull him from me, Perry alternately tried to choke me and punch me in the ribs. He was sobbing, too, or so it seemed. As he attacked, it was more like being slobbered and grinded upon than truly assaulted.

I asked him to stop. "Please," I begged. "Please, Perry. You've gone off the bucket." I pleaded with him. It was not fair to fight back when he was so diminished.

Finally, they managed to pull him from me. He stood up, saying, "Alright, alright, I'm done. This fucking pussy's too chicken-shit to fight. He just lays there like a bitch!" he cried out hysterically. "This guy?" he yelled at Indigo. "Really? This fucking mental patient?" He spat on me, and I pulled my straw hat down and pressed it firmly over my face.

"Just leave, Perry." I could see through a hole in my hat that it was Indigo who said it. Her voice was ragged and tired but resolute.

"Leave?" he yelled at her incredulously. "You fucking tell *me* to leave?" There was something raw and vulnerable in his question and my heart broke for him though I knew it shouldn't have.

"Perry," she said. "If you'd only..." She was wringing her hands. Her eyes seemed to be offering every part of her heart to him, every part but the one he wanted. Without a word, Perry struck her in the face with his open hand and stormed away.

After Perry departed, I'd tried to console Indigo, but she had held out her arm to indicate that I should stay away. The crowd parted for her as she made her way up to the road holding her cheek. Everyone looked at me silently as if I might offer some explanation, but what was there to say?

I turned and loped off to make my way home alertly along the beach, hoping that Anit or some other ruffian would accost me, so I could unleash hell on them, but went the whole way unmolested.

All Things Await

70

That morning was overcast, the sky stretched like soiled silk. I walked to Indigo's dark and quiet house, but either she had shut herself in or there was no one there. When the sunlight appeared in the treetops, I walked down to Burger Rancho to get a coffee and sit under the thatch.

"*Un café con leche?*" Océane asked sweetly once I'd sat down.

"No, thank you. Just a coffee with milk, please."

"Okay." She patted my head. "Your stitching looks less bad."

"Thanks." Aldo was looking at me.

"What?" I asked.

"You should not be embarrassed," he said. He was sitting at his little table and enjoying the day's first light with a fine joint. As usual he was facing the little television, but the television was still locked in its box.

"I'm not," I said.

"Martijn and Massimo told us about last night," Océane said from the kitchen.

"I was being the bigger man," I explained.

"Even so," Aldo said. "It is not manly in Costa Rica, as in many other places, to simply lie on the ground and allow another man to roll around on top of you and insult you."

Océane came over and placed the coffee on the table. She'd stacked as many extra cookies on the saucer around it as she could fit. She stood beside me, leaned down and pressed her cheek to the top of my head.

"I think you are sweet," she said. "And Indigo deserves a sweet man. If only more men were man enough to be as unmanly as you."

"Ha!" Aldo said, laughing pleasantly. "That's it. Unmanly, just as I said."

All Things Await

71

I didn't linger at the Rancho because Aldo and Océane's treatment of me had coaxed up a weird conflict of emotions.

When I got back to camp, Rosa and Santana Montana were both up. They'd carved a mango and were eating slices of it with their fingers from paper bowls. I sat down and told them what had happened. I explained how noble my behavior had been but lamented that my begging Perry to stop was not seen in its proper light.

"Jesus," I told Santana Montana and Rosa back at the camp. "They don't understand how I wanted to save Perry from further humiliation."

Santana Montana translated for Rosa. His notebook was out on the log between them. It was bursting at the seams with foliage and whatnot.

"Rosa says she has seen and heard of Perry and that you *should* have humiliated him."

"Damn it, Santana Montana," I said. "Sometimes people who we think need to be humiliated are the very people who've suffered the worst humiliations of all. He's got no chance falling for a genius like Indigo. You tell her that, my friend. His mother left and his absentee father is a senator, and Perry is the son who can't live up to his father's expectations and all. God, but it's been seen again and again. There's only so many ways you get fucked up as a person. You see the same ones over and over. The particulars change but the root things are always the same." Santana Montana had been translating but now Rosa was talking.

"What is she saying?" I asked him. He held up his hand for me to wait until she finished, and it was so damn chivalrous I almost hugged him.

"She asks what that makes you then, you who simply lay on a filthy floor and allowed himself to be so grossly humiliated."

"Goddamn it, Santana Montana!" I cried out angrily. "She did not say *grossly*! She's an underage prostitute with no education and would not use such a word and you fucking know it!" I was shaking my finger and squinting at him for I was furious at Santana Montana just then. "You're mad at me that I won't leave this place and so you put that word in passive-aggressively. You're the one who finds it *gross* and you're trying to get that across through her, because you lack the resolve to tell me to my face."

Santana Montana was speaking to Rosa again.

"What are you doing?" I demanded.

"Translating."

"Don't do that," I said with a dismissive wave, "she'll be offended that I said she wouldn't know the word because she's a prostitute." He ignored me and kept speaking. "Santana Montana," I said. "You stop that! What the hell are you doing? I just said to stop!"

"I know," he said quietly. "I have *resolved* to tell her." He gave me the first even, challenging look I'd ever gotten from him and finished translating, and my heart began to swell with joy.

"Good for you, Santana Montana!" I exclaimed, slapping my knee. "You've given me the screws. You've stood up to me, looked me in the eye and said 'to hell with you, this is what I want!'" I was going to expound upon, as they say, how proud I was of him and even wrap him in a big hug but I didn't. I didn't because Rosa suddenly stabbed me in the thigh with her goddamn needle and ran down toward the beach with her hands cupped to her face.

"Jesus god!" I yelled, hopping on one leg and covering the puncture wound. "I hope she disinfects that fucking thing!"

Santana Montana stood up. He shook his head at me in a disgusted way and hurried out into the *ceibos*, softly calling Rosa's name.

72

I sat around camp waiting for my friends to return, feeling terribly guilty. When they didn't, I stumbled down the beach stopping only to pick up the brightest and smoothest stones the tide had brought in. I had apologies to make, and I didn't want to stand before my friends empty handed.

When I returned from my walk later that morning, they were both there and I made my apologies to them and made gifts of the pretty rocks I'd collected.

Rosa forgave me right away but Santana Montana said, "I forgive you if you will accept the fact that I am leaving."

I told him I acknowledged that. When he offered his forgiveness, too, I wrapped them both in a crushing hug and held them firmly until at last Santana Montana began to struggle and beg for release.

All Things Await

73

We didn't hear about Perry until we ventured out to Pizza Tomate in the early afternoon. Anklebells had just come on her shift and she told us Perry had the bad luck to have locked horns with Anit outside La Lora's. Perry had been drinking heavily at the D&N, but after mauling me, slapping Indigo, and stalking away he'd returned and kept going behind the bathroom again and again to do lines.

It ended poorly for Perry just as it had for the man on the bus, but much, much worse. Rather than being knocked out immediately, Anklebells said, the cocaine had kept his body upright and allowed Anit to pummel him for much longer than he should. In the end, Anit had smashed several of his ribs and shattered that noble nose of his that I'd long considered smiting; but it was his arm that had suffered the worst damage. It had been broken very badly. Compound fracture. Indigo had tended to him until an ambulance could be arranged to take him to San Jose. He'd be there indefinitely.

The news filled me with sadness. I thought of his arms, of how beautiful they were. I didn't see Indigo that whole day.

We sat at the table in the heat brooding over the strangeness of it all. One of the strays was underneath and kept licking my toes. Sweat was rolling down Santana Montana's face.

"Will you go confront your father?" I asked him. "When you leave?"

"First to my mother's house—which was, is, and will be my home. If he comes calling, though, I will show him this new strength you have gifted me."

"What will you do?"

"My mother's great friend is the curator of the museum in Puerto Vallarta. He always said I could come work as a guide, and I will do that."

"I meant with your father."

"I will do what I must." He looked at me. "The mistakes of our fathers are not our mistakes. I will not bear the weight of them. I think, perhaps, you have taught me that, too."

"Oh. Well, what of our Rose?"

"I will work there and find a job for her. If she'll come. She loves you.

She talks of marriage to you. I try to explain to her. I hope that you will tell her to come. She needs someone who is capable of—well, I feel she would be better off if you could convince her to come."

I felt sick, abandoned and very lonely. I'd not felt those things so vividly ever before. I was a little angry, too, but I wasn't sure why. I knew Rosa would stay with me if I but said the word, and I knew it'd be exactly the worst thing for her. He loved her. I knew he would work hard and he would be noble and in a few years if she chose to love him back, then they would marry—there was only a few years difference between them. If she didn't, he would love her still and help her however he could.

"Well," I said. "If you're going to leave, you've at least got to come see the Witch's Hat first. It is a special place. Maybe the vision will come there. You've at least got to see it. Both of you."

Rosa had nodded sagaciously throughout and she was doing so now. I wondered if she understood what we were saying. I believed very sincerely that she did not.

"I'll bet there's some very interesting ecological niches on a geological formation such as that," he said.

"There are," I said. "Do you know what a gryke is?"

"Yes."

"How about clints?"

"Yes."

"Best you bring your sketchbook," I told him.

"Oh," he said, fixing me with a look of intense sincerity. "I intend to."

74

By the time Indigo came riding up to the Witch's Hat on her quad, Santana Montana was halfway through his sketch of the formation's north face, and Rosa and I were catching hermit and Halloween crabs in an old bucket we'd found on the beach. She'd handle them carefully until our little bucket was nearly full and then gently release them. She'd come a long way in a short time from that evening where she was squashing them into the road dust with her heel.

I stood up and dropped the bucket.

"Hey," Indigo said.

"Hey," I said.

"Anechka said you all had headed this way."

"How is Perry?"

"Okay. He's at CIMA." I didn't say anything. I didn't know what to say except that I felt guilty. "I was thinking of taking a walk," she said.

"Sure," I said. "Yes. Very much yes."

"Actually," she said. "I was wondering if your friend would like to take a walk."

I was very confused. Did she mean Santana Montana? I knew that she did, but still I did not understand.

"Would you mind taking a walk?" she asked him.

He glanced at my open mouth, at the blank look on my face.

"I would not mind at all," he said. With that, they turned and started walking up the beach.

"Damn," I said to Rosa. "What in the world do you make of that?"

There was nothing to do and I had a great deal of nervous energy, seeing as how I was confused about Indigo and the walk she was taking with Santana Montana. I pointed up to the top of the Witch's Hat and indicated to Rosa that we could climb up. "The view is incredible," I told her. "Besides, there's something I've been meaning to tell you. I know Santana Montana has been teaching you all sorts of practical helpful things and the like, but I've something important to tell you, especially if you are leaving. It might just change the way you look at things."

Anyway, Rosa and I started to climb up but we'd only gotten four feet off the ground when Rosa got scared. She said, "There are snakes in the crevices," or, at least, that's what I believed she said, though it could have been anything. I started to explain that it wasn't true—I even stuck my hands into all the crevices I could see, but then stopped.

I stopped because it occurred to me that telling a child prostitute that there are no snakes lurking in darkened crevices was just about the biggest boldface lie a person could manage. Rosa knew the truth: that in every crevice there lurked a serpent. Some bad and dangerous and others much, much worse. So I told Rosa, "Go ahead you tiny brutalized genius and climb onto my back." I gestured and she came over and climbed on. She wrapped her thin arms around my neck very tightly, so it was with some difficulty that I said, "I swear to you, Rosa, if there's a snake in a crevice, then I will turn into a mongoose and bite the fucker's head off." I turned my head, snarled, bared my teeth, and then made several vicious biting motions. "I'm not joking at all. You've my word on that, my little one."

Even though I'm an agile bastard, it took me a quarter of an hour to make the tricky climb. It wasn't so much that it was high but that it was straight up. You had to pick your way carefully. Once or twice I thought I felt Rosa's lips brush the back of my neck, but I couldn't be sure. In any event, we reached the summit after all and, once up there, we just sat for a long, long while, staring out into all the beautiful waste of rock-sea-sky. It was a low-slung horizon above the watery-blue expanse and beige band of beach, with varying shades of grey. I wanted to fork the side of the horizon for her, pull it away and expose all the machinery at work behind it.

I started to tell Rosa about string theory and how it could unify the quantum theory with gravity. She indicated with a shrug and tilt of her head that she didn't understand, so I told her it didn't matter if she understood but only that she listened and tried to understand. "For knowledge," I explained, "doesn't come all at once to most people, but gradually and only through knowledge dear Rosa can we be saved, can we be made humble and self-assured all at once."

Rosa shrugged again, but she scooted over to lean sleepily against me. Below us, a pack of dogs had materialized from the tree line and were trotting toward the breakwater. I told Rosa the problem with string theory was that there were, like, five different versions of it. "So, instead of one theory of everything, Rosa, you have several theories of everything, and that doesn't stir the Kool-Aide, as they say, for those brilliant physicist bastards." I told her how some pumpkin-headed genius at Princeton said that all five theories were actually the same theory when you added in an eleventh dimension or something because when you added an eleventh dimension all the string theories collapsed into one theory.

Rosa laughed and hugged my arm. I didn't know if she was laughing at me or at the pack of dogs that were leaping about in the ankle-deep water, trying to catch pale fish that were darting back out through the run down toward the waves.

"You see, Rosa?" I asked. "That would mean that our universe is like a membrane floating about in eleven-dimensional hyperspace, which means our universe might exist in a multiverse of other universes."

Rosa smiled sweetly without taking her attention away from the show the dogs were putting on.

"Just think of it, Rosa," I said and I explained, using many fantastic gestures, just how we might be living in a universe that exists on the membrane of a bubble in a vast foam sea of trillions upon trillions of bubbles. I pointed at all the bubbles the waves were frothing up along the shore below us and said, "Some of those sons of bitches even say that our whole universe came from two of those bubbles slamming into each other fourteen billion years ago or whatever but I don't know."

Rosa was gazing adoringly at me now, and I smiled at her because I thought maybe the tiniest bit was hitting home. "Good lord," I said thickly. "You're so sharp, Rosa, honey, that you could cut a hole in the sky and just walk the hell..." but I got the impression Rosa wasn't listening, because she was trying to kiss me.

"Come on now, Rosa, damn it," I said in the sternest reprimand voice I could muster. "No, no. None of that. Cut it out, little one."

A moment or two later I was holding my arm in pain and calling after Rosa.

That needle of hers was sticking out of my bicep and she'd scampered off and was climbing down. I stepped over with the thought of calling her back up, but I stopped when I saw the incredible agility with which she scarped down the side. It made me mad, too, because she'd pretended to fear snakes so that she could grope me and kiss my neck while I carted her up.

"What a tricky little rascal," I said to myself. I figured that Rosa had decided to make one more play for me since she knew the time for departures was at hand. "And damn does this needle sting." Let her climb, I thought, it'll be good exercise. I watched her progress for a few minutes then glanced away. Far off, I could see Santana Montana and Indigo making their way back. My ears burned. I wished there had been time to tell Santana Montana to put in a good word for me, to tell her I was worth the trouble after all, though I hardly felt it true.

"Damn it," I said, throwing up my arms. "Who cares anyway?"

I went back over and sat down to admire the view and it was one hell-of-a-view out over all that water like purple glass. I'd somehow forgotten the needle, so I plucked it from my arm and placed it on a rock. It was the only weapon that poor child had and I aimed to give it back even if that meant it was destined to find its way into my flesh again.

75

Well, of course it happened like that.

It was perfectly fitting that I was up there on the Witch's Hat when Anit came into view. I don't know if I heard the rattling first or spotted the movement but suddenly there he was, emerging from the jungle below. He changed in the light from a dark, lurking form among the *almendros* and *pachotes* to the crazy bastard from the bus like he was a shape shifter.

The weird thing was that he had not changed his clothes and his bag was a mountain on his back. My first thought was how glad I was to be up high and out of view. But then Anit was moving toward the Witch's Hat and then he was there and he'd gotten Rosa by the wrist and I was whispering, "Shit, shit, shit," but I wasn't moving. I didn't know why I was frozen there, but I was. I couldn't move and I was mumbling, "It's him. It's him. He's come for the little one." I knew it wasn't the fear that kept me from moving but the certainty of his victory and that made me angry.

I turned in desperation and caught something else moving in the edge of my vision: it was the movement of the leathery pinnate leaves on the high *pau-brasil* across from me. They seemed to be waving me on. Rosa was screaming now as Anit twisted her arm and there was that booming laugh of his which was oddly in concert with Rosa's shrill shrieks. Meanwhile, I was mumbling about pharaohs now and ancient stones—about quests and seven levels. The names of distant gods were on my lips. The only name I said on purpose, though, was Indigo. Her name rose as a circle in the air and I took hold of it and put the colors of it around my neck like an amulet.

Anit was forcing Rosa back around the base of the Witch's Hat for god knows what and I told my feet to move or I'd break them off and they finally did. They moved but not to begin the climb down the peak but to turn and face the *brasil* tree, for it'd take ten minutes or more to climb down and that was too long. So, I backed up to the edge with my heels and took measure of the span between the far ledge and the *brasil* tree, the limbs of it. I hopped up and down three times and rolled my neck and smiled, for in me was the knowledge, the certainty, that I could make the leap—that those limbs waving at me would spread wide for embrace, that they wouldn't let me fall.

I had four steps until the air and I made them count in vicious, long strides, that ate up ground the way black holes swallow light and then I was airborne and for it, part cloud, part bird, and so much a part of the air that, for a moment, I feared I'd become set in it like something set in stone.

But then I was slamming violently into the rough *brasil* branches and reaching desperately, grasping, clutching at limbs and leaflets as if they were the arms and fingertips of friends. I took hold of the tree and it took hold of me for it was covered with tiny thorns that had stuck in my skin and clothing. I got my balance and managed not to cry out in pain.

Anit rounded the Witch's Hat, rough-housing Rosa by the wrist, and I saw straight off how his line would take him right under me. I slunk down through the branches like a jungle cat and, ignoring the crunching thorns, positioned myself on a narrow branch. What was it? Thirty feet? More? "Steady now," I told myself. "Look at the water, how it glows with light. Steady or you'll break your neck."

Anit walked under the *pau-brasil*, and then I was falling.

It takes a long time when you fall like that. On purpose, I mean. I had time to notice, for example, how I'd spread my fingers like claws, and to marvel at how my mouth had snarled open, baring my teeth. And his back— my god, but Anit's back was so bright, so wide and obvious like prey, that I knew I couldn't miss him, that I wouldn't miss.

And I didn't.

I staggered up from the violent flash of the collision and knew straight off that I was hurt but not how bad. I was, truth be told, half surprised I'd not been annihilated along with Anit by the impact. I was dizzy as hell and it was with great difficulty that I got to my feet. It was the shoulder, I realized, that was hurt. The one from when I'd leapt for all those pine tops ages ago with Lance trailing behind and thinking I'd purposely done a seventy-foot swan dive into oblivion.

Anit was facedown in the sand and Rosa was sitting cross-legged beside him and crying like the child she was.

Without getting off his stomach, Anit started removing his backpack. I grabbed Rosa by the arm and told her to run. Santana Montana and Indigo were still hazy figures up the beach, and I told her to sprint for them and she did with her hands pressed to her face, her knobby knees bent inward and her little feet throwing the sand behind her as she ran.

Anit's backpack fell off and he still didn't rise. Instead he rolled onto his back in the sand and lay there in an oddly peaceful way with his big hands resting on his stomach as if he were enjoying pictures the clouds were painting for him. I knew enough about violent collisions from being sacked viciously time and again to know he was checking himself out internally, and that it would be folly to think he wouldn't rise, because I was sure he would. I took the time I had to get ready. I stepped back unsteadily from him. Slowly, favoring my right arm, I removed my shirt. Anit moved up to his knees and again waited in that way, and he looked a hell of a lot like a mound of stone. He was bleeding slightly from his hairline. My hands and arms had blood pricks from the *brasil* thorns.

Anit's sunglasses must've broken in the collision, because when he stood up and shook his wide head like a beast with a great, black mane, the sunglasses flew off his face in three pieces.

To ensure he'd have nothing to grab, I removed my shorts, so that I was totally naked before him. I hoisted my thick chest and moved my shoulders to set off the play of muscles along my broad, sun-kissed back the same way I had when I'd stood before Padre Johnson way back when. Only this foe was not small and kind, but big and dangerous, so I rubbed the sweat into my stomach and then passed my hands over my face.

Anit grinned ominously and his eyes were dead and black, but it didn't make a damn to me. He removed his shirt, but nothing else for he didn't wear shoes. Beyond him I saw that Santana Montana and Indigo were running now. They yelled and Rosa was screaming something to them, but their cries came only lightly to my ears. They came to me on a dim and minute scale, from the distant edges of a bonfire's glow where the darkness gathers far off and the circle of light dies.

I bent at the knees and pressed my wet palms and then fists into the sand so that the crushed stone stuck to them and I would have traction. I hunched my back and held my fists before me. I was ready for the bull rush, but instead Anit lowered himself and moved to the side.

My thighs glistened. The muscles in them were springy and alive, and, feeling golden and huge. I moved to circle with him in the sand. I was enormously excited, not just to fight but at the savageness overtaking my heart and obliterating my higher faculties with all their voices and longings.

Too late, I realized that Anit's circling had been tactical, for he stopped once he was on the higher bank and I was caught on the slope.

I laughed at such a plan and then waved him on and said, "Come on you fucker! You could be twice as big and still I'd take you!"

His lunge was sudden and ferocious like a lion leaping for prey out of the tall grass and I saw in an instant how his arms with their faded tattoos were extended for my throat. But I was quicker than he'd have any right to expect and I dove low, powerfully sending my body horizontal along the sand slope and balled up as I did so that I violently collided with his knees. There was that white explosion again as his legs struck my head and shoulders and I rolled left immediately to avoid him if he'd not been flipped but also because I believed it would help me stay conscious. I leapt gracefully to my feet but then fell over on my ass for his knees had done more damage than I'd thought. I sat there in the sand with the whole world sloshing around me as if glimpsed through a mason jar of spinning creek water. That might have been the end of it except that my dive had done its trick and Anit had been sent flipping airborne and was now flat on his back with his toes pointing toward the waves and the Galapagos Islands of Ecuador that lay somewhere beyond.

I wanted to press my advantage, but, as Anit slowly rolled to his stomach and pushed himself up, it was all I could do to stand without falling. Still, the daze wore off more quickly this time, and I began to feel, as I stood, how my whole body suddenly pulsated with waves of energy. The hair stood up on the back of my neck and my scar tingled with electric particles, which always meant the approach of something incredible. Things steadied out immediately, and I flexed my biceps and squeezed the muscles in my stomach and luxuriated in the power that resided there.

Anit approached directly this time, hobbling slightly. He moved slowly with his weighty arms outstretched. I moved toward him and there was something intimate in our slow approach, our cautious reaching toward one another. We locked arms and it was like locking horns with a big stag, no doubt. He grappled very subtly, though, and I knew he was testing my strength. He brought his weight to bear, but I matched his bulk with my sheer strength and incredible balance. My shoulder hurt like hell, but I was able to increase the use of the muscles around the hurt one and thereby reduce the pain.

I could feel his body preparing something through subtle changes in his arms, so that when he tried a leg swipe, I was able to dance my leg away. After another failed attempt—this time to step over for a hip toss—he shoved me off and we moved in a half circle again. He stepped in once more as if to lock arms, but at the last second threw a punch. I saw it too late. His meat hook clipped over my out-stretched arm and caught me square on the ear with all his bulk behind it. My legs disappeared and I collapsed to my knees but did not go over. I heard someone screaming for Anit to stop, but I also heard church bells ringing in the Greek Isles.

More than anything, though, I was astonished, because I felt no pain at all.

I was still pondering this curiosity when his knee smashed into my chest, and I lifted and went sprawling backwards. Again, though, I was surprised because I had not felt the blow. So, I lay on my side clear-headed, naked, the length of my body covered with crushed stone, mirrors of rock ground for eons over the seafloor that made me like some camouflaged crab, and prepared a surprise. Anit stepped over casually. He had every right to think I was done for. When he reached down to pull me up and, I supposed, to finish the job, I kicked him in his groin with my heel. I leapt to my feet as he bent over in pain, and I placed both hands on the back of his head, forced it down, and brought my knee up through his face with all the force I could muster. His nose exploded and he stumbled back waving his heavy arms to keep his balance.

I leapt for him and reached for his throat but he managed to get my right arm in some Honduran military lock. He steadied himself, holding me like that while his head cleared. Then he used his leverage to twist my arm behind me so that we were belly to belly and my forehead rested on his massive bosom. He stank greatly of body odor, of course, but also of stale linens and of caves, opened soil and the darker places of the earth and of liquor, too. Rum, by the smell of it. Only faintly did he smell of baby powder. He had both arms around me now, applying pressure and he seemed to be bending all his great strength and superior leverage on slowly breaking my golden arm.

I called to the fur-covered animal within, summoned the residue of that bestial thing that evolution had not yet wiped from the genes and gave over all my energy to it. I leaned back just to get Anit to pull me toward him and then suddenly I pressed my belly upon him and drove my legs to get him moving backwards. He stumbled to regain his footing but I'd already sprung forward and up in the tight space with my mouth flung open, teeth exposed. I clamped my jaws viciously on the curve of his dark, muscular neck.

Anit grunted in pain and, releasing me, fell away. A considerable chunk of his neck stayed in my mouth. My lips were wet. I spat the piece of him in the sand.

"Come on you big fucker!" I roared, "I'm not done with you!" But Anit did not come on but stood there with his arm across his chest and his palm applying pressure to the wound on his neck. I could see blood gathering at the edges of his hand and then three rivulets of it began coursing down his chest. Anit had a look on his face like someone who had been insulted by a friend. Slowly, he walked back over to his shirt. He put it on gingerly and then shouldered his huge pack. He looked from me to Santana Montana and Indigo, who I now noticed were standing there dismayed.

Anit shook his head sadly as if deciding something not in our favor and trudged slowly back up the beach. He walked hunched over with great heaviness about the feet. It was as if he'd had his feelings hurt.

I saw then, glancing in a questioning way back at my friends, that his rattle had come off his bag when I'd fallen upon him from the *pau-brasil*. I stepped over and picked it up. I turned it in my fingers and shook my head. It was old. All the baby blue paint had dimmed nearly to the vanishing point on the white plastic ball, and the wooden handle was worn low and smooth with what must have been decades of use.

"Oh for god's sake," I said to no one in particular. I ran after Anit and caught up to him just as he was entering the woods. He turned to face me with his arms hanging tiredly at his sides and the bloom of blood growing at the neck of his shirt like the swelling of some great, wet rose.

"Jesus, Anit," I said. "I'm—I mean, I guess I'm—fuck!" I spat. "It's just you can't tangle with someone like me, Anit, because I don't know moderation and I was trying—I mean, I suppose I was trying—to kill you, Anit. Hell. Anyway. Here's your rattle." I hastily brushed the sand from it and he took it from me. His nose was broken very badly. He sniffled at the blood dripping from it and it was the same sound a child made when she cried while her nose was running. "Jesus," I said. "Just stop touching little girls and beating the hell out of people. Cut back with the liquor. Anit, Anit. Maybe you've got a chance," I said though I doubted it. "Maybe there's still time for you, Anit," though I suspected there wasn't. A few *almendro* nuts fell noisily on the leaves.

There was no expression on his face. I asked him if there was an address I could write him at, but Anit cocked his head as if he'd heard something in the jungle and turned and walked away.

I thought of shouting after him that I was sorry for biting out a piece of his neck, but I didn't because I wasn't sure if I was sorry or not. And, anyway, I didn't want to interrupt him, for already he was singing one of those creepy songs, though it was sadder than I remembered, and with a quality of intense longing, as if some transference had occurred at the moment of our collision, though it might well have been the effect of the blood in his throat.

76

I went back down the beach and asked where Rosa was. Santana Montana said they'd sent her to Burger Rancho.

"In case you didn't stop Anit," Indigo added. The way Santana Montana and Indigo kept shifting their weight uncomfortably and looking everywhere but at me, reminded me I was naked.

"What is it?" I said. "My nakedness?" I put my hands on my hips and shrugged. I told them not to be uncomfortable for I wasn't inhibited about my nakedness at all. I told them, as honestly and devoid of self-aggrandizement as I could, that the only embarrassment I felt about my nakedness, was how it made others painfully aware of how comparatively out of shape or ugly they were when they beheld me. "Not that people behold me naked often," I said, "because I'm modest and don't have sex unless I'm in love. But I do feel embarrassed for them, I guess, when they happen to see me."

"It's not just your nakedness, Lightly," Indigo said gently. "It's all that blood at the sides of your mouth. You should wash it off."

Santana Montana agreed. He said that if you could get AIDS from a needle, he was pretty sure that eating part of someone would do it, too. So, I turned from them and went down and waded into the ocean, noting the nearly transparent fish darting amongst my ankles.

"Those damn dogs don't stand a chance," I said to one of them as it sped by. "Margaret was like that. So pale you could see right through her. So fleeting you could never take hold."

I waded on out to my waist and then my shoulders. My body stung all over from the salt in the thorn holes. "It hurts," I said, "because it's healing."

I dove under the waves and took in great mouthfuls of seawater, sloshing it around, and spitting it out like a whale does from his spout. I doubted just then that *spout* was the anatomical name of the aperture, and resolved to ask Santana Montana about it, for I didn't know why it wouldn't be a sphincter. Then I lay back to float and admire the white puffs of cloud above me.

When you get your ears under the ocean that's when you can really hear the Earth's machinery at work—the subduction and creation of crust and so on.

The waves lifted me gently and sat me back down and there was something incredible about it all—the pain and the bright sky with its poof of clouds, the church bells ringing in one ear and the scrape-grind of Earth's crust emerging and submerging in the other, and the sizzling of bubbles I'd heard in the breakwater. I knew, for example, our universe sizzled like that and that a wave was not the name for a single crest of water but rather the name for all of the crests and troughs stretching from one side of the ocean to the other.

I smiled, shut my eyes, and floated in all that blue-green water with its see-through fish and giggles of foam, letting the current take me playfully hither, as they say, and thither.

When I emerged from the sea a quarter of an hour later, Santana Montana was gone and it was just Indigo leaning back on her elbows in the sand with her long brown legs stretched so beautifully before her. I'd floated considerably down the beach and had a little walk before I came to stand before her.

She handed me the shorts and I put them on.

"Are you okay?" she asked.

"Yes." She gathered herself and rose before me. She turned me to inspect my cuts and scrapes.

"I'm sorry," I told her. "I didn't mean to make everything a mess for you."

"Do you mean Perry?"

"Yes."

"Don't be sorry. It was already a mess. You've given me a reason to fix it."

"I helped fix it?" She stepped forward and her arms encircled my neck.

"In a way. I gather that's something you do quite a lot. You fix people."

Her touch and the way she said it made me blush, so I asked where Santana Montana had gone. She said he took the quad and went to check on Rosa and let her know I was okay.

"What did you two talk about?" I asked. "You and Santana Montana."

"Nothing important," she said. I nodded. I had felt invulnerable against Anit. I felt the opposite of that with her.

"I'm okay," I said. "I mean there's nothing wrong with me. I'm not crazy or anything if that's what you were asking. I've had a few messed up things happen and some people who couldn't accept that I was fine and happy. It's a shame, but I'm wide open and forgiving and don't hold against broken people their failure to understand those of us who can't be broken."

She put her hand on the nape of my neck and kissed me. Then she said,

"Why don't we go to the house and I can doctor you?"

"Okay," I replied, genuinely touched. "I'll bet the press of your hands could heal anything."

She laughed. It was a quiet laugh, humbled and scarred by the goings-on of the past few days but with something husky in it that sent sparks up inside me.

She kept her arm around me as we walked along the beach.

After a while, she said, "You are odd. I mean, you are very odd, aren't you?"

I didn't know what to say other than I trusted her opinion. She felt soft and comfortable against me, familiar in a fascinating way, but also strong and protective.

She was smarter and better looking than I was. She was a more impressive and better person than me.

I was pleased to see it so clearly.

77

We climbed up the steps of her house and she led me over the beige tiles to the plush couch at the far end of the porch. I lay lengthwise on the cushions and she went into the house. When she came back, she had a little medical bag and the breeze was stirring the drapes along the corners of the porch. She dragged the wicker coffee table closer to the couch and sat on it.

"I can't do much for your cauliflower ear," she said, "but I'll fix up your scrapes."

I brought my fingers to my ear. I hadn't realized it was so badly busted. It felt huge and foreign like reaching blindly into a box to touch curiously at a water balloon. Silently she went about dabbing me with ointment all over. She did a thorough job with the clinical efficiency that only people with medical training can muster. Though, truth be told, I doubted she let her lustrous hair caress all her patients in quite the same way that it kept brushing over my skin. When she leaned across me to apply the stuff to my thighs, I really, truly thought I was going to die with love, for I don't know how else to describe what the gentle, warm press of her body against mine did to me. When she was done, she sat beside me in the rocking chair and looked out over the yard at the beach and the water, though it seemed to me she was looking at nothing.

"I had a twin," I said, for I felt something had been given to me and I wanted to give back. "Her name was Margaret and I loved her. She didn't like it when people fawned over her, but strangers would hug her because she always looked so damn cute and worried, but that was long ago."

"What happened to her?"

"She died. I slept with her body in a pool of blood, but it doesn't matter. It was my father's fault. None of us knew, but we should have. Looking back, we can see she tried to tell us a hundred times. My father set in motion her death and her death set in motion a series of invisible phenomena that led to a father that's brain dead, a mother I can no longer recognize, and a brother who can't be near any of us if he is to survive. These are the things that have washed up, but there is the history behind them. Nothing is random, but that doesn't matter either and that's the point. We all have our problems and life is hard."

I gave her my spiel about the limpet because I was really thinking about helping her with her hardships, but Indigo said, "Right, but limpets don't have the brain power we do." She asked me how vividly I thought limpets recalled their difficulties, and I admitted they did not remember them vividly, if at all.

A little later, I guess realizing I didn't want to say any more, she said, "Maybe we should be limpets then." I wanted to tell her that, more than anything in the world, I wanted to be a limpet with her. Scavenging along the seashore together and not remembering difficulties or harsh cycles sounded as lovely to me as having her always walking toward me in a floral bikini, smiling that sweet, white smile, and smelling of fruit and surf wax with the *almendro* blossoms twinkling in her hair like tiny stars in a black, black sky. I knew how sometimes the wanting and the almost having could bring you closer to perfection than having ever could, but I also knew how unfulfilled longing could become itself a type of fulfillment.

I didn't tell her any of it because my heart was fat and trembling and my throat constricted. My body ached, but my guts hurt, too, and I told myself, *Remember how you feel—really remember it—because you might never feel such tenderness again.* I lay my head back on the couch and sang a little wistful song about limpets the way I'd long ago sung songs for Pop to make him laugh. That was the trouble, the irreconcilable thing—that he could be Pop and monster in the same man.

Indigo watched me dreamily, a gentle, contented smile on her face. She was hugging her long legs and her feet were perched at the edge of the rocking chair seat and she was rocking ever so lightly. In the front yard a breeze sent a few yellow blossoms from the *pau-brasil* spiraling toward the grass— it looked like they were unwinding themselves from limb to land on invisible, diagonal strings.

78

That night Indigo and I made dinner together and ate at the table on the porch with both of us watching the particles of light diminish over the sea.

"Your friend said that he and Rosa will leave tomorrow."

"Yes, I know."

"When are you leaving?"

"Soon."

"Me, too. I wish we had longer."

"Not me. I'd rather have more lives than live longer."

"I'm not sure I follow you."

"I know. But I wish you would."

We cleared the table, then washed and dried the dishes together. She phoned Perry's father to get an update and then we sat on the porch. A few strays came to check in and we gave them what leftovers we had.

When it got dark enough, we went down and walked the beach beneath a snowfall of stars. She rattled off the names of constellations like she'd been kissed by them.

I didn't say much except to ask if I could stay the night.

"I would be disappointed if you didn't," she said.

We walked past the campground and went over to check on my friends. Santana Montana was writing in his notebook and looked up. He stood as we approached and I noticed the gun in the band of his pants.

"Where's Rosa?" I asked.

"In the tent asleep."

"She's had a scary day," Indigo said. Santana Montana nodded.

"What time will you leave tomorrow?" I said.

"The bus leaves at seven sharp."

"I will come help with the tents in the morning," I said. Indigo was staring at the pistol.

"Oh," Santana Montana explained, patting it. "In case Anit comes back."

"You're both welcome to stay at the house," Indigo said to him. "You and Rosa."

Santana Montana breathed deeply and looked up at the stars. The stubble on his face made him look rugged and the sun had given his lovely golden skin tints of antique copper. He looked like a chieftain or a well-fed castaway. With the gun in his waistband he looked like someone you wouldn't mess with. It suited him.

"Thank you," he said. "But I would like to stay here tonight—this last night—and since Rosie is already asleep..."

I understood him precisely. My heart hurt at the idea of a future without him. But all the futures with him remained, though unseen, no less real.

79

We took showers after we got back to the house and Indigo gave me a fresh shirt and shorts from the closet. By the time we crawled into bed, my body was starting to tighten and ache. The bed was soft and small. We were both tall enough for our ankles to hang over the end. That her bedroom would be located in the guesthouse suggested a unique set of circumstances, but I was happy not to know. I was happy to lie there in the orange light from the bedside lamp and luxuriate in the simple freshness of it all.

She turned off the light, and we lay there listening to the constant murmur of the waves and the occasional shrill call of the house geckos. She pulled a thin blanket up to cover both of us and smoothed the surface of it over her stomach.

"I'm going to behave," I told her. "I mean," I added after a moment, "unless you don't want me to."

She laughed beside me in the dark. "I think we should try and behave," she said. "We don't know each other very well."

We talked. We filled in our backstories like you'd fill holes in a cemetery—with corpses and wood, dirt and stone. But I didn't mind. I liked what I felt, lying there with her. I liked the sound of her voice. It was all very gratifying and sad, too, because she was to leave in three days time and then what would I do? My friends were leaving, and she was what I had come for as much as anything.

"I'm gone on you," I told her. "I want to stay with you for forty years just so I can kiss you when you are old."

"I like you, Lightly. I like you very much, but I'm starting med school in August and I've got to be moved and settled into a new apartment. There's so much to do. And I have to see Perry before I leave, if he'll see me. But we have these final days and when we are back in the States we can figure out how to see one another."

I didn't know what to say. I loved her. That was all. I didn't say it, though, and she was quiet a long time. She yawned and stretched her long body beneath the sheets and then curled and snuggled against me. It had been a rough few days for her. I listened as her breathing slowed and became deeper and more regular.

I turned to lie on my back and looked up into the dark ceiling. After a while I shut my eyes.

80

In the morning, I left Indigo sleeping and went over to help Santana Montana break down and then pack up the tents. We returned them to the office and then went back and stood looking at the bottle cap whale on the ship hull that leaned against a *ceibo* in our otherwise empty campsite.

Santana Montana put his hands up on what would be—if he were thinner—his hips and sighed heavily.

"It is as if we were never here," he said.

I laughed. "We weren't. We were here but we were also not here and a-hell-of-a-lot of places in between. We left Tommy Jeffs, but we also did not leave it. We're heading off to different places but versions of us will not leave here and so on. It's a gift to know that they'll stay here always and live out the living we would have done here, that we will, in a manner of speaking, do." His face was blank and I laughed. I laughed loudly, from the guts out into the treetops and the blue sky above us—out into space above that. The world was so small; teenagers were sailing around it and birds in flight could encircle it in tendrils of air. I looked out at the water.

"What did Indigo talk to you about?" I asked. "When you took your walk."

He studied me a moment. "You know what we talked about," he said. "Just as, I suspect, you know what your brother and I talked about back in the town of Charlottesville." He waved me off and fixed a level look upon me. "Go home," he said. "Or come with us. We are worried for you."

"But there are already *mes* in those places," I told him. "This me has other paths. It's all about entanglement and parallel universes, and Schrodinger's cat, you see? We're here, there, everywhere—alive and dead as long as there's no one to observe us."

Rosa was watching my mouth, and I raised my eyebrows at her. A pained look played across her face, and she threw her arms around my waist, suddenly whispering *mi mangosto* lovingly into my ribs again and again.

"What does she say?" I asked. "That I am very manly?"

"She is calling you a mongoose," he said. His voice was thick with something. "She is saying, 'My mongoose, my mongoose'."

I knew that I'd shaken Santana Montana from the paralysis of his life, beaten the shadows from him, and I also felt as though I'd snatched Rosa from the mouths of wolves, but why—considering how I'd arranged things for them—did I feel so much as if I'd lost?

I hugged Rosa against me. Something in me, at my very core, ached. I felt broken, broken, broken. I knew I was lucky to feel it.

We made it in time to catch the morning bus and stood beneath the big mango tree at Soda Taunos. When the bus came I walked them to the door. The driver was out loading the bags in the side compartments. Santana Montana and Rosa stood there looking at me.

"You sure you won't wait and ride up with me tomorrow when I go to fetch Crampton and the others?"

He shook his head. "The future cannot wait until tomorrow," he said. "It must happen now."

"But the future can never be now because now is always the—oh, damn it, Santana Montana, you've given me a cramp in my pumpkin! Okay, listen up then," I told him, putting my hands on his shoulders, "remember that you may not be a bullfighter, but that even your grandfather would not have stared down a croc the way you did."

"It was a caiman," he said.

"You don't know which it was," I said. "That was braver than that stupid nonsense with the bulls. I guess you are genetically inclined to such things after all. Greater things, in fact."

A few locals climbed on the bus and a few more were still slowly making their way up the road in the dust toward it. A girl in a bikini sped by on a quad with a surfboard across her lap. There was a basket affixed to the rear and there was a small dog sitting in it. I caught our reflection in the dark glass of his eyes. He watched us until he, the quad, and the driver disappeared in the rising twist of dust.

Santana Montana took out the folded picture of my beach. He handed it to me.

"I am sorry you did not find what you sought."

"I'm not done seeking," I said.

"Come with us."

"In another world I do go with you, my lovely friend."

"Why not come in this world," he countered seriously, "and stay in the other?"

I laughed. I would miss being able to talk with a genius of Santana Montana's ilk. I would miss being understood.

"You know why," I said. "You are the one that knows best."

"I anticipated that response," he said. He held out something to me. It was a filthy envelope which was worn and filled to the bursting point with something that felt like paper.

"What's this?" I asked. "I'd rather you'd give me that gun. I don't want you getting into trouble."

"No," he said gravely, glancing at Rosa. "I may need that. This is a gift."

"For what?"

"For everything. I don't know if you know what you've done for me, but I have been helped through something by you and by this thing you think you are on. You have gotten me to this point, and if you had not become my friend, I would have found it necessary to invent you." He looked away. I smiled and started to open the old envelope, but he said it was for later.

"Okay, well, don't worry about me," I said. "Are you sure *you've* thought all this out, Santana Montana?"

"Yes."

"What of Tommy Jeffs?" The bus hummed. The air was full of fumes. He looked around him as if really seeing the place, not just the "here," as they say, but even all those cities that lay beyond, as if he were taking a photograph of the moment that he might pull from the album of memory in his old age and admire with fondness.

"There are little suspension bridges between Isla Rio Cuale and the Vallartan mainland," he said. "People come to picnic beneath the island's big trees and to walk through the flea market with light hearts."

"What do you mean?" I asked.

"I mean that Thomas Jefferson College is not 'school'." He waved his arm to indicate the whole wide world. I knew then what he meant.

"Jesus," I said. "That is kind of sappy, Santana Montana, but, even so, I give you praise for your brave thought. Take care of my Rosie." I realized immediately I should have been asking Rosa to take care of him, for whereas he was brilliant and sensitive Rosie was savvy and tough. Rosa put her arm around Santana Montana and smiled up at him. He didn't put his arm around her or look at her though, so she gave his rotund body a shake and loosed a foamy giggle into the air. What had happened that day? By what invisible phenomenon had he gotten her to come? I saw them—Santana Montana, a museum director now, old and bald, and Rosa with liver spots and her hair pulled back—lounging in the shade on the little Vallartan oasis, or walking through the flowers to the spot where Santana Montana would deliver another of his lectures, which were approaching the status of famous in the guidebooks to the area. I saw them, too, crossing a narrow suspension bridge over the Rio Cuale with Rosa leading Santana Montana by the hand to that little island of flowers. From that image came a single word that did not begin or end but was always in the process of being said. That word was *love*. The word—the sound of it—formed a halo around my head and hovered there.

I nearly cried. Very truly, nearly did, because I could see suddenly the whole bright and beautiful arc of their life as they grew, loved, aged, begat and, finally, passed away, leaving behind them a cavalcade of accomplishments and three of the most brilliant and resourceful children imaginable. "God," I said. "You two give me more hope—you give me more hope," but then I gave up because some strange bubble had formed in my throat. "Goodbye, goddamn it," I said, giving him a big hug and then I turned and walked back down the road.

I stumbled back along the rutted track in the direction of Indigo's house until I heard the bus rumbling up behind me and was forced to step aside. I looked up and saw Rosa and Santana Montana sitting together. I was about to wave but stopped short when I noticed the handsome young man leaning over the back of the seat in front of them and speaking intently to them. They looked like they were plotting. They looked like a little family. It was the young man who caught my attention because he looked, though it might have been the effect of extra moisture in my eyes, awfully similar me.

I hustled on back to tell Indigo about what I'd seen.

She was raking *almendro* leaves in the yard, preparing for her own imminent departure, and after I explained what I'd seen on the bus and in the weight room at Tommy Jeffs, she said, "So you're saying this has happened before?"

"On occasion, darling," I said.

"Maybe it's the stress of parting?"

"It's not stress and I'm not crazy, either. I think it's a sign the vision approaches."

81

We went for *casados* at Burger Rancho and I tried to convince her to pursue the vision with me.

"Lightly, I can't," she said. "I have so much to do. Why not come with me? It's just a couple more days here and we could fly back together. You could help me get settled in and we could figure out how to see each other."

"I can't," I said. "I've got to meet my friends at the airport tomorrow and then find that beach."

It was obvious that we were at an impasse, and to push it further would be to ruin what precious little time we had left in Santa Teresa. So we dropped it and after our meal we went out to surf the La Lora break. I came in when the waves got big but Indigo stayed. Dark clouds were wandering up from the south. I went and stowed my board at Mrs. Engdahl's and walked into town.

I stopped by Tres Olas and picked out a batch of postcards. There were people I had messages for.

When I came back, I dragged the whale art Rosa and I had made from plastic bottle caps to Indigo's house and leaned it against an *almendro*. Gusts were pruning in the treetops all around.

I looked up and saw Indigo running up over the rippled sand with the board under her arm as the rain squall moved up from the south over the headlands. Threatening clouds towered over her and her hair twisted and blew about behind her as the first drops of rain came in on the stiff wind. From my dark and sheltered spot beneath the canopy of *almendros* I watched her come and breathed in deeply of the turbulent air for I could feel how the Gulf of Nicoya curled its way in eddies and rills behind the peninsula. I knew from Santana Montana that beyond the gulf lay Puntarenas and the Cordillera de Tilaran, and beyond those mountains, the pasturelands of Alajuela and Heredia, then Limon and the Caribbean coast.

On that bighted beach with Indigo running swift and easy while lightning pulsed silently in the clouds behind her, I felt I was witnessing the absolute heart of a wild, lovely summer. And I told myself, *Keep this image. Take it and cup it gently and it will be a talisman in darker days,* for I had known right then that if all the pain of living—what, if anything, I'd endured so far and what was yet to come—was the price for that glimpse, then I'd gotten the better of the deal.

82

We went to Meli Melo for dinner and the easy way we were with each other felt right. It felt comfortable. We held hands across the table and it was like what I felt when I was with her was something that I'd known once but had been separated from. All my rushing about, my bumbling heart and head full of insistent voices, were merely the devices by which I would be returned—not to her exactly—but to the feeling that came over me when I was with her.

We went back to Mrs. Engdahl's and I dragged the ship hull from the tree and muscled it onto the porch.

"What is it?"

"A gift," I said.

"Are those bottle tops?"

"Yes. I didn't tell Rosa, but I was tracking the colors of the bottle caps we found. In here," I said, pointing to my temple. "They are the most prevalent trash item on the beach."

"I know," she said. "I grew up here."

"Yes," I said, "but I doubt you've ever broken down the numbers. Sixty-one percent of the bottle caps Rosa and I collected were some shade of red. About eighteen percent were blue. Six percent were green and four percent were yellow—you get the point."

"That's an extraordinarily random thing to do."

"That's the point, though. It's not random at all. There are reasons and logic behind seemingly random phenomena. We could probably tie these statistics to the production and sale of these products in this area."

She looked out at the water a moment.

"You'd need to account for things like sea current and littoral drift," she said.

"You are a genius," I said. "You're absolutely right. If only we had time we might explore it. There are endless miracles all around us and everything is depth, history and complexity, and there is reason behind it all and logic and science."

83

We lay in the bed that last night beneath the scent of leaves wet in the treetops while the crashing waves loosened coastal perfume from the splintered sand. I kissed her magic eye and the scar that curled from it. Our warm, sweet breath mingled in the intimate space between us, the air hovering and electric. Her body fragrant, her voice green and blue, the tone of it sheaving me in velvet as she murmured the secrets of her heart.

After we had made love we lay there beneath the ceiling fan and the breeze kept lifting the curtains into the room. She asked me again to come back to the US. Her hair lay across my chest and I stroked it delicately as if it were the parchment of a sacred text.

"Do you mean to Massachusetts?" I asked her.

"No, to your school. We could work out how to see each other."

"Oh, I'm not going back," I said. "You come with me. I'll gather up my friends, save them, and then we'll track down the vision."

"You really believe in this vision?"

"Yes. I even have a picture." I went and retrieved the photo. She propped up on her elbow to study it in the dim light and her hair came cascading over her shoulder. "I only know that it is on the peninsula," I said. "I have to keep looking."

She lay back with the photo. A house gecko called from the porch and another answered, two frail creatures trying to find one another in the vast dark. I wished them well.

"Regarding your scar," I said. "Santana Montana said that you have heterochromia. That it was from a wound. And Dr. Jorge told me about the crash. Reading the signs then, my theory is that..."

"I know this beach," she said quietly.

"You do? Where is it?"

"It's on the Oso Peninsula."

"Another Peninsula? How do I get there?"

"It's very remote—just jungle and sand. One of the wildest places on Earth. There are few roads, fewer houses. No electricity once you're beyond Puerto Jiménez."

"How can I get to it?"

"I can show you on a map. It is pristine, but totally off the grid. I went there with friends several years ago to surf the river mouth breaks. At mid-tide Cabo Matapalo has a steep and powerful right hand wave. It's a point break. See the point in your photo? That's it."

She handed the photo to me, and I studied the rocks closely.

"We got stuck in a river and our car got washed out. You could spend a year there and not see a soul. We were there two days until the rains stopped and they could get to us. The rivers were so bad they had to send a little plane."

"It had to be deserted," I said. "I didn't realize that until now."

"Do you really believe in this vision?"

"Yes," I said.

"But why?" she asked.

"I just do."

"What is it a vision of?"

"The nature of things as they are when the veils fall away. There are other dimensions all around us. Right now. Here in this room. It's a problem of perception that we can't see them."

She was quiet then. I listened to the run-up and backwash of the waves in the distance, and imagined the Witch's Hat all silent and pointed like a seamount in the air above the dark, cuspate beach. I wondered if Anit's mother was tending to his wound in the jungle nearby or if she'd sent him out again to ride the buses.

After a while she said, "I don't know that I would want to see such a thing."

"Me either," I said, "but I've got to know." She turned and lay her arm across my chest and kissed me sweetly and my scar tingled mightily.

84

When it was time to go, I stood on the porch holding Santana Montana's guidebook, pointing to a spot on a map inside and looking at Indigo.

"I think you should go home," she said.

"Come with me."

"I can't," she said. "We've gone over this already."

"I'll look for you in three days," I told her. "You can clear out and lock up here, check on Perry in San Jose, and then follow me down the next day."

"I'm not coming. I have to get back. I mean, my father has been to space, Lightly. There are big things that I want to do."

"I'll be in Cabo Matapalo. Right where you said. Hopefully my vision will have already come. Otherwise we can wait together."

"Lightly, come with me. At least wait and ride up with me to San Jose day after tomorrow."

"But my friends arrive tonight, and anyway I'm in a rush to complete an inner alchemy, and I've got to go now, but I'll wait for you on the beach that day."

She put those mismatched eyes in me and I felt the twist of doubt in my gut—what did Rampage and Biggs and Crampton matter compared to this? There was a catch in her breath and then she said, "I think this is goodbye, Lightly. Find me when you get back." She enveloped me in a fragrant hug and pressed her sweet lips to mine for a long time until finally I had to break away and run at a dead sprint just to make the bus.

All Things Await

85

The bus ride was long and lonely. It shuttered over the ruts, and I only managed to scrawl a few of my postcards. If we made decent time, I would arrive in San Jose about an hour before the last flight from the US touched down at 10:30 that night.

I'd waited that whole time to open Santana Montana's gift, so I stuck my cards away in the guidebook and took out the envelope. It came apart easily. It was full of money, as I had guessed it would be. Very practical. Crisp new colones no doubt fresh from the ATM in Playa Carmen. He'd written some things on the inside of the envelope in his purple script. *Did you know CR money was named after Cristóbal Colón?* he'd penned. Below that he'd written, *Did you know that's Spanish for Christopher Columbus?* Jesus. There was no doubt that he was a sweet genius. A fleshy golden god and a guide of sorts for Rosa just as sure as she would be a guide for him. It was enough money to last a well-lived week. He'd also written that he anticipated a letter at some point and included the following: *Write Rosa and me at: Museum Rio Cuale, La Isla de Rio Cuale, Puerto Vallarta, Jalisco 43810.*

At half past eight, I was herded along with the other passengers onto the ferry at Paquera, and we crossed back over the Gulf de Nicoya under the cover of darkness. I wrote the rest of my postcards on the well-lit ferry. We climbed back on the bus at Puntarenas and I tried to get in the right high-energy mindset that I'd need to greet my friends. We arrived at Coca Cola bus station in San Jose a little later than expected but I still had enough time to prepare properly for the arrival of Rampage, Biggs and Crampton. Though I had no desire to make signs and hold them up as they walked through the baggage claim doors, if I were to make a sign at all, it would have been on a big poster board, and it would have read, NEW RELIGION: JUST DON'T BE AN ASSHOLE. I wouldn't have taken it to the airport but to a street corner and I would have held it up all day.

But I didn't have the time.

Just opposite the station was a dense maze of shopping kiosks. There were a couple of items I wanted to pick up, so I hoofed it on into the labyrinth of backpacks, tennis shoes, electronics, and stacked pet food. At a corner kiosk, I found and paid for an old pack of pastels and a sketchpad.

On my way out, a man came up and opened his coat to reveal an expensive looking camera—no doubt stolen. "You buy?" he asked—though he might have been saying Dubai. I just wasn't sure. I waved him off.

I got turned around in the narrow network of passages on the way back and stumbled upon another Jesus behind glass. This one stood in a little open area at the center of the market and was just as tall as I was. I went over and pressed my forehead to the glass. It was cool amidst the humidity, the fumes, the smell of plastics and leather, and the stench of armpits and of the things men and women put in their hair or whatever it is they do.

"Unless you plan on helping at some point," I told the robed figure who was crowned with golden thorns, "then I'm going to have to ask you to stop following me, Jesus."

Finally, I emerged from the jumble of ramshackle shops and hailed a cab.

By repeating the word *airport* over and over like a simpleton, I was able to make my destination known.

As we made our way along, I eyed the cabber suspiciously. He spoke to me once but I pointed at my tongue and shook my head. When we pulled up to the airport a little later, I waited in the cab right outside with the meter running.

A tall girl entering the airport in an orange frilly skirt caught my eye. She seemed so cool and easy among the noise, fumes and bustle. One long braid of gloriously dense dark hair hung to her waist, and she was carrying a stack of brightly wrapped packages and both the packages and braid tied up in the same pale blue ribbon.

Something about the composition coaxed up a sea-foam of longing. It bubbled and fizzed just below the surface of perception. I wished I could follow her or put myself inside those packages, to be bound for people or places unknown, to be a gift in many elsewheres. But I'd timed my arrival pretty well because just as she entered through the glass doors, Rampage emerged toting his green duffle. I leaned out the window and waved him over.

"Did you spy Biggs and Crampton?" I asked.

"If I tell you they weren't on the plane," he asked, "can we leave right now?"

Our cabber got out and went around to wrestle Rampage's bag into the trunk.

314

"What do you mean?" I asked. "Didn't they come? Don't lie to me, Rampage," I said. "How many goddamn times did I audible to *fullback dive* when we got near the end zone, so you could have the glory?"

"Biggs wasn't on the plane," he said. "I'm sure of that because he texted me while I was boarding to say he'd surrendered his seat to someone more deserving, whatever that means. Crampton was, though." He shook his head and didn't try to hide his frustration. "You could have said something, Light. Why the hell did you have to invite him?" he asked. "Of all people."

"Because of all people," I said, "he needs help most."

"I *hate* you," he said.

"I know, Rampage, but you love me more."

A few minutes later Crampton emerged from the airport. I waved to him, too, and sang out his name, but he flicked me off and slid in up front without a word, leaving the cabber to his bag.

"Cramps, old buddy," I said, leaning forward. "I want you to let down all those slabs of hate you've built up about your heart and brace yourself for something amazing."

"You are fucking crazy," he said matter-of-factly. I didn't tell him how his brown words smelled like the inside of a dead pirate's old dancing boot.

The cabber got back in the car and said something, his eyes watching me in the rearview.

"You leave those poor, goddamn girls alone," I told him, shaking my fist at him.

"What are you talking about?" Crampton said. "He wants to know where we're going."

"Oh, that. Calle Central," I shouted, repeating the name of the shitty hostel I'd located in Santana Montana's travel book. "Tranquilo Backpackers."

He nodded and we were off.

"What happened to your face, Light?" Rampage said.

"What?" Crampton turned to look at me.

"It's all busted up," Rampage said.

"That ear," Crampton said, pointing, "is much larger than the other one."

"Oh, I just fell out of a tree."

"Yeah, well, I hope it was a tall damn tree," Crampton said, turning back around.

Rampage passed the tips of his fingers over the scratches on my forehead. He shook his head.

"I came because you asked," he said, taking out his phone and thumbing through his music, "but you didn't say a damn word about that hick right there coming or how long I had to stay. I'm leaving first thing tomorrow."

He put on his earphones.

86

We coasted amid heavy traffic back down the hills into the city basin. There was a dark, tense vibe from everyone including me. Leaving Indigo still felt the opposite of right. It wasn't the best start, what with everyone hating everyone and Biggs not showing up. I considered it a Herculean effort on my part not to just abandon them to their hate, insecurities and their depressions—especially now that I knew the exact location of my vision. But they needed me and I did not need any of them and still I stayed for I was secure about the good I saw in things and in people, in the work of art imprisoned in all that shit stone.

I nudged closer to Rampage to put my arm around the massive bulge of his shoulders, which—even sitting as we were—did not quite reach the height of my nipples and watched the night pitch its tent all around us. Outside, the city lights underlit the clouds, turning them not so much sunset pink as Pepto-Bismol pink.

The cabber and Crampton were conversing in Spanish.

"No, no," I told Crampton, "don't speak to the man."

Crampton waved me off and kept talking.

"Okay then," I said, speaking over their conversation. "Well, ask him where the nerve center of Chepe is—that's where we must go. Tonight is tricky and Chepe is mangy and wild."

87

Calle Central was a real shit-hole of a place. We checked in and, after a short awkward ride in a rickety elevator, we found our room and dropped off our belongings. I put the narrow package of pastels I'd bought in my back pocket and carried the sketchpad under my arm as we headed back down. Crampton received directions from the hostel manager to the places the cabber mentioned—the Key Lounge and a place called the Blue Marlin Bar in the Hotel Del Rey—and I asked for an envelope, which I took, folded, and stuck in my front pocket.

"What do you want that for?" Crampton asked.

"To put something in it, of course," I said. "What else?"

We went back out to the street. The air of tense hostility had been nearly unbearable in the cramped hostel and so it was liberating to step out on the pedestrian thoroughfare.

We moved through a bustle of people and the bustle was heavy, no doubt.

"The Key Lounge is just up ahead," Crampton said gruffly. "That and the Blue Marlin are the two main spots. You can go somewhere else if you want." We followed him, though, knifing through the crowd. We were only accosted once. A man dropped in beside us to ask in accented English if we liked "the green" or "the white."

"Jesus," I yelled, shooing him with my free hand. "What is it with you people and your colors!" He veered away immediately aided by a rough shove from Crampton. The man recovered nicely, though, and fell in step with a couple walking in the opposite direction, hocking his wares beneath the dark sky of a youthful, uncertain Costa Rican night.

In my heart, I missed Indi and Santana Montana and Rosie. The presence of Crampton and Rampage only enhanced my loneliness, but I was determined to play my part, to orchestrate for them what they could not on their own, direct.

"Listen to me, Cramps," I said, drawing up beside him. "There are now billions of known galaxies today and, like people, they come in different sizes—some are much smaller than our galaxy, some much more massive. One weird thing about galaxies is how they cluster together like people at a party or something. All this clustering is going on even as we're tossing pigskins, peeling potatoes, taking in a movie or out the trash, or shuffling into the nerve centers of Central American cities. Hell, even now the individual galaxies—ours and billions upon billions more—are in motion as are the larger clusters of them as a whole."

He looked at me as if I were crazy, as if I were speaking the language rain makes when it falls on leaves in remote forests. I knew, though, it was really that I was speaking a language that folks like Cramps were not yet alive to. Or perhaps it was a language to which man had grown deaf, and, as such, could only hope to one day hear again. And that wasn't the same thing. It wasn't the same thing at all.

88

It's an odd thing for sure, though—all this shuffling into the heart of Chepe, Central America, I mean. It can make you see, for example, how varied and how small places on Earth truly are all at the same time because what you are seeing are the worlds that exist within a world you thought you knew.

I mean, you take in San Jose in June like we were, for example, and you come on down toward La Central and if you take Calle Avendo 10 you'll see the city's heart pulsating in bright lights. To get to the center you have to go through a dangerous patch of city where the crackheads hang out, but three blocks more and you're at the thoroughfare which is well-lit and heavily traveled.

Near the fleshy center is a little place called the Key Lounge and you have to get through the muscle-bound bodyguard who is wearing a nice suit and brandishing a metal detector wand. His skin is as beautifully black as the remotest reaches of space and maybe later you'll realize he's probably from the Caribbean coast but it's more likely that you won't.

Inside you'll think for a moment—if you go there—that you are in Cuba, what with all the dark wood and floor length red curtains and the smell of cigars, but you're not in Cuba at all. There are three pool tables at the front of the Key Lounge and maybe you and your companions go play a game. Maybe everyone orders the Espinaca Ravioli or maybe they don't. Who knows? Hell, maybe you give up on the pool since you can't concentrate on it or because your friends are god-awful at it anyway. If you do, you'll go sit at the back bar beneath a full-length photograph of Humphrey Bogart, but who cares?

89

I'd had two Imperials at Key Lounge but I could never get a feel for the place as a whole which was frustrating. Also frustrating was that Rampage, still furious at me, kept his earphones in and Crampton sat up at the bar with his big back to us.

So, after a while, I collected my friends to say that we should make haste for the Blue Marlin in the bottom of the Del Rey.

I was not prepared for what I saw inside the Blue Marlin—which was the name of Hotel Del Rey's bar—because I'd not seen the like before. The exterior of the hotel was the same peach heart color that Dr. Jorge's scooter had been and the bar was baffling. What baffled me most were the women. Not just women but beautiful, otherworldly women. Lovely women with hardly anything on, women with breasts bursting from blue or red or pink or yellow tube tops; thin, willowy young girls with flat chests, slender arms, skin-tight pants; voluptuous women. God, you name it, and I saw it. It blew my mind, to be sure, but not because I'm horn-dog at all, which I'm not. No, the thing that really destroyed me was the nearly incomprehensible fact that these women were all here in one place and seemingly outnumbering the males twenty to one. That I had never seen at any party, and my failure to understand it produced an uncomfortable shock to my system.

I stood on the big pink tiles, while a healthy stream of newcomers pushed past and opened my mouth to say something but found I couldn't. I was very happy to see Crampton and Rampage's mouths hanging slack, too. Rampage pulled the earphones from his ears and stood there dumbly.

"I need to sit down," I said. "I can't wrap my mind around this place and I need a beer and some time to figure something out, but I'm not sure what."

As we made our way slowly through the log jam of people, we passed by a stretch of green, felt-covered card tables, a roulette wheel, and a spinning, tire-shaped wire cage with balls or dice or something inside which an employee in a black vest and matching bowtie turned with a crank handle. Beyond those we saw the carnivalesque flash and blink of row upon row of slot machines.

There was loud music, of course, and banter, along with the bells and sirens of the slot machine area. The result was a deafening mix which might have seemed hypnotic to some, but managed to produce in me a nearly unrivaled sense of anxiety because all of those sounds mixed into loud, obnoxious colors in the air, in my ears and before my eyes.

"Stay with me!" I yelled over my shoulder. We snaked and wound our way haltingly through the packed crowd. I moved us up toward the bar area, which was entirely raised on a platform and had massive fish mounted here and there on the photo-filled walls and a huge, wooden canoe hanging from the ceiling of the bar itself. The bar area was even more densely crowded than the entrance and casino areas had been and since I found myself stuck in traffic I began yelling over the people sitting at the bar to get the bartender's attention.

Finally I got it. "Imperials!" I yelled. "Imperials, goddamn it! Six of them. Please! And fast!" I held up six fingers and in this way was able to make the bartender understand me. She went to fill my order.

"Did you see the bartender?" I heard Rampage ask. "She is drop-dead gorgeous!" I twisted my head around, taking in all the additional beauties that I'd not been able to see due to the half wall separating the bar area from the casino floor.

"What in the fuck is going on? What is happening here?" I yelled angrily at my companions. "If I don't get an explanation my head is going to explode on my shoulders!"

By the time the beers arrived, we had snailed our way to the opposite side of the bar and were looking down upon a half-dozen round, wooden tables which were thankfully dark because of a low slung ceiling. The waitress unloaded our Imperials from the tray and stood there, so I nodded to Rampage. "He'll give you his card," I screamed into her face. "Start a tab. A tab! A tab, you understand?"

"What?" Rampage yelled.

"Don't worry," I said. "Next round's on Cramps."

Rampage handed over his card but the look on his face told me I'd never be forgiven for any of this.

"I don't like being called Cramps," Crampton said.

"I know, Cramps," I said. "And I don't like having a bottle of Wild Turkey smash the heavenly fuck out of my pumpkin head."

"Yeah, well..." he replied.

I raised the Imperial to my lips and didn't take it away until half was gone. I clutched the other Imperial tightly by the neck. Beside us, two old, overweight gentlemen were sitting with two lovely girls with dark hair and dark skin. They all suddenly stood and made for the back of the bar, presumably to try their luck on the tables or the slot machines.

When I was done with the first Imperial, I pushed it from me and said, "Well, gentlemen, I suppose this is where the action is, indeed. What do you say, buddies? Good lord, but we weren't expecting this at all."

90

As our night at the Blue Marlin progressed and our drinking along with it, the weirdness of the place applied a consistent pressure to my mind and I felt increasingly ill at ease. Also of concern was the behavior of Crampton. When, for example, the lovely waitress brought us our third round of drinks, Crampton asked her if she spoke English. She shook her head to indicate she couldn't and Crampton said, "You have a great ass. I'd love to fuck the shit out of you."

"Jesus, Crampton," I said once she'd gone back into the crowd. "What's your problem?" Crampton had mumbled something about her not being able to understand him anyway.

"Oh, you're surprised?" Rampage mocked. "I mean what a fucking shock that the biggest asshole at Thomas Jefferson College is also behaving like a complete jerk in San Jose. I, for one, could not see this coming at all."

"Listen to your friend," Crampton said but there was a quiver of nervousness to his voice.

"Friend?" Rampage repeated. He hadn't even looked at Crampton once and he wasn't looking at him now but at me. "Did you hear that, Light? Now he's calling me *your friend*, but how many drinks before it's *nigger* this and *nigger* that? And I'm buying this stupid hick drinks thanks to you. I'm telling you right now, Light, if I go crazy on someone tonight, it will be your fault entirely. It will be totally your fault."

Crampton looked angry, but I felt something coming. I really did because he looked uncomfortable, too. He had seemed agitated the whole evening, which I knew was a necessary way to look if any change were ever going to take place. And there was something hopeful in the way his mouth moved as if there was something to be said. He rubbed fiercely at his cheek for so long it turned red. Then, suddenly, he made fists with his hands and slammed them into the table.

"All right," he said. "I am not proud of what I called your friend, Rampage." He spoke as if a confession were being tortured from him. "I was brought up a certain way. I am who I am. I have my own ideas, but what I did was wrong. I came here—flew all the way here—as much to say that as to avoid prosecution, which, in the end, I don't care about at all. Fuck the other AAs." He looked at Rampage now and said, "I'm sorry, damn it. I was drunk and I'm abrasive and I'm loud. I won't apologize to anyone for that, but I'm sorry I called you what I did and I'm sorry if I call you it again. It's who I am. Don't you understand? That stuff was put there and now it's who I am." He stood to leave. "And I don't give a shit if you forgive me or not." He grabbed his beer by the neck. "I'm going to drop off my credit card at the bar then go to the blackjack tables. The next few rounds are on me, okay? Come and get me when we're leaving."

"Oh, my god," I said as Crampton made his way through the women. "We are on to something. Don't you go anywhere, Rampage," I added. "We're making real progress here, and, besides, there's this hotel in San Tana with a painting of a blue nymph in a blue pool, and I think you should see it. The whole hotel is dripping with original works of art, and I know you're the only one alive who can explain them to me. I hope Elena will let us in. Her opinion of me is not high."

I really did know that about Rampage: That he could explain it. The thing I didn't know was that the whole evening was about to collapse.

After Crampton had left, with a beer clutched in each hand, Rampage shook his head reproachfully at me and announced he was going to spend the next two rounds sitting alone at the bar.

Apparently, a few ladies had their eye on me and saw an opening, for no sooner had my friends departed then two came to sit with me. One was small with brown skin and hair darker than the absence of dreams when asleep, the other was tall with blonde and pink highlights in her dark hair. She had a little low-slung purse hanging from a delicate gold thread over her shoulder.

They smiled in such a friendly and interested way that I was automatically partial to them and on their side in whatever matters they might have at hand. The smaller of the two said something to me that I didn't understand and I put my hand on her forearm and yelled, "I know, sweet lady, I've got to head to the Peninsula, but it's too late now for public transportation."

They giggled and pointed to the rear of the bar.

"I'm leaving first thing in the morning by bus bound for the Oso." I said. "I mean it. It's the first goddamn thing I do. Here," I said. I took out the tattered picture of the beach and carefully unfolded it. As they studied it, I told them, "I saw you noticing me from the bar, and I'm very flattered but I have to tell you I'm in love already and I am a decent and honorable young man.

Sort of old fashioned in that way." The girls smiled and I smiled, too, feeling as though there were ways I had of understanding, of making myself understood.

Jeez, but I sat there talking with those girls like I'd talked to all those foreign nannies and babysitters, which is to say I would listen to them intently, try to guess at what they were saying, and respond accordingly, and earnestly, in English. We started out hesitantly but I was soon enjoying it because they laughed a lot and because it seemed we'd become engaged in a math game of sorts with each other. I reckon I'd been speaking intently with them for about a quarter hour before I felt a hand on my shoulder. It was a new waitress.

"Yes?" I said. "My friends have skipped out on the bill, haven't they? Damn it!"

She shook her head and put her mouth in my ear. "Speak Spanish?" she asked over the din.

"No," I said.

"I thought not."

"What is it? Have you heard my conversation with these fine ladies?" She nodded.

"Am I responding appropriately? I am for the most part, aren't I, kind waitress lady? I know. It's incredible. I've always had this gift of getting the gist of people no matter what language they speak."

"They are prostitutes," she said. "You are deciding a price with them. I want to tell you this because you seem like you know nothing."

"Ah, wait, what!" I couldn't believe it, but one look at the waitress told me it was so.

"Damn," I said. "Really?" I gave the entire bar area a good going over with my eyes and it was as if I'd slipped on magic glasses. All the women were just as beautiful, to be sure. But now I noticed little odd things. Like how they were all together in teams of two, for example, and how none of them were engrossed in conversation with each other but scanning the crowd for a gaze that would meet theirs. Suddenly, all the tumblers fell in place and the Blue Marlin unlocked its secrets to me. The atmosphere of the place changed for these were not lovely women proud of their bodies and flaunting it. No, no, these were young people showing off what their bodies were worth by wearing very little and by standing in ways to accentuate breasts or posteriors or both.

"Prostitutes?" I said again.

"Brothel," she said. "See the swiping machines on the wall? Must have a card to prostitute in the Blue Marlin."

I'd noticed how some young, local men stood along the wall of the place and I asked the waitress if these were male prostitutes. She explained that they were drug runners—that the prostitutes would call them if a customer also wanted drugs and then they'd come running.

I looked around the place. The ratio of women made sense now and the pudgy tourists in their dark slacks, white colored shirts, and the silver-haired grandpas with gold rings on their fingers that moved among them suddenly filled me with revulsion. I looked at a group of men at the table beside me. They looked like imitations of Floridian fishermen. I studied their fingers until I could see the pale skin where their wedding bands had been.

"Sweet lord," I said. "What the hell have I stumbled upon here?"

Of course, I wanted to leave right away. After thanking my waitress and hugging and apologizing to the two prostitutes for taking up their time, I set out to gather my friends, but I couldn't find them. I'd gone around the cavernous and packed bar several times and was nearly to the point of assuming they'd gone ahead and left when I finally spied Crampton at the black jack tables which I'd already checked twice. He'd evidently been getting up to buy shots for himself because empty shot glasses where lined up before him at the table. I believed that the apology had been massively difficult for him. When I rushed over to tell him that we were, in fact, in a brothel, he snarled, "Of course we're in a goddamn brothel. It's the most famous brothel in Central America. Didn't you see me go upstairs with one? You think it's my personality winning them over?" He then explained that there was a private elevator at the rear of the place and how you and your lady had to sign in on a sheet when you left and also when you returned. "By the way," he said, "I've rented a room up there for the whole fucking night. You can use it if you want."

"I can't find Rampage anywhere," I said. He'd looked off in the direction of the bar with eyes that were blurry with beer and liquor. "Rampage is right there. He can use the room, too, I guess."

I went back over to where Rampage sat on his barstool and wrapped my arms around him and squeezed.

"Where the fuck have you been, buddy?"

"Outside on the phone with my girlfriend," he said.

I gave him the scoop about the place being a brothel, but he didn't seem all that surprised either. "I sort of figured," he said. "That's why I called Amber: Guilt. Now, let's get out of here."

We agreed to have one last drink for the road and turned to watch Crampton take more shots of whiskey. He had gotten pretty bad. He was falling off his stool and cursing loudly, accusing the dealers of cheating. A minute later he called a group of Australian men *witless cunts* and then grabbed a waitress by the arm. She managed to twist free, and he poked at the private area of another woman who was just trying to make her way to the slot machines. She turned and slapped him hard on the cheek, and he roared out curses at her.

"There's a kid whose mother never loved him," I said to Rampage.

"Wrong," Rampage said. "There's a kid deeply loved by racist, sexist, stupid parents."

Anyway, it was so bad that a group of locals—whether pimps or drug runners I didn't know—came over and stood menacingly at his table and I thought that was the end of him, no doubt.

"Come on," I said. "Let's get Cramps."

He stood up.

"I'm coming," he said. "But only to back you up. I hate that big redneck." I nodded and we made our way toward Crampton.

I was prepared to get thrown out or have to pick Cramps up after the drug runners had wiped the floor with him, but when we reached the tables I saw Crampton had come up with a brilliant plan, for he had ingeniously picked that moment to throw up on his shoes and collapse on the floor.

"That's it boys," I said to the drug runners once I was standing over him. "Really and truly it is. I swear to god. He's a terrible bastard. Look at him down there. I'd like nothing more than for us to drag him out into the San Jose night and beat him with long pieces of PVC pipe but we won't, because someone might need the pipes for plumbing and whatnot but also because I want to try and fix him. I promise you I'll take him upstairs right now and pack him away for the night."

The card dealer, who apparently knew some English, translated and slowly the runners left us to our job. Not because they were the forgiving sort but likely because they were working and couldn't spare the time. I leaned over and pulled Crampton up to a sitting position so that his back rested against my legs. The security guard at the rear elevator came over and reminded me in passable English that Crampton had paid for a room for the night.

331

"I know," I told him. "Thanks." I squatted down and put his arm over my shoulder. I asked Rampage to get his other arm. "He's a big boy," I said, "and all his hate makes him heavier than burlap sacks of wet sand, but we've got to get him to the elevator for he is in the black, as they say."

"I'm not touching him, Light. I won't lay a finger on him."

"Why get angry at his stupidity?" I asked. "Do you rough up children who can't read? Do you beat new Earth creationists who say dinosaurs are a thousand years old? Do you sniper out fools who say the holocaust is a myth and gays should be hung? No, you try to help them. You work your ass off to bring them the light and hope they'll come around. Gandhi and MLK would know what I mean. Crampton may need a beating, but he needs some teaching even more. Hell," I said, "he basically told you that he's sorry and finds it impossible to change because of how he was raised. Can't you see him out there hunting with his daddy, whom he loves terribly? His eyes are big and lovely like the eyes of children always are and here's this old bastard father of his nipping at a flask of Wild Turkey and pouring that racist shit in the porches of his ears like Claudius poured that cursed *hebona*, or whatever, in King Hamlet's ear while the vain King was napping in his well-tended garden and what not? Whatever. My point is racism's almost genetic in the sense it is passed from generation to generation. You and I have to show him different."

I could see Rampage was weakening a little. Not because of the strength of my argument, but because he loved me greatly as evidenced by the earnest, pleading way I was asking him to help. "That little boy," I said, "is still in there and needs our help and that should soften the heart of an artist like you, Rampage."

"Alright," Rampage said. "I'll take him up, but not because of any of your overly dramatic, sensitivity bullshit, but because I want to be at the airport first thing in the morning and am ready for bed." He shoved me, not gently, aside and squatted down. He pulled Crampton over his shoulders and maneuvered him into a fireman's carry. He came up slowly but very steady.

"God, Rampage," I said. "You are stronger than a tank."

He held his hand out. "Well?" he said.

"What?"

"The room keys?" I searched Crampton's pockets and got the keys out. I held them up and said, "I want you to do something for me."

"What? Something else?" he demanded. "Don't you think it's enough that I've come to another country for you, that I'm toting a fucking racist on my back for you? You didn't even tell me this dumb-ass was coming. Now I'm leaving. What a fucking waste of time."

"I want you to sketch him for me tonight."

"Oh, *fuck* you," he said in disgust and started to turn away.

I stepped in front of him and said, "Do you remember spring break behind the Food Lion Super Grocery, Thelonious?"

"Yeah, yeah," he said, "the Pabst, the marshmallows, getting me on the inside at Tommy Jeffs, blah, blah, blah. You used that to get me here. You can't keep using it, Light."

"Okay," I said. "I love you and you're right. Just do this last thing for me and I'll never use it again. Please, buddy. It'd mean the world to me."

Rampage was giving me a hard look now and I knew it was because I was putting the spotlight again on an area of great vulnerability. Rampage was *very* smart. I knew he'd refigured that spring break in his head, that time we'd spent together, which had been a little oasis for him during a time of drought and isolation and hardship. He'd thought I'd hung out that whole spring break behind a grocery store without plan or intent and very much as if I'd nothing better to do. Surely he was seeing now in that marvelous mind behind his lovely, gold-flecked eyes that it was not so. That it'd all been by a design of sorts and with gentleness and love.

"I don't have any supplies," he said quietly, shifting the enormous weight on his shoulders.

"Shit, Rampage," I said. "I don't know where the sketch pad went, but..." I stuck the keys in his shirt pocket. I pulled the pastels from my back pocket and held them up.

"You've crushed them to pieces," he said.

"I know."

I put them in his waistband.

"I really hate you," he said. "You bought all this shit and planned it all out. You think you're so clever, don't you? Oh, how I really do hate you." He pushed his way past me and made for the back with the aid of the helpful security officer. The officer spoke to the man with the clipboard and then Rampage, hefting all that hate on his broad shoulders, disappeared into the elevator without a backward glance.

I turned to the card dealer. "Have you got a mop?" I asked. "I would like to clean this mess because I'm the one responsible for bringing it into your fine establishment."

All Things Await

91

My heart was heavy as I mopped up Cramps' sick from the floor. This—the bar, the music, the girls, the chaos of it all, was not my scene. After Indigo, with her intelligence, quiet strength and beauty, it all just felt profane. I missed her terribly. After I stowed away the bucket, I went to the bar to close out Crampton's tab and collect his card, but first I thought it wise to run the tab up a little more. After a few more Imperials, I made my way to the elevator with only the number on Cramps' room key in my head.

The security guard was kind enough to let me in. When I stepped into the room I saw Crampton lying on the floor. He'd torn the drapes off the wall and had pulled them over him like a blanket. Rampage had stripped to his boxers was in the double bed. I slept in the double bed with Rampage and it was a fitful sleep because I awoke three times before finally rising for the day. The first thing that woke me was Santana Montana's rapid breathing. I immediately sat up to shake him violently before realizing it was a dream and that my friend was no longer with me.

I loved Rampage, for sure, but I missed Santana Montana more. I missed Rosa, her wonderful impatience, the light that lived in her eyes.

I woke again in the early morning dark when Rampage placed something beside the door and slipped out. There must have been complimentary toiletries in Del Rey for Rampage had showered and shaved. I could smell the crisp, fresh odor of his aftershave even after he'd stepped quietly from the dank, musty room.

Some time later that morning I awoke a third time to Crampton vomiting in the toilet. He moaned and cursed and spat, and it was with great difficulty that I went back to sleep.

At last, I awoke on my own to an empty room. Crampton was gone.

I showered and when I came out I noticed the piece of paper folded by the door. I went and opened it. The sketch was on the back of what appeared to be a room service menu. I stood there in my towel and held it away from me and gave it a thorough going over with my eyes.

Rampage had sketched Crampton where he'd lain on the carpet against the wall. Crampton's body was ursine and there was a bulkiness to all his features—including his eyebrows, lips, nose—that made him seem thick, heavy, primitive and dumb. The almost total absence of color seemed to reinforce the impression. I studied the eyes, though. Closed of course, for he was sleeping. I brought the sketch to my face. Though Crampton's eyes were closed, there it was—the thing I was looking for. It was in his lashes—in the shading just below the eyes. Rampage had made the lashes longer then he should have, thinner than all the other features. There was tenderness in the representation of those eyelashes, the slightest hint of beauty, innocence, goodness. The untroubled, cleanly unshadowed cheekbones were like those of a child. I noted that Rampage had given Crampton's lips just the slightest color of pale rose.

"He's done it!" I said. "He's studied him and he's seen the thing inside. He didn't want to, but he had to." I believed that if he'd looked at him long enough, if he'd stared at Crampton when Crampton was weak and undone on the floor, then I knew he'd see the thing, just as I knew he'd done the lashes and shaded the lips and cheeks last—after his disgust had melted away.

I was so excited that I threw the door open. There was a fat, bearded old chap in slacks with his shirttail untucked backing out guiltily from the room a few doors down.

"Mister! Sir!" I called. He recoiled instantly and his discomfort grew as I jogged toward him in my towel.

"Hold on," I said, taking him by the arm as he tried to move past me in the direction of the elevator. "Take a look at this."

I shoved the sketch in his hand and he looked at it as if coming out of a daze. He looked like I'd just put a poisonous snake in his hand.

"Jesus, old man," I said. "Snap out of it! I'm not judging your philandering and whatnot. Just look at this sketch a minute will you? Right here. Focus! See the face, how sweetly the eyes and eyelashes are done?"

"Uh," he adjusted his spectacles and looked closely at the sketch. "No," he said finally. His lips were dry and cracked and his breath was the air from a linen trunk in a dusty garret.

"The faint blush of red in the lips?" I said, looking at his teeth.

"No, I'm sorry."

"Well, anyway, he gets it now," I said. "He can't help but feel for Cramps no matter how terrible he is."

"Please," he begged. "I don't see it. If it's money you want—"

"You look like Santa," I said, folding up the sketch and regarding him.

"Only, what would Santa be doing in a brothel?"

"Look, I'm not— I just slept here. That's all. The other hotels were full."

"Oh, okay," I told him, stepping back. "That's none of my business, sir."

He hurried past me and punched the elevator button three times, tucking in his shirt as he waited. I went back to the door to my room. "By the way," I said. "We have pictures of you from last night and we know your family." A fresh look of horror appeared on his face. "The room mirrors," I explained. "They're all two way so we can record everything. That's how I knew you were leaving your room. Anyway, if you don't start donating twenty-five percent of your earnings to assisting underprivileged youths in Central America and addressing your halitosis, we're going to email the video to people you know. It's extortion for a good cause—just this new thing the guys and I are doing."

The elevator went *bing* and yawned opened, but the man just stood there gawking in the hall.

92

I sat at the little shabby desk and searched the drawers. I found a pen and a Bible in the top drawer and on the back of Rampage's sketch, I wrote, *It was Rampage who carried you on his shoulders when you passed out & he got your card back for you.* I retrieved the folded envelope from the pocket of my jeans. I put the sketch and Crampton's credit card in the envelope. I wrote Crampton's name on the front followed by the Tommy Jeffs address.

"It's the start of something maybe," I said, licking the envelope and pressing it shut.

All Things Await

93

I could not bear to be in the rank and enseamed sty of the Del Rey room alone—something in it brought the pain of Rosa's past to the forefront—so I walked back to Tranquilo Backpackers to retrieve my meager belongings and check out properly. Rampage and Crampton must have both come by and collected their things before setting out for the airport, too, because their bags were gone.

There was a note on top of my bag written in Rampage's handwriting. It said: *text from biggs this AM. gave his ticket info & room # to a doc. biggs says the doc is coming to Tranquilo's. r looking 4 u. biggs says post nude photos of him if u want, but make sure his penis looks big pls. and that u should talk 2 the doc. good luck light. IMO u should see ur mom's friend. At least ur parent wants u. still kinda hate u. Rampage*

Back at Tranquilo's and with my belongings once more in my care, I went and checked out in the atrium with the bearded man behind the glass.

"I'm wondering," I said, "if you could tell me what room my doctor is in?"

"You rented a room here," the man said.

"Yes."

"You and three friends."

"Two friends. Yes, I know."

"But you did not stay here last night."

"Okay, so you're right. What are you doing! We were at the Blue Marlin and it was terrible, okay? But what about the doctor?"

"Which is your doctor?"

"Tall, slicked back hair. Meticulously groomed and in a suit."

"Oh, yeah," he said, "Bernie mentioned him this morning. We don't get many suits at the hostel." He looked at a clipboard. There were two coffee mug stains on the back of it. They looked like the circles birds draw in a November sky. "Number twelve," he said.

94

I knocked on the door of room twelve, and after a few moments Dr. Crispin pulled it open. He was in creaseless, mint-colored pajamas, but otherwise his appearance shocked me. His hair, normally slicked back carefully, stuck out in all directions. He had stubble on his usually clean-shaven face. The face itself was pale and drawn. There was a tiny sticky note on his lapel and he regarded me with eyes that were not sharp and clear and focused, but devitalized, enfeebled.

"Lightly," he said, tiredly. "Oh, thank goodness."

"Jeez, Doc. May I touch your stubble?" Before he answered I gave his cheek a couple of light strokes. "Just as I expected—like the rind of a kiwi. You look awful."

"Getting your mom here was a challenge. I'm sure you can empathize."

If I'd had coffee in my mouth I might have sprayed it all over him.

"Mom's here? You're joking. She can't leave the damn house and would never stay at a hostel! Where is she?"

"Shower." There was a little door beside the bed and I could hear the water now.

"She was quite sedated for the flight. I had to wheel her to the cab in a wheelchair."

"Damn," I said looking at the door to the bathroom. There was a yellow sticky note on it, too, and, now that I was looking, there were some on the walls. "How did she do the sticky notes if she was sedated?"

"Very slowly," he said. "But I think she can do them in her sleep. Actually, she might—I've woken up with them on me occasionally."

"Wow," I said, shaking my head at him. "I don't know what to say."

"Well, say how you are," he said. "She's worried sick."

"Biggs told you where I was?"

"Yes. We went by the dorm room. I understand Biggs and your mother traded some letters. Once I explained things, he seemed really eager to forward me the email with the flight and hostel information you'd sent him. Stella is going to be enormously relieved."

"Listen, I can't believe you got her here. I mean, it's incredible. Really.

But you do know I'm not coming back with you, if that's why you've come. I'm too close now."

"Look, Lightly. I know you've never liked me very much and I understand that. But I do hope you know that I genuinely care for your mother. She has been through an awful lot. You both have."

"So you keep saying." I pulled the sticky note off his lapel. It read, *good color for casket linings*. "I don't know how you can stand being around her so long."

"She likes these particular pajamas," he explained.

"Okay."

"But that doesn't mean I like them."

"I understand." I gave him the note and looked at him. A cockroach went up the peeling wallpaper and disappeared in a crack where the wall and ceiling met. "How is she? The delusions and all?"

"She hasn't talked about them for a couple of months, Lightly, but there's still a lot of work to do, and I do understand if you don't want to come back, but will you just talk to her, please," he said. "Just try and put her at ease. It's a very big thing she has done to come here. Only you could have done it."

He looked like hell with his stubble and bleary eyes. Mom was putting him through her psychological ringer, and I thought of exposing all that to him—of asking him if she could break down a learned psychologist, what chance did any of us kids have. He looked so worn that I thought maybe he wasn't as bad as I'd made him out to be. Nobody ever is. Not as bad or as good as we'd like to think. The problem, of course, was that it cost me an awful lot to put my mother at ease. It damaged me to take that trip inside her head.

"I tell you what," I said. "There's a shitty little soda right across the street. I saw it coming in. Tell her I'll take my stuff and wait for her there, but there's no chance in hell I'm leaving with her. Tell her that, too."

"Okay," he said tiredly. "Thank you, Lightly." *The poor man*, I thought. *To find himself entangled with such a family.*

"You do know, Doc—don't you?—that her condition is likely incurable."

"That's strange," he said absently rubbing one of the buttons on his pajamas. "She said the same thing about you."

344

95

The *tipico* soda proved to be just as rundown on the inside as the outside had suggested, and the old man falling asleep at the table next to me got me feeling a little depressed. But since the interior matched the exterior, I knew this place was trustworthy and honest—fulfilling its unspoken promises— and there was a pleasant fresh scent in the air. I couldn't make much out of the menu but managed to order the *pinto gallo* and a coffee from a waitress who, by the look of it, had just been informed her only daughter had stone man's disease.

"What is wrong, lady?" I asked after giving her my order, but she just looked at the big surfboard and bag I'd carried in, shook her head sadly, and padded back to the kitchen. "The poor, lost thing," I said fondly, watching her go.

96

Having traveled to all those exotic places as my mother pursued back-grounds for her horny romance novels, and having—for huge portions of my time in these places—been in the care of various nannies as my mother worked, I was quite familiar with seeing Stella coming toward me after a long absence. And so it was that as I watched my mother cross the street, holding onto Crispin's now suited arm, I felt the press of images and certain familiar feelings raising their heads inside the vault of memory. Breezes of Grand Canaria filled my nostrils and on the back of my neck I could feel the cold rains of winter in Portugal and so on. In her giant sunglasses, my mother looked very much like a wealthy blind woman being led through a foreign city by an attendant, which was not, I knew, very far off the mark.

Ah, Mother! In her immaculate black and white striped sleeveless dress with red belt and expensive shoes! Her black, full-bodied hair and her skin just as iridescent as Margaret's was in my dreams. Her beauty marked in the eyes of men, in how animated they'd become when they met her.

She swept through the door, Crispin at her heel now, and stopped until her eyes found me sitting there smiling at her. She came briskly forward, ran her fingers through my hair, and encircled me in her arms.

"My son," she whispered into my ear. "My dear little boy. Let me breathe you in," and with her nose buried in my cheek and small hands pressing against my back, she drew in a long steady breath.

"Okay, Mom," I said, feeling her tears through the silent tremor of her perfumed body. "Okay, now. It's all been arranged. Sweet lady."

She straightened and moved her thumb beneath each dark lens, and I no-ticed the pen in her hand.

"Are you well," she asked as she sat opposite me.

"Mom?"

"You look like a dashing island dweller."

"When you were hugging me just now, did you happen to put something on my back?"

"I'm sure I don't know what you mean."

I reached behind me and removed the note. *Wash*, it read.

"Lightly," she said, ignoring the note. "It's so good to see you."

"It's good to see you, Mom. It has been a long time."

"I know. I've not gotten out much."

"Yes," I said. "I know."

"I've so many things to inform you about and helpful guidance to offer, and you've not come home."

"I know that, too, Mom, though of late I've felt prodded to return."

"My attempts to prod you? Are you being clever? Always such a clever boy," she said. I watched her write *clever boy* on the little pad in her hand. She reached over and stuck it on my wrist.

"Thanks, Mom. You're clever, too. To track down my trip info from Biggs was genius. I should have known better to give that to a kid unlikely to come." I tried to keep a sweet tone, but in my head my mother was a great, beautiful fanged creature and I had no intention of venturing into her web. That's exactly what going home would have been doing—going right to the center of it.

"Not like you to slip up, dear," she said.

There was a cough behind me. "Should I..." Crispin asked. He'd been standing there uncertain whether to join us or give us privacy.

"Oh, I'd forgotten you were there," Mom said and made a dismissive shooing motion with her hand. Then, seemingly catching herself, she added sweetly, "I'm fine, Thorn. You can go back to the room or maybe eat at that table over there." She pointed to a dark corner of the soda where a dim wall sconce hung upside down. She wrote *Thorn leaves* and reached for him but he was too far away, so I took it from her and placed it on his trousers, though I winced as I did. "Sorry, Doc."

"I'm used to it," he said and turned away. I watched him make his way to the back.

I leaned toward Mom. "*Thorn*?"

"Didn't you know his name was Thorn?"

"He was my doctor. I called him Dr. Crispin."

"In retrospect," she said, watching him, "it was probably a mistake to make him change his name."

"You made him change his name? What was it before?"

"Steve or Stephen or something. Regardless, it was probably also a mistake to have him counsel you about Margie and your father."

"You mean because you were sleeping with him?"

"No, darling, because he wasn't very effective. I think he's more hopeful and brave than helpful and bright."

"Shit, Mom, you ought to go easy on that poor bastard."

"Please don't talk like that, Lightly," she said, scribbling another note. "No one says *ought* anymore." She handed it to me. Note: *poor diction.*

"You're probably right," I said, setting it aside. "As am I." The waitress appeared, looking more strained and unhappy. She placed the plate and coffee in front of me and I took the waitress gently by the wrist. "I'm sorry about your misfortunes, dear sweet soda waitress," I said, offering her a sympathetic smile. "Things will improve. We'll arrange something." She wrangled her hand free and looked at my mother.

"*¿Quieres algo?*" she asked. Stella recoiled instantly. She wrote quickly on her pad.

"*No gracias,*" Mom replied placing the note on the hem of the waitress' dress. "*Estoy no comiendo.*"

Note: *Leave.*

"Sorry," she said once the waitress had left.

"It's okay, Mom."

She watched me. "Always trying to arrange things for others," she said. "You have a good heart, son. It's good to be with you again finally, even if none of it's real."

"Thanks," I said, forking some rice and beans into my mouth.

"What is your plan?" she asked.

"I'm on a quest," I said, "which is driven by a longing of great intensity."

"So I've heard. Is there anything I can do to get you to come home?"

Note: *Home*

"Not at the moment, Mother." I cut the eggs into squares with the edge of my fork.

"Will you come home?"

"No."

"Please?"

"Nope. Hey, I met a girl. She's super smart."

"Do you know you're unwell, son?"

Note: *Unwell.*

"Let's consider the logic," I said, "of me coming to stay with you. If I am unwell—which I'm not—but if I am, then it makes little sense for me to come stay near you considering how unwell you are."

"I'm getting better. I came here, didn't I?"

"Yes, Mom," I said gently. "Yes, I'm proud of you for that. How are you with the delusion?"

"Tell me about this girl you met."

"Do you still believe this is your story?"

Note: *Story.*

"But if this is your book and I'm your character then why not just write that I come home with you?"

"I told you. You are my Lightly as I remember him. Everything I know of him. I can't change what he—what you—would do in certain situations. I'm just following the tuneful patch of your voice in this narrative. The moment I make you do something you wouldn't do, it all becomes inauthentic."

Note: *Tuneful patch.*

"Why write about me?"

"You're gone, Lightly. Not here in this book I'm writing but in real life. You left school and came here and disappeared. This was year before last. I want to understand what happened to you and writing is a highly imaginative investigative tool that is just as valid as science or history. Besides, it's all I was ever good at."

As expected, my head was starting to hurt and I could feel that pressure rising in my chest. Who could survive such ideas.

"Why not write about Margie?"

"Because I know what happened to Margie and why she did what she did and don't ask why I don't write about Dad—he's a monster and doesn't deserve to be understood. Besides, he's in your story already. He's the dark thing you run from. He pushes you ever forward."

"So you really believe you're writing all of this? That this—right now—is a scene of yours?"

"It is."

"Are you here now? In Costa Rica?"

"Yes. I've written a version of myself here inside this story, but I'm also in Costa Rica in real life finishing it up. The end is near, I think, and you know I have to travel for backgrounds in order to complete a book. The Spanish for the local characters is not good yet either."

"But you're a romance writer, Mom. This isn't a romance novel, believe me."

"Didn't you say you met a girl?"

Note: *Romance*.

"Funny," I said, but it wasn't funny at all. It did my head in, this delusion of hers. This idea her brain had created to escape facing what her husband had done. Her manuscripts always had sticky note tabs everywhere—it was how she wrote and revised. Now those sticky notes were all over everything around her in real life. She couldn't tell the difference.

"Why do you want me home then, Mom? I mean if you're writing this, then you're with me at all times, so why try and force me home?"

"Isn't it obvious, son? I don't leave the house. I didn't want to come here for the background. I wanted you in a locale I knew already. The condition I have here is the same as the one I have out there."

"So, in this story now and in your real life as the writer of this story, I've gotten you to leave the house for the first time in years?"

"Yes. What are you after, son—this vision? Why won't you let me understand?"

"There are six more dimensions knotted up in our four, Mom, and there are parallel worlds I have eyes in. I want them all to be opened at once. Does that help?"

"No. There is only one world, son. One reality."

Note: *One*.

"Not so, Mother. You're claiming to live in two, and, besides, you live in a world where I'm a character of yours; I live in a world where I'm not. We're haggling over our own variant realities even now and each is equally real to us."

"We both live in a world without Margie," she said.

Note: *Margie*.

"Yeah, Mom, I know."

"Do you remember the time she found the bag of drowned puppies in the creek?"

"Yeah. Some asshole didn't want them, I guess."

"She carried that bag all the way to the house. At least a mile. Crying the whole way."

"I remember," I said. "She laid them all out in a row."

"Six dead puppies. Golden and bloated and wet. She said—and I've never forgotten this—'How could he do it?' She said, 'How could he do it to such small, beautiful things?'" She faltered.

"Steady, Mom. Steady now." She was rocking back and forth. She wasn't talking about puppies anymore.

"I should have known, Lightly. Just because she told you and Lance doesn't make you responsible. You were both young and scared and he was your father. It's my fault. My fault I didn't see it. Me with my head stuck in the other worlds, in those stupid books."

"Quiet now, Stella. It's okay. It's okay."

"I know, son, but I want to tell you that."

After her big cry, I talked with Stella for as long as I could stand it. After a good while, exhausted from guilt and hysterics, I could take it no more and I told her I was going.

"I'll be watching," she said. "I'll need to stay here until the end."

"I know, Mom," I said. She came over and hugged me tightly. I ignored her fingers pressing another note onto the back of my shirt and hugged her warmly.

"I know I can't force it, son, but it'd be nice if it ended with a pretty image."

"If what ended?" I asked.

"Maybe of the sea. Or of flowers—what were those flowers that Margie loved? The ones that grow in the mountains?"

"Bluebells," I said.

"Lightly, there's been so much awfulness. It'd be nice for there to be something pretty at the end."

"Good luck, Mom," I said into her cheek. "I love you."

She went over to the door and motioned for Crispin. He came by and shook my hand.

"Thank you," he said. "We tried to stop you, I know, but I think it may have been a stroke of luck, your trip here. Maybe leaving the house will open up the world for Stella again. It's a big first step."

"Luck?" I said shaking my head at him reproachfully. "Huh." Maybe Mom was right about him not being all that bright. There was no luck in it at all—just hidden designs. Despite his ignorance, I hoped the best for him all the same.

I pulled the note from the back of my shirt. It read, *Love.*

97

I had just enough time to locate the post office, send off my postcards and the envelope for Crampton, and sprint back to the Coca-Cola bus stop before the bus bound for the Oso Peninsula set off beneath the pale gold glow of morning light.

I settled in for the long, slow trip. There were only a few passengers. No tourists, just tired local men with serious faces. Eventually the bus let us out in a small town and I transferred to a big, white SUV driven by a local man whose name I didn't catch. It was a rusty old thing he drove with big tires and a powerful engine. It was rough going. Miles of difficult terrain, of washouts and places where there was no road—only hills and pastures that you drove through. My big u-boat of a surfboard banged back and forth against the sides like the pendulum of a grandfather clock.

We were silent—which was fine by me—I needed my mother's voice out of my head. I needed for the excitement to build, to kindle inside. I'd suspected that the peninsula I was searching for was some place undiscovered. So I'd go on down to the Oso and see what was what, gather my vision to me and maybe after Indigo arrived we'd work down there for a while. There'd be time for med school. Until then, we could rent a little place on the beach. We could lie in the dark in a hammock on the outside porch and swing, and swing, and swing, until we got folded into the sound a wave makes when it breaks—all that transference of force again, and again, and again, forever.

And I found such a place in Cabo Matapalo. I'd walked the road after being dropped off and had eventually come upon a little bungalow with a mango tree and a hammock in the yard. It was for sale, but it was also for rent.

I went across the dusty, potholed road to the *tico* Gringo soda—the only other building around. There was a filthy, rusted solar panel on the thatched roof, and gorgeous black and white photos of old Costa Rica taking up one whole wall. A rattling little fridge with a glass door had foodstuffs for sale—beer, mangos, lettuce, a block of cheese, Trits, fresh eggs in a basket. It buzzed loudly.

I held up the rental flier to the proprietor and he nodded toward a balding man with glasses set in thin, circular frames who was reading a little paper.

He saw the flier as I approached. "The Planck Bungalow?" he asked.

"Yes—could I rent it?"

"Of course. It is very lovely, no? You go down path and the beach is there. Locals call it Playa Matapalo, but I call it Planck Beach." His heavy German accent turned his words the color of copper as they issued forth beneath his thick mustache like a strange guttural music.

"You're Planck, aren't you?" I asked him. He laughed, so I did, too.

I had enough money to rent the house for three days, but in the end I only rented it for two. Indigo would be here tomorrow—I believed that.

After I'd settled things with Planck, I went over and bought a tomato, a few eggs, a box of *leche*, and two sixers of Imperials, then I borrowed a black marker from the proprietor and crossed out the word *Not* on my shirt.

He looked at me like I was a fool. I looked at him like he wasn't.

98

I wanted to rush right down to the beach, but I was travel-weary and somehow afraid. My mind felt cold and raw, like someone was unwrapping layers of gauze from it, and besides, I was holding out hope that tomorrow Indigo would appear on the beach. I wanted to share my vision with her. I'd run so long. I could wait until morning.

So I put my meager groceries in the cold box, and opened a beer. I could feel the vision on the other side of the trees. It throbbed there over the beach in the center of the sky.

"You can wait one day," I said.

I opened all the windows and doors and swept out the bright, little bungalow. I opened a narrow closet: a wire hanger, an old shoe and some empty beer cans at the base of a rusted file cabinet. I opened the file cabinet. It contained a single file. Inside the file was a sheet of paper and on the paper was written the word *blank* and nothing else.

"Jesus," I whispered. I went over and stood in the doorway. Two spider monkeys watched me from the tress.

Indigo might come, but I did miss Rosa and Santana Montana terribly. I drew pictures of them in the sandy yard. How would they get to Mexico without Rosa having a passport? Neutrinos passed through my body, through entire planets, untouched. They would drive, of course. But how would they do it? I set the beer cans on a low wall and knocked them down with rocks from twenty yards away. *Mi nombre es Ligeramente.* There was no one here to save. *Ojos estrellados.* Things circling in the Hadron Collider, people in white coats searching for answers in black holes, in the invisible things collisions produce.

I collapsed into the hammock.

It creaked back and forth, slowly swinging in the waning light. My thoughts drifted unchecked, sought connections. Frogs chirped and howlers filled the treetops with their throaty calls. Wind moved gently through my hair. I listened as my breathing slowed, as it had come to my ears from a great distance. In. Out. In. Out. A slow, steady pull into the shadows.

In my vulnerable state between sleep and wakefulness I asked for something gone to return and suddenly Margaret was there—six years old, beautiful as first snow, pale as the dust on the moon. She stepped from the shadows to touch my hand. We were at Cub Creek. The farmhouse and Blue Ridge Mountains lay somewhere behind us.

It had been so long, this flight from her, and I was rotten tired of it. So, I took her hand, as I always had, as I did before she'd go into the woods, as I did when she lay dead in cool blood on the white bathroom tiles, and she sank quietly into the water with me, a scrawny, freckled thing. The scent of her shampoo filled my nostrils.

"You're confused," she said. "I never did. It was you. You've jumped selves before. You jumped here for her but you forgot. You'll jump again for me. And so it goes. My Lightie, quantum schizophrenic, junky for longing, for that flicker, that instant between variant *yous* when you are all of your selves."

The dead make little sense when they speak, so I started whispering those sweet things to her just like I had to quell her whimpering. My heart was swollen, trembling, the exact opposite of invulnerable—if you'd squeezed it in your hand you'd know what I meant. I knew how Margaret was Uluwehi, Emmy, even Rosa and Indigo. It was obvious, of course. I saw how those girls ghosted behind her transparent skin, trapped there like smoke in a jar, or like the faded faces imprinted on poor Anit's arms.

"It snowed the night before we buried you," I whispered. "We stood beside your grave. The trees were dark against the blanket of snow and all the branches were encrusted in ice. They tinkled like little bells."

"No," Margaret said. "It snowed the day you jumped."

I asked her dreamily if the clover had stopped screaming beneath the snow, but she just said everyone went to space when they died. Her voice was creepy precisely because her words formed bridges the dead slunk over, but still I loved her so. I asked her who held her hand out there because I knew she hated the dark and she said, "You do, Lightie—can't you feel it?" and I smiled because I knew all along that it was exactly so.

I asked her if she could see those lights now, the ones I'd seen retiring in pairs long ago on the bedroom wall of a Tenerife flat overlooking the Puerto Deportivo where the boats had lifted and dropped to the water's gentle swell and the ropes had whined and groaned.

"Yes," she said.

"Do you know what they are?"

"You and I."

"But we were in the room watching," I said.

"I know, Lightie," she said. "We've done this all before. We drift in tangles this way to the end."

"I don't want to hear it, Margie. It's hard for me to understand you."

"I know," she said soothingly.

The waves were busy as ever about their shorelines in the distance, going on with what it was they did and as heedless of us as tomorrow is of today. Maybe at that moment Mother was punching keys so rapidly it sounded like a tin roof in a rain squall and Pop was bundled up safely in the dark cloth of oblivion. Lance was probably at work, eating his bottom lip right off his face with worry and maybe that tricky psychologist—what was his name?—was sitting on a couch in his ridiculous suit with his elbows on his knees and just the tips of his fingers touching.

But who cared for them? I wiped them from the table of my memory as easily as one brushed the sand from his feet. I smiled and for tonight, just tonight, I held my dear twin close and let all that sweet, obliterating pain scaffold around my trembling heart.

All Things Await

99

I awoke to sunlight creeping into my bones. In a month or two Coach Sanford would be blowing the hell out of his whistle and barking at the freshmen, making them run suicides until one of them puked. Maybe he'd let me come back and maybe he wouldn't. It was hard to say and what did it matter? Today Indigo would come or maybe she wouldn't come at all, for you could never tell about such things. In one universe she would and, I supposed, in another she would not. The tricky thing was in not knowing which universe was the one in which this version of me resided.

I rolled out of my hammock and drank some warm *leche* and fried a *huevo* on the *estufa eléctrica* and ate it along with half a *tomate*. I could hear the morning smoothing out its dress in the treetops and feel the Earth turning shyly toward the sun.

I put on the shorts Indigo had given me, and went outside barefoot. I pulled a mango from the tree in the yard and walked down the sandy lane under the *almendros* and the muscular *ceibo boles* and took to the Matapalo beach—Planck beach—because I'd told Indigo I'd meet her on it but also because millions of years ago my ancestors dragged themselves from these waters. I knew in my genes, in the roots of my teeth, in the cuticles of my nails that that was true.

It was a fine morning and very cool. Cabo Matapalo's heat had yet to pin the midnight's coolness for the count of three. The light pressed on all it touched. The whole place deserted and filled with light, horizon, sea sparkle.

The beach itself was wide and crescent shaped. I could see the dark bumps of a reef stretching a ways into the water to the south. Palm trees leaned out over the beach as if they longed to touch the water—to be kissed deeply by its foamy lips. I watched the long break line of a wave move left to right, then went over and sat on a washed up stump and shut my eyes.

The silence of this remote coast, of the crisp sky above it, of outer space above that. I twisted my feet into the sand. I wanted my scar to tingle but it wouldn't. Still, though, I felt the electric thing move inside me for it was all there—not just in the composition of the beach but within me, too. The noises of my body boomed and swelled in my ears against the outer silence—the rushing of blood through vein, the passing of air through lung, the machinery of my brain, the hum and pulse of me.

I squinted at the far off shelving clouds that rested on all that bright blue.

There was no vision. I'd already had the vision. The vision approached. I heard laughter, the scattering of distant applause. I caressed my bronze arm. Both my wrists were covered in bits of washed up netting. The ridges and swales of muscle, blonde hair like gold-wire trees. I remembered a summer day in golden sunlight when Mother had blown the thistles from a dandelion and directed Margaret and me—all thin and little and beautiful and laughing—to collect them and bring them back. I remembered Pop shaking the dogwood trees on some long gone October afternoon, alternately yelling encouragement and laughing as Lance and I tried to catch the leaves before they hit the ground. Who would arrange things now for Santana Montana and Rosa—even people like Perry and Gus McGovern? How was it that there had never been a kind-hearted person who had the presence and power to arrange things for me?

I stretched out in the sand, rested my head on the tattered husk of a coconut. Thistles once blown cannot be returned. I lay there in the sand and listened to Pop's voice whispering in my ear.

Listen, it said, *sticks crackle in a blue fire*.

100

The vision materializes from the sand's heat haze, loosening its hair, brushing it out into streams that lengthen like afternoon shadows. It's far up the beach and moving as a dark, distinctly feminine disruption at the center of all the bright things. Instantly I feel myself lift from the ground, begin to drift toward its nuclear bulge.

I wave to the form down the beach, which is still too far off to be sure of anything. My scar is tingling like it's bursting with electricity and soon enough I'm moving at incredible speed, around and around—orbiting ever closer to this thing I've sought.

A minute more and I'm inside it and it's like being inside many places all at once—everything, everywhere transposed. I'm on the practice field at Tommy Jeffs throwing perfect spirals to Rampage in the flat; I'm at the farm and Mother is crying quietly in the other room; at the Outer Banks and I'm tan, grown up, and putting shells in a bucket; I'm watching the outrigger canoes with Uluwehi in Waikiki; on a veranda in Georgia with Emmy's well-loved face staring up adoringly from my lap; baring my soul to Dr. Crispin; meeting with Padre Johnson and his arm is on my shoulder and I'm crying; I'm bearded, wild-eyed and living in a shack I built on top of Margaret's grave; on a plane with Indigo and we're arguing excitedly about wormholes and time travel; in the backseat among baggage in an old beater and Santana Montana and Rosa have taken Rosa's sister and all of them are up front talking quietly; in Ireland, Spain, Belize, Hawai'i, the Azores —it goes on and on, all these places, all these Lightlys, all these *mes,* seeking the perfection of themselves in worlds of their own making.

My head feels hot, like lasers are burning into it and they're proliferating—all these parallel *mes*—yet remaining distinct, drifting toward and away from each other as they divide and divide and divide. Each one branches into a trillion futures and my mind races to remove the veils in twirls of silk streamers, and I know I'll have to choose one soon to inhabit. So I give it my all, bear down in one last effort against collapse with all that—for better or worse—is me and I perceive it.

For the slightest moment, I catch the glimpse: all these infinite universes bubbling within and without, and in each and every last one of them a singular, conscious, euphoric, *me*.

101

I open my eyes. I'm standing in a field that I know well. It's the farm, only the field is in better shape, the rich grass recently mown and pistachio green. I see Margaret up in the distance. She's near the creek. She's grown up and lovely and there's a guy with her. A boyfriend maybe.

Still skinny, but look how tall she is!

She sees me and gives a wave. Six full-grown yellow labs bound and roughhouse around her, dashing up and down the bank.

I wave back and think how it would be more fitting if it were raining, so that I could be seeing her, exactly as she had promised, through the raindrops. In another variant reality it is, but in this one it isn't raining. It's a sun-drenched field and I'm running across it, waving like a lunatic.

There are trillions of bubbles and raindrops that I have eyes in. Trillions of alternate lives at the ready. I understand now how one can move between them, but cue the credits, let them roll over bush and field and sky because I'm staying here. At least until that feeling rises again. At least until the calls of some new, distant place coax me from this dream.

"Margie!" I yell, running at a dead sprint. The dogs freeze, tails straight up. "Margie! Honey! You have no idea!"

What else?

High in the mountains a hidden forest of bluebells. Swaths of African purple and French sky blue among the russet and gold of fallen leaves. Little spring ephemerals to sweeten the air, to make, for a moment, the impalpable less uncanny, then die back to root.

All Things Await

About the Author

Seth Clabough is a professor and published scholar, poet, and fiction writer. His work appears in a wide range of journals, magazines, and anthologies. He has a MA in English from USC and a PhD in English from the University of Wales, Aberystwyth, where he won the LBA Prize for Fiction. He lives with his wife and four children in Virginia and on Hatteras Island.

Author website at www.sethclabough.com

If you enjoyed *All Things Await,* consider these other fine books from Savant Books and Publications:

Essay, Essay, Essay by Yasuo Kobachi
Aloha from Coffee Island by Walter Miyanari
Footprints, Smiles and Little White Lies by Daniel S. Janik
The Illustrated Middle Earth by Daniel S. Janik
Last and Final Harvest by Daniel S. Janik
A Whale's Tale by Daniel S. Janik
Tropic of California by R. Page Kaufman
Tropic of California (the companion music CD) by R. Page Kaufman
The Village Curtain by Tony Tame
Dare to Love in Oz by William Maltese
The Interzone by Tatsuyuki Kobayashi
Today I Am a Man by Larry Rodness
The Bahrain Conspiracy by Bentley Gates
Called Home by Gloria Schumann
Kanaka Blues by Mike Farris
First Breath edited by Z. M. Oliver
Poor Rich by Jean Blasiar
The Jumper Chronicles by W. C. Peever
William Maltese's Flicker by William Maltese
My Unborn Child by Orest Stocco
Last Song of the Whales by Four Arrows
Perilous Panacea by Ronald Klueh
Falling but Fulfilled by Zachary M. Oliver
Mythical Voyage by Robin Ymer
Hello, Norma Jean by Sue Dolleris
Richer by Jean Blasiar
Manifest Intent by Mike Farris
Charlie No Face by David B. Seaburn
Number One Bestseller by Brian Morley
My Two Wives and Three Husbands by S. Stanley Gordon
In Dire Straits by Jim Currie
Wretched Land by Mila Komarnisky
Chan Kim by Ilan Herman
Who's Killing All the Lawyers? by A. G. Hayes
Ammon's Horn by G. Amati
Wavelengths edited by Zachary M. Oliver
Almost Paradise by Laurie Hanan
Communion by Jean Blasiar and Jonathan Marcantoni
The Oil Man by Leon Puissegur
Random Views of Asia from the Mid-Pacific by William E. Sharp
The Isla Vista Crucible by Reilly Ridgell

Blood Money by Scott Mastro
In the Himalayan Nights by Anoop Chandola
On My Behalf by Helen Doan
Traveler's Rest by Jonathan Marcantoni
Keys in the River by Tendai Mwanaka
Chimney Bluffs by David B. Seaburn
The Loons by Sue Dolleris
Light Surfer by David Allan Williams
The Judas List by A. G. Hayes
Path of the Templar - Book 2 of The Jumper Chronicles by W. C. Peever
The Desperate Cycle by Tony Tame
Shutterbug by Buz Sawyer
Blessed are the Peacekeepers by Tom Donnelly and Mike Munger
The Bellwether Messages edited by D. S. Janik
The Turtle Dances by Daniel S. Janik
The Lazarus Conspiracies by Richard Rose
Purple Haze by George B. Hudson
Imminent Danger by A. G. Hayes
Lullaby Moon (CD) by Malia Elliott of Leon & Malia
Volutions edited by Suzanne Langford
In the Eyes of the Son by Hans Brinckmann
The Hanging of Dr. Hanson by Bentley Gates
Flight of Destiny by Francis Powell
Elaine of Corbenic by Tima Z. Newman
Ballerina Birdies by Marina Yamamoto
More More Time by David B. Seabird
Crazy Like Me by Erin Lee
Cleopatra Unconquered by Helen R. Davis
Valedictory by Daniel Scott
The Chemical Factor by A. G. Hayes
Quantum Death by A. G. Hayes
Running with the Pack edited by Helen R. Davis
Big Heaven by Charlotte Hebert
Captain Riddle's Treasure by GV Rama Rao

Coming Soon:
Libido Tsunami by Cate Burns
The Adventures of Purple Head, Buddha Monkey and Sticky Feet by Eric and Forest Bracht
Cereus by Z. Roux
In the Shadows of My Mind by Andrew Massie
Finding Kate by A. G. Hayes

www.savantbooksandpublications.com

WITHDRAWN

Made in the USA
San Bernardino, CA
19 July 2016